About the Author

This is her fourth book. She began writing five years ago. Her first book, Hooves and Hands, was published in 2020.

Fetlocks and Fisticuffs

S. V. Brown

Fetlocks and Fisticuffs

Olympia Publishers
London

www.olympiapublishers.com
OLYMPIA PAPERBACK EDITION

Copyright © S. V. Brown 2024

The right of S. V. Brown to be identified as author of
this work has been asserted in accordance with sections 77 and 78 of the
Copyright, Designs and Patents Act 1988.

All Rights Reserved

No reproduction, copy or transmission of this publication
may be made without written permission.
No paragraph of this publication may be reproduced,
copied or transmitted save with the written permission of the publisher, or in
accordance with the provisions
of the Copyright Act 1956 (as amended).

Any person who commits any unauthorised act in relation to
this publication may be liable to criminal
prosecution and civil claims for damage.

A CIP catalogue record for this title is
available from the British Library.

ISBN: 978-1-80439-783-1

This is a work of fiction.
Names, characters, places and incidents originate from the writer's imagination.
Any resemblance to actual persons, living or dead, is purely coincidental.

First Published in 2024

Olympia Publishers
Tallis House
2 Tallis Street
London
EC4Y 0AB

Printed in Great Britain

Dedication

I dedicate this book to all my friends.

Acknowledgements

I would like to thank all those who have supported me and my publishers for their help, their patience and excellent work.

Chapter 1

Bernard had gone to the Wine Rack restaurant Friday evening, greeted and spoken to his staff, had dinner there, and even entertained customers playing piano. After informing his restaurant manager, he was spending the night in the vineyard flat, he said goodnight.

Wandered across the courtyard, unlocked the door to the flat but didn't immediately go inside, leaning instead on the porch railing to watch the moonlit sea. His eyes dropped to the Mustang parked nearby, thoughts and visions of Maria and him having fun in the front seat making him smile. Heaving a sigh, he turned to go in, shutting the door behind him and flicking on a light switch.

Stood staring at the sofa and remembered her again, shaking his head before entering the bedroom. Lying down on the bed fully clothed he closed his eyes and wished that she was there beside him, felt the longing like a deep pain in his chest. He dozed and dreamt of her, felt her kiss and hands on him, saw her smile and heard that sexy laugh he loved. Woke with a start to find himself alone, groaned, and buried his face in the pillow.

Muttering he got up, went to the kitchen for a glass of water and sat at the table for a while. Next morning, he found himself undressed and in bed, wondering how he'd got there. In the bathroom, he splashed his face with cold water to clear his head and got dressed before leaving. He drove the Mustang slowly through the empty restaurant carpark, along the driveway to the road and once on the highway throttled the big engine, driving at speed to his seaside cabin where he showered, dressed in fresh clothes, and had breakfast on the deck, oblivious to the chilly air. The sea was rough with huge, ragged breakers and gulls screamed overhead, imminent of a storm somewhere. He went back inside after finishing his coffee, tidied up and decided to head for the local car racing track, named the Strait.

At the workshop garages, he found his son bending over a racing car engine and hearing the growl of the Mustang, Jason looked up with a welcoming grin. Bernard alighted, gave his bad leg a stretch and walked across, barely limping.

"Hey, Dad, you're up early." Jason greeted him with a man hug.
Bernard smiled. "Get up with the birds these days."
"Glad you're here, you can give me a hand," Jason chuckled.
"Get in your way more like." Bernard slanted him a wry look.
"Nah, I'll let you supervise."
"Aw, thanks. You're so kind."
They both laughed and chatted for a while.

Jason was pleased to see his dad looking surprisingly chipper, noticing too he'd made an effort to shave and his visit to the Wine Rack was also a positive sign. Jason had seen his dad deteriorate after his mum died three months before and understood; he felt her absence terribly himself and thought about her every day. Their whole family missed Maria, but Jason knew his dad felt it the most; without his wife he'd changed overnight and often spent all day alone living a reclusive life at the cabin.

An hour later, Bernard hugged his son goodbye and roared away, tyres squealing on tarmac. Watching him go, Jason shook his head.

Dad's driving never changes, that's for sure, he thought with a rueful grin. Looks like things are on the up. The old fella's off to the farm, doing the rounds. Maybe he'll be back on the racetrack soon and then watch out!

He turned back to the engine still grinning, wondered what his mum would be saying, probably scolding his dad about doing wheelies.

Bernard drove fast to the farm, tyres spitting gravel as he braked in front of the homestead and waved at Anna, his sister-in-law, who looked up from her gardening. Quickly removing her gloves, she hurried to meet him, throwing her arms around his neck and giving his cheek a resounding kiss. She talked non-stop as they made their way to the homestead door where Zoe, Bernard's daughter in law stood waiting to welcome him. While they sat at the kitchen table enjoying a cup of tea his two grandsons, Matthew and Daniel, burst in to wrap their grubby hands around their opa for a boisterous hug. Granddaughter Kate was not far behind and wriggled herself onto his lap, giving him a kiss and snuggling into his arms. He refused Zoe's offer to stay for lunch and with hugs all round waved goodbye as he drove out, more discreetly this time with the kids watching.

He looked across at the passenger seat, wanting so desperately for Maria to be there beside him. He could almost see her, frowning at him and telling him to stop driving so fast. His lips curved at that and lifting his foot off the accelerator, the engine's growl dropped a few notes. The car took the next corner without a murmur. Punching his foot down again, he felt the kick of power and grinned boyishly. Barely aware of the roadside flashing by faster and faster, his attention began to wander again.

I miss you so much, sweet witch, he thought, feeling the ache inside. Why did you have to leave? I wish you were here with me, with us all. I saw Jason today and the grandkids. Little Kate, she looks so like you.

He turned off the main highway onto the coast road, taking the big car through its paces like always. It gave him some sort of release to feel the Mustang's response, the backend slewing a little on fast corners. It also made him concentrate, changing gear quickly, accelerating hard and letting the steering wheel slide through his hands.

"Hey, Mr Big Bad Wolf. This is not a racetrack!" Maria said into his ear.

"It isn't?" He laughed ruefully and slowed down.

"Think of other motorists!" she scolded.

"Yes, witchy poo. Whatever you say," he nodded, driving on more sedately.

Pulled into a layby, braked and switched off the engine. Clenching his hands on the wheel he breathed deeply, leaning back to rest his head against the seat. Felt tears sting as he closed his eyes.

"Hold me," he murmured. "Please, just hold me."

"I'll always hold you," she said softly. "I love you, forever."

He opened his eyes, turning his face to the passenger seat. Imagined her there, smiling and reaching her hand to his cheek. Relaxing his arms, he dropped his hands to his thighs. Closed his eyes again, let himself drift and remembered how it had all started.

She'd been with his best friend, Jason Sandford, the first time he'd seen her. Those solemn grey eyes had hit him smack bang in the gut. There'd been no pretence about her, a stunning natural woman with a beauty all her own and he'd wanted her right there and then.

Jason, mate! His immediate thought had been. You lucky bugger!

Then he'd seen her outside Jason's flat the morning after a hard night of partying and drinking. Felt the same shock of lust. Told himself she was just another lecherous little gold digger after his mate's money and made a point of doing more than insult her. He shook his head ruefully at the memory of him totally losing control and ending up rolling on the floor in agony, clutching his rearranged gonads. He grinned at another vision of her drenching him with the Sandford Veterinary Clinic's high-pressure hose and then later at the Lawson farm's river, his next attempt to get up close and personal where she'd fooled him, dumped him in water and supposedly left him to drown. Jason warning him off with a few well aimed punches had been part and parcel of the experience and he'd sported a black eye and a split lip for a few days after, but it hadn't stopped his obsession. With a grimace of self-disgust, he remembered using other women to ease the wanting but kept watch, waiting for another chance to get near her.

Karl's wedding had been the catalyst, by the Sandford homestead's swimming pool, when he'd locked his faithful walking stick around her waist and laughed when she threatened to castrate him. Then Jason had turned up, pissing him off big time. He'd got blotto purposely after that, and in the haze of alcohol and frustration, he'd taken Jason's car, driven off at speed and wrapped it around a tree. The head injury he'd sustained had scrubbed out all memory of her for a time, but strangely enough, it had brought his best mate back to him and they'd patched up their differences. Until that terrible, shocking day when Jason had been killed flying his own helicopter. He remembered the sadness of the funeral, hardly able to take it all in.

Then the next shock at a Sandford dinner when he'd heard her laugh, the sound bringing his memory flooding back, how he'd recognised her again. Later unable to sleep, appalling thoughts of his past behaviour had blown his mind. Unbelievably, he'd had a chance to apologise and make it right somehow. He'd been dumbfounded when she'd agreed to go out with him; the thrill he'd felt inside was something he'd never known before and although she hadn't made it easy their relationship progressed.

The look on her face had been priceless when he'd shown her the new tattoo on his chest, the heart with her initials inside. She'd attempted bolting like a nervous filly but instead they'd made love for the first time; the beginning of a togetherness he couldn't get enough of. She'd been scornful about the other tattoo, a naked female on his bicep, and wouldn't believe it had anything to do with her, although he said it had. He chuckled softly at the memory.

Everything about her had been so incredibly special, her company a delight and constant surprise. He thought about the ups and downs they'd gone through, their separation, the horrendous shock when she'd been kidnapped and then his almost fatal assault, but they'd made it through together and loved each other more. The joy of having a son with her had been something he'd never imagined possible and now here he was with grandchildren. His thinking and ideals had changed; a beautiful feisty witch had made his life complete. But she'd gone, dying of cancer and all he had left now were memories of her, precious memories to treasure until he too met his end.

A bird calling roused him. Blinking, he narrowed his eyes against the sunlight and sitting up straighter whispered, "Thank you, my dear. For everything."

The engine fired immediately as he turned the key, the Mustang rolled forward onto the road, tyres squealing as he floored it. He approached the first corner too fast. Felt the car slew and right itself. At the next familiar bend, he didn't ease up either, the car sliding sideways again. Fighting the wheel, he got the Mustang under control, letting his breath out through his teeth as she snaked and straightened. The next left-hand corner was another one he knew like the back of his hand, but it came far too fast. Lifting his foot off the accelerator, he pumped the brake lightly. Turned the wheel to control the skid, but he knew instantly that he'd overcooked it. The car didn't slow. Sliding wildly with tyres screeching protest, the car spun off the road into gravel, a hail of stones clattering underneath.

Time seemed to stand still, resuming in slow motion with muffled sound. Bernard turned his head without haste to look out the side window. Didn't even blink.

Smiled instead. The shark's smile that Maria had found so infuriating.

The tree at the side of the road was suddenly there. Close, too close. The shattering impact reverberated through the bush, birds squawking in fright. Silence descended abruptly. Then the sound of steam hissing, cooling metal ticked while the wind rustled in the bushes.

Several minutes later, two cars left the beach and came across the wreckage, a mangled blue Mustang almost split in half and wrapped around the tree. The first car braked hard, driver gawping at the sight before switching on hazard lights and frantically clambering out. He waved down the second car which skidded to a halt, the passenger immediately calling emergency services. Both drivers rushed to the Mustang to look inside, staring with wide eyed shock and horror. They knew that help when it came, emergency or otherwise, wouldn't save the man inside.

His life was over.

Chapter 2

Time ticks on but our world and the way we live in it doesn't change, only circumstances and people do. I'm one of those people, the next generation of Von Meerens.

My parents, Jason and Zoe, had three children: two boys and a girl. Matthew Frederik, the eldest by fourteen months, Daniel Bernard next and sixteen months older than me, Kate Maria. We weren't just close in age, we got on well together and although we gave each other heaps we'd fight tooth and nail to stick up for each other.

At age ten, I found out from my brothers that the Von Meeren males weren't supposed to be able to have children and infertility laboratory tests done on Dad and Opa Bernard had proved it. Proved it to be a whole load of bull, that was if my two brothers and myself were anything to go by, not forgetting Dad who shouldn't have been born either.

During those early years, our home life was idyllic living on the Lawson farm in New Zealand. After my great grandmother Sarah died, my great aunt and uncle, Anna and David, shifted into her cottage, and Dad, Mum and us kids took over the homestead. Second cousin Ben and his wife Olivia also lived on the farm with their daughter Stephanie in the house Morgan Lawson, my dad's long-gone cousin had built. Olivia, Leon Sandford's daughter, worked at the Sandford veterinary and quarantine clinic across the road from us doing the administrative work.

I didn't remember the matriarch of the clinic business, Alicia Sandford, but I knew her sons Leon and Karl well, good friends of our family and like uncles to us kids.

The other farm cottage used to be occupied by the farm manager Wade and his partner Yvonne, but she became ill whereupon they moved back to her family down country. She died not long after, and Wade never returned, although he kept in touch.

My paternal grandparents died when I was seven, although young and not completely understanding of all the goings on I would never forget the disbelief and sadness at that time.

Oma Maria Jean went first; she had melanoma cancer which spread to her internal organs and died within a few short months of diagnosis. Opa Bernard Ranolf found life difficult after her passing and seemed to change overnight, becoming reclusive, which was very unlike the extrovert I remembered. Three months later, he was driving home from the farm to his seaside cabin and crashed his car, writing off the beautiful Ford Mustang that he loved. He was killed instantly after leaving the road at high speed and hitting a tree broadside. Apart from the shock of his passing, talk of him having done it deliberately was even more upsetting; the gossip tabloids had a field day, and none of our family believed a bar of it. Opa had simply been doing what he'd always done; driving too fast, and for once he'd misjudged the corner and simply couldn't control the skidding car. Dad wondered too if his father had been distracted, perhaps even been thinking of Oma, which in some unexplainable way was a comfort.

We missed them both terribly; they'd left a deep void, and our family unit would never be the same. The memories were always there of my Oma, so lovely, kind and understanding with her passion for animals, and my Opa, so handsome and such fun, his teasing grin, the trademark limp, scars and tattoos. Dad vowed to keep Opa's legacy alive, continuing to work as mechanic at the Strait racetrack workshops, testing and racing cars. The apartment Opa owned there was still in use, occupied mostly on race weekends. A public museum was built at the track showcasing all types of automotive paraphernalia, with Opa's racing Mustang and Dad's Escort also on display. The rundown vineyard that Opa had transformed into a boutique winery with its ever-popular restaurant, The Wine Rack, also continued on with efficient management and staff, funded by the Von Meeren Trust. The seaside cabin Oma had inherited and where she'd spent her married life with Opa would never be sold. It was very precious to our family—our bolthole and beach playground.

Being Von Meerens hadn't made life easy for us kids, but it was certainly interesting. We'd learnt to cope with other people's opinions, less-than-truthful gossip, and the odd spate of bullying during our years in school.

I remember a time in the playground when Matthew stood up to a boy called Douglas Willard who was hounding me about being a witch just like my grandmother.

"Don't talk to my sister like that!" Matthew said with a ferocious scowl.

Having never quite seen him look so threatening. I eyed his balled fists in surprise.

"What are you going to do about it, Von Meeren?" Was Willard's scornful reply.

There were two other boys with Willard, Matthew's age and known to be bullies.

"This!" Matthew said and punched him in the nose.

Immediately thereafter, it was all on with legs and arms flailing in every direction. I promptly joined in as well, even landing a few punches, scratches, and slaps of my own. We were pulled apart by two teachers and sent to the headmaster's office for a lecture, Dad arriving shortly after to take us home for the remainder of the day.

Matthew sat up front of Dad's car, sporting a purpling eye and fat lip, staring belligerently down at his lap and said not a word. I was in the back seat with my hair on end and a hand that still smarted from landing blows on Willard's person somewhere, think I'd even manged a good hard thump on the back of his head to my morbid glee.

"What was that all about?" Dad asked Matthew once we were on our way.

"They were picking on Kate," Matthew muttered.

"Said I was a witch," I volunteered indignantly.

"You'd have been better off ignoring them, don't you think?" Dad reasoned.

"They're always picking on other kids." Matthew was surly. "They deserved it."

"It's about time someone stood up to those bullies," I agreed, curling my lip.

"And you think this is the way to deal with it?" Dad frowned.

"I had to do something, Dad," Matthew shot him a frowning glance.

"I understand, son." Dad sighed. "But retaliation isn't the answer, best you keep away from them if you can."

"But they follow us around," I protested. "Especially that Douglas guy! He's a beast."

"You should tell a teacher as soon as he annoys you," Dad countered.

"Easier said than done, Dad," I told him. "He's cunning! Waits for the right time when there's no teachers around."

Matthew turned to look at me. "You know something? I reckon he's got the hots for you, sis," Tried a smirk, wincing at his fat lip. "He picks on you, so you'll notice him."

I screwed up my nose in disgust, "Ugh! He's a creep! He can go get…" Promptly shut my mouth as Dad's eyes met mine in the rear vision mirror.

"Stick close to your friends, my girl," he said ignoring my outburst. "If he hassles you again speak to your teachers; otherwise, I'll deal with it."

Nodding, I dropped my bottom lip sulkily.

Dad frowned at his son. "And Matthew, please try to do the same. I understand you sticking up for your sister, but using your fists isn't the way to deal with things.'

Matthew turned his head away to stare out the side window.

"It's not a good look for one thing and it'll cause more problems, not just for you but also for your brother," Dad continued. "Do you understand, both of you?"

"Yes, Dad," we muttered in unison.

"I'm going to have to tell your Mum about this and I suggest you only speak when she asks you to, okay?"

"Yes, Dad."

"Otherwise, I'll be in the frying pan as well." He suddenly grinned ruefully. "You know what your Mum is like."

"Sure, Dad." We both grinned back at him.

I thought my dad adorable, the coolest one in the world, and loved his wicked sense of humour which so exasperated my mum. People often commented on his similarities to Opa Bernard—not just the handsome Von Meeren looks but his easy-going manner. Daniel was Dad all over again, same lean build, thick black hair and grey eyes. I'd inherited the grey Lawson eyes too, reminding people of Oma Maria when they looked at me, the same slim to the point of being skinny figure, and long wavy dark hair with its distinct touch of red. Matthew was the fairest of us three, his curly hair lightened to blonde streaks in the summer sun, and his eyes were blue like Mum's.

At age nineteen, I proved to have true-blue Lawson blood flowing through my veins, completing a veterinary course at a university campus down the country to be accepted for employment at a large and small animal clinic just out of our town. My great love for anything four-legged and furry, especially dogs and horses, had been fulfilled, my work with animals ultimately enjoyable. Driving was another passion of mine, inherited through the Von Meeren bloodline, it seemed, and travelled to work in my blue Suzuki four-wheel-drive jeep that Dad helped me choose.

My brothers had also done good, both working as soon as they left college. Matthew loved anything with a motor and wheels, followed Dad into mechanics, and took on an apprenticeship at the racetrack garage. He purchased an older-model Subaru Legacy as his gad about vehicle and raced Opa's Mustang in partnership with Dad. Daniel, on the other hand, bought himself a Ford Ranger four-wheel drive Ute, moved into the farm manager's cottage with cousin, Jonathan, and helped him run the farm. Although as mechanically minded as his brother, he preferred the outdoors, his deepest love being for horses of the four-legged variety. His rapport with them always amazed me; he rode without saddle or bridle, hung off the back of a horse fearlessly like in the cowboy movies and had an innate ability to communicate with them. People described him as another Morgan, our family's long-ago horseman and hero.

Great Aunt Anna's daughter, Bella, who married Roman Antonovich, the local farrier, also had that same love of equines, Morgan having taught her everything he knew before he died. She was a qualified vet nurse, worked at the Sandford clinic part-time and trained horses, teaching Daniel all the Morgan tricks. She and Roman had no children, contented with their nieces and nephews and busy working lives.

Great Aunt Anna was the only oldie still living on the farm, in her eighties but remarkably sprightly and abhorred being called Aunty, demanding that everyone including us younger lot call her Anna. She lived alone since her husband, David, died a few years before from a chronic blood disorder which affected his liver.

Our long-time friends, the Sandford brothers, were also still with us, Leon Sandford and his wife Jacqueline, Roman's mum, were in their senior years but led active lives and continued to reside at the Sandford homestead. Karl Sandford lost his wife Nell to bowel cancer some years back and lived with his sons Tobias and Luis on the farm next door to ours. Tobias married Glenys, and they had two sons, Tony and Jack. Luis and his partner Rebecca had a daughter, Natalia.

The late Jason Sandford, elder half-brother of Leon and Karl, originally set up the quarantine clinic, my Oma Maria, the love of his life, before he was killed in a helicopter crash. He bought her a standard-bred trotting mare to breed from, and several stallions from the same Shadow lineage were still continuing as notable sires. Oma eventually stopped breeding horses herself, left it to the expert stud owners and reverted to past times, grazing only rescue horses on the farm, although shadow horses unable to race because of injury or other circumstances and needing a place to retire were also included.

Three horses resided on the farm nowadays, two of which were progeny from stallions my Oma bred. First was Kingston, Shadow King's grandson, a big black and handsome, kind-natured gelding whose racing career ended because of a damaged hoof. Second was another retired racehorse, a grey mare named Moon River and Shadow River's granddaughter. For reasons unknown, she bucked, hence her nickname BB, or Bucking Bronco for short. Nobody ever found out why she did it, but Bella surmised she'd suffered trauma to her back during race training which became ingrained in her memory. She'd caused mayhem, demolished a sulky or two and was sent to the farm for a spell, but never left and became Bella's favourite ride. On occasion, her bucking high spirits got the better of her, but for the most part, she wouldn't harm a fly and behaved. Our third resident horse, Delta, wasn't a Shadow horse. She'd been abused, left badly neglected in a paddock without barely enough grass and rescued by animal welfare. They'd approached Bella to help, as Delta was understandably anti-human and difficult to handle, it took several weeks to gain her trust and when Bella was given the first choice to keep her, she did. Although the beautiful bay mare had physical scars, she proved to be obliging, a wonderful horse to ride and became my favourite.

My happy place was with the horses. I also loved to watch Bella and Daniel work them; they had something special going on, and when they freerode, no saddle or bridle, just communicating through body and voice, it was magical. I didn't have their confidence or ability, simply enjoyed riding to relax, especially across the farm atop a comfortable western saddle.

In the farm's top paddock stood beautiful trees planted to commemorate all the horses that had been and gone. I spent quiet times there, sitting in the grass or leaning on the fence, remembering the many stories I'd heard about them. There were fond memories told about other past pets, a favourite being the Wolfhound cross dog named Wolf that Dad grew up with. He gave me my first puppy, Pirate, a part husky/shepherd we got from the SPCA who looked like he had a patch over one eye, hence his name. His death when I was fourteen hurt terribly for a long time, I missed him like a brother. Less than a year later, a girl at school found an abandoned pup in the park and took him home but when her parents wouldn't let her keep a dog, I offered to take him. Dad laughingly told me that my new pet was going to be huge, judging by the size of his feet. He was right. Trojan, as I named him, thought to be a Mastiff/Shepherd cross, stood almost level with my hip once fully grown, handsome and brindle in colour with gorgeous dark chocolate eyes. He followed me everywhere if he could, loved to ride in my jeep and was so laid back that my boss didn't mind me bringing him to work on occasion. He appeared to have a calming effect on the patients, stretched out contentedly on the clinic's kennel floor, got fussed over by everyone and lapped it all up with his happy doggy grin. Although super friendly, he proved to be a surprisingly good watch dog too, barking at unexpected noises or strangers.

I had no intention of moving out of home, the homestead was spacious with plenty of room for everyone. Matthew also still lived there, but his more frequent overnighting at the Strait had something to do with a girl, I was certain, although he denied it. Surmised it to be the daughter of another race-track workshop owner who also owned an apartment there; she raced go-karts, which was right up Matthew's alley.

"Have you heard from Matthew?" Mum asked one Friday evening before dinner.

"He's staying at the track tonight, he said," I told her.
She frowned at Dad. "Well, I'm glad someone knows what he's up to."
"I know as much as you do." Dad spread his hands.
"I reckon he's chasing a girl," I informed them both casually.
"Chasing?" Mum stared.
"Yes. Martina. Her father owns one of the racing teams."
"Vinnie Bertolini's daughter, you mean?" Dad cocked an eyebrow.
"Just guessing," I nodded. "He eyes her up, I've seen him."
"Nothing wrong with that."
"What's that supposed to mean?" Mum gave him a narrow-eyed look.
Dad grinned. "It's perfectly normal male behaviour, isn't it?"
"What happens if he does more than look?" I asked innocently.
"Kate!" Mum's eyes swivelled to me.
"What?" I eyed her back, shrugged. "Just curious."

With an amused sidelong glance at Mum, Dad said to me. "What happens is your brother's business. He's old enough to decide."

"Ugly enough too."

"There's that." Dad snorted a laugh.

"I hope he knows what he's doing," Mum still had Dad in her sights, frowning. "I really think you should speak to him, Jason."

"He's not a kid any more, Zoe. He's over the boy talk thing."

"There's never been a girl around before."

"Boy talk thing?" I queried. "Sex and stuff, you mean?"

"Kate!" Mum blinked at me.

I pouted. "Is the boy talk thing more interesting than the girl talk thing?"

"Leave it please!"

I tilted my head at Dad. "Can you talk to me about it?"

"No! That's completely unnecessary," Mum said sharply.

"Aw, why?" I dropped my lower lip.

Dad shot me a suitably serious frown, to which I screwed up my nose, and that was the end of the subject. Wishing them goodnight later that night, Dad sent me a wink from behind Mum's back, which had me skipping to my bedroom, grinning from ear to ear.

At Saturday breakfast, Dad said he'd be working in one of the farm sheds, gave me another wink on his way out the door and I joined him discreetly soon after. He proceeded to boy talk which incidentally wasn't much different to the girl talk but his poker face and innuendos had me in fits of hysterical laughter and almost falling off the haybale while Trojan wagged his huge tail with hilarious enthusiasm.

Chapter 3

Delta had arrived at the Lawson farm suspicious and on edge. She wondered what was in store after all she'd been through, and this morning's disagreement with three humans hadn't put her in a good mood. They put her in a crush, pricked her neck with a needle, and she woozily remembered stumbling into the horse float with them pulling and pushing.

She heard an engine start up, the horse float rolled forward, and after a few jerks gained momentum. She braced her legs to keep her balance, alternatively leaning her shoulders on the outside wall or middle partition and her chest against the front railing during the long drive. Feeling weird in the head, she almost fell asleep on her feet, but as the horse float slowed, crunching gravel, she came to. It gradually stopped before reversing, with tyres whispering over a different surface. As the engine cut out, she heard human voices, turned her head to eyeball the rear of the horse float, and went into defence mode.

The familiar soothing voice of her late friend popped into her head: "It'll be okay now, Delta girl. Trust me. You'll be all right."

"How do you know that, Riva?"

"I can feel it. This is your last stop."

"My last stop?" Delta was doubtful. "And you think that's okay?"

"I don't just think. I know."

Delta shook her head as Riva faded from her mind. She heard someone at the front access door, and as it opened, a stranger's face and upper body appeared quietly without haste. Delta glared, laid her ears back, and mock lunged, but the female human didn't retreat as quickly as expected or give the usual gasp or yelp of fright.

That's strange! Delta thought. Not the normal human reaction.

The woman murmured and stepped inside, her movements deliberate and non-threatening. With her head still groggy from the sedative, Delta decided not to make any more sudden moves and watched the stranger the lead rope from the wall ring. Delta heard her speak to someone outside, then the sound of the horse float ramp unlocking and slowly opening to sunlight and more human figures. Delta's focus was no longer on the woman, hardly noticing the lead rope unclasping from her halter. Tensing her hindquarters as the ramp touched the ground, she made her move to rush backwards and out, hooves sliding on the lowered ramp. Outside she swung to her left, careering off towards the high fence line with nose in the air and snorting. The ramp was quickly raised, the horse float left the area and a gate swung shut immediately behind it.

Delta followed the rounded fence at a gallop, eased to a canter and then a trot. She realised soon enough that there was no way out, jumping the high wooden railings not an option. At a fast walk, head jerking from side to side she took in her surroundings. She noticed people watching her from outside the fence, recognised two from the place she'd left that morning but the others she didn't know. Shaking her head to clear the leftover fuzziness, she halted, flattened her ears to her skull, and gave the spectators a baleful unfriendly stare.

A young man spoke, "Wow! You've got yourself a handful there, Bella."

The woman who Delta recognised from the horse float stood closest to the gate and spoke softly in reply, "Yes, she'll be a challenge."

Delta couldn't understand the words but knew they were talking about her, didn't much care for their scrutiny and whirled away.

Watching her, I felt a thrill go through me. She was beautiful, dark brown with a white star on her forehead but thin with a gauntness about her head and neck. She also bore scars, along one side of her body and down a foreleg. Her eyes were big and bold but held distrust and a look that I could only describe as fear or even hate.

It saddened me, felt tears stand in my eyes as I asked with a catch in my voice. "What happened to her?"

"Knocked around and left in a paddock to rot basically," Bella told me.

"How horrible."

"Some people shouldn't be allowed near animals," Daniel growled.

"Don't deserve to look after their own children either for that matter," Bella said.

"Excuse me?" A man standing by the horse float waved a hand. "Can we go now?"

"Of course." Bella nodded, waving back. "Thanks so much for bringing her over."

"No worries," he smiled. "Good luck."

He and a second man turned to the towing vehicle, climbed in and drove away.

"Who found her?" Daniel watched them go before looking at the horse again.

"Someone walking a dog noticed her," Bella sighed. "There were two horses. The other mare had to be put down, she was in such a bad state they couldn't help her."

"Some owners are bastards!" Daniel snarled.

"That's one description," Bella shot him a look. "I could think of others."

He grimaced distaste, shaking his head. "Do you want any help with her?"

"I'd be very glad if you would."

"Cool." He looked at me. "K will too, won't you, sis."

"I'd love to help," I nodded, adding a question. "What's her name?"

"Delta." Bella watched Delta turn her head to us, smiled. "She knows her name."

"And her friend, the one that died?"

"She was Riva, a beautiful grey. Thoroughbred, apparently."

"Why would anyone do this?"

"Who would know. Some people seem to think that a horse can be left in a paddock without being looked after." Bella compressed her lips. "The trough water was stagnant, I was told. There was mud to their knees and weeds up almost to the top of their heads. They were in a sorry state and hadn't seen a farrier for ages."

"What's happened to the owners?"

"They've been fined and won't be owning another animal for a while."

"That's pittance! They should be strung up!" Daniel snarled again.

"Exactly, it's just a rap over the knuckles," Bella agreed. "Apparently some kids were abusing them, chasing them and throwing things. Riva couldn't run away, she was arthritic and very sore on her feet, but Delta attacked them if she could. I'd say she was trying to protect her friend."

"So, she hates humans pretty much." I frowned.

"She certainly doesn't think much of us." Bella nodded. "They had to sedate her each time to do anything medical or otherwise and she's been confined which hasn't helped her mental state."

"How are you going to make her like us again?"

"I'll ask good old Morgan," Bella smiled.

"Morgan?"

"Yeah. Uncle Morgan Lawson, the horseman. He helps me every time."

"How?"

"In here." Bella tapped her forehead, grinning.

"He's still talking to you, then?" Daniel grinned back.

"Yep."

I looked from one to the other. "You mean, like, telepathically?"

"Hey K, enough of the big words," Daniel gave me a playful shove.

The sudden movement spooked Delta, flinging up her head to glare at us.

"It's okay, girl," Bella called softly.

"Can't she be put in with the others?" I saw Kingston and BB eyeing the new arrival from the adjoining paddock.

"Not yet, but hopefully soon," Bella told me. "I'll start working with her tomorrow."

"Do you want us here, tomorrow?" Daniel asked.

"I'd like someone to watch from outside the arena for starters, for my safety," Bella squeezed his shoulder. "How about eight thirty in the morning, just a short session."

He nodded enthusiastically. "I'll be there."

"Oh, blast." I pulled a face. "I have to work."

"Don't you worry, Kate. I'll be working her in the evenings too."

"Tomorrow?"

She nodded. "How about we make it six o'clock. And don't forget, you two, there's always the weekends."

"You're on," Daniel grinned. "Do you think Morgan will talk to me and K, too."

"Wouldn't be surprised if he does," Bella laughed. "He'll be keeping his eye on us, that's for sure."

Watching Bella doing what she did was remarkable. I'd seen her at work before but never with a horse like this one and even the first session was an eye opener. Delta was having none of it too start with and kept her distance, running along the fence as though her life depended on it. The subtle change in her manner surprised me, not so much her reaction when it happened but the fact that I saw it. Bella was in the centre of the arena swinging a long rope that kept Delta circling at a distance. Her inside ear swivelled on Bella and then she lowered her head, loping along with her nose to her knees almost. As Bella stopped swinging the rope and broke eye contact, I watched Delta slow and halt. Her whole attention was on Bella for several minutes, standing completely still and staring. As soon as she looked away Bella turned back to her and began all over again, swinging the rope and pushing her forward in the opposite direction along the fence. Each time Delta communicated that she'd had enough of the roundabouts Bella would ease off the rope and wait. Bella worked with her for perhaps fifteen minutes, crossed to the gate and the session was finished.

"Short and sweet," Bella said, looking back at Delta. "She's communicating."

"I saw it," I breathed. "It was magic."

"Magic, that's a great word," she laughed. "We'll try again tomorrow."

"Did she do the same this morning?"

"She certainly did. Daniel picked it too."

"Amazing," I grinned. "Shall I see you the same time tomorrow?"

"We'll be here," Bella laughed.

The next day, Delta behaved the same way, but this time she wasn't distracted. With all her attention on Bella, who had halted in the arena's centre she took one first tentative step and then another until she reached to touch Bella's shoulder. Hand to my mouth, I felt tears choke me. Bella responded slowly, kept her eyes downwards before turning to touch Delta's neck lightly with her hand. Something wondrous happened between horse and human right then that I'd never fully understood until that moment.

Days later, Bella showed me how to communicate with Delta myself, I would never forget it. Daniel rode her before I did, without saddle or bridle and his lack of fear as usual amazed me. She loved him, it was obvious in the way she blew her nostrils into his hair and nudged him. I would never dare to do what he did, but I thoroughly enjoyed my first ride in the saddle, her long loping strides breath taking.

"Wow! It's like she's walking on air," I marvelled.

"Good shock absorbers as Morgan would say," Bella grinned at me.

"Good description," I chuckled. "Smooth and bouncy at the same time. In slow motion."

"So, you like riding her?"

"You bet!" I laughed. "I love her."

"Then she's your ride from now on."

I halted Delta to stare wide-eyed at Bella. "You mean that?"

"Of course. I can't ride every horse."

"What about Daniel?"

"He can ride her too if he wants, but you both know Kingston is his favourite."

"True." I beamed. "I'm rapt. Thank you, Bella."

"And I must thank you for helping me."

"I'd do it all again."

"I think Delta's appreciated it."

I gave Delta's neck a rub. "Do you think she's truly happy now?"

"She looks more than happy to me."

"She must miss her friend, though."

"She will, they never forget." She looked over at Kingston and BB. "But she's got herself two new friends now."

"They clicked right from the start, didn't they?"

"Yep. We now have ourselves a cool little herd."

Delta had settled in with the other horses no problem, appreciating their company and was a good listener with Kingston especially having some interesting stories to tell about his racing days. BB tended to stress, chatting non-stop if she was given the chance and having Delta's easy-going calming presence around settled her down.

"I'm glad you came," BB told her. "You're so chilled."

"Am now," Delta corrected. "I was pretty screwed up and stressed out before."

"Really?" Kingston was surprised. "I would never have guessed."

"This place has changed me."

"It's a cool place, all right," BB nodded. "Awesome owners too, eh?"

"Bella's special, for sure," Delta agreed. "Daniel and Kate are great too. They've all helped me."

"We're a lucky lot."

They lapsed into silence, dozing under the shading trees until Delta's eyes suddenly popped open, hearing a voice in her mind.

"What did I tell you, Delta girl?" Riva spoke quietly. "Isn't it wonderful?"

"Truly wonderful. I wish you were here with me."

"I am, right here. With you forever."

"Physically would be nicer."

"It's better this way. I would still have had all my problems, arthritis and that."

"I suppose. But I miss you."

"You have two good mates now. Don't miss me too much."

"Excuse me?" Kingston was ogling. "Are you okay?"

Delta jerked her head to look into his worried questioning eyes.

"You're talking to yourself," BB eyed her too, looking baffled.

"Oh, yes. Sorry," Delta nodded. "I have a friend in my head."

"You hear voices?"

"Yes. She talks to me."

"Shadow horses do the same, it runs in the family we've been told." Kingston said.

"Shadow horses?"

He inclined his head to BB. "We're both Shadow horses."

"Oh, so you hear voices too. Your family talk to you?"

"We think so."

"You're not sure?"

"Horses are buried here, these trees are memorials to them," Kingston swivelled his head to look around the paddock. "We think we hear them sometimes."

"Wow!" Delta followed his gaze.

"Wow, indeed," BB nodded. "And weird."

"I know Riva gave me a fright the first time she spoke."

"Like being haunted, eh? But we're getting used to it slowly."

"So, do you know who they are? I mean do you know whose buried here?"

"Shadow horses mostly and a few others," Kingston told her.

"All Standardbred racehorses, like you?"

"Not all."

"Do you know their names?"

"A famous racehorse named Obsidian is one of them," BB said, grimacing wryly. "He can get quite grumpy."

"How do you mean?"

"Kind of grumbles and mutters about his mates, especially when there's a full moon."

Kingston rounded his eyes. "And he shows up, too."

Delta was surprised. "You've seen him?"

"Well, he's like a shadow, big and black."

"Wow! That's even more amazing."

"He's a bit like me eh, Bronc?"

BB shook her head scornfully. "You're tame compared to that dude."

Kingston eyed Delta again, "What happened to your friend?"

"Riva and I were best mates and together for ages, but we weren't looked after or fed properly and she got very thin and sick," Delta answered. "They had to put her down."

"I'm sorry. That must have been very sad losing her."

"It was, but now I'm here in this wonderful place," Delta said quietly. "I'm happy again and she still talks to me."

He nodded. "Cool!"

"We're also happy and glad to have met you," BB added.

"Thanks, I'm glad I met you both too."

"May the good times roll," Kingston said.

"I second that," BB agreed.

Chapter 4

The tabloids were forever interested in the Von Meerens, especially since Bernard had come on the scene, nicknamed, the Playboy. Dad was known as the Playboy's son or alternatively the Wolf's son, Matthew and Daniel have been targeted simply as the Von Meeren boys and not surprisingly I was the Von Meeren girl, the Von Meeren witch or the Wolf girl.

My grandparents had nicknames for each other too and I remembered Dad liked to tease his parents about them. Oma called Opa, Big Bad Wolf or Mr Wolf and she was Witchy Poo or Sweet Witch to him. When these names were bandied about by strangers it felt like an affront to our family's privacy and annoyed me more than I cared to admit.

Mum and Dad have tried their best to help us kids deal with the publicity, they'd done a fairly good job too, and I'd learnt to ignore the name-calling to a certain degree, gave the offenders an icy stare and frigid silence to match, which usually worked; most of whom either shut up or back tracked quickly. There were of course always exceptions; the pea-brained ignorant and arrogant variety who amused themselves at our expense, and although I wasn't one to make a spectacle of myself, they would feel the lash of my tongue if the occasion demanded.

I did, however, meet my match; a smart arse so and so who simply found my killer stare amusing, even laughing at what I had to say afterwards. Not a journalist, nothing to do with the tabloids or press but someone who worked for our family.

Roman, Bella's husband, was not only a farrier and great at handling horses but also artistic, dabbling in wrought iron work. His farrier business centred around the race-horse industry and in times past he'd taken on several young apprentice farriers to ease his workload, it was supposed to give him more time at home in his workshop but inevitably the staff moved on.

The latest help wasn't an apprentice this time, he'd drifted all over the country for years, working as farrier, stable hand and at other horse related odd jobs. Roman met him working at one of the racing stables he frequented, liked the guy immediately and offered him employment which he'd accepted for an indefinite term.

Two weeks later, he arrived in an old faded blue Ford Courier ute towing a caravan, parked it behind Roman's workshop to live in and was given access to the toilet and bathroom facilities inside, settled in no problem and proved to be a reliable and efficient worker. Bella was most relieved Roman had found someone to help him at last, thought the new man wonderful and invited him into their home for a meal most weeknights.

I met him about six weeks into his job after Bella, Daniel, and I had been at the farm together riding. She invited us home to have a look at the horse she was training, a handsome Appaloosa called Blade, and we stayed for lunch, Roman and his help also there.

At my introduction to Kenneth Hawke, something I'd never felt before made my hackles rise, making me wonder why some people just seemed to rub others up the wrong way right from the start. His appearance surprised me too, had expected someone older of perhaps Roman's age, but this man looked to be in his mid to late-twenties. Not being the kind of girl to judge a guy by looks, my reaction to his obvious good ones put me on immediate edge. It felt like someone had scraped their fingernails over a blackboard and made the hairs on my neck stand on end. I didn't like it one bit.

This guy oozed hunk from his head to his toes and knew it. His dark curly hair was too long and needed cutting or at least tying back, his deep blue eyes were the colour of a summer sky, but it was the something lurking in his stare that I didn't much care for.

"Nice to meet you," he greeted in a drawl that had more than neck hairs reacting.

When he shook my hand, I snatched it away which only served to amuse him.

"Likewise," I returned without smiling.

"You're another vet nurse, I believe?"

"That's right," I said coldly.

"It's a family thing," Bella laughed. "Us Lawson girls adore animals."

"And Lawson boys," Daniel piped up.

"Good on you," Kenneth chuckled. "So, you're a vet?"

"No way." Daniel shook his head with a snort. "Not brainy enough for that."

"Don't listen to him. He could be anything he wants." Bella wagged her finger at Daniel indignantly. "I'm lucky. He decided to work with me and on our family farm."

"Another horse whisperer, then?"

"If you call it that." She pulled a wry face. "Morgan was the horseman of the family. We're just trying to continue what he started."

"Morgan? I've heard stories about him."

"Yeah, amazing guy," Roman nodded.

With Kenneth's attention no longer on me, I gave him the once-over and couldn't help but wonder what Roman saw in him. Personally, I wouldn't have trusted this drifter as far as I could throw him; he had that I'll do what I want and don't give a shit kind of look.

When Kenneth's eyes suddenly locked on me again, I wasn't prepared for it, felt my face flush and his knowing smile at my scowl didn't help.

After lunch, Daniel and I went with Bella to admire Blade, Roman stopped to make a phone call in the shed while Kenneth disappeared to his caravan, which was parked nearby in full view of the yards. Wondering what it looked like inside, I wrinkled my nose at the visions in my brain of an untidy mess and hippy clutter. When Bella suggested Daniel take Blade through his paces, I left the yard to watch from outside the fence, but my eyes kept drifting to the caravan. Kenneth's sudden appearance at the door made me jump, and the way he looked straight at me with that enigmatic curve to his mouth had me wondering how long he'd been watching me from inside. His approach had my nerves tightening, but as he halted beside me, I ignored him, pretending to be solely focused on Bella explaining something to Daniel, wishing at the same time that Roman would hurry up and join us.

"Kate," he said quietly. "That's a nice name for a girl." At my lack of response, he leant closer, murmuring. "But I think Wolf girl or maybe witch, suits you better."

That was all I needed to confirm my suspicions—here was another pea-brained, arrogant so and so. I faced him with a killer stare, letting him know without words what I thought of him.

"Ah, I see," he said into the chilly silence. "Methinks you prefer Kate."

I curled my lip in disgusted disdain, shifting along the fence away from him.

He wasn't at all put off and shifted along with me, speaking quietly again. "There's something about those eyes of yours."

It took all my willpower not to turn on him and do some damage. He hadn't finished. "Wild and untamed, just like a wolf."

"Why don't you piss off?" I hissed.

His unexpected chuckle had my eyes popping wide. "Now, that's not friendly."

"I'm not being friendly," I spat. "Call me names again and you'll be sorry."

"Sorry, how?"

"You'll find out."

"That sound promising."

"Get lost."

"Very friendly."

"Ha! I knew Bella would have Daniel working as soon as she got the chance," Roman said, coming up behind us.

Forcing a calming breath, I turned to him quickly with a tight smile. "Good on her, I reckon. Why not make use of my brother while he's here?"

He laughed, "Are you going to have a go?"

"I'd confuse the poor horse," I told him. "Daniel's way better than me."

"Bella tells me you're pretty good."

"Not like my brother. He has a gift and he's fearless."

"Like this guy," Roman gestured to Kenneth. "Horses roll over and play dead for him."

My look of disbelief made Kenneth grin and roll his eyes. "The man exaggerates."

"No, mate." Roman shook his head. "Horses behave better with you than me."

Kenneth laughed. "You get the naughty ones."

"Ah, but even the naughty ones like you."

"Must be my deodorant."

"What deodorant?" Roman chortled. "BO, you mean?"

"Fillies especially, like it." Kenneth laughing eyes were on me.

Their camaraderie took me aback, made me realise then what Roman saw in him. He's good with horses, I thought in surprise, replacing that instantly with scorn at myself. Duh! He is a farrier after all and has worked with horses for years. What did you expect? It doesn't change who he is, an obvious smart arse who very likely treats women like nothing if his arrogance is anything to go by. I'm not changing my opinion!

I was more than glad to be back in Daniel's ute on our way home soon after.

"Is something wrong?" Daniel asked at one point, noticing my lack of conversation.

"Nothing's wrong," I assured him. "Just thinking."

"About Kenneth?"

"No!" I said too quickly.

He gave me a sidelong grin, "Aw K, come on. I thought you'd like him."

"Why would I?"

"Being a horseman and all."

"And all?"

"Good looking too."

"You think?" I was sarcastic.

"Not me," Daniel smirked. "Bella says the girls do though."

"The girls?"

"You know, females. Roman says they're after him, ring him up all the time."

"Isn't he lucky?" Doubly sarcastic this time. "And for your information I am not one of those girls."

"He likes you."

"What?"

"Sis, are you blind? He was ogling you the whole time."

"He was not!"

"He was. Couldn't keep his eyes off."

"Oh, stop it!" I snapped. "Why would he be interested in me? I'm way too young for starters."

"He's not that old. Twenty-eight, I think."

"Nine years older than me!" I curled my lip.

"That's nothing these days," Daniel grinned.

"Whatever!" I snapped. "I don't know where you're going with this, brother but I advise you to give it up."

"Aw, I'm just helping my little sister get hooked."

"Hooked?" I glared.

"With a nice good-looking dude."

"I do not want a dude, thank you very much!" I bit it out. "And even if I did, it wouldn't be Kenneth Hawke."

"Ah, that got a reaction." Daniel's look was sly. "That's always a good sign they say."

"A good sign?"

"That deep down you really do like him."

"Oh, shut up!" I hissed. "For your information, I do not think he's good-looking or nice and I certainly do not like him!"

"Okay, okay! Keep your hair on!" He laughed. "Just trying to help."

"Don't help!" I said coldly. "If I ever want a guy, I'll deal with it myself."

"Sure, K." He nodded vigorously. "Whatever you say."

That was the last thing said about the subject, thankfully. Daniel dropped me at the homestead door before planting his foot with a wide cheeky grin, skidding the ute over to his cottage. To my relief, I met no one in the house, scooting up to my bedroom to strut in front of the mirror and wonder what exactly guys would find attractive.

Figured my delightful brother, who loved to tease, was having me on about Kenneth Hawke ogling me. There was nothing to ogle at for starters; guys liked bouncy curves, which I had none of, and they liked pretty things, which I wasn't. I pulled a sour face at the mirror. But I do have my Oma's looks, or so I've been told often enough, and she hooked one of the hunkiest men on the planet. Who knows, maybe one day I could get lucky! That had me snorting a derisive cackle. Not now! There's more to life than the opposite sex, and who wants to get involved at my age, far too young!

My lack of interest or attraction to boys at college had never worried me, I'd known of girls there who'd been doing far more than just going out with boys and not only had one but several on a string. Even at work, most of the girls were attached or having men problems with me, thinking they needed to get a life. If I ever did hook up with a guy in the future, it wouldn't be with anyone remotely like Hawke, I could guarantee that.

Chapter 5

Family get-togethers, parties, and barbeques, for whatever reason, were always fun, and Tobias's birthday at the Sandford homestead was no exception, a cracker of a party with laughter, music and plenty of food and drink.

I sat listening to Olivia, Glenys, and Rebecca having an aminated discussion about kids and schooling when Roman and Bella arrived. My enjoyment went right out the window when I saw who was with them. There'd been no need for me to see the man again, had made sure of it by excusing myself twice now from visiting Bella's place with Daniel.

Unexpected as his presence was, his appearance was even more of a surprise; he'd had his hair cut, and although it still threatened to curl, it was short all over and only just skimmed his collar. The blue shirt matched his eyes, and the grey trousers hugged hips and butt nicely. Whatever was I taking notice of that for? Looking away, I tried resuming an interest in the conversation, but my eyes had a mind of their own, watching him shake hands with Leon, Karl and several others.

"Is that Roman's new workman?" Rebecca asked. "Rather good-looking, isn't he?"

I realised then that it wasn't only me eyeing him up.

"Good looking is too tame a word," Olivia noted. "Have you not met him yet?"

"No." Rebecca shook her head. "Have you, Glenys?"

"Not yet but I've heard talk about him," Glenys told us. "He's shod horses for one of the ladies at the library and she thinks he's hot."

"Have you met him, Kate?" Olivia asked.

"Once at Bella's." I was brusque.

"What do you think?"

"Roman likes him."

"I meant you." She locked eyes with me, smiling slyly. "What do you think?"

"Good catch for you, girl." Rebecca was also smiling.

"I doubt that." I pretended a laugh. "He's old."

"Old!" Olivia snorted. "He's only in his twenties."

"Twenty-eight actually." I arched my eyebrows. "Nine years older than me."

"What's nine years?" Rebecca scoffed. "My hairdresser's man is twelve years older than her, and she loves it."

"Oh, yes. Imagine nine years of experience." Glenys licked her lips.

"Hmm, indeed." Olivia did the same. "Wonder what he's like in the sack?"

"La-de-dah." Rebecca rolled her eyes. "Probably knows every position."

"And the rest!" Glenys chortled.

My jaw dropped, eyebrows hitting my hairline.

"Good kisser too, I bet," Olivia said.

"With that mouth," Rebecca agreed with a vigorous nod. "For sure!"

"Got it all going on, hasn't he?" Olivia sighed. "What more could a woman want?"

I found my voice at last. "Aren't you lot supposed to be married?"

"Eyes, girl. Husbands look, so can wives." Olivia smirked at my disbelieving frown.

"You call that just looking?" I pulled a sceptical face.

"Looking and talking," Olivia laughed. "Sex is always such an interesting subject."

Glenys patted my arm. "Don't worry, Kate."

"Yeah, take no notice of us old married ladies," Olivia said. "He's all yours."

I couldn't say a word, my mouth opening and closing like a fish.

"A word of advice. Guys your own age are too immature," she added.

"I second that. Older is better," Rebecca grinned.

"And nine years is nothing," Glenys added. "Go for experience. That hunk over there fits the bill perfectly."

I said not a word, my sense of humour having all but left me. When Bella suddenly steered the subject of our conversation towards Olivia who was waving out, I went into panic mode, looking for an escape route. Too late!

"Hey, girls. Have you met Kenneth?" Bella greeted us.

A positively glowing Glenys was first to step forward, shaking his hand. "Hello, I'm Glenys, Tobias's wife. So nice to meet you at last, we've heard all about you."

"Should I be worried?" Kenneth laughed, blue eyes twinkling.

"Nothing bad, I can assure you," Glenys giggled.

"Hi, Kenneth." Rebecca was next to fawn over him. "I'm Rebecca, Luis's partner."

"The lovely Sandford ladies," Kenneth grinned. "Glad to meet you."

"Nice of you to come and meet our families." Olivia took his hand.

"Thank you. It's a privilege."

I attempted to disappear into the background, but his eyes had me in their sights.

"You've met Kate, I believe." Olivia gestured at me. "Jason's daughter."

"Of course. Who could forget meeting the lovely Von Meeren girl," His teasing grin had my hackles rising. "Good to see you again, Kate."

"Hi," I said coolly which only served to amuse him more.

"You've meet Jason, Kate's dad?" Olivia asked him.

"I have indeed." Kenneth nodded. "Another good guy who appreciates horses."

"Yes, like his mother Maria did," Olivia nodded. "Mind you his father Bernard liked them too but didn't ride."

"I believe the Von Meeren family were avid horse racing people."

"That's right. Avid supporters of animal charities too."

Kenneth's eyes returned to me. "I understand your father was named after the eldest Sandford son, Jason."

"He was." I spoke as coolly as before.

"You've heard the story then?" Olivia asked. "That Maria was Jason's girlfriend before he died?"

"I have."

"You know about the helicopter crash?"

As Kenneth nodded something changed in his eyes, sending a chill down my spine but it was so fleeting I wondered if I'd imagined it. "A tragedy," he murmured.

"Yes, it was. A difficult time for everyone, especially Maria."

"And then she married Bernard."

"Maria met Bernard when she was with Jason. Those two boys were old friends from way back when they were children." Olivia sighed. "It's quite something, naming your child after a memory."

"Hey, ladies." Roman appeared. "Give Kenneth a break will you."

"He's loving it," Bella grinned as he put his arm around her.

"What guy wouldn't?" Roman tweaked her nose.

Everyone laughed, and the conversation turned to other things. I was relieved at the interruption, discreetly slipping away as more people joined our group. Although Kenneth and I met three more times during the party, I was never alone and hardly spoke, leaving those with me to do most of the talking. It didn't stop him looking, though; his eyes speaking a language all their own. It made me squirm.

Arrogant chauvinist, I sneered deep down. Those pretty-blue eyes of yours aren't going to make this girl slobber over you. Ever!

Several times I held his gaze deliberately with the iciest stare I could muster, hoping to break his scrutiny, but it only prompted that infuriating little smile of his. Would have loved to wipe that look off his face, but each time someone came to his rescue and distracted me.

Later at home in bed, I couldn't for the life of me understand why the man got me so wound up; the wolf and witch name calling was one excuse but hadn't previously incited quite the same reaction. Perhaps my senses were working overtime, as if I felt something uneasy lurking below the surface of the man.

It was three months later that my suspicions about Kenneth Hawke proved conclusive. Dad received a phone call from Leon asking all our family, Roman and Bella included, to attend a meeting at his place Sunday afternoon, but wouldn't say why.

The homestead dining table was laden with finger food; we were all offered a drink by the kitchen staff, and once we'd settled down in the lounge, Leon and Karl took the meeting.

"Thanks for coming along," Leon smiled, holding a folder in his hand. "Karl and I have some news."

"We wanted you to hear it from us and not some other source," Karl added.

Dad slanted his head. "Good news, we hope."

"A big surprise, but we think it's good, yes," Leon nodded.

"Another thing." Karl crooked a rueful smile. "Leon and I have known about this for weeks, but we do hope no one gets their noses out of joint at the secrecy."

"Especially our wives and kids." Leon pulled a wry grimace at everyone's bemused faces. "Before we continue, please accept our humble apologies; we meant no offence."

Jacqueline, Leon's wife, gave him a mock frown. "Secrets, huh?"

Leon laughed. "We simply thought it was better this way, and not just for us."

"So, let's get started." Karl inclined his head to his brother. "You first, Leon."

"Right." Leon cleared his throat. "Most of you haven't met our big brother, Jason, in the flesh. Anna, of course, would remember him well." He gestured to Anna, who smiled and nodded in reply. "But I'm sure you're all familiar with the history. Jason's mum died when he was very young, his dad, Tony, then remarried our mum, Alicia, and subsequently Karl and I came along." Leon took a long breath before saying on a gruff note. "As you also know, Jason died in a helicopter accident."

"This news we have concerns Jason," Karl continued. "It's taken approximately two months to clarify and now we want to share it."

Leon cleared his throat. "We've found out that Jason had a son."

All eyebrows shot up, but no one said a word. I noticed Dad's blank look of astonishment, his eyes riveted on Leon.

Leon spoke again quietly. "Jason's son, Karl and my nephew died twenty years ago, but he also had a son who is still alive."

"My cousin then? Second cousin?" Olivia gasped.

"Yes, my dear," Leon smiled gently at his daughter. "Tobias and Luis's too."

"You've met him?"

"We have," Karl nodded.

Tobias, Luis and Olivia all looked at each other in astonishment.

"Let's carry on shall we?" Leon said. "Jason's grandson only recently found out his true identity from his grandmother, she died just days later. He wrote everything down, which is what I have here." He opened the folder, scanning paperwork inside. "As the story goes, a twenty-year-old Jason and his mates went camping in the summer holidays, an open-air concert was held at the campsite where he met a girl named Valerie, but it seems they never saw each other again afterwards." Leon paused to take a breath. "Valerie gave birth to a son whom she named Adam, but she kept the father's identity to herself, didn't even tell her parents and on her son's birth certificate, the father was listed as unknown."

Leon stopped there to let Karl take over, handing him another sheet of paper. "Adam was living with the mother of his son, but she left them both not long after the birth. From then on, he began drinking heavily, and we understand he died of alcoholic poisoning several years later, which resulted in Valerie taking over her grandson's care." Karl paused to let that sink in. "After he got in touch with us, we had all the facts checked over and verified. Valerie's dates are spot on; the campsite and concert are legit. She also mentioned the names of Jason's friends who were with him at the time, one of whom was Bernard."

"Dad was there?" Dad said in surprise as Mum took his hand.

"Yes, he was," Karl nodded. "And both Leon and I knew some of the other guys."

"We're able to do a more thorough investigation if we need to," Leon said. "But at this stage, we have no reason to believe that this isn't true."

"This grandson, our second cousin, what's his name?" Tobias wanted to know.

"Now this will come as a real surprise." Leon pressed his lips together, turning his eyes to Bella and Roman. "Especially to you both."

They both looked at each other with puzzlement.

"He works for you, Roman."

"What?" Roman looked dumbstruck. "Kenneth?"

"Yes, Kenneth Hawke. His grandmother was Valerie Hawke."

"Kenneth is Jason's grandson?" Bella gasped.

I echoed her gasp, staring disbelievingly at Leon.

"Of course!" A voice piped up, clear and precise. "He has Jason's eyes."

We all turned to stare at Anna, who smiled knowingly.

"You're right, Anna." Leon smiled at her. "Exactly what Karl and I thought."

"So, how will this affect our family?" Tobias wanted to know.

"Yes, Dad. What happens now?" Olivia frowned.

"We haven't got that far yet." Leon smiled at her. "Kenneth just wanted us to know about his father, Adam."

"That's all?" She sounded disbelieving.

I sympathise with you, Olivia, I thought. I can't imagine a drifter like Kenneth Hawke will settle for nothing. Now he's found out he's a Sandford, he'll probably bleed the family dry if he can. My feelings about him were right, Trouble with a capital T.

"Don't worry, my girl," Leon shook his head. "He doesn't want money from us, if that's what you're meaning."

"I'm not worried about that, Dad." She pursed her lips. "But if he's family he's entitled to something, isn't he?"

"Shouldn't we be seeking legal advice?" Tobias asked.

"You're right, Tobe." Karl turned to his son. "And we are seeking legal advice. We'll also do DNA testing if required and that may involve you, Luis and Olivia as well."

"Blood tests?" Olivia pulled a distasteful face.

Like me she detested blood tests and had fainted once or twice before.

"They do saliva and hair too, these days." Luis piped up helpfully.

"Won't they need DNA from your brother, Jason? How will they get that?" Daniel was interested to know.

"You'd be surprised," Leon told him. "Old clothing, even things from inside his apartment, after all most of his stuff is still there."

"Going back to Olivia mentioning entitlement," Dad narrowed his eyes on Leon. "Jason left things to Mum, like the beach cabin. Should that have gone to Kenneth, perhaps?"

"No." Jason shook his head. "What Jason did for Maria was his wish at the time and done legally. We must remember Valerie chose not to let Jason or his family know about Adam, and it's our sincere belief that Jason would have provided for his son if he'd known. What's happening now has nothing to do Maria."

"I understand." Dad nodded. "Well, I hope things work out for you all."

"Thanks. It'll take time, but we'll sort everything out."

"In the meantime, we're getting to know, Kenneth," Karl spread his hands, smiling at us all. "We like him so far and to be honest, he already feels like family."

"You're right," Olivia beamed. "I like him too."

"And, so do we, he's a great guy." Roman said. "Is he planning on staying?"

Leon shrugged. "That's up to him but we're hoping he'll stay for a while at least."

What's wrong with you lot? I thought with incredulous disdain. Can't you see what the guy is really like, he doesn't belong with us? Am I the only one that doesn't like him?

It seemed I was because suddenly everyone was talking at once about how wonderful Kenneth was, Kenneth this and Kenneth that. I despaired, hoping with a vengeance that he would move on like the nomad he was.

"Just one more thing everyone!" Karl raised a hand for quiet. "As we all know this will get out eventually, more fodder for the tabloids. So, be prepared, okay?"

"I'll let you know when the gossip hits," Anna laughed.

She'd always loved to keep up with the news, still did and sure enough, days later, the story was out, it never ceased to amaze us how the press got hold of their information, and we read all about it, huddling around the farm homestead's computer.

"The Sandford Secret" was the caption. It went on to mention details about Jason Sandford, the eldest son, who had been tragically killed. Him having met Valarie Hawke during the summer holidays so many years ago and her having his illegitimate child in secret. There was even more about the grandson, a photograph of Kenneth with those blue eyes looking directly at the camera.

"Goodness me!" Anna chortled. "He's Jason all over again."

"Very yummy," Olivia laughed too. "Pity he's related."

As Ben gave her a suspicious sidelong look she fluttered her eyelashes at him.

"I agree. Gorgeous indeed," Mum laughed.

Dad gave Ben an eye roll, shooting Mum a suspicious frown thereafter.

"Well, that's a matter of opinion," I said snootily. "He doesn't appeal to me."

"Really? That's unusual." Anna cocked a disbelieving eyebrow at me. "One thing you don't have in common with my sister then. She found Jason most appealing, especially those wicked eyes of his."

Feeling uncomfortable at her scrutiny, I shrugged without replying and broke eye contact. Left the room shortly after for some fresh air, wandering across to talk to our horses in the paddock. They nodded, sighed and nudged me gently with their noses but were no help in removing a pair of wicked blue eyes out of my head.

Chapter 6

When stressed or thinking hard, I tended to mutter to myself, which was how Dad found me one morning inside the tractor shed having a good old conversation. I wasn't exactly talking to thin air as Trojan was with me, sprawled out nearby, listening politely, but when he unexpectedly leapt to his feet, I spun around, heart to my mouth.

"It's only me!" Dad threw up both hands. "Giving Trojan a pep talk, are you?"

Sighing, I shook my head ruefully, "Just talking to myself."

"Sounds interesting." He propped himself against the wall.

"It's not really."

"Everything you do or say is interesting to your old dad."

"You're not old."

"Thanks."

He waited patiently, watching me.

"Aren't you worried about this Sandford stuff?" I blurted.

"About Kenneth, you mean?"

"Yes, him."

"You really don't like him, do you?"

I looked down at my feet, frowned, "Maybe I just don't trust him."

"So far everything he's said is true."

"I know." I sighed again. "I understand him wanting Leon and Karl to know he's Jason's grandson, but do you really think that's all he's after?"

"It seems so. He's not interested in inheritances or money Leon says."

"Look at him though." I spread my hands. "He lives in a caravan and drifts around doing odd jobs all over the place. Surely, he must want something."

"The Sandford boys will sort it." Dad eyed me. "Why does it worry you so much?"

"Our cabin," I stated bluntly.

"It's ours, like Leon said. Jason left it to your grandmother, legally."

"But he could fight to get it, couldn't he?"

"I suppose he could. What makes you think he will?"

"I don't know," I let out a long breath. "There's something about him."

"Which you don't like."

"I suppose so."

"Daniel reckons he likes you."

My eyebrows shot up. "He told you that?"

"Yep." Dad smiled gently. "And I think he's right. I noticed at Tobias's party."

"Noticed what?"

"Him giving you the up and down."

"I'm sure he'd give any girl the up and down," I scoffed, adding snappishly without thinking. "He's an arrogant smart arse!"

"Ah!" Dad's smile turned knowing. "Now we're getting somewhere."

"What?" I could feel my face flushing.

"Has he come on to you?"

"No!"

"Talk to me, my dear." Dad straightened up from off the wall. "He's obviously done something."

"He called me Wolf girl and said the witch word."

"Ha! Now I really do see." Dad chuckled. "Silly boy!"

I gave him a baleful stare but kept my mouth shut.

"That's all?" Dad was still grinning.

"All?" I was indignant. "Isn't that enough?"

"I thought you'd got used to ignoring the names?"

"I have, sort of," I muttered.

"Then along comes an arrogant stranger who gets under your skin."

"Well, yes."

"You know your mother thought I was an arrogant one of those, too?"

I gaped. "What?"

"She didn't want me near her at first."

"Are you kidding?"

"Nope."

"What happened?"

"My considerable charm," he grinned. "And she couldn't keep away in the end."

"You have charm?" I rolled my eyes.

"Sometimes us males get lucky."

I snorted a laugh, mock punching him. "So, what are you saying?"

"Arrogance can be a cover." Dad narrowed his eyes. "I think that boy has been through a lot, maybe he's searching for something."

"What do you mean, searching?"

"Stability in his life, a name, a father he hardly knew."

"You feel sorry for him?" I was surprised.

"Sorry isn't the word, but I do feel for him."

"And you think I should too?" I screwed up my nose.

"Just give him a chance, learn more about the guy before you judge."

"Learn more about him?" I yipped.

"You know what I mean. Get to know him," Dad smiled. "He might surprise you."

"I'm not sure I want to be surprised."

"If he gets fresh just use your knee, that's what your grandmother did."

"Pardon?" My jaw dropped.

"Apparently she used hers on Dad and tried drowning him too."

"You're joking!" I gasped and at his head shake, squeaked. "That's priceless!"

"Yes, she was. Very priceless," he murmured. "And you're so very like her."

"Oh, Dad." I put my arms around him. "You still miss her so much, don't you?"

"I do. She was a wonderful mum." He squeezed me tight. "I miss them both."

I pulled back, cocking an eyebrow, "Why did Oma use her knee on Opa?"

"He got fresh."

"And the drowning?"

"Same again."

My burst of laughter had Trojan wagging his tail in earnest, face split in a big doggy grin.

"Well," I spluttered. "If Oma can do it so can I."

"Just don't put him out of action for life."

I tilted my head. "Did Oma tell you much about Jason?"

"She told me a little." He smiled. "He was her first love."

"And she named you after him so that's saying something."

"She missed him terribly after he died," he told me. "Lived in his apartment for a while and then moved into the cabin."

"She lived alone at the cabin?" I was surprised. "Wasn't she there with Opa?"

"Opa and her had their ups and downs before I came along, something went wrong and they split up for a time, but she had Wolf for company, the dog I was brought up with."

"She told you about that?"

"Some."

"But they turned out okay, didn't they?"

"They sure did."

"She would have felt safe with Wolf at the cabin."

"I think so. He was very loyal."

"Like Trojan here." I put out a hand to ruffle my dog's ears.

"You're just like your Oma," Dad chuckled. "So fond of animals."

"Hey, I'm fond of some humans too!" I tapped his nose.

"If you want to know more about Oma you should talk to Bella, she and Maria got on well," Dad suggested. "She could help you too, with boys."

"Boys?" I screwed up my nose. "Why would I want help with them?"

"A certain boy." He chuckled at my look. "Mr Hawke or should I say Sandford."

I heaved a sigh. "That is so weird, isn't it?"

"It must have been a real surprise for Leon and Karl, for sure."

"I really hope he doesn't cause problems for them or us." I knit my brows.

"I don't think he will." Dad lifted a teasing eyebrow. "But you could always try distracting him, have him eating out of your pretty little hand."

"I do not have pretty little hands!"

Dad chuckled at my scowl. "Yes, you do, little girl. You are very beautiful."

"You're biased!" I made a face. "And I doubt he'd eat out of anyone's hand."

"You'd be surprised what us males will do." Dad teased.

"I don't think I want to know!" I shot him a disgusted look.

"Just be nice to the guy. I'm sure he's not as bad as you think."

"Are you trying to matchmake or something?" I eyed him suspiciously.

"Would I do that?"

"I understand most dads would have their shotgun at the ready."

"If any guy even thought to hurt you, I'd use more than a shotgun," he said quietly, adding as my eyes widened at his sudden seriousness. "But I don't think Kenneth would hurt you. I like him and actually feel like I've met him before somewhere."

"You've met him before?" My eyes went wider. "Where?"

He shook his head. "It's just a feeling, maybe to do with Mum, I mean, her having known Jason, his grandfather." He shrugged. "I don't know."

"A feeling?" I eyeballed him worriedly.

"Oma had feelings too, you know." He tipped his head, all seriousness gone. "She used to talk to Jason in dreams."

"Yikes! This is getting creepy."

His eyes twinkled. "Dad didn't call Mum Witchy poo for nothing."

"Oh, please. I thought the witch thing was a joke!"

"It's okay, little girl, it was and still is." He chuckled. "But Mum did have a way about her, those grey eyes could read your mind."

"The same eyes as ours," I muttered, staring into Dad's. "But I don't have feelings and I can't read minds, or at least I haven't noticed so far."

"Maybe it comes with age," Dad smirked.

"Something to look forward to then." I rolled my eyes.

"Come to think of it, even Dad had dreams about Jason."

"Really?" I squeaked.

"That's what he told me."

"Jason seems to have left quite an impression." I arched my eyebrows.

"And now he's back via his grandson."

"Brilliant!" I said, not quite able to keep the sarcasm at bay.

"Anna seems to think they're very alike." Dad's teasing smile had me narrowing my eyes suspiciously "And she said something else to me after Leon and Karl's meeting."

"What was that?" Did I really want to know?

"Imagine it all coming full circle, that really would be quite something."

"Meaning?" Knew what was coming.

He chuckled. "As in, Maria's granddaughter with Jason's grandson."

"She's dreaming!" I scoffed. "That's not just quite something, that's over the top!"

"An interesting observation, don't you think?"

"Not!" I poked him in the chest.

"She could be onto something you know." He grinned, tweaking my chin. "And Mum would be laughing about it."

"No way! Not going to happen!" I shook my head vehemently. "I will try my best to be nice to him, but nothing else. Okay?"

"Okay, my girl." He pulled me into a bear hug. "I hold you to that."

His mum may have been laughing but I certainly wasn't. Deep down I doubted my best would be enough as I rarely changed my mind once I'd made it up about someone; Kenneth Hawke Sandford or whatever he called himself was no exception.

I'd promised Dad, however, so when Bella invited me to her place a fortnight later to meet a mare and foal that she was looking after, I accepted. As Daniel had something else planned, I arrived on my own, parking my jeep beside Bella's Land-rover and Roman's classic Ford Jailbar truck. After a quick chat with Roman who was busy in the workshop, Bella and I entered the back paddock to cluck over the beautiful Arab mare and her adorable foal. Couldn't help but notice the door of Kenneth's caravan was closed with no sign of life, his ute not parked anywhere in sight either which concluded my being nice wouldn't be happening this visit rather to my relief.

"Roman's helper hasn't moved out then?" I couldn't resist asking.

"Not planning to as far as we know," Bella looked across at the caravan. "He's out at the Brooms' stable this morning."

"Doesn't he want to shift out of his caravan into the Sandford house." I couldn't keep the sarcasm out of my voice.

"I doubt it, not his style," Bella raised her eyebrows at my tone.

"Jason's apartment then. It isn't used, is it?"

"I suppose he could park his caravan next to it." Bella laughed.

"Have they done the DNA tests yet?"

"Last resort, I think." Her eyes narrowed on me. "He is telling the truth, you know."

"I'm sure he is," I nodded quickly.

"You don't like him, do you?" Her sharp look stayed on me.

Oh dear! Not another one. I obviously wasn't that good at hiding my feelings. Shrugging, I averted my eyes. "I hardly know him."

"Well, you should get to know him," she said quietly, echoing Dad's words. "He's a good guy, Kate."

I forced my eyes back to her, saying with a tight-lipped smile. "Of course."

"You get used to him." Bella grinned wryly. "He's straight up, says what he thinks and isn't so different to Roman." When I didn't reply she added. "Or your very forthright grandfather to be honest."

"Hmm," I was noncommittal, eyes on the horses. "How long are they here for?"

"Another month. I'm working with the mare, she's difficult to load and not a good traveller. It's good for the foal as well."

Phew! I was glad the subject of Kenneth Hawke had been dropped.

We chatted about the horses, what we were both up to at our respective jobs until lunch time. While helping Bella prepare food in the kitchen, the sound of a vehicle pulling in had us both turning to look out the window, my heart sinking at the sight of a faded blue ute and its driver alighting. Kenneth went straight to the shed's open door, disappearing inside without so much as a glance at the house.

"That's good timing," Bella smiled at me. "Would you like to ask him if he wants some lunch?"

I didn't want to ask him anything but forcing an enthusiastic nod made for the shed, poked my head in with some trepidation and saw him talking to Roman, his back to me.

Roman acknowledged me with a grin. "Hey, Kate. Lunch ready, is it?"

"Yes, just about. Bella wants to know if Kenneth is coming in as well."

Kenneth turned around, his eyes lighting up. "Hey, you're a nice surprise!"

You'll get more than a surprise if you're not careful, I thought belligerently. Why do you have to look at me like that? You're not helping, I'm trying to be nice!

I plastered on a cheerful smile, "So, you're here for lunch then?"

"How could I refuse with two lovely ladies for company? I better go and clean up."

Roman laughed, giving Kenneth a friendly punch as he made for the bathroom. Watching his butt in the faded blue jeans, I became aware that Roman was watching me, watching him and spun on my heel, flapping a hand to cool my embarrassed cheeks before re-entering the house. Told Bella Kenneth was coming for lunch, helped her set the table with hands that weren't quite steady and both men strolled in minutes later, minus their boots.

"Hello, you," Bella welcomed Kenneth. "How were the Brooms this morning?"

"Not bad. The old lady was hanging around but got told to shut up," he chuckled.

The sound of his laughter had my knees going weak. What the heck! Nobody had ever had that effect on me before!

"She's a hard case, that one," Roman laughed too. "It's a wonder her family haven't tried breaking her walking stick yet to stop her interfering."

"That'll never happen. She'll kark it in the stables first."

"You have to like her though, don't you," Bella said. "Such a sprightly lady."

"She's harmless. I just say yes and no at the right times," Kenneth grinned.

"What would you like to drink?" Bella asked him. "You've finished work for the day, haven't you? How about a wine?"

He nodded. "Won't say no, thanks."

Unfortunately, I ended up sitting opposite him and avoiding his eyes during lunch was a mission. Be nice, be nice! Kept resounding in my head. I let the talk wash over me to start until Bella drew me in to the conversation.

"What was Daniel up to today?"

"He was going to the Strait with Matthew; some go karting competition."

"Oh, fun! Did your dad go?"

"No, he's visiting a friend with Mum."

"The Strait is our local car racing track," Roman told Kenneth.

"Yeah, I've heard about it." Kenneth looked at me. "Your dad races cars as well as works on them, doesn't he?"

"Yes, he does."

"Very good at it too, like his father Bernard," Roman added.

"I've heard a lot about Bernard from Leon and Karl."

"He was your grandfather's best friend," Bella said.

"Did Bernard ever talk to you about Jason?" Kenneth asked her.

"He did. Mum talked about him too, but I'm sorry I didn't take much notice."

"I totally get it. Us young ones are all the same, eh? We don't take enough notice of the olds until it's too late."

"Aren't you lucky your grandmother had a chance to talk to you, then," I couldn't help the snide remark. "Before it was too late."

"Very lucky." His eyes drilled. "I'd never have known about my family otherwise."

Bella sipped her wine. "Leon and Karl are over the moon about you."

Kenneth's eyes stayed on me. "They've been very welcoming, really great guys. My dad would have been impressed." His slow smile made my nerves jangle. "You remember your paternal grandparents well, Kate?"

I didn't smile back. "Yes, they died when I was seven."

"Your grandmother Maria was quite something I'm told."

"She was the best Oma anyone could have." I told him haughtily.

"Oma?" He slanted his head. "Is that German for grandmother?"

I nodded sharply once, before dropping my eyes to drink some wine.

"She was a beautiful person, we all loved her very much," Bella said. "And Kate, is very like her."

I almost choked on the wine. Thank you, Bella! Did you have to add that in?

"They must have made a striking couple," Kenneth said quietly. "Your Oma and my grandfather, Jason, I mean."

I looked at him again coldly. "I wouldn't know."

"Yes, they did. I've seen photographs," Bella informed him cheerfully. "I'm sure Leon would know where they are and show you."

Kenneth held my stare. "I'll ask him. Would be good to see them."

"I think your dad has some too, doesn't he, Kate?"

"Probably," I turned my head to give her a forced smile.

Roman changed the subject thankfully, the conversation flowing over me again.

I'd totally lost the enthusiasm to be nice, however, wanting to leave right then but endured for another hour. As Kenneth's eyes locked on too often for my liking, the feeling inside of me got worse each time, nerves stretching but with something else I couldn't fathom. Didn't want to fathom.

Glad to make my escape eventually, I went home to seriously unwind.

Chapter 7

Bella was slumped face down over Roman on one of the deck loungers, both of them naked and still catching their breaths.

"I think we should stop doing this," Bella spluttered, lifting her head a little.

"Why?" Roman croaked against her neck.

"I don't like audiences."

"We have an audience?" He wasn't perturbed.

"Not right now." She blew out her cheeks. "But we most likely will have one day."

"Who?"

"Who do you think?"

"Kenneth?" Roman snorted a laugh. "Nothing embarrasses him!"

"Maybe not, but it will embarrass me!"

"Aw, why? He'll only wolf whistle."

"That's exactly what I mean!" Bella levered herself up on her elbows to glare down at him. "Doesn't that worry you?"

"I'd probably do the same."

She rolled her eyes. "Of course, I should have expected that!"

"He's harmless."

"Roman! That's beside the point." She scrambled off him. "I do not want anyone watching us, thank you very much!"

He rolled onto his side, made a grab for her but missed. At her squeal, he grinned, watching her shapely backside disappear inside. He sat up to rub a hand over his face, taking deep breaths of night air.

Kenneth was definitely at home, his ute was parked out front and, although the caravan was out of sight, Roman could hear the faint sound of a guitar playing. He wondered if his workmate had more than music entertaining him, there'd been no sign of any females lurking, but Kenneth did have eyes on Kate and made no secret of his interest.

Woohoo! Good luck with that man, Roman thought with a chuckle. She's another Bella or, more to the point, another Maria. Watch yourself.

They're feisty women!

He stood up to go inside, locking the door before going in search of Bella. She was in the shower and not overly welcoming when he joined her, but soon stopped her protests.

Later in bed, he lay on his side contentedly studying his wife's face and seeing his mouth curve, she gave him a suspicious up from under look. "What?"

"Just glad you're here," he murmured.

"As long as that all you're thinking."

"Now, what else would I be thinking?"

She screwed her nose at him, reaching a hand up to his face. "We really should be toning down the exercise, don't you think?"

"Why?"

"We're not spring chickens any more, Mr Antonovich, haven't you noticed?"

"And?"

"You are unbelievable. You work full days, and you still have the energy!"

"As do you."

"Yeah right!" She rolled her eyes. "I can hardly get out of bed in the mornings."

He laughed, "You've had that problem since I've known you, Lady."

She sighed. "Can we just not get energetic on the deck any more?"

"What's wrong with the deck?"

"Roman!" She frowned frustratedly. "Please, be sensible."

"Explain sensible."

"I don't feel comfortable out there, we're not on our own any more."

"Kenneth would probably join us if he could." As her eyebrows shot up in horror, he snorted. "I meant with his own lady."

"He's not joining us ever!" She glared. "With or without a lady!"

He laughed softly. "There was music playing in the caravan, I wonder if he's with someone right now."

"Well, don't even think about going over there to look!"

"I thought it might be Kate."

"Kate?" Bella blinked. "You've noticed it too, then?"

"That he's after her. Hasn't everyone?"

"I don't think she's quite as enthusiastic about him."

He smiled slyly. "Reminds me of someone else I know."

"Really?"

"She's a spitfire that one. Like you and her grandmother."

"A spitfire?" She creased her forehead.

"Apt description I reckon."

She pursed her lips. "Funny! He reminds me of someone too."

"Jason Sandford, you mean?" he grinned.

"I never really knew him, so I can't say." She wrinkled her nose. "But there's a certain man around here with the same smart-arse attitude."

"Now who would that be?"

"I'm sure you'll figure it out."

"Why isn't Kate keen on him, do you know?"

"I think he called her names to start with."

"Names?"

"The Wolf girl, Witch girl. She hates those names."

"Aha, I see." He chuckled. "Is that the only reason?"

"I wouldn't be surprised if she's annoyed about the Jason and Maria thing."

"What thing?"

"Haven't you heard the gossip? Another Sandford Lawson hitch up, neither of them have the name but they have the blood." Bella paused a moment to think. "Actually, Daniel did tell me Kate reckons Kenneth's too old, as in, for her, but I don't think that's the only reason she's playing hard to get, there's something else going on."

"Maybe she's got a crush on him and doesn't want him to know."

"Ha! You are so very funny." She punched him lightly on his chest. "I doubt she's anything like me in that way, besides she's only just met him remember."

"True." He took her balled fist and kissed it. "Anyway, I'm sure they'll figure it out."

"I agree," she grinned. "You know, I think they'd make quite a couple."

"And your Mum would be rapt if they got together."

"She's the one who started all this history repeating stuff, talking about Jason and Maria back together. I really think she believes it will happen."

"Why did Maria and Jason never marry?"

"I suppose they never got around to it. Mum told me they split up once but when they got back together, they were inseparable."

"Then he died." Roman frowned. "That really was tragic."

She heaved a sigh. "Yes, so very sad."

"But then along came Jason's best mate."

"And did Bernard rock the boat!" Bella had to laugh. "Maria gave him a hard time."

"So, I've heard."

"It's legendary, you know!" She pouted, fluttering her eyelashes. "A Lawson girl thing, giving their men a hard time."

"I've noticed."

"You've got broad shoulders, haven't you?"

"Broad enough." He chuckled. "Your Mum's not as much of a Lawson, is she?"

"Mum takes after Gran's side of the family, outgoing but placid."

"I can see why she used to say Maria should have been your mother and not her."

"Hmmm." She pulled a wry face. "I suppose."

"Admit it, you are very like your aunt." He tweaked her nose. "As is Kate."

"So, like it or not!" She eyed him smugly. "The Lawsons are here to stay."

"And I'm glad." Grinning, he got busy with his hands. "I love my Lawson lady."

"Hey, enough!" she squeaked. "We're too old for all this exercise!"

"Never too old or enough," he murmured, silencing her with his mouth.

While having breakfast next morning, they saw Kenneth glance across to the house windows from the shed door. He returned Roman's raised hand greeting before going inside to return with supplies, loading up his ute and driving off with a grin and salute.

"Works hard that fella," Roman said, munching toast. "Doing more than twelve-hour days lately."

"You were lucky to find him," Bella replied. "Hope he stays."

"Yeah, so do I."

"I have a feeling it may depend on his personal life."

"His family you mean or Kate?"

"Both, I think."

"Well, it seems the Sandfords all like him." Roman took another bite of toast.

"Olivia especially really feels for him, she told me," Bella said. "I guess she understands Kenneth's father situation, born to a single parent who later dies."

"True. She was lucky Leon found out about her."

"Very, at least Kenneth had a grandparent to take over his care. I don't think Olivia would have." Bella sighed. "She's very grateful for her dad coming to the rescue, it could have been so different."

"Now she not only has her dad but also your brother."

"The poor girl!" Bella snorted a laugh.

"Come on now. Ben's a good guy."

"You didn't have to grow up with him."

"And you didn't grow up with my sister."

"Lara is a darling and the kindest friend."

"Whatever."

"The joys of siblings, eh?" She poked him.

"Yep," he grinned.

Grinning back, she sipped her coffee. "Kenneth suddenly finding out he's got family must have been strange for him."

"Very strange," Roman agreed with his mouth full.

"All he had was a grandmother up until recently." Bella shook her head. "And now he finds out he's got a whole bunch of other relatives."

"He seems to be dealing with it okay, so far."

"Olivia was saying the lawyers are still sorting out all the legalities."

"I suppose they have to," Roman grimaced. "Inheritance stuff."

"I wonder how that will affect Kenneth?" Bella eyed him.

"He'll inherit something for sure," Roman sighed. "Who knows what he'll do after that though, maybe settle down."

"Stop living in his caravan, you reckon?" Bella slanted an eyebrow.

"Something like that. Buy his own piece of land maybe."

"And find himself someone to share it with."

"You could be right about Kate, you know. She could make all the difference."

"Well, here's to him settling down and staying here." Bella raised her coffee mug.

"I second that." Roman nodded, touching his mug to hers.

The next day Bella went to visit her Mum at the farm. Anna complained ruefully about her weary old bones after tending the vegetable plot that morning, thankfully sitting down with her daughter for a welcome cup of tea.

"How's Roman and Kenneth, still keeping busy?" Anna asked.

"Put it this way, they're not taking on any new clients." Bella pulled a face. "Roman would be scaling down even more if Kenneth wasn't here."

"Just as well that lad turned up."

"Certainly was, and we're hoping he stays."

"You think he won't?" Anna frowned.

"He's always moved around. I'm not sure his family will keep him here."

"But Kate will!" Anna nodded her head with certainty.

"You think so?" Bella was doubtful. "It looks like a one-way street to me."

"One-way street?"

"He's keen on her, but I'm not sure she's that keen on him."

"Ah, she's Maria all over again." Anna laughed. "My sister was never keen either."

"She wasn't?" Bella raised her eyebrows. "Not even about Jason?"

"Jason was a hunk and she eyeballed him all right, but she certainly wasn't expecting him to be interested in her."

"Why?" Bella was astounded. "She was a beauty!"

"She never saw herself that way." Anna shook her head. "Guys did, but she found them more of a hassle than anything. She had a couple of relationships before Jason but after they ended, she opted to stay single."

"But then Jason came along."

"She didn't make it easy for him." Anna tipped her head. "Sound familiar, doesn't it? I always did feel sorry for Roman."

Bella wrinkled her nose in reply. "Do you really think Kenneth's like Jason?"

"Oh yes! Very much so especially those eyes." Anna chuckled. "But even his nature, he's got the same charisma and hard-working ethic."

"A hard worker indeed." Bella nodded. "We think he's wonderful and one out of the box but we're not sure Kate's on the same page."

"She's like Maria, doesn't do complicated, runs in the opposite direction if she can."

"Naïve."

"There's that." Anna smiling knowingly. "But he's not."

"You're right there, he's been around."

"He's told you?" Anna was avidly interested.

"Not me, but he talks to Roman." Bella wrinkled her nose.

"Man talk, eh?"

"He's had a few short, sweet and move on kind of relationships I'm told."

"But nobody now?"

Bella shook her head. "And I don't think he's after short, sweet and move on with Kate somehow."

"That's exactly it, I think he's found the one he wants."

"But she's not playing ball, is she?"

"Maybe we could help things along a little."

"Mum!" Bella creased her forehead. "I don't think that's a good idea."

"Why not?" Anna smiled slyly. "Just a gentle nudge in the right direction."

"If she finds out she'll never speak to us again!"

"She doesn't need to know."

"Know exactly what?"

"We'll work it out." Anna tapped her nose. "You could ask Roman to help Kenneth."

"Help Kenneth!" Bella squeaked. "He doesn't need any help, Mum!"

"Right time, right place and all that."

"No, no and no! I am not getting involved." Bella shook her vehemently.

"Oh, come on, Bella dear. Kate's family after all and we are involved."

"I have a bad feeling about this."

"Now you really sound like your aunt Maria."

"What's new?" Bella looked rueful. "I've heard that heaps of times before."

"It's true," Anna nodded. "And neither of you got it right every time, did you?"

"Got what right?" Bella was indignant.

"Your feelings! Especially about your men."

Bella sighed deeply but didn't reply.

Anna tipped her head. "We can't have Kate getting it wrong as well, can we?"

"Please Mum, let's just leave it. Let her and Kenneth sort themselves out."

"Okay, okay." Anna shook her head resignedly. "Don't say I didn't try to help."

Bella departed soon after, arriving home to poke her head into the workshop where Roman was fabricating a wrought iron eagle. He didn't notice her ogling his butt or tiptoeing into the office where she made herself comfortable in his chair, waiting for him to finish. Ten minutes later, he put the wing of the eagle down, removed his goggles and earmuffs before turning from the bench to find her watching him.

He's still got it in spades, she thought, as his lips curved in a slow sexy smile. And I'm not the only one who notices, older women especially. Don't forget you're not so far behind them these days, she told herself ruefully. Where have the years gone? From a teenage crush to this, and I'm as infatuated as ever.

He approached the office to lean against the door jamb, saying quietly, "Hello, Lady."

"Hello, Mr Antonovich," Bella breathed. "You look busy?"

"I feel like getting busier."

"Oh."

He stepped forward to lift her out of the chair and onto the desk, her legs pulling him close as his mouth took hers in a kiss that went deep.

They were at the naked to the waist stage when Kenneth strolled in, calling out. "Hey, Roman, have you seen...! Aw, shit!"

Neither Roman nor Bella had heard his ute pull up, going rigid at the sound of his voice. Roman groaned, screwing his eyes shut as his hands tightened on Bella's behind. She yelped in panic, almost tipping off the desk as Roman took a step backward. He recovered quickly, shielding her with his arms and brought his head up to give Kenneth a glazed stare through the office's internal window.

Kenneth raised both hands, palm up. "Sorry, man! I'm out of here."

"Hey!" Roman croaked. "Wait!"

Kenneth strode out without a backward look. Squeaking incoherently, Bella squirmed out of Roman's arms to bend down for her top and bra, picked up his shirt as well which she handed to him with hands that shook.

"Are you okay?' he asked, pulling it on.

"I should have known this would happen!" she wailed.

"Don't worry about it." He crooked a grin, cupping her cheek.

"Don't worry!" she glared. "I'm embarrassed! He's embarrassed!"

"I'll go talk to him." Roman smothered a laugh.

"We are never doing this here again!" Bella told him with a snap, finished dressing and stalked to the outside door red in the face and scowling. "I'll be in the house!"

Roman grinned at her indignant back before going in search of Kenneth who he found rummaging in his ute. Hearing him, Kenneth spun immediately with another apology on his lips but Roman raised his hand, shaking his head.

"It's okay, man." Roman grimaced wryly. "These things happen."

"Do they what!" Kenneth eyebrows shot up. "You're not going to deck me, then?"

"Nah, not this time," Roman laughed.

"Bella?" Kenneth looked over at the house. "Is she okay?"

"A little wound up but she'll get over it."

Kenneth frown worriedly. "Is she going to speak to me again?"

"She will." Roman clapped his shoulder. "Come over for dinner later."

"Do you think I should?"

"Of course. Don't stress, man."

Kenneth arrived for dinner looking sheepish, again wanting to apologise.

Bella shook her head at him. "Don't say a word! You saw nothing, okay?"

He nodded agreeably, took the beer Roman offered and their meal together was as companionable as always. After dessert they relaxed in the lounge until Kenneth took his leave, turning at the door to eye them both for a long thoughtful moment, eyes twinkling.

"You know it's really nice to see an old married couple still at it," he said slyly.

Bella hissed a venomous breath as Kenneth moved out fast, Roman doubling up laughing as the door slammed. Leaping to the window she returned Kenneth's grin and thumbs up with a baleful glare, watching him saunter to his caravan.

"Smartarse!" She turned her scowl on Roman. "I'm so glad you find it hilarious!"

"Well, it is." Roman chortled. "Aw, come on, sweetie, lighten up."

"Lighten up? What if we'd been…" She waved her hands about wildly.

"Past the point of no return?" Roman grinned.

"Yes!" She shuddered at the thought.

"He would have got more than an eyeful. The old married couple starkers and giving the desk a workout."

"Oh, please! I don't even want to think about it!"

"Why not?" Roman got to his feet with a certain glint in his eye.

She shook her head. "No, no and no! I've had enough of that for one day."

"We didn't get very far if I remember."

"And we're not getting any further now."

"Aren't we?"

"Roman!"

"No desk and no deck," he assured her. "What about the bed?"

She glared, sighed and finally muttered, "Dishes first!"

Chapter 8

Dad told me DNA tests had been done at Kenneth's request, proving he was indeed Jason Sandford's grandson. He wasn't planning to change his surname, however, or move on, and he still lived in his caravan at Roman and Bella's place.

Slowly but surely, the gossip column's interest in the Sandford Secret died down with life resuming a semblance of normality. At least for everyone else, but not so much for me.

Kenneth Hawke was a pain, upsetting my secure little world. I'd always enjoyed visiting Bella at home before he turned up, wished he would leave or at least park up somewhere else, even move into Jason's apartment at the Sandfords across from our farm, where I'd be less likely to bump into him.

Hadn't yet figured out why I reacted so badly to the guy—my neck hairs standing on end whenever I heard his voice and the funny kind of shiver going on whenever his eyes met mine—that my brain really couldn't analyse.

Like butterflies in your tummy when you're nervous, maybe. No! It was worse than that, the butterflies were gigantic for starters and sat lower. Crap! Just go away!

Apart from that, he made no attempt to hide his interest in me, and to top it off, everyone that knew seemed to think it was wonderful, making unreasonable assumptions that had me digging in my heels with a vengeance. Why would he even be interested in a naïve nineteen-year-old like myself? There were loads of suitably aged females available in the district who were way more man-savvy than I could ever be.

Stressing about it wasn't helping, convinced myself to get my act together. For starters, I hadn't tried hard enough to get to know him; my promise to Dad had kind of soured. Who knew? Once Kenneth realised how boring and not his type I was, he'd likely run in the opposite direction. Perhaps he could even be my first boyfriend, then dump me quickly.

Yikes! I shuddered at the thought. Not happening! That's way out of hand!

Relationships with guys hadn't really interested me before, still didn't and although it didn't worry me a great deal, I felt like the odd one out at times and thought my female instincts were stunted, maybe worse, non-existent, or perhaps late-developing. It wasn't the sex that put me off either, there was enough information out there, and besides parents and schoolteachers, my darling older brothers could also be decidedly enlightening and crude at times. Biology was very much part of a vet nurse's job after all, I'd seen animals mating since I was small, so no big deal.

All part of life, wasn't it? Yes, but getting intimate with Kenneth Hawke was not part of my life plan! I snapped a shutter down hard on those thoughts, but the shutter snapped back open. I heard Olivia's voice in my mind. "Wonder what he's like in the sack?" Rebecca's voice too. "He'd know every position." Glenys adding. "And the rest?" What did they mean? How many positions were there? I knew humans were more adventurous than animals; I'd spied Mum and Dad doing more than canoodling in their bed often enough.

Why don't you find out what he's like yourself? a sly little voice whispered in my ear. Are you crazy? Nope! Think long and hard—the shivers, that feeling in your gut when he's around—maybe your female instincts aren't so stunted after all. No way! Dare you to find out, I bet you want to! Did I? Only one way to find out.

On Friday morning, I went shopping, my boss having given me the day off as a thank you for working overtime each evening the week before, after which I decided to call in to see Bella on my way home. She was in the pen with a lanky red gelding, waved out when I arrived, and stopped working the horse to approach me at the railings.

"Well timed." She wiped her brow. "I need a break and a drink."

"New horse?" I gestured to the gelding.

"Yes, the mother and foal departed three days ago," she nodded. "This boy is just starting to race, but he likes to rear and throw riders for some reason."

"Hard work?"

"A little, he's nice natured but touchy around his back."

"Something sore there?"

"No sign of anything and he's been vet checked."

"Something he remembers then?"

"I think so. I've got to change his thoughts about that somehow."

"You'll get there, you always do," I smiled reassuringly. "Has Morgan been talking to you yet?"

"You bet he has." She smiled too. "He keeps telling me to chill."

"Well, that's good advice." I laughed.

"Isn't it just?"

As the gelding snorted, she looked at him. "Yes sir, we need to chill, eh?" She turned back to me, "Are you in a hurry?"

"No, it's my day off."

"Oh, lucky you! I'll just clean him up and put him away, won't be long."

"Okay," I nodded.

She walked back to the horse, attached a lead rope, and, after brushing him down quickly, threw on a rug and took him to the paddock. With Bella's attention elsewhere, I scrutinised Kenneth's locked-up caravan, wondering again about the interior. My mind quickly began running riot, imagining the bed with him sprawled across it naked.

I blinked hard. Where did that come from? No PJs indeed! Wonder if he's had women in there? Caravan's rock, don't they? What? Stop it now! Gave myself a disgusted mental shake back to reality as Bella returned, suggesting we go to the house for a cool lemonade.

Once settled down with our drinks, she got a phone call from Roman asking for her help with a difficult horse he was shoeing.

"Isn't he lucky, having you?" I grinned as she stood up to go.

"Why don't you come too?" She grinned back. "Two women giving him a hand would make his day, I'm sure."

"Thanks, but I think I'll make tracks."

"Well, stay as long as you like, finish your drink at least."

"I'll do that. Have fun."

She gulped down her drink, collected her car keys and purse and called on her way out. "We'll do this another time, eh?"

"You betcha."

After finishing my drink, I rinsed my glass and locked the door behind me, leaving the key under the planter on the deck. For some unearthly reason, I didn't immediately leave, skirting my car instead and heading for the caravan, which was, of course, locked. Glancing around to make sure no one was watching, I stepped to the large front windows but could see nothing as the curtains were drawn. There was ample room between the shed wall and caravan, allowing me to sidle further to a side window which wasn't covered. Let out an involuntary gasp at the neatly made-up bed in full view, taking up most of the caravan's width, and it wasn't just the tidiness of the interior that surprised me but it's muted colours, not the clutter and gaudiness I'd expected. Pressing my nose against the glass, I tried for a closer look and was so engrossed the sudden sound of a vehicle's engine turning into the driveway made me jump.

Scrambling out from behind the caravan to hide behind the back of the shed, I heard the sound of a car door slam, followed by the shed's utility door opening. Had a sinking feeling I knew who it was, tiptoed across the house lawn until the front parking area came into view, and sure enough, Kenneth's blue ute stood beside my jeep.

Panic had me veering quick smart to the house deck, keeping one eye on the shed door, and once at the steps, I turned back, pretending as if I'd just come from that direction. Was about to open my car when he spoke from behind me. "Hey, Kate. Thought I recognised your car."

I turned oh so nonchalantly with a polite little smile, waving a hand at the house. "I was visiting Bella, but she had to go out."

He glanced that way. "Didn't see you when I drove in."

I ignored that. "We had a drink together, er, she gave me the key to lock up."

"Day off?" he asked.

"Yes."

"Nice."

"Bella was working the new horse when I got here," I said. "He's a beauty."

He slanted his head, smiling slowly. "As are you."

I blinked, asked on a colder note. "Do you flirt with every female you meet?"

"Wasn't flirting." His smiled widened. "And you are very beautiful."

"Whatever." I was curt. "So, what are you doing here?"

"Picking up some more supplies to stock the ute." He cocked an eyebrow.

I glanced away feeling foolish. Of course, stupid! Did I really think he was up to no good? The guy works for Roman, remember.

"Well, have a good day," I muttered, turning to my car.

"If you only have to ask if you want to look inside the caravan."

I went rigid, eyes stretching wide. Made myself turn around again. "What?"

He pointed up the road. "I saw you. There's a good view from the road up further."

I didn't have a clue what to say, could only stare like an idiot.

"Here." Pulling a bunch of keys from his pocket, he identified one. "That's the caravan door key. You're welcome to have a look."

He held them out to me, his mouth curving in an enigmatic little smile.

Eying him doubtfully, I mumbled. "I'm sorry. I was being nosey."

"I really don't mind." He jiggled the keys. "Have a look. I'll be in the shed for a bit."

Taking a deep breath, I reached for them but wasn't prepared for the unexpected tingle as our fingers touched and snatched them away, prompting a soft snort of laughter from him. Without a word, I turned on my heel towards the yards, walked quickly to the caravan but hesitated at the door to look over my shoulder, half expecting him to have followed me. There was no sign of him. Unlocking the door, I opened it cautiously before going inside.

Realised ruefully on entering that my assumption about his living habits had been very wrong; the place was not only tidy but scrupulously clean. Opposite the door was the kitchen area with only one mug upended and a teaspoon on the sink bench. There was a stove top and oven, microwave, kettle and toaster, all spick and span. To the left was the dining and sitting area, cushioned bench seats along the front windows and a fold up table in between. A TV screen hung on the kitchen cupboard wall, with a radio/CD player on a shelf underneath. To my right at the other end of the caravan was the bed I'd seen, and again, the lack of clutter and feeling of space surprised me. The caravan's décor was tasteful too, cream walls with varnished wooden doors.

Moving in further, I opened a door opposite the kitchen bench to find a small shower/toilet room with his toiletries on the basin shelf underneath a wall mirror, and as everything was bone dry, I figured he made use of the shed's facilities instead. In the bedroom area, the bed itself filled up most of the space, with just room enough on either side to get by, two bedside cabinets with fitted lamps on the back wall, and propped on the floor in one corner was a guitar. Nosiness got the better of me, opened a cupboard to find clothes hung up neatly and piled on side shelves, his underwear, and other personal stuff in a bedside cabinet drawer, which I promptly snapped shut after a quick guilty look.

I'd half expected it to be musty inside, smell like stale BO and horse or something, but the air was fresh with a trace of his cologne lingering. Deciding I'd seen more than enough and not wanting him to come looking for me, I quickly made my way out.

Had to return his keys, though. Bugger! Could always leave them in his ute. Ah, don't be such a wuss. Just tell him you liked it and get out of here.

Bracing myself, I walked back to the shed door to peep inside and call out. He stood at a bench sorting shoeing gear, the clanging noises making it impossible for him to hear me. Stepping inside a few paces, I called more loudly, and this time he heard me, looking up before leaving the bench to approach me. Handing him the keys, I dangled them daintily to make sure our fingers didn't touch, his knowing little smile immediately putting me on the defensive.

"Nice caravan," I told him coolly. "More room than I expected."

"It's a good size. Ideal for me."

"You haven't thought of moving then?" I couldn't quite keep the mockery out of my voice. "Into the Sandford mansion maybe?"

He slanted his head, the smile turning to a grin. "Too big."

I grimaced snootily. "Really. I thought you'd be all for change these days. Don't you want to join the family and the Sandford life?"

"Not my style." His eyes narrowed a fraction. "So, are big houses your thing?"

Here's your chance to be nice, have a decent conversation, I told myself, taking a breath. "Well, I love our farmhouse. It's big I suppose but it's homely and no mansion."

"You wouldn't live in a caravan?"

Frowning, I shook my head.

"Why?" he laughed. "Too small?"

"Actually, our cabin isn't that much bigger than a caravan and I'd live there."

"So why don't you?"

I shrugged. "Our family use it for weekends and holidays mostly. Although we haven't lately, I suppose we're all too busy."

"Where's the cabin?"

"On the coast not far from here. It has an awesome sea view, great sunsets too."

"Sounds cool."

"It is."

"Maybe I'll see it one day."

I blinked at the look in his eyes, felt uncomfortable. "I better get going."

"Sure." He smiled. "Any plans for tonight?"

"What?" I blinked again. "Um, no."

"Would you like to go out for dinner with me?"

"What?" I said again, eyes popping wide. "Why?"

"Why not?"

"Do you know what they're saying already?"

"They?"

"Um, our families."

"What are they saying?"

"Talking about us," I swallowed. "Um, like, us together!"

"That worries you?" He cocked an eyebrow. "Us together?"

"There isn't an us, okay!" I bit out. "And I don't like rumours."

"Just ignore them," he said mildly, shrugging. "And there's nothing wrong with us being friends, is there?"

I swallowed. "Ah, no."

"Good. So, dinner tonight?"

"Um, are you sure?"

"Yep. I'll pick you up from the farm if you like."

"No!" I shook my head vigorously. "I mean, I'd rather meet you somewhere."

He grinned. "The passenger seat in the ute is clean, you know."

"Oh! I didn't mean it like that." I flapped a hand. "I'd just rather drive myself."

"Fine. So, do you like Italian food?"

"Yes."

"Bonitos in town at seven o'clock then. Okay?"

"Okay."

"Great. See you then." He smiled cheerfully.

Didn't return the smile, jumped in my car and saw him salute as I drove off.

What the heck had I done? I asked myself, spending the afternoon thinking up all sorts of excuses not to go. Oh, stop being pathetic! This is just another rung on the ladder of experience and life. Be brave!

Chapter 9

I was as nervous as a skittish foal by the time I'd had a shower, dressed and toned down my unruly hair, tying it back in a single ponytail. With no desire to draw attention to myself, I'd chosen a loose grey blouse, slim-fitting black trousers, and ankle boots to wear, slipping on a dark grey thigh-length cardigan against the chill of the evening before departing at six thirty on the dot.

Had lied to Mum about the outing, said I was going to dinner with friends, and hoped desperately that I wouldn't meet anyone I knew during the evening.

Parked at Bonito's but didn't immediately leave my car, breathing deep and slow to calm myself. It didn't help much. I got out, locked up, and, walking hesitantly to the restaurant entrance saw his empty ute in the next row over.

Nerves began to scream. Get a grip, girl. I chastised myself. It's only a dinner. Get it over with. Stay cool, keep it friendly and it probably won't ever happen again.

I found him waiting just inside the door by reception; I didn't recall answering his greeting and could only stare. He was wearing a black leather jacket over a grey shirt almost the same colour as mine, black jeans, and boots, and looked jaw-droppingly gorgeous. His slow scrutiny from my face to my toes had me fizzing inside.

A waiter distracted him, gave me a second to clear my head before we were ushered to a table for two. Once seated, I glanced around at the other diners but, with relief, didn't recognise anyone.

"You're looking very lovely," he said softly.

That brought my attention back to him pronto, said stonily. "Flirting again?"

"No. Stating a fact."

Made myself say. "You don't look too bad yourself."

"A matching pair," he drawled softly.

"Pardon me?" I blinked.

"We're wearing the same colours."

"Fluke," I said dropping my gaze to his shirt.

It fitted him snugly, had me imagining the body underneath. Biting my lip, I didn't dare raise my eyes and fumbled to pick up the menu.

"Kate?"

Looking up into shadowed blue eyes, the rather unwelcome funny shiver did its thing again, making me react with a stare straight out of the artic.

"Don't get any ideas." I heard myself hiss. "Just because your grandfather went out with my grandmother." Oh, well done! Super friendly!

He wasn't at all perturbed, asking mildly. "And if I already have ideas?"

"Excuse me?"

"There's something about you, Kate," he said softly. "Right from the start."

"What?"

"You interested me as soon as I saw you."

"Why would you even be interested? You're way older than me."

"That bothers you?"

"Bothers?" I gawped at him. "You're what, twenty-eight? I'm nine years younger. It's not so much the age, it's…" I shook my head lost for words.

He waited with an enigmatic half smile.

"I'm just a naïve girl." I flapped a frustrated hand. "Er, you're experienced."

"Experienced?"

"Yes!" I glared. "Like heaps of girlfriends."

"I wouldn't say heaps." He slanted an amused eyebrow. "A few maybe."

"Whatever! Anyhow, I don't think I'd even begin to know how to satisfy…" What was I saying? How had the subject even got this far?

"Satisfy me?"

"Evening, sir," The waiter hovered. "Would you like something to drink?"

Kenneth didn't even flinch, studying me momentarily before glancing up at the waiter and ordering two glasses of Chardonnay. He waited until we were alone again before saying quietly. "Maybe we should check out the menu before he returns."

I dropped my eyes on the menu without taking it in, wanting to crawl under the table and disappear. This was no friendly outing; this was me making a fool of myself.

"Relax." He spoke again. "We're just having dinner remember."

Blowing out a breath, I gave him a suspicious up from under look but his teasing smile and the slicing of his hand across his throat had me jerking up my head to stare.

"Let's start again from now, eh?" He inclined his head. "Hi, I'm Kenneth."

A surprising laugh welled up. Couldn't help but reply. "Hi, I'm Kate."

"Nice to meet you." He held my gaze for a long moment before looking back at the menu. "The food is highly recommended here. I see they have a beef dish."

I blew out another breath. "Where?"

"Mains, third one down. Would you like an entrée? The scallops look good."

"Um. I don't usually have entrée."

"How about we share?"

I looked up at that, nodding without hesitation as his smiled again.

"Good," he said. "Scallops to start. I'm thinking the beef for a main, how about you?"

"The beef has mushrooms," I read.

"You don't like mushrooms?"

"Love them. I'll have the beef too."

"Matching pair again." He sounded amused.

He got a silent stare from me.

The sudden loud cackle of a woman at another table had his eyebrows shooting up, and the silly cross-eyed face he pulled had me smothering a giggle. The waiter returned with our drinks, took our meal order, and thereafter Kenneth began regaling stories and jokes about his job, which, as well as the wine, began to relax me. The scallops were divine and gave me the warm fuzzies, not least because I was sharing them with him.

This is more like it, I sighed inwardly. Friendly and getting to know each other.

The beef was also delicious, but at his suggestion to have dessert, I shook my head.

"Aw, gotta have dessert." He dropped his lower lip, eyes puppy dog cute. "Will you share on with me, please?"

I giggled, eying his flat torso. "Where do you put it all."

He gave his tummy a pat. "I work it off."

"You would with your job, it's very physical."

He let his gaze slide down my front. "As is vet nursing."

"Nothing like shoeing horses but yes I suppose we're both on our feet all day."

"So, let's work off a dessert together, then."

I relented with a pout. "Oh, all right then. Nothing too fattening, please."

"A little fat won't do you any harm, beautiful. You have a very lovely body."

I didn't answer, eyes widening before narrowing suspiciously.

"Whoops! Couldn't resist." He grinned. "It's true though."

I said in clipped tones. "You're getting personal again."

His chuckle made me shiver. "Hasn't anyone ever told you?"

"Told me what?"

"How very beautiful you are?"

"Has anyone ever told you that…" I broke off.

"Carry on."

I drew in air. "That you're very forward."

"Is that all?"

"And a smart arse." I bit my lip. "And way too good looking."

"Is that what you think?"

I looked down at the tabletop, avoiding his scrutiny, "I suppose."

"Too good looking?" His voice went low. "What does that mean exactly?"

"It could get you into trouble."

"Really? What sort of trouble?"

"Can we please stop this?" I refused to look at him, shook my head.

"Into trouble with you?"

"Kenneth!"

"Sexy."

"What?" I jerked my head up.

"The way you said my name."

"Stop it!"

I thanked my lucky stars that the waiter appeared at our table again.

"Would you like dessert or coffee?" he asked politely.

"We'd like one chocolate mousse with two spoons, please" Kenneth said.

As the waiter left us, I deliberately pretended interest in the other diners but felt decidedly uncomfortable, feeling Kenneth watching me. Made an excuse to use the ladies, quickly getting to my feet. While there, I took off my cardigan, cooled my flushed face with a splash of water, and gave myself a talking to in the bathroom mirror. To my relief, Kenneth was on his mobile as I returned to our table and apart from shooting me a glance as I draped my cardigan over the back of the chair before sitting down his concentration was on the call, obviously to do with work and treatment of a horse's hoof. It gave me time to study the man and his good looks, with thoughts racing through my head.

Oh, yes! I think you're good-looking, all right, Kenneth Hawke. I've been trying to deny it since I first saw you. Getting into trouble with you would be more than exciting, except I don't want trouble or exciting! You admire beauty, but I'm by far not the only beauty in the world, and as I said before, I wouldn't satisfy you. Wouldn't know how, for starters!

As he finished the call, I lifted an oh so casual eyebrow. "Everything okay?"

"Yeah. Just checking on a patient."

"Sore foot?"

"Very, but it'll come right."

"That's good."

"Here's our mousse," he said as the waiter arrived.

Something profound had changed in the air between us since sharing the entrée. It wasn't just the jitters in my stomach stopping me from taking more than a few mouthfuls, but the tremble in my hand I didn't want him to see.

"Don't you want any more?" he asked as I put my spoon down.

"No, thanks. I'm full," I replied, concentrating on the tabletop.

"Would you like a coffee instead?"

"No, I'm fine."

"What's wrong?"

"Nothing's wrong?" I looked up, heart doing a little flip at the look in his eyes.

He narrowed them. "You really don't like personal, do you?"

"What?"

"When things get personal, you run."

"I do not!" Watching him lick mousse of his spoon, I shivered.

"Okay, so, let's try this." He tipped his head. "Any boyfriends?"

Swallowed down another shiver as he licked his lips. "No!"

"None?"

"None."

He took another spoonful, swallowed. "Something wrong with us guys?"

Watched his mouth, clenching my hands in my lap. "Of course not! I love my dad and brothers."

He grinned. "I'm talking unrelated?"

"I don't mind those either."

"But no serious boyfriends?"

"No."

"Why not?" He licked mousse from his lip.

Oh, please, don't do that! The shiver went ape. "I don't know," I mumbled. "Too young probably."

"Most nineteen-year-olds would think they're too old."

"I'm not most."

He laughed softly. "No, you surely aren't."

Indignation flared, my voice bouncing back with a snap, "Is that a problem?"

"Not for me, it isn't."

"Meaning?"

"You're unique. I like that." He smiled. "So, talking of being too young or old, have you got an age in mind?"

"For what?"

"A boyfriend."

"Why are you asking me all this?"

"Getting to know you."

Gritting my teeth, I shut up. Pretended interest in my purse, opening it to rummage while he finished off the dessert.

"Lost something," he asked politely.

I stopped fumbling to glance up, shaking my head as he put the spoon down.

"What are you doing tomorrow?" He wiped his mouth with the napkin, eyes on mine. "Tomorrow?" I repeated inanely.

"Saturday night." He lifted his eyebrows. "Everyone goes out, don't they?"

"Do they?" I felt pathetic.

"You don't?"

"Not really."

"Unique indeed." His lips twisted. "Why don't we give it a try? Could be fun."

I curled my lip. "Your kind of fun?"

"What's my kind of fun?"

"Not mine!"

"Aw, I'm not so bad." He grinned. "Try me, you might like it."

"Like it?" I scoffed.

He chuckled, leaning towards me. "I'd just like to get to know you better."

"I don't think that's all you want."

"Clever girl."

I blinked.

"So, what do you think I want?" There was something burning in his eyes.

I didn't reply, attempted a glare.

"You're not such a naïve nineteen-year-old after all, are you?"

"I'd like to go now!" I bit it out.

"Sure."

His amicable reply was unexpected, as was him pushing his chair back and getting to his feet. Waiting politely for me to do the same, I quickly grabbed my purse and cardigan and followed him to the cashier where he refused my offer to share the bill. Once outside in the carpark, he pulled his phone from his jacket pocket as I turned to thank him.

"May I have your phone number?" he asked.

"Why? I really don't want to go out tomorrow," I said peevishly.

"No problem, we'll go out another time," he shrugged, a smirk on his lips. "And I could always ask Bella for your number, I guess."

Glaring balefully, I snatched the phone out of his hand and punched in my number before handing it back. The warmth of his fingers tingled and lingered, annoying me.

"Would you like mine?" He grinned evilly.

"No!" I snapped.

He laughed. "Where are you parked? I'll walk with you."

I shook my head. "Don't bother. Thanks for dinner, I enjoyed the food."

"But you didn't enjoy the company?"

"I did actually," I told him snootily. "Most of the time."

"That's nice to know," he chuckled. "So how about most of the time enjoying my company again?"

"You don't give up, do you?"

He cocked an eyebrow. "Like I said before, there's something about you, girl."

"There is nothing about me!"

"Hook, line and sinker," he murmured.

"Pardon?"

"You have me hooked."

"Hooked?" I snorted. "Are you not feeling well or something?"

"Never felt better."

"I can't imagine you ever being hooked." I scowled.

"First time for everything." He leant closer.

I stepped back hurriedly, his chuckle standing my neck hairs to attention.

"Don't I get a kiss good night," he drawled softly.

"No, you do not!"

"Aw, what a shame." His grin teased. "I'll phone you tomorrow."

"I told you! I'm not going out tomorrow."

"Maybe I'll change your mind."

"Good luck with that!" I snapped.

I turned quickly to my car with his sexy laugh in my ears. Deliberately didn't look back and drove out, shaking my head. I slept not a wink, going over and over the evening. Felt shivers, tingles and hot all over at the memory.

Chapter 10

Didn't even bother trying to figure out how he changed my mind. He also insisted on picking me up in his ute; so much for keeping things secret.

Mum was delighted at my going to an out-of-town music event with Kenneth, her delighted welcome over the top when he arrived to collect me that evening. I felt much less delighted or welcoming, and Mum cooing over him certainly didn't put me in a better frame of mind. At least Dad wasn't home to join in, that would have been the last straw.

"Your daughter's in safe hands," Kenneth assured Mum.

"Oh, I'm sure she is," she tittered.

He caught me rolling my eyes in exasperation behind her back with an almost imperceptible lift of an amused eyebrow, my embarrassment at him having seen my reaction turning to a defiant glower.

"We'll see you later, Mrs Von Meeren," he smiled politely at Mum.

"Call me, Zoe," she oozed. "You must come in for a chat when you get back."

He nodded affably, I gave Mum a quick hug and we left. Couldn't use a ute's dirty passenger seat as an excuse not to go out with him again, it was as clean as he'd said.

Again? I'd make sure this was the last time! I'd done my dash at being friendly.

"Your Mum's a sweetie," he said once we hit the road.

I flicked him a sarcastic look. "I'm sure you think every female is."

"Not every female." His glance was amused. "Some are sweeter than others."

"Really?" I curled my lip. "I'm sure you'd know."

"She's a lovely lady. Zoe, is a nice name too."

"Why don't you tell her that." I was sarcastic. "She might go weak at the knees."

"Do you?"

"Do I what?"

"Go weak at the knees when a guy says your name?"

"Don't be stupid!"

"Kate."

No noticeable problems with my knees but felt the shiver. Giving him a very cold stare, I wasn't telling him anything about my reaction that was certain.

He merely laughed softly. "Your mum is definitely sweeter."

My stare turned positively icy to which he chuckled again.

"If this is the way things are heading," I snapped. "I suggest you turn around and take me home right now."

"Why?" he grinned. "Things are just getting interesting."

"Interesting?"

"Spicy and tart with a hint of sour, better than sweet any day."

I scowled my bewilderment, keeping silent for the rest of the drive while churning over what he'd said. Arriving at the venue, I still had no idea what he meant.

He parked the ute, switching off the engine before turning to me in his seat. "Before we go in how about we talk, hmmm?"

I shrugged, eying him suspiciously.

"What's annoying you? Me picking you up from your place or your Mum?"

"Nothing's annoying me!" I said indignantly.

"Come on, talk to me. I'd like us to enjoy the night."

I blew out my cheeks. "Everyone's watching us!"

"Everyone?"

"My parents, family, friends. Whoever. All because of this Jason and Maria thing."

"That bugs you?"

"Yes!"

"You don't want them to know we're dating?"

"We're not dating!" I snapped. "We're just having a…um, a night out together."

"As you say. So, what's the problem?"

"Being watched, what they're thinking!" I answered indignantly.

"Let them watch and think," he said, quietly reasonable. "Jason and Maria are history. We're not them."

"I know that, but everyone else seems to think we are. Like they're expecting history to repeat itself."

"Look, it's no secret that I'm keen on you. We'll deal with it."

"Keen?" I frowned. "Deal with what?"

"I think you know and if you don't, you will."

"You're very sure of yourself," I stated coldly.

"This time I am." He smiled.

"This time?" I gulped at the heat in his eyes.

"Let's talk about it later. We should go in." He reached for his door handle.

I got out quickly to take a calming gulp of air.

The large, covered pavilion and pleasant surroundings with manicured lawns, trees, flowering shrubs, and an olive grove surprised me; I'd seen the property advertised as a venue for concerts, weddings, and the like but never been before.

At the entrance, Kenneth handed over tickets to a smiling attendant, who showed us through the well-lit interior to our reserved table where we had a good view of the stage and judging by the crowds arriving, the event was popular and fully booked. A waitress offered us a glass of white wine each while several waiting staff moved between the tables with platters of food. Despite my earlier tension, I was surprisingly peckish, heaping up a plate with several little savouries and snacks which made Kenneth grin.

"What?" I eyeballed him, frowning.

"It's nice to see a girl with appetite."

"I like food," I said indignantly.

"Good." He nodded, biting into a savoury of his own.

The waiting staff retreated as the show began, the stage lighting up as all other lights dimmed. There were several different acts—solo musicians and bands—all playing good music, old and new. My favourite were two young men from Mexico playing guitar and pan-flute; found the poignant, beautiful music mesmerising and hardly noticed Kenneth move his chair along to my side of the table for a better view. During the applause, I became aware of how close he was, staring at his profile just inches away in the dim light. The sudden turn of his face to mine had me recoiling so badly I almost fell off my chair, glaring as I slid my bum back on feeling idiotic.

His teeth showed in a grin. "Relax, beautiful."

"I am relaxed, thank you very much!" I hissed. "And stop calling me that."

He shrugged. "Enjoying it so far?"

"Very much."

"You like guitar."

"Yes, especially played like that. It's very moving."

"Music does that," he murmured. "Moves you."

"Do you play?" I asked. "There was a guitar in your caravan."

"You noticed?"

"It was in plain sight!" I pointed out defiantly.

"True," he nodded. "And yes, I do play sometimes. What about yourself?"

"I play piano but not well," I told him. "Dad plays both, like Opa did."

"Ah, yes, Leon told me Bernard was very musical."

"He entertained his customers at the Wine Rack restaurant some nights."

"What about your brothers?"

"Daniel's musical. Matthew, not so much."

As he put his elbow on the table to lean closer, I jerked away again.

"You're quite safe." His mouth curved slyly. "I won't jump you in the dark."

"If you so much as tried," I hissed. "You'd be sorry!"

"See what I mean?"

"What?" I scowled.

"It's much better."

"What is?"

"Spicy, tart and a little sour," he said softly.

"I have no idea what you're talking about," I spat.

He grinned but said nothing more.

Another act came on, his attention thankfully diverted. The woman singer wore a low-cut bright red dress which showed an indecent amount of cleavage, sang a sultry number and exaggerated the sway of her hips which I thought quite unnecessary. Kenneth's obvious fascination had me screwing up my nose but at least with her on stage he'd have no cause to jump me in the dark. The standing ovation she got plus plenty of wolf whistles from the male contingent had me scornfully tight lipped, eyes deliberately averted from the man beside me.

"Whew!" I heard him say. "That's some hot lady."

I curled my lip. "A spicy sickly-sweet tart with not a hint of sour, if you ask me."

He heard, chuckled. "Touché."

I didn't respond.

"Now if you were up there on stage doing that I'd be sweating."

That made me look at him. "Excuse me?"

His suggestive grin had my heart doing a flip, but he didn't elaborate thankfully. From then on until the end of the show I was even more aware of him and once back in the ute felt ridiculously nervous, wishing the journey home would hurry up and be over.

"Still hungry?" he asked.

"No. I had more than enough to eat," I mumbled.

"Do you mind if we stop in town?"

"What for?"

"I've got the munchies. Need something else."

I shook my head. "You men are all the same, always hungry."

"You have a pretty good appetite yourself."

"Sometimes."

He laughed. "Come on, humour me. Let's stop for a pizza or something."

I sighed. "An ice-cream would be nice."

"Pizza and ice-cream, it is."

We ended the night on a good note with a small pizza shared between us and scrummy hokeypokey ice-cream. He dropped me off politely at home, asked me to apologies to Mum for not coming in siting an early start on Sunday with plans to meet friends down the line. Promising he'd be in touch; I went to bed with my mind jumping hoops.

So much for the last time or me having enough of being friendly, we went out again and again. As our friendship grew for all to see, I couldn't deny how alive he made me feel or how much more than interesting he was. We talked, debated and laughed together with the constant banter and inevitable sexual innuendos not only entertaining but exhilarating, but he made no demands on me, keeping it light and casual.

One time at the movies, however, I grabbed his arm for the third time during a scary scene, and he took my hand, slipping his fingers between mine, which gave the tingles a workout. I attempted to dislodge my fingers as the movie credits rolled out and the theatre lights came back on, but he was in no hurry to let go.

"Can I have my hand back, please." I eyed him.

"Such a beautiful little hand," he murmured, lifting my knuckles to his lips.

I stared at his mouth for a stunned second, snatching my hand away as my neck hairs did their thing. Standing up abruptly, I bolted outside to wait at the ute.

"How about something to eat?" he asked as he joined me there. "Do you like Thai?"

"I think I'd rather go home." I said, not looking at him.

"I'd rather take you out to dinner, besides I'm hungry."

"Well, I'm not!"

"There are ways to work up an appetite."

That prompted a mindboggling vision of him naked, not lying on his caravan bed but a front view of him in the driver's seat of the ute breathing hard. I was in the frame too and what I was doing had my eyes out on stalks.

I gave my head a quick shake, croaked. "Excuse me?"

"Ah," he smirked. "Methinks your mind is working overtime."

"Really?" I snapped. "And what exactly are you thinking then?"

"Walking to a restaurant."

"Oh."

"If that's okay with you?" He raised his eyebrows teasingly.

I didn't answer except to shrug, stalking beside him in silence all the way to the restaurant with the distinct feeling he was laughing at me. Sitting down opposite in a booth, I stared at the menu as if my life depended on it, head down and feeling stupid.

"It's not very comfortable," he said softly.

"What?" My eyes shot up to his.

"The front seat of the ute."

I gawped, swallowed hard and finally croaked. "What are you talking about?"

"What you were thinking about."

Desperately pretended ignorance. "And what was that exactly?"

He grinned. "Of ways to work up an appetite inside it."

"You've lost me!" I looked away, face flushing.

"No, I haven't," he drawled softly. "Like I said once before, you're not as naïve as you make out."

My eyes snapped back to his. "What's that supposed to mean?"

"You know exactly what I mean, beautiful." He held my gaze for a long moment before dropping his eyes to the menu, saying casually. "Let's order some food."

My eyes were riveted on him. How on earth did he know what I'd been thinking? How had I even come up with the thoughts anyhow? He could suggest what he liked, but I was naïve and knew nothing about working up appetites inside a ute or any other vehicle for that matter. Something weird was happening here. I didn't much like it!

"Relax." He didn't look up. "We'll eat first and sort it out later."

I gulped. "Sort what out?"

"Whatever's bothering you."

"Nothing's bothering me."

"Read the menu then and stop staring." He still hadn't looked at me.

"I am not staring!"

"I can feel your eyes, beautiful," he murmured.

"Stop calling me beautiful!"

"What would you like me to call you then?" His eyes remained on the menu.

"Nothing!" I snapped.

"Have you seen anything you like to eat?"

"I'm not hungry!" I said petulantly like a spoilt child. "This is a waste of time."

He looked up then, said mildly. "You don't want anything to eat?"

I scowled. "I'd rather go home."

He stood up so abruptly I jumped in my seat. "Let's go then."

On his way out, he spoke to a waiter, leaving me to scramble up and rush after him. Halting outside the restaurant entrance, I watched him stride away towards the movie theatre carpark and knowing I'd have to run to catch up, stubborn pride kicked in. Whirled in the opposite direction until I was out of sight around a street corner, muttering rudely as I fished out my phone.

What are you going to do now, ring up family to collect you? That's adding insult to injury, don't you think? You'll be laughed at, I derided myself. Best you find a taxi, it'll drop you off outside the farm gate, and nobody will be any the wiser.

Except there was no taxi in sight, and apart from the odd car driving by no sign of life either. Feeling suddenly vulnerable, I shivered in the chill air and wished for a warmer jacket. Heard a car approaching, but as the ute rounded the corner, did a U-turn, and pulled up at the curb next to me, I blatantly ignored it, not even looking up when he called out.

"Get in, Kate!" His voice sounded harsh. "I'm not leaving without you."

I continued staring stubbornly at my phone, heard a door open and slam.

"You're being a bitch, Wolf girl," he growled softly from close by.

My head came up at that, but whatever I was planning to throw back at him died on my lips. The anger in his eyes made me recoil a pace.

"I'll take you home." He jerked his head sharply to the ute.

"You don't have to!" I said through my teeth.

"Yes, I do."

"You don't have to worry about my Mum. I won't tell her."

"I'm not worried." He shook his head. "I took you out, I take you back. Simple."

"Such a gentleman." I glowered.

"Don't push your luck." He narrowed his eyes, moving to open the passenger door.

With my heart tripping at the deadly look, I didn't argue and got in. We sat in silence as he drove, with me feeling worse about the whole evening with every passing moment.

"I'm sorry," I finally muttered. "For being a bitch."

He didn't say anything, but when he veered off suddenly onto an unfamiliar road, I shot him a quick worried glance. He was frowning, eyes narrowed. Felt decidedly nervous, not sure if he was still angry or just concentrating. Winding up a hill, he pulled into a lookout area with a partial view of the town below, switching off the engine.

"Why are we here?" I heard the tremble in my voice.

"To talk if you don't mind."

I let out a long sigh but didn't reply or look at him.

"What triggered that reaction?" His voice was quiet, controlled.

I shook my head, kept silent.

"You don't like me kissing your hand?"

I looked at him then, shook my head and mumbled. "You just surprised me that's all."

"No shit!" He raised his eyebrows.

"Guys don't usually do that!" I said defensively.

"So, what do they usually do then?"

"Let's forget it, please," I whined. "I'm sorry if I reacted."

"Go for the jugular, tongue down your throat, is that what you mean?"

That shocked me speechless, my jaw dropping.

"I'm not a wham, bam and thank you ma'am kind of guy, beautiful." He smirked at the look on my face. "Just so you know."

"Um," I croaked. "I don't want to know!"

"Well, keep it for future reference." He tilted his head. "And don't panic next time."

"Next time?"

"Yeah." He laughed. "Now how about some food, huh?"

I blew out my cheeks. "Okay."

"Cool bananas." He started the engine. "I'm starving."

I enjoyed the rest of the evening. Food, good company and no more hand kissing.

Chapter 11

Douglas Willard, the school bully, hadn't left the district. He worked at the local sawmill and lived on an acre of land at the edge of town in one of the dilapidated old sheds that his late father once owned. The place was quite literally a junkyard, with car wrecks, machinery parts, and the like strewn about. As gossip would have it, he'd been in trouble with the law for drunken and disorderly behaviour, including assault, since leaving school, and neighbours periodically complained about the goings on at his property, namely loud parties and fights.

Willard's supposed thing for the Von Meeren girl since school was the reason, he kept hassling me whenever he got the chance, or so my dear brother Matthew reckoned. Suffice to say, I headed in the opposite direction if I saw him in the street, wasn't afraid of him but simply thought him an annoyance that I preferred to stay away from.

I couldn't deny that his looks had improved with age; remembered he used to be podgy with a piggy-eyed sneering face at school. He'd lost the puppy fat, sported a toned well-built body, and if you were into shaved blonde hair, ice blue eyes and a wicked sardonic grin that seemed to be permanently plastered to his face he was probably quite a catch nowadays. His biceps were often on display in muscle shirts showing off the grinning skull tattoos on his arms which I shuddered with distaste at the sight while other females it was rumoured, thought differently.

After stopping in town on my way home one day to pick up something for Mum, I returned to find the jeep's front tyre flat to the wheel rim. There was nobody about in the small off-street carpark to give me a hand and muttering my displeasure, I got out the jack, brace and spare wheel. After some minutes of huffing and puffing, the car was up on the jack but undoing the nuts on the wheel was giving me grief.

"Well, well. Look who we have here," a man drawled.

I shot Douglas an unfriendly sideways glance without replying.

He grinned. "The Von Meeren witch has got herself a flatty."

"Aren't you so smart," I said sarcastically.

He snorted a laugh, bending over to look down my front. "Nice view."

"Piss off, Douglas!" I said through my teeth.

He didn't move. "Rear view's nice too."

I stood up abruptly, gripping the brace and turning threateningly to face him. "Come any nearer and I'll use this on you!"

He took a quick step backward, but his grin didn't change. "Oho! Witchy is bitchy."

"I mean it! Go away." I scowled, lifting an arm to wipe my clammy forehead.

"Hot and bothered?" His grin widened.

Turning away, I squatted back down to slot the brace back on the wheel. Tried again to undo the nut but it wouldn't budge, my arm trembling with the effort.

"Want me to give you a hand?" He leant closer again.

I gave him a baleful up from under look to which he raised his eyebrows slyly. I had a feeling there was more to his offer and shook my head, trying again to turn the brace.

"How about I change the tyre for a witch's kiss."

"Get lost!" I snapped, letting out a long breath of relief when the nut moved.

"Aw, come on. Be nice." He placed his hand on my shoulder.

The brace came away in my hand as I jerked out of his grip, turning on my haunches at the same time. Heard the sickening clack of metal connecting with his kneecap. With a horrible animal howl, he staggered back against the car beside mine and doubled over, clutching his leg. Without thought, I leapt to my feet, reaching out to him.

"Oh, crap!" I gasped. "Sorry. Are you all right?"

He ignored my hand, stared at me with pure venom and turning away snarled over his shoulder. "Fucking bitch!"

I watched him lurch away, half hopping and muttering obscenities. Realising that he could return at any moment, possibly with backup I hurriedly got back to my wheel and for some reason found the other nuts a whole lot easier to undo.

Nothing like a good shot of adrenalin, I thought.

It was with relief that I finished the job, piled everything back into the jeep and took off home, Dad taking the flat tyre to the track next day to have it repaired. I made no mention of my unfortunate encounter with Douglas.

That weekend the racetrack held a two-day car racing event which Kenneth and I went along too with free tickets courtesy of Dad and Matthew. It was busy, loud and fun to watch with all kinds of race classes, touring and vintage cars, V8 classics and trucks.

We left our vantage point near the finish line for lunch, stood waiting in the queue at the kiosk when Kenneth bent his head to say in my ear. "Someone's got their eye on you."

"What?"

"There are some guys at the Toyota stand. The blonde dude on crutches keeps looking."

I peered past his shoulder, recognising who he meant immediately.

"You know them?" Kenneth lifted an enquiring eyebrow at my disdainful grimace.

"Douglas Willard and his mates. Know them from school, they used to bully me and my brothers."

"Nice!" Kenneth eyed me. "He still bullies you now?"

"Not really," I muttered. "I keep my distance, mostly."

"Mostly?" He narrowed his eyes at my tone.

I pulled a rueful face but shook my head, not wanting to talk about it.

"What happened?"

He was too astute for my health. How did he know anything had happened?

"You can tell me," he added softly.

"I hit him with a wheel brace last week."

His eyebrows shot up. "Interesting. Why a wheel brace?"

"I had a flatty. He kind of offered to help."

"Kind of?"

"I didn't want his help, told him to go away," I muttered waspishly. "I don't like him. He calls me the Von Meeren witch."

"Aha! I'm beginning to follow." His lips twisted. "But he didn't go away?"

"No, he didn't!" I averted my eyes. "He touched me."

"Touched you?" His voice sharpened. "How?"

My eyes shot back to his. "Oh, not like that! He just put his hand on my shoulder."

"Why?"

"He wanted, er...um." I shook my head. "It doesn't matter."

"He wanted something for helping you?" He frowned. "Like what?"

"A kiss!" I bit it out.

"Ah." His mouth curved. "But, not on your hand like?"

I scowled. "It's not funny!"

"No, it's not," he nodded agreeably. "So, you hit him?"

"I didn't mean to. I just turned around and the brace caught his kneecap."

He couldn't hide his grin. "What did he do?"

"He wasn't very happy. I think it hurt."

"And now he's on crutches."

I pulled an unsympathetic face.

He laughed. "Did he leave you alone after that?"

"Yes. He kind of hobbled away and called me an ef…" I bit my lip. "A bitch."

"I get it!" he snorted. "No wonder he's giving you the evil eye, you busted his leg."

"I said I was sorry," I protested. "It just happened somehow."

"You just reacted, huh?" He tweaked my chin. "Lady, you're really something else."

I eyeballed him in silence, my chin tingling where he'd touched me.

"That wasn't a kiss." He instantly raised his palms. "Please, don't hit me."

I curled my lip. "You're so hilarious."

He was suddenly serious. "Next time you need help for a flatty or whatever, call me."

"Oh, right! You're going to drop everything and come running?" I was sarcastic.

"I mean it." He frowned. "And any trouble with that fella, you call me too, okay?"

I nodded, surprised at the vehemence in his voice.

"Have you told your dad and brothers about this?"

"No."

"I suggest you do."

"Can I help you?" The lady in the kiosk called out.

We ordered our food, a scoop of fries, club sandwiches and a coffee each. Kenneth didn't pursue the subject of Douglas, thereafter, finding us another good spot to munch our lunch and watch the racing. Later we made our way to the pit garages, chatted with Dad, Matthew and Daniel before they got back to the organised chaos of being racetrack mechanics and during the afternoon, I noticed Douglas twice more in the crowd. His scrutiny made me feel distinctly uncomfortable and rather glad of Kenneth's company.

Bugger! I grimaced resignedly. Don't think the bully will be forgetting me in a hurry.

After work weeks later, I dropped off a cat for an elderly customer; her beloved moggy had been collected that morning by another vet nurse for dental care at the clinic and as she lived across town, it meant driving through the main thoroughfare on my way home.

While waiting at the first set of traffic lights behind another vehicle, a station wagon throttled up alongside in the right lane with loud music blaring. Glancing across, I recognised the front-seat passenger with a groan. He'd already seen me. Wound down his window. Showed his teeth in an evil grin and mouthed something distinctly crude. Giving him a cold look of disdain, I looked away and tried my best to ignore him.

As the lights turned green, we moved off to stop at the next set of lights with me now first in line. The station wagon drew up alongside again, but this time Douglas opened his door to get out at which point I quickly locked mine, glaring when he rapped on my window.

"Hey, Von Meeren witch! Want some of this?" Grinning salaciously, he made a lewd gesture with a pumping fist at his crotch right in front of my eyes.

"Oh, gross!" I spat. "Get lost! You, dirty creep!"

I jerked my face away, wishing desperately that the lights would hurry up and change. They did, and I floored it. At the last set of lights, which were thankfully green, I made a split-second decision to turn left, laughing gleefully as the station wagon hurtled past straight ahead. Continuing on in excess of the speed limit, I eventually headed out of town and slowed down on a road that wasn't exactly familiar, arriving at a t-intersection to stop and take stock. To my right were distant wooded hills, recognised the pine forest block near the sawmill and was fairly sure a secondary road led to the coast, and from there I could loop back home.

The sawmill itself was to my left, but the forest it serviced stretched for hundreds of hectares in the other direction, and as I swung right, it wasn't long before a side accessway appeared, signposted Sawmill Forest

Road. Relieved I'd got my bearings right, I turned in, driving at a more leisurely pace along the quiet road, but soon became aware of a vehicle approaching at speed behind me.

It was the station wagon.

Of course! I realised with dismay, heart leaping to my throat. This is Douglas Willard country; he probably knows every road around here like the back of his hand.

As I pressed my foot down hard on the accelerator, my little jeep responded, but the station wagon edged ever nearer. Glancing in the rear-vision mirror for the hundredth time, I saw it was almost upon me, so close the front grill was out of sight.

What I could see was Douglas, head and shoulders leaning out the passenger window, grinning like an ape with his tongue hanging out. The unexpected tap on the jeep's rear made me yelp with fright. Had to wrestle the steering wheel to keep her straight, letting out another shriek as a second tap came. The third time was different, as if the Suzuki was being shunted, sliding out of control and my attempt to brake didn't help much.

Something snapped in my head. Baring my teeth, I took my foot off the brake and gripped the steering wheel hard. I didn't have a dad and brother who drove racing cars for nothing, all they'd taught me suddenly taking over. I straightened her up again somehow and accelerated away, preparing myself for the next onslaught. Felt surprisingly calm although my whole body trembled, the initial shock and fright gone.

We were going too fast. At the next corner, tyres screeched on the tarmac, my little car wobbled and tipped sideways. Thought for a crazy second that we'd go over. Didn't happen. As she dropped back on all fours, I touched the brakes and let out a thankful whoop.

The feeling didn't last long. Saw the station wagon in my mirror, moving out onto the wrong side of the road.

Yipped. "Oh, shit!"

As they drew up alongside, I knew exactly what they were planning and decided right then that hitting a tree was preferable to being spun around by them. Braced myself for impact as the station wagon veered my way, the forest track suddenly there as if by magic. Jerking the steering wheel, I sent the jeep careering wildly, bouncing and juddering off-road.

The track headed downhill at a slight incline at first, rutted and full of potholes. I could feel my bum leaving the seat, my teeth clacking together and at each bump I yelped. Constantly fighting to keep the car on track, I took my off the accelerator as it got steeper, touching the brakes to round a blind corner. Wasn't prepared for the huge tree root. It lifted the front wheel, shooting the jeep upwards to land sideways with a jolt and run straight into a bank. The force of contact winded me. Sat stunned at first, heaving air into my lungs. The sound of the Suzuki's engine still running cleared my head, I shifted gear and hit the accelerator. She was stuck fast. Tried reverse and first gear again, but she wouldn't move.

Something in my brain told me to get out. I switched off the ignition, undid my seatbelt in a panic, grabbed my bag from the passenger seat and threw open the door to tumble out. Took one look back the way I'd come.

Approaching fast down the track were three men, one of them Douglas. Wasn't hanging around. Spun on my heel and bolted.

Heard him shout. "Hey, witch! Come back here!"

Skidding to a halt, I whirled to see them at my car. He stood in front it, hands on hips and even from a distance I could see his teeth showing in that familiar evil grin of his. His two mates stood slightly behind him on either side, one said something I couldn't catch to which they all laughed. The initial fear I'd felt at seeing the station wagon behind me on the road was back in spades.

"Stop running!" Douglas yelled. "You can't get away, witch!"

He took one step forward. It was enough to motivate me, breath leaving in a whoosh as I whipped around and away. Sprinted along the track, a minefield of ruts and protruding rocks, hoping desperately not to break a leg. There seemed to be no other sound but the thudding of my feet and tortured breathing. Had no idea if they were closing in, but even in my panicked state, when the moment came, I took it.

As the track veered suddenly to the right, I leapt in the opposite direction. Dived into the undergrowth, lost my footing, and hurtled down a slope, managing somehow to stay upright. Huge tree ferns closed over me, and at the bottom of a small gully, I slithered to a stop, immediately crouching low in the foliage. Forced control of my breathing to listen.

Could hear their heavy footfalls close by above me, but they didn't stop. Heard voices, and then nothing, sound fading to silence. Not daring to move, I waited until they returned at walking pace, muttering amongst themselves. Car doors opened and slammed shut. Figured they'd returned to my jeep, cringing at what they might do to it.

"You won't get away next time, witch!" Douglas shouted again. "Do you hear me!"

Held my breath, but he didn't come closer. Heard footsteps moving off, more doors slamming, and a big engine firing up with a roar, tyres squealing on tarmac. Listened to their vehicle driving off into the distance, silence soon replaced by welcoming bird song.

Leaving my hiding place cautiously, I began to climb, but not back onto the track. Stayed in amongst the undergrowth until I came to a clearing amongst the trees, made sure there was no one about before crouching down to search in my bag. Found my phone and tried it. No reception, not a bar. Needed to go somewhere higher or back to the road, but risking another encounter with Douglas's lot wasn't an option in my book. Decided to stay in the shelter of the trees, heading uphill, and at the top of a rise amongst taller stands of pine forest, I tried again. The phone showed a weak signal but there was no connection to Dad or either of my brothers. Knowing Mum was out of town that day, I tapped in Bella's number, but again, no luck.

As reaction suddenly set in, I went through my knees and slumped to the ground, feeling nauseous.

Chapter 12

How long I stayed there I had no idea, but it was Kenneth's voice resounding in my head that shocked my wits into gear. Tried his phone number. It rang.

His drawl almost made me weep. "Hey, beautiful. How about a date tonight?"

I tried to speak but could only croak.

"Are you there?" His voice sharpened.

"Yes." I managed a louder croak.

"Kate? What's up?"

"Kenneth."

"Kate? Hey, are you okay?"

"No."

"What's wrong? Where are you?"

I swallowed. "Please. Can you ring, Dad."

"Ring your dad? Sure." He sounded worried. "What's happened?"

"I crashed."

"What? Your car?" he asked harshly. "Where?"

"In the forest by the sawmill."

"Forest?" Worry turned to bafflement. "You're in the forest?"

"Yes." I let out a long trembling breath. "They chased me."

"Chased you? Who chased you?"

"Douglas and his mates."

"The guy at the track?" He bit it out. "Kate? Tell me! Are you okay?"

"I'm okay." My voice was beginning to shake.

"Is he there?"

"No. I got away."

"You're in your car?"

"No. I had to leave it." The shake was getting worse, all over.

He must have heard my teeth chattering or something, "Kate! Try to stay calm, breath slowly. Take slow deep breaths."

I gulped air.

"Do you know where you are?"

I closed my eyes, breathed in and out. "Off the sawmill road."

"Right. Are you anywhere near your car?"

"I'm not sure any more. The phone wouldn't work, I had to move."

"Okay. But your car is in the forest, not on the road?"

"Yes."

"How far down from the town end?"

"Um, ten, twelve kms, I suppose."

"I'm on my way."

"Please, just call my dad or my brothers."

"Don't worry, I'll call them." He paused. "Those guys, do you know where they are? Are they still in the forest?"

"I don't think so. I heard them drive away."

"Okay, stay put. I'll ring you soon."

I swallowed, breathed. "Please hurry."

"You'll be fine, Kate. I won't be long."

I sat down against a tree trunk to wait, watch and listen. The only sound was the wind in the trees, birds twittering and my own breathing. As my body slowly relaxed, I stopped shaking.

Less than twenty minutes later he rang.

"Hello," I croaked.

"Hi, beautiful. Everything okay?"

"I think so." The relief at hearing his voice set off the trembling again.

"Good, I'm nearly there," he said cheerfully. "Your dad and Matthew are bringing one of the track recovery vehicles over. They'll call me when they get to Sawmill Road."

"Okay."

"You think the forest track is about ten kms in?"

"Yes. You might see my tyre tracks. I turned in pretty fast."

"Right. Be there soon. I'll phone you again."

I heard an engine in the distance less than ten minutes later, straining my ears to listen, and as it got closer, it sounded familiar. Kenneth's ute. The breath left my lungs in a rush, I stood up quickly on wobbly legs.

The engine note changed as he slowed down to stop, but I didn't wait for him to ring me, punched in his number, and before he could say a word, it squeaked. "I can hear you!"

"And I can see a track and tyre marks," he said. "There's nobody else here. How about we both stay put until your dad arrives, hmmm?"

"I'm up the hill further along, I can start walking down."

"Okay but be careful and keep your phone handy."

I picked my way as quickly as I dared down through the trees, slithering to stop to listen as another engine approached. The vehicle slowed down, changed gears and braked. Men's voices.

I grinned like a Cheshire cat when Dad shouted. "Kate! Can you hear me?"

"Yes!" I yelled back. "I'm nearly at the forest track. I can see it now."

"Kenneth's on his way." Dad called again. "We'll drive the truck in."

I saw Kenneth before he saw me. Burst out of the trees onto the track, raced towards him and leapt into his arms, not caring who might be watching.

He kept his balance commendably, whooped. "Like the welcome!"

I didn't speak, pressing my face into his shoulder and holding on tight.

"Hey, it's okay," he murmured. "You're safe now."

I sighed deeply and let go, stepping back to look at him. "Thank you."

"Anytime," he grinned, taking my hand.

We walked down the track together without words but catching sight of my jeep nose into the bank had me gasping. Pulled out of his grasp and ran towards it just as a four-wheel drive tow wagon emblazoned with the racetrack logo appeared, reversing in.

Dad was riding as passenger, saw me in the side mirror and leapt out as Matthew braked. We met halfway, his hug almost cracking my ribs. Matthew clambered out from the driver's side to do the same, holding me at arms-length afterwards.

He grinned part teasing, part relieved. "Since when have you been into off roading, sis?"

"Wasn't." I said with a wry little laugh. "Until now."

"You're not hurt?"

"I'm okay, really. Just a little shook up."

Dad nodded at Kenneth who had joined us, but his attention immediately returned to me, anger in his eyes. "This Douglas fella, he ran you off the road?"

Matthew snarled. "Bloody bastard!"

I shook my head. "Actually, he wasn't the one driving."

"Doesn't matter," Matthew shook his head. "He would have been egging them on!"

"What happened?" Dad asked, frowning.

"I saw them in town first at the lights." I took a breath. "Thought I'd left them behind, but they followed me out here and then things got silly, they er, bumped my car."

Matthew looked livid. "They rammed you!"

"Not rammed, well not at first." I blew out my cheeks. "It wasn't until they came up beside me on the wrong side of the road that I took off down the forest track."

"Wise girl." Dad's lips twisted. "Kenneth said they chased you on foot, too?"

"Yes, but they didn't get close."

"What is it with you and that dickhead?" Matthew shook his head at me.

I snorted an indignant laugh. "Hey, I didn't do anything!"

"You sure know how to wind him up, sis."

"It's not my fault. Don't blame me!"

"Okay, enough talking for now, best we sort your car out." Dad intervened. "Can you back the truck up closer, Matt?"

"Yep. No worries," Matthew nodded and got back into the tow wagon.

Kenneth had been inspecting the Suzuki, opening both driver and passenger doors to check inside before turning to me. "Have you got your car keys?"

"Somewhere," I said, finding them in my bag.

He put it in the jeep's ignition, helped secure a rope to both vehicles, and with Dad, supervising Matthew, very capably pulled the jeep backwards and out of its predicament.

I grimaced dismay and annoyance at the bent bumper and grill while Kenneth got in to try starting it, the motor spluttering a few times before firing. He gestured for me to get in while Dad undid the rope, the Suzuki following the truck out onto the road under its own steam. After all three men had another good look underneath, they agreed it was fit to drive but Dad wasn't keen on me taking the wheel.

"I'd rather you let me drive right now, Kate." He put at hand up at my frown. "We'll take it to the garage, check it over and see what needs fixing. And we'll run by the police station on the way, let them know what happened and show them the damage."

"What will the cops do?" I wrinkled my forehead dubiously. "I didn't recognise the driver or get the number plate."

Dad shook his head, saying adamantly. "They harassed you and we need to report it. It could have been a lot worse."

"Yeah, it could!" Matthew agreed, scowling. "And the cops will want to know about Willard, they've got a dossier on the dickhead."

"I told you; he wasn't driving." I said sharply.

"He was there, wasn't he?" Matthew narrowed his eyes on me. "Do you happen to know what kind of car it was?"

"A station wagon, older model Holden Commodore. Matt black."

"Good spotting, sis." He commended before pursing his lips in thought. "Doesn't ring a bell, though. Can you remember what the driver looked like?"

"Long dark hair, a goatee and wearing a cap," I sighed. "Didn't get a good look."

He shrugged. "I'll ask around. Daniel might know."

"Even if I recognised him, it's my word against theirs," I protested.

"Doesn't matter, you should still tell the cops. These guys could try this again, maybe not to you but someone else," Kenneth said quietly. "Go now and get it sorted."

Matthew nodded. "He's right. Go on, sis. It won't take long."

"Oh, all right then." I relented grudgingly.

"Good girl." Dad put out a hand to shake Kenneth's. "Thanks, for all your help."

Matthew clapped Kenneth's shoulder. "Yeah, thanks mate. Good of you to help my little sister."

"You're welcome, anytime." Kenneth grinned at my pout and eye roll.

"How about coming over for dinner tonight for a catch up?" Dad suggested. "I'll phone Zoe, she won't mind an extra at the table."

"Sure, I'd like that," Kenneth nodded.

With a honk of horns and waves we set off, my jeep to the police station where Dad was immediately greeted by several cops he knew and within the hour I'd filed a report and answered their questions. The police assured us the incident and Douglas Willard would be investigated which left me feeling more trepidation than relief. Antagonising the guy wasn't going to improve relations between us, hated to think how he would retaliate.

From there we departed to the track where Dad sorted a loan car for me to use during which time my jeep would be thoroughly inspected and repaired, Matthew already rubbing his hands together at the chance to practise his panel beating and painting skills on my car.

"You be careful with my little car," I told him.

"Don't you worry, sis. I'll treat her with kid gloves," he grinned.

"You better. I'm very fond of her."

"Don't worry, Kate. I'll keep an eye on him," Dad reassured me, laughing. "Now you take care driving home, won't you?"

"Don't worry, Dad, there'll be no more off roading." I rolled my eyes at him. "I better get moving, Mum will be wondering where I've got to."

"Thanks for reminding me." Dad whipped his phone from his pocket. "I better let her know we have an extra for dinner."

"She'll love that. Kate's boyfriend's coming over." Matthew slanted me a sly look.

"He's not my boyfriend," I scowled.

"As good as," Matthew grinned. "You're going out with him."

"We're just friends. Nothing else!"

"Friends? Yeah right."

I thumped him on the arm, smiling unsympathetically at his protest of pain. Heard Dad speaking to Mum and by the look on his face, he was getting an earful. Hiding my mirth, I turned to the loan car with a quick wave, bracing myself for my own earful as I drove home but Mum was remarkably subdued however, seemed Dad had borne the brunt.

Dinner turned into a rowdy affair, with Daniel and Anna also contributing to the noise. My brothers, bless them, found my afternoon excursion more than entertaining and wouldn't leave the subject alone. Kenneth, bugger him, wasn't letting it go either.

"Douglas just can't help himself when you're around, sis," Daniel grinned.

"He's always had the hots, since school." Matthew rubbed it in.

"It's nothing to do with me," I pointed out. "He's a bully who picks on anyone."

"Nah, not just anyone." Daniel shook his head. "How did you lure him out there?"

"I didn't lure him out anywhere." I was indignant. "He followed me."

"He followed you from work?" Dad frowned.

"No. I dropped off a cat for a customer after work. Him and his mates came up beside me at the lights in town, that's all."

"Did you give him the finger or something?" Matthew's grinned slyly.

"Matthew!" Mum scolded. "Kate wouldn't do that."

"Ha! Don't you believe it, Mum."

Kenneth who'd been listening avidly slanted a look at me, my chilly stare warning him not to say anything prompting an amused eyebrow lift.

"Who was driving?" Daniel asked.

"Sis, said it was some guy with long hair and a goatee." Matthew answered for me.

"Sounds like Poke, he's a friend of Willard's."

"Poke?" Dad lifted his eyebrows.

"It's his nickname, don't know his real one."

"How did he get that name?"

"He chopped off an index finger at the sawmill, still works there with his oldest brother, Axe."

"Don't tell me he chopped his finger off too." Dad said wryly. "With an axe."

"Nah, he's good at throwing axes apparently."

"Nasty about the finger." Anna piped up.

"Very." Mum agreed, shuddering sympathy.

"Their father and uncle work at the mill too, I think or used to," Daniel continued. "You may have heard of the family, Dad. Thornton's the name, father's Pakeha, mother's Māori."

"Can't say I have."

"Anyway, sis," Daniel looked at me. "What kind of car was it?"

"A Holden station wagon, black." I told him.

"Don't know that one," Daniel frowned. "Poke used to drive a Toyota Hilux."

"How many guys were there?" Mum wanted to know.

"Three," I told her.

"Three!" She looked horrified. "What on earth were they planning?"

"With Willard around I'd hate to think." Matthew grimaced.

"Let's not go there." Dad gave Mum's hand a squeeze. "It turned out okay. Kate did the right thing and got away."

"We'll sort those dickheads out, Mum, don't you worry," Matthew muttered.

"There will be no vigilante stuff, son!" Dad frowned. "Adrian and

Wayne know what happened. We'll leave it to them to sort out."

"You mean, the cops?" Anna asked.

"Yes, Adrian is Evan Martin's son."

"Ah, yes, I remember Evan." Anna nodded. "Another of Maria's friends."

"Sounds like she was a popular lady," Kenneth said.

"She had her admirers," Anna smiled knowingly at him. "But only your grandfather and Bernard got anywhere."

Kenneth smiled back but didn't comment.

Matthew's mind was on one track mode. "I still think we should do something and give those dickheads a kick up the arse. Willard especially."

"Matthew! That's enough!" Mum scolded.

"Could be fun," Daniel grinned. "We could use K as bait."

"Daniel!" Mum was suitably shocked.

"He won't be able to resist." Daniel rubbed his hands together gleefully.

"Whatever!" I gave him a filthy look. "I will not be going anywhere near him!"

"You didn't tell them, did you?" Kenneth was looking at me again.

Everyone stared at him, turned to stare at me and waited. I knew what was coming, gave Kenneth another don't you dare icy scowl, but he took no notice.

"She hit him with a wheel brace," he said into the silence.

Matthew made a strangled sound before bursting into hysterical laughter, Daniel's eyebrows shot to his hairline before he too promptly doubled over in a fit of the same.

Dad blinked at them both, turned on his serious face with a deep sigh and narrowed his eyes on me. "Is that true?"

"Maybe," I muttered, shooting daggers at Kenneth.

"On the kneecap," Kenneth added for good measure.

Mum stared at me as if I'd turned into an alien, Dad shook his head and Anna simply smiled.

"No shit!" Matthew recovered first, spluttering. "No wonder he's after you."

A wheezing Daniel managed to speak. "Priceless! How did that happen."

"Can we not talk about it now!" I whined.

"Aw! Please, tell us." Matthew grinned from ear to ear.

"That sounds like something Maria would do," Anna offered the information mildly.

"Really?" Kenneth raised interested eyebrows.

"She stuck up for herself, my sister."

"What did she do?" He wanted to know. "Who to?"

"Don't worry, she never hurt your grandfather as far as I know," Anna chuckled. "Only Bernard got picked on."

"So, I've been told." Dad's grimace was rueful. "My poor father."

Kenneth tipped his head. "You mean she assaulted him."

"She used her knee once and also tried to drown him," Anna told him. "Before they got married, that was."

"Wow! Don't mess with a Lawson girl, then?" Kenneth grinned.

"Not all Lawson girls, my lad. I'm the nice one." Anna's glance at me was sly. "But it does run in the family. Bella's feisty and it seems our dear Kate has the same tendencies."

"So, why did you hit Douglas, sis?" Daniel asked, smirking.

I looked down my nose at him. "I didn't. It was an accident."

"She got a flatty," Kenneth told him, grinning at the slicing gesture I made across my throat. "He turned up and offered to help, I was told, but he got too close."

"I didn't mean to hit him," I hissed. "The brace caught his knee as I turned around."

"How close was he?" Matthew snorted a laugh.

"Close enough to want a kiss," Kenneth offered, grin turning malicious.

That set off another raucous bout of brotherly hysterics. Anna chortled, Dad clamped his lips together to stop from laughing and Mum simply looked dumbfounded.

I scowled balefully at my brothers. "Oh, shut up, you two! Control yourselves!"

Daniel controlled himself first, shaking his head. "Aha! Now that explains everything. The guy just wanted a smooch."

"Why don't you just put him out of his misery, sis?" Matthew spluttered, hands clutching his belly. "One smooch and he'll probably never come near you again."

"Sweet aren't you, brother dear?" Tilted my head with a smirk as I remembered something. "By the way, did you know he went out with Martina before you came along?"

Matthew's laughter died abruptly. "What? How do you know that?"

I tapped my nose. "Wendy at work told me, she's Martina's friend."

"Girl's gossiping like usual," he scoffed.

"Douglas's a good kisser too, apparently," I added snidely. "So, Martina told her."

"Eh!" He looked suitably poleaxed.

I smiled evilly. "Not bad in bed either."

"Kate!" Mum yelped.

"Love you too, sister dear!" Matthew glowered daggers at me. "No wonder Willard calls you a witch, the name suits you."

Dad shook his head resignedly as Mum closed her eyes in despair, Daniel and Anna grinned at each other and Kenneth kept a straight face.

"Witch or bitch," I gave him a snooty stare. "What do you think, Kenneth?"

"Okay, children! That's enough," Dad was authoritative. "Be nice."

"Siblings, eh?" Kenneth's mouth twisted. "Seems like a whole lot of fun."

Daniel sniggered. "Yep, it is. Most of the time."

"Word of warning, mate," Matthew muttered to Kenneth. "My little sister bites."

"Just like Maria," Anna murmured.

"I'll be careful," Kenneth grinned.

I poked my tongue out childishly at him.

Of course, my brothers thought that hilarious too and got back to doubling over. Mum clucked her tongue at me but as Dad got up to clear the dishes quickly left the table with him. During dessert, us siblings called a truce and the conversation reverted to normality and nicer subjects. Kenneth departed soon after with a long teasing look at me, letting me know without words that he'd be in contact sooner rather than later.

It wasn't memories of the day's antics or Douglas Willard that kept me awake that night but Kenneth in my head. Eventually slept to dream about him, us in a forest doing mind-boggling stuff I didn't even know about and woke in the morning decidedly jaded, shuddering to think how my brain could even conjure up images like that.

Chapter 13

I wasn't in a good mood when he called me the following evening, his greeting and subsequent question not helping one iota.

"Hi, beautiful. Are we still going on a date?"

"No, we are not!" I snapped. "And stop calling me that."

"Beautiful?" He sounded amused. "But that's what you are, Kate."

"I don't care, just stop it!"

"How are you? No sleepless night after what happened?"

"No!" I lied. Certainly, wasn't telling him the reason for my lack of sleep.

"No nightmares?"

"No!" It was a dream, actually. No thanks to you!

"Not dreaming about car chases in the forest?"

Forest? That was way too close for comfort. "I have not been dreaming about anything!" I spat. "I slept like a log, thank you very much! Anyway, what's it to you?"

"Okay, okay, just asking?" He chuckled. "Not a good day at work, then?"

"Nothing wrong with my day at work either."

The chuckle turned into a sexy laugh, made me shiver.

"What are you doing tomorrow night?"

My breath hissed through my teeth. "Staying home."

"Friday nights are for going out."

"Well, I'm staying in."

"What about relaxing and unwinding?"

"I can relax and unwind at home," I told him nastily.

"Shall I ring back and start over?" His amusement grated.

"No! Hang up and don't ring back at all." The bitch in me snapped.

"I'm sorry you've had a bad day; you really should take some time out."

"I haven't had a bad day and I don't care for time out!"

He ignored my belligerence. "I'll pick you up tomorrow at seven."

"Don't bother!" I spat.

"If you aren't ready when I get there I'll wait until you are," he said quietly. "I'll even come in and dress you myself."

My jaw dropped. "Excuse me?"

"And if you hide, I'll find you," he continued. "Got that?"

My mouth closed and opened again but no sound emerged.

"Did you hear me?" he said softly.

"How dare you!" I croaked.

"Oh, I dare, beautiful." His laugh was evil. "Don't keep me waiting, okay?"

I disconnected without a word, breathing fast to a thudding heart. Half expected him to ring back, but he didn't, and when I headed for bed my mind churned. Another night of almost non-existent sleep all because of a man who I still didn't really trust or like.

Oh, get real, girl! Like? That's so tame, he's in your head, and you want him. What? I do not want him! Yes, you do! Desperately! Sure, you don't trust him but that's all part of the fun. He's exciting, and don't forget, he wants you too. Meet him halfway, you'll love every second! Are you crazy? No, truthful!

Burying my head under the pillow, I devised a plan. Packed a small overnight bag when I got up and lied to Mum at breakfast, saying that I'd had a surprise text inviting me to a friend's party and would be staying overnight.

There! I thought spitefully. That'll teach you, Mr Smartarse Hawke. I'll hide all right and you won't ever find me, not tonight anyway.

I didn't exactly know why I wanted to run from him, perhaps the niggling distrust had intensified because he'd peeved me off at dinner or maybe I just needed space. More to the point things were moving too fast, not only did I barely understand the thoughts and feelings he evoked, but they also scared me.

I ran to the cabin after work, picking up a Thai takeaway meal on my way. The smug feeling as I drove in, waiting for the automatic gate to close behind felt good. Stopped to look across the sea before going inside, left my bag in Dad's old bedroom at the cabin's southside before going for a walk down the cliff steps to the beach, sighing at the sound of the waves.

Later, I showered and settled down in comfort clothes, reheated my meal in the microwave and ate as the sun lowered, gold and orange reflected in the sea.

When my phone rang just as I finished eating, my bum leaving the seat in a hurry. Heart flipped at his number, but I didn't answer, waiting for a message with bated breath.

"Hello, beautiful?" he asked with the familiar infuriating amusement in his voice. "Your Mum said you had a surprise invite to a party. That's nice."

I knew he didn't believe a word, the text soon after confirming it: **Where are you really, beautiful?**

I didn't reply.

The next text had my heart in my mouth: **I like playing hide and seek.**

Something made me stand up abruptly, reaching for my car keys. Outside my eyes shifted down the driveway in trepidation, another text coming through as I drove the loan car into the garage and out of sight.

My heart tripped when I read it: **What should I do when I find you?**

Eek! He was beginning to really scare me. I had to stop this, replying smartly: **I'm at the party, I'll talk to you another time.**

Where's the party?
Why do you want to know? It's girls only.
That's okay. I like girls.
No boys allowed.
Why do I think you're telling fibs?
Think what you like.
I think you're on your own someplace.
Whatever. Why don't you go relax and unwind?
I will when I find you.
Leave it please.
Leave you alone all night? Never!

I screwed my eyes shut, puffing out my cheeks but refrained from sending a rude reply. Was sure he wouldn't find me here, wouldn't even think to look at the cabin and as far as I knew he'd never been near the place. Checked every door and window was locked but couldn't stop myself from peering from behind the curtain of the north bedroom window closest to the driveway every few minutes, hoping that the cabin looked deserted if for some unearthly reason he did come looking and jump the gate.

Began to relax a little half an hour later as the sun disappeared, settling in an armchair to watch the sky turn to indigo blue when a rapping came at the door. Let out an almighty shriek and sat bolt upright, fingers digging into the armrests.

Thought I was going to faint as he called out. "Kate, open up! I know you're in there."

There was no hiding; he would have heard me, and judging by the tone of his voice, he'd probably bust down the door or break a window to get in.

"Please, just go away!" I yelled back.

"I'm not going anywhere. Open the door!"

Screwing my eyes shut, I took a long breath to ease the panic. Got up to the door, hesitating before forcing myself to unlock it with a hand that shook, opening it tentatively to a man who wasn't overly happy but whatever he saw in my face damped down his anger almost instantly.

Staying where he was, he said softly. "Thank you."

I felt strangely lightheaded, hoping desperately that I wasn't going to drop at his feet.

"Hey!" He drew his brows together. "I just want us to talk."

Got myself together, mumbling. "How did you find the cabin?"

"Leon told me where it was a while ago."

"Oh." I breathed, adding inanely. "He used to swim here."

"Yeah, he said that."

"How did you know I'd be here?"

"I guessed." His lips twisted. "The way you spoke about it, I figured it was your place to relax and unwind."

"Oh."

His grin flashed. "And as I said before I like playing hide and seek."

I shut my mouth, holding his gaze for several tense seconds before he turned abruptly.

Staring out to sea, he murmured. "You were right, what an awesome view."

"It's even better in daylight," I murmured.

"I can imagine."

Watching him, I decided to risk it. "Would you like a look inside?"

"You're letting me in?" He turned back with raised eyebrows.

Pressing my lips together, I stood aside without replying.

After a moment's hesitation, he entered, shutting the door behind him, but he didn't go far, standing still to look around slowly.

As the silence lengthened, I needed to say something. "This front area is the original cabin, just one room," I gestured to the far wall. "The two bedrooms and hallway were added after Dad was born."

"I see. Who built it originally, do you know?"

"A farmer, I think," I shrugged. "Jason, your grandfather bought it off him. There's land as well, up along the bluff behind and down to the beach."

"Interesting." He inclined his head, watching me. "So, this is your idea of a party with friends?"

My eyes narrowed defiantly but I but didn't speak.

"Don't worry, my lips are sealed," he grinned. "Where's your car?"

"In the garage," I muttered defensively. "I put it there when you phoned, er, tried to make it look like nobody was here."

"Clever girl," he chuckled. "You're happy staying here on your own?"

"Yes. It's quite safe," I told him.

"I'm sure it is," he nodded. "Are the lights working?"

"Yes. I haven't turned them on yet."

"Of course not," he grinned. "You wanted to make it look like nobody was home."

I gave him a peeved look before switching on lights. "There's a generator for power. I'll show you."

There were three doors along the back wall, I led him through the middle one into a hallway with laundry facilities, shelves, and cupboards on the right. Another door to the left opened into a storeroom, which housed the diesel generator.

"Very efficient." He opened the back door, spotting the huge water tanks. "Good water supply as well."

"It's a very user-friendly home. I'll show you the rest if you like." At his nod I took him to the south bedroom with its ensuite and walk-in wardrobe.

"You sleep here?" He noted my overnight bag on the bed.

"Yes. This used to be Dad's room," I told him.

He wandered to the glassed bi-fold doors which opened onto the deck, looking out at the view again. Watching his profile silently, I wondered what he was thinking but wasn't going to ask.

Back in the living room, I pointed to the far door. "The north bedroom is a mirror image of this one."

"Right." He stood still, hands in his pockets. "I'll have a better look some other time."

"Make sure you check out the beach when you do."

"Good idea." He smiled slowly. "I'll leave you to it, then. Enjoy your party."

I pulled a derisive face but didn't reply.

We walked across to the front door, but before opening it he gave me a sidelong look. "Tomorrow, at your place. Same time, okay?"

I rolled my eyes. "You don't give up, do you?"

"Never," he laughed.

As he strode out, I flicked on the outside light and stood in the open doorway, eying the view. Not the sea, but him and his tight butt disappearing down the driveway. Shook my head, shut the door quickly and returned to the south bedroom, staring at the bed with visions of him on it, the sight of which did funny things to my insides. Gave my head another frustrated sake and went to the kitchen, making myself a hot chocolate before settling in the armchair again but couldn't relax and began pacing the floor instead. Spent most of the night with more visions of him on the brain.

As Sunday rolled around, I went home and lied to Mum about how good the party had been. Felt guilty and pathetic, took Delta out for a long ride to sort myself out and by the time he arrived that evening my nerves were under some semblance of control. Our night out was fun, I couldn't deny it and had to wonder why I'd got so uptight.

This guy likes me for some reason, I grinned to myself. And he's not so bad really. Is that all? Okay, he's much better than not bad, even cute and nice. Ah, and you're falling for him! Stop right there! I am not. Don't kid yourself, girly.

Chapter 14

When Dad told me the news, I didn't take it well, which was an understatement. The feeling inside was something I'd never felt before, like a wound ripped open and left bleeding.

I'd returned from a ride on Delta the following Saturday morning, brushed her down, taken her back to her paddock mates, and was cleaning tack when Dad turned up.

"Hi," he said. "Nice ride?"

Had a feeling he'd sought me out but wasn't concerned. "Hi. Just a short one to the river, but yeah, it was nice."

"Good," he smiled. "Got a minute, I've got something to tell you."

"I'm listening." I hoisted the saddle up on the wall rack and turned to him.

"Mum and your brothers already know about this," he said quietly. "Would have told you too but you weren't home for dinner."

"We had a going away party at work for someone leaving to go overseas."

"Yeah, I heard, how was that?"

"Nice. Didn't see you when I got home, you went out too?"

He nodded. "To Leon's for a couple of hours."

I slanted an eyebrow. "Family business?"

"Something like that."

"So, what is it, good news or bad?"

"We all think it's good."

"Okay, shoot."

"I've decided to make use of the cabin, have someone live there permanently."

"Live in the cabin?" I was surprised. "Rent it out, you mean?"

"No, not exactly." Dad shook his head. "Kenneth's taking it on."

My throat constricted, I tried to speak but nothing came out.

"He and I talked just this last week." Dad's voice sounded weird, almost distant. "He said it would suit him down to the ground, his kind of place."

Found my voice, speaking almost to myself. "I showed him the cabin."

"Yes, I know. He said you loved the place and so did he."

"He loved the place?"

"Yes. Didn't he tell you that?"

I swallowed hard. "He said the view was awesome, but then everyone says that."

Dad didn't appear to notice my shock. "Well, he's looking forward to living there."

"It's actually happening?"

"Definitely. It's a good idea, don't you think? Someone there all the time?"

"So Mum, the boys and Leon think it's okay?" My voice shook.

"They're all happy about it." He picked up on my agitation. "Kate?"

"You should have asked me?"

"I didn't think you'd mind." Dad frowned at my tone. "I thought you and Kenneth were getting on well."

"Getting on well!" I snapped. "Yeah! He made sure of that."

"Pardon me?"

"I knew he was up to something! I knew it!"

"Kate, what do you mean?" He put his hands out to me. "What's wrong?"

I warded him off, bared my teeth. "It's not a good idea at all!"

"Why on earth not?" Dad's eyebrows shot up.

"He's what I always thought, a user!" My voice rose sharply. "He used me to get to you, Dad. To get the cabin!"

Dad shook his head. "I don't think so, Kate. He's not like that."

"Yes, he is!" I was losing it, almost shouting. "He's a user and a bastard!"

"Kate!" Dad's voice sliced through me. "That's enough!"

"It's true! He got friendly with me just to get what he wanted!" I snarled. "You said you'd never give the cabin away!"

"I'm not giving it away," he protested.

"Yes, you are!"

Dad put his hands up to quieten me down, his eyes worried and shocked. "Kate! You've got this all wrong."

My breath rasped. "How long is he staying there?"

Dad hesitated. "I'm not sure. We didn't talk about that."

I snorted a bitter laugh. "How convenient. He's found his place and he'll be staying for good!" My voice rose to a screech. "He's got our cabin! Our cabin, do you hear me!"

"Please! Calm yourself." Dad's voice was harsh. "The cabin is ours and always will be. We don't use it enough and Kenneth will look after it for us."

"We do use it!"

"Kate! Think about it. When was the last time anyone was there? It'll be good to have someone on site all the time, good for security as well."

I stared at him, hardly believing what I was hearing. "When is he moving in?"

"In a fortnight."

I turned without another word, pushing past him on my way out. Ran to the bush behind the sheds and down the shortcut to the river, to Paradise and my favourite spot amongst the ferns. In the past, I'd spent quiet times on my own there mulling over things, but never before had I felt so angry, frustrated and bewildered. Never argued with Dad quite like that before either, which was the worst thing of all. I sat there for an hour at least, calming down and slowly getting my head around my thoughts.

Needed to make my peace with Dad that much I knew and returning to the house found him in the kitchen with Mum. As we eyeballed each other, Mum took one look and left the room without a word.

"I'm sorry for what I said before," I told him, tears threatening to spill. "I'm sorry I yelled at you."

He immediately stepped forward with open arms to hold me tight. "It's okay, my dear girl. It's okay."

Felt secure with my cheek against his chest, the despair inside ebbing. "I didn't mean to get so upset about the cabin," I sniffed, lifting my head.

"I understand." His smile was gentle. "I know how you feel about the place."

"But I shouldn't have lost it like that."

"We all lose it sometimes, better to let it out." He tweaked my chin. "Don't worry, your dad's got broad shoulders."

"Just as well." I grimaced ruefully.

"So, it's all good?" He looked deep into my eyes. "About the cabin?"

Heaving a sigh, I nodded. "Yes. I think I can handle it."

"That's my girl."

I reached up to kiss his cheek. "Love you, Dad."

"Love you, too."

He wasn't to know I'd lied to him. It wasn't good, I'd never handle or accept what was happening to the cabin and the reason for all the angst needed to know how I felt.

On Sunday morning, I told both my parents I was going out to see my workmate one last time before she departed overseas. Another lie. Headed in the opposite direction towards Roman and Bella's place, knowing they were away that weekend making my plan that much easier.

Kenneth was my target; knew he didn't often go out on Sunday, and although I could have phoned him to confirm he was home, I didn't. The surprise visit would give me the upper hand, or that's what I hoped.

As I parked in front of Roman's shed, the initial rush of trepidation had me wanting to reverse straight back out. Instead, I reluctantly got out of the car, deep breathed to compose myself and stalked towards the caravan. The sight of the door latched open stopped me in mid stride. Wanted to turn tail and run.

Get on with it, coward! I told myself. This is exactly how you wanted it, he's home and you've got all the privacy you need.

After knocking on the door and no reply, I cautiously peered in to find the caravan empty, decided he couldn't be far away, and sat down on the window bench seat to wait. Minutes later, I heard him whistling a tune outside and braced myself, eyes popping saucer wide as he appeared at the doorway, stark naked with only a towel slung over his shoulder.

"Sweet crap!" he said.

I think I was more shocked than him, jerking my embarrassed face away to stare blindly out the window. Felt a sudden fizz in my belly and clenched a hand there.

"Hang on a minute!" He spoke again, sounding amused.

Feeling ridiculously uncomfortable, I didn't move a muscle. Upper hand indeed!

Soon after some noises and rummaging he slid into the seat opposite, saying with distinct laughter in his voice. "All present and correct."

I gave his teasing grin and fully clothed self a scowl. "Do you always walk around like that?"

"Not always," he chuckled. "Had an urgent call out to a hoof injury this morning and just got home. Needed a shower and voila!"

"Whatever!" I snapped. "I don't think Bella would appreciate it."

"She'd probably crack up." He cocked an eyebrow. "Besides they're not home."

I didn't reply, opting for a snooty stare.

"Anyhow." He smiled cheerfully. "Nice to see you, you've made my morning."

"I doubt it." I gritted my teeth.

"Ah, but you have, beautiful lady. You should do it more often."

"I will not be doing it ever again."

He snorted a laugh. "Phone me next time and I'll make sure I'm dressed."

"That's not what I meant!"

He slanted an eyebrow. "So, what's up?"

"You're an arrogant piece of work, just like I always thought." I curled my lip.

"And?" He looked slightly baffled but still amused.

"You went behind my back."

"You've lost me." The amusement faded.

"The cabin!" I spat it out.

He frowned. "What about it?"

"You got me to show you the place and went sniffing over to my dad afterwards."

"If I recall you offered to show me the cabin, I didn't ask you to." He narrowed his eyes. "And your dad and I had a random chat, it wasn't planned."

"I bet it wasn't!" I snapped. "You're conniving. I knew it from the start."

"Conniving?"

"A cunning drifter who wheedles himself into people's lives."

His eyes changed abruptly, went cold. "That's what you really think?"

"That's exactly what I think, what I thought when I first met you," I sneered. "And look at where you are now, in the Sandford good books. Our family was next, wasn't it? You had the cabin in your sights all the time, my Oma's place!"

"Your father offered me the cabin," he told me on a harsh note.

"Like I said, you're cunning." I spoke through my teeth. "You did your homework before you came here, checked us all out didn't you?" I curled my lip, dripping sarcasm. "Such a wonderful guy is Kenneth Hawke. Everyone loves him!"

"But you don't?" He was just as sarcastic.

"No, I don't!" I bit out. "But you tried to make me, didn't you?"

His sudden show of teeth wasn't pleasant. "Thought I was getting somewhere too."

"Well, you weren't!" I spat. "And you never will!"

"What a shame." He barked a sardonic laugh. "I may have even got you used to me walking around naked. Should have tried harder."

"You really are a piece of work!" I leapt to my feet, staring daggers down at him.

"If you say so." He slanted a contemptuous smile. "You know something. I'm really looking forward to living in your cabin."

I gawped at him in shocked distaste, unable to get a word out.

His smile turned sly. "Even thought that you might like to live there with me."

"What?" I croaked.

"Yeah, that did cross my mind." He growled, getting to his feet. "Once!"

Seeing the anger in him, I stepped quickly sideways and backwards. "I should have known how much of an arrogant bastard you were!" Hated the quaver in my voice.

He didn't reply, his flat blue stare sending a chill through me.

I hadn't finished. "A bastard who stuffs everything up! Our lives, our families!"

He took a step towards me, brows drawn together.

"Don't come near me!" I shrieked it, hands up to ward him off. "I hate you! Never want to see your face again!"

His lip curled in a sarcastic snarl. "Just my face?"

Ignored that. "You won't last long in our cabin, my Oma and Opa will haunt you forever!" Sounded pathetic but I was past caring.

His snorted a derisive laugh. "Are you gonna haunt me too, witch girl?"

"Why don't you just drown in the sea or fall off the cliff!"

"Think I'd rather be haunted." His grin was infuriating.

"Go screw yourself!"

"Aw, but I'd rather screw you."

Aimed a vicious open-handed slap at his face but he was quicker, clamping my wrist in his hand. Unable to get loose, I lashed out like a mad thing. Several choice words and grunts later, he had both my wrists caught, hauling me up against him. I tried kicking instead, but it was a losing battle. With our faces just centimetres apart, we eyeballed each other. I seemed to be way more agitated than him, breathing harder and faster, and his sudden harsh laugh served to incense me further.

I hissed through my teeth at him. "Arsehole bastard! Let me go!"

He wasn't listening, shutting my mouth instead. With his.

I wasn't exactly practised in the kissing department but knew instantly that this was way out of my league. Went rigid with shock as the kiss went deep, his mouth doing things that made my belly do more than fizz. Wanted more but desperate self-preservation wouldn't let me succumb. I bit him. He grunted, instantly wrenched his head away and let me go, pressing the heel of his hand to his mouth. As he removed it, I saw the blood on his lip, staring with wide horrified eyes into his livid ones.

"Bitch," he said softly, stepping forward.

"If you so much as touch me again, I'll have you up for rape!" I spluttered, staggering backwards up against the wall.

"Just for touching you?" He curled his lip. "Why not have me up for the real thing?"

His angry face was too close. Letting out a strangled yelp of fright and terror, I jerked my head sideways. Heard my heart thudding in my ears as I cringed, eyes screwed shut.

He stepped back just as abruptly, snarling. "Get out!"

My eyes snapped open to see him jabbing a finger at the doorway and in my panic turned awkwardly to leap out, misjudging the step. Lost my balance and crashed to the ground outside. Cried out at the shock of it, lying stunned with my foot twisted under me.

He was suddenly there, squatting on his haunches beside me. "Shit! Are you okay?"

Thought he was going to reach for me and jerked hands up to stop him, hissing. "Don't you dare touch me!"

He didn't move a muscle as I half slithered, half rolled to my knees to scramble up. Stared into blue eyes gone dark and deadly. Whirled away, sucking in air as pain shot through my left knee. Ignoring it, I stumbled to my car, wrenched open the door and fell in. Could hardly turn the ignition key, my hand was shaking so badly but at last the engine fired. Revving the car madly, I took off in a spray of gravel without bothering to fasten my seatbelt. Kilometres down the road, I pulled over, rested my head on the steering wheel, and eventually calmed my panicked breathing, fastened my seatbelt and drove off.

Shaking my head in disbelief and derision, my mind raced. What a pathetic little girl, you are! Did you really think you'd make a fool out of him? He must think you're deranged. Well, at least he won't come near you any more now, he now knows exactly what you think of him. That's done and over with. It's what you wanted, isn't it?

How I functioned during the next weeks, I would never know; work was an effort and I struggled to concentrate. The last scene with Kenneth kept on and on in my head, thoughts of him at the cabin making things even worse. My state of mind was noticed at home, especially by Dad, who watched me with worried eyes, but after somehow reassuring him, I kept my secrets.

Bonnie, the workmate who had departed on her OE, sent me a message from London two weeks after her arrival, said she was having fun but wished she had company. Something clicked in my brain. Knew what I had to do. When I messaged her back to ask if I could join her, she was more than enthusiastic, and after informing my rather surprised family of my decision, I handed in my notice at work and booked a flight to London in May, less than a month away.

Dad was relieved my mojo had returned, was supportive of my OE plans, and suggested I also make time to visit Austria, Opa's homeland. He jotted down some contact addresses for me, pulled up images of the Von Meeren Estate and surrounding areas on his computer while I peered over his shoulder, oohing and aahing at the beautiful scenery.

"Do you need any help with finances?" he asked.

"Thanks, but I'm good." I told him. "I've been saving money in my piggy bank."

He laughed. "Thrifty girl. Just remember to call me if you need anything, okay?"

"Sure, Dad. I'll do that." I ruffled his hair.

"It's so good to see you happy again." He gave me a sidelong glance.

"I'm happy." I assured him with a little smile. "Who wouldn't be doing this?"

"Well, you enjoy it and have fun. It's a great time to travel when you're young."

Mum was thrilled for me but worried about me travelling on my own and when Daniel said he was envious and hoped to do the same thing one day I suggested he come with me, but he'd already made plans for his twenty first birthday party in July.

It suddenly occurred to me that I wouldn't be there. "Oh no! I'll be away."

"It's only another birthday, sis." He shrugged, tapping my nose affectionately. "Don't stress about it."

"But it's special," I pouted sadly. "And I've never missed any of your birthdays."

He chewed his lip a moment. "Hey, I've just had a thought."

"What about?"

"How about I meet you in Austria afterwards?" He grinned. "We can have our own party over there?"

Whooping, I threw my arms around him. "Great idea. That's so cool!"

He chuckled, squeezed me. "I'll start making plans for August then. How's that?"

Dad approved wholeheartedly, and the idea seemed to appease Mum too, both saying they'd make sure my brother kept his promise even if it meant organising the travel plans themselves.

I flew out from Auckland to London, met up with Bonnie, and squeezed into the small flat she was temporarily sharing with two others. She planned to move out the following month, would be staying with family in Edinburgh, with a job lined up as well. We made the most of our time together, sightseeing through the south of England by train and bus. It was full-on and tiring, but a blast, and we thoroughly enjoyed our travels. She insisted I go with her to Scotland; we travelled by train, and after spending a fortnight with her family, I said my goodbyes. After enjoying an organised tour of the Scottish Highlands, I travelled back down the coast, booked a ferry, and headed across the channel to Belgium.

The journey gave me time to take a breather and reflect. Standing at the deck railing, I stared blindly out over the water, feeling suddenly homesick, a vision in my head of the cabin's ocean view and wished for my old life back, knowing it would never be the same.

Times change; you've changed things yourself, made choices. Accept it! And stop thinking of home, I scolded myself. Make the most of your holiday—this chance to see the world. People would die to do what you're doing right now.

Sighed deeply but couldn't stop my thoughts churning. Made a resolution there and then to act like the grown-up I was supposed to be when I got back home, to apologise to Kenneth for my behaviour and with that sorted I felt better, the sadness easing.

I made my way through Belgium by train, overnighting along the way in reputable hotels within walking distance of the railway stations. Spent several days in some places, enjoying the sights and marvelling at the historic buildings, something not seen in New Zealand. I preferred my own company at night and didn't go out, had dinner late most evenings, and made a point of contacting Mum and Dad regularly by phone. I was looking forward to Daniel's arrival in three weeks, planning to meet him at the Von Meeren Estate. From Belgium, I travelled to Paris, had a wonderful time exploring the city for a week, and boarded a train to Munich. On my way to Salzburg, my eyes were glued to the passing scenery, picturesque and breath-taking.

At the Salzburg railway station, I made a call to the Von Meeren home as per Dad's instruction, waited in the railway café until a chauffeur-driven Mercedes drove up and its young driver smilingly helped with my luggage, holding open the car's back door for me. He introduced himself as Darius, was very polite and answered all my questions along the way in accented but good English.

When the mansion came into view it struck me as austere, perhaps even forbidding but it had character and a commanding presence that I rather liked. The grounds were immaculate with beautifully kept gardens, a huge ancient forest stood as a backdrop closely bordering the land and the mountain views were stunning.

Von Meerens no longer resided there, at least not living ones but a ghost or two would have suited the place, I thought. The property was opened to the public during weekends by the estate trust, but one mansion wing was kept private and at the ready for us to use, the only existing Von Meerens left. A housekeeper/cook and gardener/handyman also had quarters there, but the Mercedes driver Darius lived in the local village, as did other staff who worked on a casual basis maintaining the buildings and gardens.

Darius dropped me off at the door of a turreted wing to the right of the main entrance, where the waiting housekeeper introduced herself as Stella, a stocky grey-haired woman of perhaps sixty who was smilingly cheerful but spoke stilted English. She ushered me through to a huge high-ceilinged cream and gold bedroom with terrace doors opening out to the gardens and view of the distant hills. She informed me that lunch would be served in an hour, gave me directions to the dining room and left me to unpack and settle in.

I had three days there before Daniel arrived in Salzburg, where he would be met and driven by Darius, as I had been. I was sure once my brother arrived it would be all gone, and made the most of the quiet time on my own, taking walks through the gardens, along the edge of the ancient forest, and down to the village.

Chapter 15

Daniel texted me once his plane landed in Munich, then again from the Salzburg railway station, and I was excitedly waiting when the Mercedes drove in. He exited the car with a huge grin, opening his arms to give me a bear hug. Stella smiled a welcome and took him along to the bedroom next to mine, similar in size and tastefully furnished in green and gold.

I watched him flop down full length on the bed after she departed, curling myself into an armchair. "So how did you find the flight?"

"Long and exhausting," he sighed. "Should have done a stopover, I think."

"Next time, huh?" I replied. "I guess you should phone home soon."

"Yeah, I will," he nodded. "So, what do think of this place?"

"Like something out of a Gothic movie but I kind of like it."

"Count Dracula could live here, or Frankenstein."

I mock shuddered. "I reckon, but it doesn't seem to be haunted."

"Cool view." He lifted his head to look out the terrace door window.

"It's beautiful. The forest and mountain view out the other side is awesome too." I pointed in the general direction. "Let's go for a walk later and have a look."

"Sounds like a plan." He settled back down, stretching. "What's the food like?"

"We had a yummy casserole last night," I told him. "Stella's a good cook."

"Looking forward to it. The meals on the plane weren't great."

"Really? I was quite impressed on my way over."

"It tasted okay." He pulled a face. "Not enough though."

"All you growing lads have the same problem, food disappears into hollow legs," I laughed. "Talking about food, how was it at your twenty first party?"

I'd phoned him on the morning of his birthday to wish him all the best but hadn't caught up on any detailed news about the party.

"You bet there was," he grinned. "Plenty to drink too."

"Got drunk, did you?" I slanted him a mocking eyebrow.

"Not too bad." He grimaced wryly. "Matthew was way worse, he got blotto."

"He would." I snorted. "How's he getting on with Martina?"

"It's all still on, I think. She was there anyway."

"Exciting stuff! My brother actually has a steady girlfriend." Tipped my head. "So, what about you, anyone yet?"

"Why have one when you can have heaps?" He smirked suggestively.

"Spare me the details, please!" I wrinkled my nose. "Don't get anyone pregnant whatever you do. Mum won't be impressed."

"Nah. I'm careful."

"I've heard that one before." I scoffed, adding with a smirk of my own. "Make sure you watch for pinholes in your condoms."

"Eh?" His eyes went wide.

I giggled. "That's an old trick, girl nabs boy fair means or foul. Didn't you know?"

He shook his head, eying me suspiciously. "You females are cunning."

"Some are." I giggled. "And some males are too."

"Are they?"

"So charming and nice when they want to be."

"And you know this how?"

I didn't answer him, looking down at the patterned carpet.

"What happened between you and Kenneth?" he asked quietly.

His question was a surprise; jerked my head up to stare at him but didn't answer.

He wrinkled his brow. "We all thought you were an item."

"We?"

"Everyone, the whole family."

"Oh." I shrugged. "Well, we weren't an item."

"You fooled us then," he murmured. "I really thought you two were meant to be."

I felt something stab and twist inside, bit my lip and kept quiet. Yes, brother dear, I thought so too, at times. Maybe when we get home, I'll have a chance to put things right.

"You know he's gone?" Daniel sat up, narrowing his eyes on me.

"Gone?" This time it was shock I felt, gawping.

He frowned at my reaction. "I'm sorry, I thought you knew."

I blinked. "No, I didn't."

"Thought Bella would have said something."

"He's not working for Roman any more?"

"No."

"Oh, um. So, where's he gone?"

"Down the line somewhere. Took another job as far as I know."

"Down the line?"

"Miles away down south," he said. "He keeps in touch with Leon off and on."

I felt at a loss, couldn't think what to say. Had very obviously blown my chance to see him again, the stab inside twisting again deeper.

"There was another Sandford family meeting by the way, Jonathan told me all about it," Daniel continued. "There were lawyers present, everyone got given their share."

"Share?" I asked inanely.

"Inheritance money. Kenneth included."

"Kenneth was there, too?"

"He is a Sandford after all." Daniel shrugged. "Jonathan told me Kenneth didn't really want to be part of it, but Leon and Karl insisted. Insisted he was family and that his grandfather would have wanted him there."

"What did the others think? Jonathan and Olivia?"

"They were fine with it. Everybody loves the guy."

"What about the Sandford house and quarantine clinic?"

"That belongs to the family trust, Jonathan told me. That will never change, it'll carry on as is. No assets were involved, only money."

"So, Kenneth took his money and left."

"Yes, basically," Daniel raised his eyebrows. "Can you believe it? Almost half a mil each, imagine what you could do with that?"

"A lot I suppose," I muttered. "I wonder if he's still living in a caravan?"

"He still had it while he was at the cabin, he shifted it there from Roman's place."

"Did he actually live in the cabin?"

"As far as I know he did."

"He wasn't there long, then?"

"About two months, I think."

"Did he ever approach Dad about buying it?"

Daniel shook his head. "Dad will never sell that to anyone."

"No, I suppose he wouldn't." I sighed deeply, staring pensively into space. Wondered where Kenneth would have gone, what he was doing.

"I'm not sure where Kenneth went, K," Daniel said into the silence. "You'd have to ask Leon or Bella."

I gave myself a shake, told a lie. "I wasn't thinking that."

The look in his eyes told me he didn't believe a word.

I heaved a sigh, flapped a hand. "By the way thanks for telling me all this, it's nice to be back in the know." I also decided it was time to change the subject. "How about we go for that walk now?"

We went out to the forest, and no more was said about Kenneth, but what I'd learned affected me more than I cared to admit. That night, it took me a long time to get to sleep with my mind full of the man, that last horrible meeting, and my vow to make things right on the ferry across from England. It seemed life at home had certainly moved on without me.

Fortunately, I didn't have a great deal of time to dwell on things, as Daniel had plans almost from the next day forward, and I was thankful to be part of them.

We stayed for another four months, touring around a good chunk of Europe together—Greece, Italy, France, and Spain most of all. Daniel hired a car and had no problem driving on the other side of the road whereas I found it a little daunting and left him to it most of the time. While we were in Spain during the first few weeks of November, I celebrated my twentieth birthday with my brother in a small village by the sea, the memory of which I would treasure for the rest of my life. The following week, we headed back through France to Austria to farewell the Von Meeren Estate and staff before flying out from Munich. We arrived home to a joyous welcome at the airport from Mum, Dad, Matthew, and Bella, and throughout the day everyone else came along to catch up and hear about our travels.

A week after my return home, I approached my previous employer, but there were no vet nursing jobs available. It was Olivia who mentioned the vacancy at the quarantine clinic, arranged an interview for me, and when offered the position, I accepted gratefully.

"All in the family." Olivia smiled her delight. "Stephanie works at the clinic too, these days."

I was surprised. "She's no longer at the opticians in town?"

"No, the new optometrist and Stephanie didn't get on."

"That's a shame. Stephanie usually gets on with everyone."

"Yes, she does," Olivia nodded. "But this woman is quite obnoxious I believe. Another of Stef's work mates there is also thinking seriously about resigning."

"Oh, dear!" I shook my head. "Some people make life difficult, don't they?"

"They do indeed," Olivia agreed. "Why, I have no idea but I'm not complaining. Stef is a real help to me in the office and she seems to be loving it."

"That's great, then." I laughed. "And I'm looking forward to joining you."

I began working there the following week, soon slotting into the role nicely. The business was no longer only a quarantine facility, but a fully equipped equine vet clinic open to the public and extremely busy. Clifford was the resident vet in charge and two others Jeff and Riley worked split shifts with three full-time nurses and several part-time and casual staff, one of which was Bella. My mum had been employed there too before we kids were born but after being diagnosed with a similar heart condition to her father's discontinued working.

Being able to walk the short distance from our farm to the clinic and back was an added privilege, the time I'd taken to travel home from my previous job was now spent with our own horses and Bella.

Chapter 16

Christmas and New Year celebrations were as usual loud, fun and all about family. We ate, drank and cooled off at Paradise during the long, lovely summer days, but there were moments when I felt a lingering sadness, as if something was missing. Figured it had something to do with Kenneth having changed our lives so profoundly.

Little did I know that something else was to change my life forever, so sudden and shocking I could hardly believe it.

I arrived home from work late afternoon as per usual, walked into the kitchen and froze. Mum was lying motionless on the floor.

Lurching forward with a strangled sound, I fell to my knees beside her, but knew immediately there was nothing I could do for her. She was as cold as ice to touch. I remember screaming hysterically for help, somehow grabbing the phone with shaking hands and calling Daniel and emergency services. We were told she'd suffered a fatal heart attack and had been dead for several hours before I found her.

It was the first time I really saw Dad cry, heart wrenching sobs that shook his body. My distraught brothers and I were hardly able to speak but thanks to Olivia and Bella we got through those next days, helping to organise the funeral and inform Mum's only living relative, an elderly aunt.

The day of the funeral was wind still, the chapel hushed and sombre. Both my brothers got up to stand beside Mum's coffin, sharing memories with us in voices that shook and broke. Bella too, spoke about her dear friend Zoe with laughter and tears, them working together at the clinic and how she'd been Mum and Dad's matchmaker. Lastly Dad thanked everyone for attending and once outside people came to offer their condolences.

It was only then that I realised who was there. Saw him speak to Dad first, my brothers and then his eyes were on me.

"I'm so sorry about your mum," Kenneth said, making no attempt to touch.

I couldn't say a word, simply nodded and took him in. He looked no different, dressed in black with his hair cut short but still threatening to curl.

Someone else moved in to speak, distracting my attention away from him and when I looked again, he was gone. At the graveside I wasn't aware of anyone, wishing so much that Mum was still with us as the coffin lowered.

Refreshments were provided in the chapel's lounge, the gentle hum of voices filling the room as I sat passively listening to Anna and Leon. Watched Dad talking to my brothers and Kenneth, but Olivia and Stephanie joined them and blocked my view. Perhaps twenty minutes later Kenneth appeared into my line of sight again speaking to Roman and Bella at the entrance doors but when Daniel joined our group, leaning on the back of my chair he distracted me and the next time I looked it was only Bella I saw, Kenneth and Roman had disappeared.

Felt a sudden need to find Kenneth, to at least talk to him properly and apologise for the past if I could. Excused myself from our group, weaving my way through the crowd towards Bella who smiled at my approach.

"Kate." She put a gentle hand on my arm. "How are you doing?"

"I'm okay," I smiled back. "I must thank you for what you said about Mum."

"I'm glad I could, she was such a good friend."

"And I'm really glad you gave Mum and Dad a push in the right direction."

"So am I." She laughed ruefully. "I never thought I'd be any good at that."

"Well, you were. They were very happy together."

"A beautiful couple," Bella agreed. "And great parents."

Nodding, I changed the subject. "You've lost Roman?"

"He's outside somewhere, talking."

"Is Kenneth with him?"

She peered at me. "Kenneth left about ten minutes ago."

"Oh." My heart sank. "He didn't stay long."

She eyed me more closely. "He would have liked to stay longer but he had some business to attend to before flying home."

I pretended a calmness I didn't feel. "Do you keep in touch with him?"

"Oh, yes, we talk to him most weeks," she told me, frowning a little. "Is there something you want to see him about?"

"No, no. Not really." I shook my head. "Some other time, maybe."

"Do you have his phone number?"

"I think so," I muttered, dropping my eyes. "But it's not important."

"Well, if he comes up our way at all, we'll let you know."

I nodded with a thin-lipped smile, "I'd better get back. See you later."

The numbness I felt right then had nothing to do with Mum's passing. I wanted to hide away somewhere but made myself walk across the room, smile at people along the way and sat back down with family. The day passed in a surreal haze until much later that night I made my way to bed, knew I'd grieve for Mum forever, but the tears that seeping into my pillow were for Kenneth. Eventually they dried but as sleep was out of the question, I got up to pull on trackpants, sweater and socks before heading to the back porch for my boots.

The horses pricked up their ears at my unexpected visit, nickering softly. There was something so therapeutic about running my hands over each one, their sighs making me smile and in those moments, I found a measure of peace. Sat down on the grass amongst them to stare heavenward at the night sky and get my head together.

Life changes, I told myself. Drastically sometimes, that's obvious. So, now it's time you adapted to the changes, girl. That includes life without Mum. And Kenneth.

I went back to the house in the early hours more resolute, better able to deal with whatever came along. Made a promise there and then to Mum that I would do my best to look after Dad and my brothers, or at least be there for them.

As we noticed Dad withdraw into himself during the next weeks, Matthew came back to live at the homestead, Daniel dropped in regularly for meals and with both their help he seemed to regain some of his vitality. He coped remarkably well in the end, we all did, returning to work and getting on with our routines. I tried my best to manage the household chores, Dad and I shared the cooking with the occasional delicious hotpot from Anna, but it soon became clear that the big house and garden needed attention.

Deciding to hire help, we found Patsy who also waitressed at the Wine Rack two days a week. She was a lively brunette in her mid-forties with three kids and a husband who worked in hardware retail, lived on our side of town and was more than happy to supplement her income as our housekeeper cum gardener. She fitted in like she'd been there all her life, taking the load off us nicely, once again giving me more time with our horses and Bella.

Dad and I also spent more weekends at the cabin after Mum died; our bolthole seemed a fitting place for both of us to unwind in, somewhere to talk or simply just sit quietly and think. To be honest, I'd been dubious about going there at first, wondered which bedroom Kenneth had used but decided against asking Dad about it and slept in Oma and Opa's bedroom without having nightmares or experiencing any bad vibes. There was no sign the caravan had been there, no bare patches of grass or tyre marks and nothing of his left behind. Sometimes with a pang I almost wished there was.

Hey! What's with that thought? I admonished myself. Move on remember. He's gone.

The horses felt the grief of Zoe's death, the friendly lady from the big house no longer appearing in the garden or at the homestead windows and Kate also talked to Delta about her Mum on their rides together.

"She worries," Delta told her paddock mates. "Especially about her dad."

"That's what people do," BB pointed out. "Worry about anything, not just their family."

"But she worries more now that her Mum's gone."

"Mums are special."

"So are dads," Kingston piped up.

BB eyeballed him. "You're so observant for a guy."

"What's that supposed to mean?" Kingston muttered, eyeballing her back.

"You surprise me every now and then," she smirked. "The things you say."

"Whatever." He rolled his eyes. "Anyway, Delta, what does Kate say?"

"She feels sad for her dad, thinks deep down he's unhappy."

"Well, of course he's unhappy. His mate's gone."

"See, what I mean," BB sniggered. "You just surprised me again."

Kingston was indignant. "Well, it's true. He's lost his mate."

"Okay, okay. Keep your hair on! I get it."

"Kate's sad too," Delta ignored them, sighing to herself. "She doesn't say much about her own feelings, but I know she's putting on a brave front."

"She's sad because of her mum but there's that other guy too," Kingston said.

"Other guy? Oh, you mean Roman and Bella's friend?"

"Yeah. The other farrier man who used to visit Kate a lot."

"But he disappeared ages ago, while she was away," BB frowned.

"He made her sad before then. That's the reason she took off, I reckon."

"I think you're right, Kingston," Delta nodded. "Something went wrong between those two, remember how uptight she was just before she went away."

"She's had a rough time lately, hasn't she?" BB murmured.

"We'll have to try and cheer her up," Delta said.

Kingston rounded his eyes excitedly at a thought. "How about we act up? Like buck, do wheelies and skid around the paddock when she comes tomorrow?"

"That's a cool idea!" BB nodded enthusiastically. "I can do bucking. Easy."

Delta laughed. "Sounds like fun."

"That's sorted then." Kingston bobbed his head. "I can't wait.

"We better go and practice."

Delta and BB grinned as Kingston wheeled on the spot, did an almighty buck and sent clods of grass flying as he took off around the paddock. His antics soon had the girls joining in, prancing on their hindlegs and kicking up their heels.

On reaching the gate the following day, I stopped dead to stare, hardly believing what was happening. One minute, the horses had their heads to the ground, supposedly grazing, and the next, they were cavorting around the paddock like they'd gone mad. At first, a giggle welled up, then I began to laugh until my stomach hurt.

"Oh, you lot!" I caught my breath. "You're priceless."

They slid to a halt in front of me, shook their manes and snorted. Eyes wide and ears pricked to attention, they looked positively pleased with themselves.

"You're magic all of you! Do you know that?" I giggled again.

"Well," Delta puffed. "That worked!"

"It sure did. She's laughing," Kingston wheezed.

"She should bring her dad next time," BB said. "We'll make him laugh too."

"I'll try telling her that." Delta nodded.

One day shortly thereafter, they saw Kate's dad watching from the house terrace and immediately went into fun mode, the sight of him staring gobsmacked and then bursting into a fit of laughter made their day.

He told me all about it later at dinner. "I've never seen them act quite like that before, as if they were putting on a show just for me."

"Funny," I chuckled. "They did that to me too, the other day."

"Maybe they're trying to cheer us up."

"They're good like that." I enthused, nodding. "Bella reckons they're super sensitive to our moods, probably know about them before we even do ourselves."

"That sixth sense that only animals have, eh?" Dad grinned. "Well, whatever it is those horses are up to, they can carry on. I haven't laughed like that for a while."

"I'll let them know," I grinned back.

Chapter 17

Not long after Mum's passing, I was in town running errands, rounded a shop corner in too much of a hurry, and walked slap bang into Douglas, standing on his foot hard.

He grunted something rude as we bounced off each other, squinted at me before showing his teeth in the trademark grin. "Why hello, witch."

"Arsehole!" I hissed.

His eyebrows lifted, grin widening as he gave me a slow up and down. I deliberately did the same to him, the eye up that was, not the grin. Had to admit he looked surprisingly presentable; the horrible tattoos were covered with a long-sleeved shirt and he actually had hair on his head, not the number one shave to the scalp like normal.

He laughed. "Very friendly as usual."

"What did you expect? You almost killed me!" I hissed. "And you wrecked my car."

He tipped his head. "That makes us even then, doesn't it?"

"What?" I scowled.

"You started it, busting my kneecap."

"I didn't mean that to happen," I told him. "Your leg was in the way."

"Yeah right!" He snorted a derisive laugh. "Not to mention, the cops came calling."

"What did you expect, you're on their books."

"So, you did report us?"

"You deserved it."

"Aw, come on! It was just a bit of er, fun. Stupid fun."

"Fun!" I spat. "Stupid, I agree, not fun!"

"Wanted to ruffle your feathers, that's all."

"Feathers?"

"Yeah, you know?" he smirked. "Scare you a little bit, get a reaction, like."

"Well, then you'll be pleased to know you succeeded and not just a little!" I snapped accusingly. "What exactly, were you going to do to me if

I hadn't got away?"

"Get my kiss."

"And the rest!"

The grin slipped as he wrinkled his forehead. "The rest?"

"Assault or rape!" I hissed. "Isn't that what you and your mates do?"

"Hey, give us a break!" he protested, scowling. "No, we don't!"

"You have a reputation for assaulting people!"

"Fisticuffs, fights with guys," he growled. "Pub brawl stuff, that's all."

"How civilised!"

He ignored that. "I like girls, I'd never hurt them!"

"But you scare the shit out of them, right?"

"And?" His lips twisted.

"Plus, you're rude, crude and disgusting!" I snapped sarcastically. "Or you were to me, or don't you remember?"

"When?"

"At the stop lights!"

"Aw, that. Sorry, didn't mean to offend." He didn't look at all sorry, shrugged. "Still, it worked!"

I blinked. "What?"

"Got you all fired up for a car chase, didn't it?" His grin was back in full force. "Must say you're a bloody good driver for a girl."

I curled my lip. "Why pick on me?"

He tipped his head again. "Don't you know?"

"Know what?"

"There's something about you." He said it softly.

"What? Not you as well?" I stared with disbelief.

"Me as well?" He cocked an eyebrow. "Ah, so your boyfriend thinks the same?"

"Boyfriend?"

"The Sandford guy, he's your fella, isn't he?"

"No, he is not!"

"So, it's true. You've split?"

"We weren't ever together!" I snapped. "It's none of your business anyhow."

He shrugged, then frowned. "Sorry about your mother by the way."

That surprised me. "You know about my mum?"

"Everyone knows, Von Meerens are always news."

I screwed up my nose. "But, of course."

"Are you in a hurry?" He changed tack. "How about a coffee?"

"What?" I snorted derisively. "Me have a coffee with you. Are you kidding?"

"Why?" His eyes went cold. "Not good enough for you, am I?"

I gaped. "What's that supposed to mean?"

"Madame up herself, Von Meeren wouldn't be seen dead with us working class."

That grated. "Excuse me!" I stepped towards him threateningly. "How dare you! I am not up myself and just so you know the Von Meerens are working class. My dad and Matthew are mechanics, Daniel works on our farm and I'm a vet nurse!" I took a breath, adding with a snap. "We are no different to anyone else and don't call me madame!"

"Bloody Nora!" His eyes stretched wide, no longer cold. "You are something else."

"What's that supposed to mean?" I eyed him balefully.

He laughed softly. "Even more gorgeous when you're fired up."

I was taken aback, stared.

He pursed his lips. "Your boyfriend's a lucky dude."

"I do not have a boyfriend!" I told him sharply.

"Is that why you went overseas, because you split?"

"There was no split!" I narrowed my eyes. "How do you know I went overseas?"

He spread his hands without replying, his grin rueful.

"Oh, right! We're news, everyone knows." I curled my lip.

"So, working class lady, how about a coffee?"

Gave him a mocking look. "My brothers would kill you if they saw us together."

"I'll risk it," he countered with a chuckle.

"Why?" I frowned suspiciously.

He shrugged. "Maybe we could be friends at last."

"Friends?" My eyebrows shot up. "Me and you?"

"Yeah, why not?" he beamed. "Come on, let's get that coffee."

Went along with some misgivings to a nearby café, where he ordered and paid for two flat whites and following him to a corner table, I also got myself more than an eyeful of swagger and his backside in jeans.

Wow wee! I thought. So, the rumours are true about girls clamouring for a piece of him. No wonder with that rear view!

We sat down at the table too soon for my liking, instantly forgetting about his butt as we faced each other. Cast a quick nervous eye around at other customers but saw no one I recognised, turned back and found him watching me with a sardonic little smile.

"You're quite safe, you know?"

I narrowed my eyes. "I could always kick you in the kneecap again, I suppose."

"Nasty." He pulled a pained face. "Sorry about your car. Is it okay now?"

"Yes, it's been fixed," I answered waspishly.

"And you?" His brow creased. "All good I hope?"

"You hope?" I curled my lip. "Pull the other one."

He sighed. "Like I said, I don't hurt girls."

"Whatever." I glared. "I wasn't hurt, just petrified. It wasn't nice."

His lips twisted. "Sorry."

"You don't look sorry." I peered at him for a moment, thinking. "Why do you pick on me and my brothers? You always did at school?"

He shrugged offhandedly. "Good targets, I guess."

"Good targets?"

"You lot are different."

"Different?"

"Yeah, rich and famous."

"No, we're not!"

"Yes, you are. Rich and famous, like your grandfather."

"That wasn't his fault, being famous." I was indignant. "The press hounded him."

"The Playboy, huh? I remember my grandmother and mother going gaga over him."

"Gaga?" I snorted, adding snidely. "They had good taste then, didn't they?"

He ignored that. "And your grandmother, the Witch. Guys drooled over her, too."

"How do you know that?"

"Like I said your family were, are always news."

I didn't bother replying, gave him a long unsmiling look which made his eyes twinkle. I was beginning to see quite clearly why he had a reputation, the blonde bad boy with girls supposedly panting after him had turned into quite the hunk.

He tipped his head. "What are you thinking?"

"A chick magnet these days, aren't you?"

"Eh?" His eyebrows went up.

"Hmmm." I pursed my lips. "Better looking than when you were at school."

"You think?" He narrowed his eyes suspiciously.

I nodded, screwed up my nose. "Except for what's under your sleeves."

He looked down at his arms. "You don't like tattoos?"

"I don't mind them, my grandfather had some," I said. "But skulls all over. Ugh!"

"I'll keep them covered just for you." He grinned.

"Are you telling me other girls like them?" I frowned in disbelief.

He laughed softly. "Some think they're works of art."

"Art?" I wrinkled my nose. "Weird!"

"Turns some on too."

"Oh, gross!" I waved my hands in disgust. "Way too much information."

Rather liked the sound of his chuckle as it came again, low and sexy. Gave him a long-measured look and wondered. Friends? Now there's a thought. Maybe he's right, we could give it a try.

"You're thinking again?" He slanted an eyebrow.

I smiled as our coffees arrived, stirred mine and asked. "You're not working today?"

"Working nights." He put three heaped teaspoons of sugar in his.

My eyebrows shot up. "Sugar with your coffee or coffee with your sugar?"

"I like it sweet." He shot me an amused glance.

"Obviously." Couldn't resist adding. "Don't think it'll help much."

"You don't think I'm sweet enough?"

"Enough?" I snorted a derisive laugh. "You'll never be. Full stop!"

"Want to give it a go?"

"Give what a go?"

"Sweetening me up?"

I wrinkled my nose at him. "Waste of time."

"Why?" He smirked. "Cast a spell, witch and I'll be eating sugar out of your hand."

"How many times?" I hissed. "I am not a witch. I don't cast spells and I doubt you'd eat out of anyone's hand."

"I'd eat out of yours." He leant closer. "Not just sugar either."

I scowled in exasperation. "Oh, shut up and drink your coffee."

He obligingly leant back and drank, his eyes laughing at me over the cup's rim. "So, how about you? Is there anything you like sweet?"

I shook my head eying him coolly.

"What about men?"

"That's none of your business!" I was sharply indignant. "Are you always this forward?"

"Depends," he said softly. "But this chance was too good to miss."

"Meaning?"

"You're actually here." He gestured a hand at me.

Frowning, I opted to say nothing.

"Didn't you know?" he asked.

"Know what?"

"That I had the hots." His mouth twisted. "I mean, I've liked you for a long time."

My eyes widened in disbelief. "You have a very funny way of showing it."

"Yeah, well. I'm not much good at showing my feelings." His grimace was wry. "Unable to express himself, the teachers used to say, or some shit like that."

I raised my eyebrows. "But you're good at showing your fists instead."

"I guess." His eyes held mine, his mouth curving.

"Well, I've heard the teacher got it wrong, that you are able to express yourself." I curved my own mouth in a smirk. "With the girls that is." Oh no! Did I really say that?

"You heard?" His lips tightened.

I ignored him. "And that you're good with your hands." Shut up now, please!

He didn't speak, simply staring with the ice blue eyes showing a touch of heat.

"Just gossip, you know," I quickly explained. "Girls talk at work."

"About my hands?"

"And the rest." My mouth wasn't listening.

"The rest?"

"Er, body too." What on earth was I saying?

"Who told you that?" His stare remained fixed.

I shrugged. "Oh, I don't remember, it was ages ago," Decided it was high time to change the subject. "Those guys in the Holden, friends of yours?"

"Yeah, sawmill mates." His eyes narrowed. "Are you bullshitting me?"

I ignored his question. "The driver, was that Poke?"

"How do you know Poke?" A touch of surprise in the intense blue stare.

"My brother Daniel knows of him. Was it him driving?"

"Yeah." He put his elbows on the table, leant forward. "You really talked about me?"

"You should tell your friends to behave." I looked down my nose at him.

He leant closer. "What did you say?"

"I said, tell your friends…" I broke off at his abrupt hand gesture.

"What did you say about me?"

"Nothing, I was only listening," I said innocently. "Look, some girls like blabbing their personal stuff to their friends. The friend, she used to work with me."

"What's her name?"

"Wendy." I told him reluctantly.

"Ah." His lips twisted. "Martina's buddy."

"You know her?" I was surprised.

"We've met." He grinned. "Martina's hooked up with your brother, right now, eh?"

"And you were hooked up with Martina too once, eh?" I threw back at him.

"Nope." The smile turned smug. "We only slept together, er, twice."

I blinked, pouting disdain. "How nice for you!"

"Must have made an impression, if she remembers that much about me." His chuckled at my disgusted look. "Don't worry. I don't do that often."

"Do what?"

"Two night-stands."

Gave him another disgusted look. "I'm so very glad to know that."

"With you," he said, for my ears only. "It would be more than two nights."

I blinked again rapidly, scowled. "In your dreams. Don't even think about it!"

He leant back in his chair, still grinning. "You started it. Getting me all excited."

"Typical male behaviour!" I scoffed. "Doesn't take much to get you lot excited."

He laughed through his nose. "You must give your brother's grief."

"That's what sisters are for."

Without answering he looked down at the table top abruptly, all laughter gone.

I knit my brows at his reaction. "Do you have any sisters or brothers?"

"I had a sister, two years older." He heaved a breath. "She drowned when I was nine."

"Oh!" That jolted me. "I'm sorry. I didn't know that."

He shrugged, eyes still on the table. "Shit happens."

I didn't really know what to say. "You must miss her."

"Yeah, I did. Still do," he muttered. "My family went off the rails after it happened."

"I can imagine. That must have been terrible."

He lapsed into silence, his thoughts elsewhere. Watching him I felt a strange empathy, beginning to understand a little more about what made him tick.

"Um, well, I better go," I said softly, getting to my feet. "Thanks for the coffee."

He came back to the present instantly, pushed back his chair and stood to his feet. "You're welcome. How about we do this again sometime?"

I gave him a studied look., "Maybe we will, if you behave."

"I can behave." He crooked a grin. "Are you going to tell your brothers about us?"

"Hmmm, I think I just might," I smirked. "I suggest you lay low for a few weeks."

"Why?"

"Ah, I almost forgot!" I rolled my eyes. "Fisticuffs and brawls, they're your thing, right?"

"Well, yeah." He chuckled. "They, er, kind of clear the air."

Shook my head in exasperation as we walked from the café together, unprepared for the reaction outside. Two women on the pavement nearby did a double take, eyebrows shooting to their hairlines, another female stared out from a shop window with her jaw hanging open, and suddenly it seemed heads were turning our way from every direction, making me feel instantly uncomfortable, his snort of amusement not helping.

"See," he murmured in my ear. "Von Meerens are always news."

"Ha!" I gave him a baleful glance. "Methinks, so are you."

"Wonder how long before everyone knows?"

"Bugger!"

"We could start a rumour."

"Excuse me?"

"Witchy woman has a new boyfriend."

"That is not my name," I snapped. "And what is it with you and boyfriends?"

He chuckled. "Want me to walk you back to your car, sweetie?"

"No, thanks!" I glowered. "Sweetie? I think I prefer witch."

His laughter followed me as I stalked away.

I must be mad! Fraternising with the enemy. My brothers will be horrified. A giggle erupted. Wait until I tell them! The look on their faces will be priceless.

Chapter 18

Didn't need to tell them; they found out soon enough via the inevitable local gossip, and horrified was too tame a word for their reaction. If I thought I was mad, they thought I'd lost my marbles completely, and even Dad voiced his concern.

We were sitting at the dining table at home, having a family meeting of sorts to iron out the angst. Matthew's appalled eyes kept throwing daggers in my direction, Daniel simply looked totally bewildered while Dad kept trying his best to make sense of it all.

"Oh, get over it!" I shook my head in exasperation. "I talked to the guy, that's all."

"He wants more than talk." Matthew scowled. "What if he comes to the farm?"

"Why would he?" I protested. "We met in town. It's hardly likely to happen again?"

"Yeah right! That dickhead never gives up."

"He's not a dickhead!"

"Bugger me! I don't believe it!" Matthew looked stunned. "You like him now!"

"Okay, you two. Calm down," Dad interrupted. "Kate, please explain. He almost ran you off the road and wrecked your car. Why the turnaround?"

"I'm as surprised as you," I sighed. "We just got talking and well, he's not so bad."

"Not so bad?" Matthew bellowed. "The guy's a first-class arsehole!"

Dad's deadly look shut him up but didn't stop him glaring at me.

"He told me his sister drowned," I explained to Dad. "It really affected him."

"A sob-story, you mean?" Daniel finally found his voice.

"I don't believe it's a sob story!" I frowned. "Did none of you know about it?"

Dad creased his forehead. "How long ago was this?"

"It was years ago," Matthew commented grudgingly.

"It is true, then?" I narrowed my eyes on him. "So, what happened?"

"His sister got caught in a rip at a beach near here, they found her washed up further down the coast days later," he told me.

"That was Willard's sister?" Daniel widened his eyes in surprise. "Didn't her...their mother have a mental break down and leave town not long after?"

"That's the one and years after the father drank himself to death," Matthew nodded, adding for good measure. "Choked on his own vomit."

Dad frowned at him before saying. "Now you mention the drowning I do remember it. Some teenage lads nearly got caught in the rip as well trying to save her."

None of us spoke, each with our own thoughts. Tears overwhelmed me without warning, the talk of death bringing back the recent rawness and finality of Mum and I had to leave the room to compose myself, Matthew surprising me by knocking on the bathroom door moments later.

"Are you okay in there, sis?" he murmured.

Sniffing, I wiped my face and opened up to eye him silently.

He looked worried and sad. "Sorry. I didn't mean to get so worked up and upset you."

"I'm okay." I sighed. "Just thinking about Mum."

"Yeah," he nodded. "Me too."

"Look." I heaved a sigh. "This stuff with Douglas, it's nothing, really."

His lips twisted. "It's just weird, him of all people."

"We just talked." I shrugged. "I think maybe he's changed too."

"He must have, if he's being nice to you." Matthew raised his eyebrows.

"Like you say, weird," I grimaced ruefully.

Dad and Daniel looked suitably relieved at our amicable return to the kitchen table.

"So, where were we, my girl?" Dad reached for my hand with a gentle smile.

"Don't worry about me, Dad," I squeezed his fingers. "We should be talking about you and your holiday."

He'd made the surprise announcement recently that he planned to travel to Austria for a break, us kids more than pleased at the idea. Daniel and I were also trying to persuade Matthew to go with him, felt he should experience a visit to Opa's homeland like we had but he hadn't so far been that easy to convince.

I looked at Matthew. "You really should think seriously about going with Dad, Matt. It's about time you had a holiday overseas, you'll love it."

Matthew chewed his lip resignedly. "Okay, okay! I get it."

"No pressure from your sister, son," Dad chuckled.

"Will you be okay in the house on your own?" Matthew eyed me.

I arched an indignant eyebrow. "I'm old enough to look after myself, thank you."

"K's right, bro," Daniel agreed. "Besides, I can stay in the house with sis anytime she wants me to and don't forget we're not the only ones on the farm."

"Very true." Dad nodded, eyes on me. "As long as you're happy with that."

"I'm happy, Dad." Smiling, I patted his hand. "We'll manage just fine."

"There's Trojan too, remember," Daniel pointed out. "He won't let anyone near, sis."

"And you know where the gun's kept if you need it, eh?" Matthew peered at me.

"Oh, you!" I threw him a mock punch. "I doubt I'll be needing it."

"Don't be too trusting of Willard, sis."

"Douglas won't come here, brother dear." I shook my head at him.

"I'm just saying. Be careful."

"Why? Because he's got a reputation with the girls?" I asked innocently.

"Reputation?" Dad cocked an eyebrow.

"I've heard things," I smirked at Matthew. "Martina's one of them."

"Martina and I are over." Matthew said abruptly, lips tight. "Just so you know."

That floored me. "Oh! I'm sorry. When did that happen?"

"A few weeks ago." Daniel wasn't so sympathetic, his grin gloating. "My poor big brother cried on my shoulder."

"I did not!" Matthew snarled, giving him the evil eye.

"That's a shame, son." Dad was sympathetic. "But it could be a good thing. There's nothing to stop you coming with me now, is there?"

Matthew let out a long breath. "No, you're right, Dad, there isn't."

"Good." Dad stood up. "I'm glad we've sorted ourselves out then."

Later I got Matthew to myself. "I'm sorry about Martina. Why did you break up?"

"I caught her with someone else?"

"What?" Did he mean Douglas? I suddenly understood his antagonism. He read my mind. "Not Douglas. A mechanic in another workshop."

"Really? You actually caught her?"

"Yeah." His lips twisted. "They were at it in the toilet."

"Oh, gross! What did you do?"

"What do you think?" He grimaced. "I walked out and confronted her later."

"Oh, well. Who needs a girl like that? You're better off without her, Matt."

"So, they say." He sighed dejectedly. "He wasn't the only one I've heard."

"I'm sorry." I hugged him. "It'll be okay. You never know, there could be a lovely girl waiting for you overseas. A beautiful Austrian fraulein."

"Give me a break," he muttered, his return hug threatening to break my ribs.

"Here's a better idea." I squirmed, puffing out air as he loosened his hold. "Lay off girls all together, for a while at least."

"Promise me." He held me away at arm's length. "Don't get involved with Douglas."

"I'm not getting involved with anyone." I screwed up my nose at him.

"You should have held onto Kenneth."

That surprised me from him. "There was nothing between us!" I protested. "Nothing to hold on to."

"Aw, but you were made for each other." His mouth curved teasingly.

"You've been listening to Anna, haven't you?" I accused.

He smiled wider. "You're meant to be, Sandford boy and Lawson girl."

"Stop it!" I punched him. "That's history and over, besides I'm a Von Meeren."

"With Lawson blood in your veins."

"Whatever." I rolled my eyes, wagging a finger in his face. "I like my life the way it is, okay? I'm not getting involved with Kenneth, Douglas or anyone else."

"Okay. Single it is then." His finger wagged in mine. "For both of us."

"Ha! You'll be the first to unsingle yourself," I scoffed. "Some cute bird will bat her eyelashes and you'll go weak at the knees."

"Do you wanna bet?" he laughed, holding out his hand. "Whoever hitches up first gets dunked at Paradise in the winter."

We shook hands. "You're on," I told him. "Prepare to freeze your nuts off, brother."

Dad and Matthew departed for Austria about five weeks later with plans to stay away for at least three months, Dad phoning two or three times a week to let me know what they were up to, the enthusiasm in his voice pleasing.

Daniel stayed over at the homestead with me to begin with but didn't sleep well, eventually returning to his own bed in the cottage at my reassurances that with Trojan on my bedroom floor every night, my mobile within easy reach and the house securely locked I felt more than safe. Didn't, however, mention to him that I'd met Douglas again while out grocery shopping one time.

I let out a yelp of fright when he tapped me on the shoulder in the supermarket, whirling to scowl as him fell about laughing at my reaction. "I'm so glad you find that funny!"

"Your nerves are shot." He dragged in air. "Who were you expecting?"

"Nobody! That's why I jumped."

Feeling conspicuous and uncomfortable as other customers sent curious looks our way, I quickly pushed my trolley into a quieter aisle while frowning indignantly as Douglas began inspecting my purchases.

"No chocolate biscuits?" he said.

"Why would I need chocolate biscuits?" I snapped.

"Aw!" He dropped his lower lip. "Chocolate ones are better with coffee."

"Get your own. Where's your trolley?"

"Wasn't shopping," he grinned. "I followed you in."

"People are watching us!" I glowered. "Doesn't that bother you?"

"Nah." He shrugged. "Who gives a shit what people think?"

"I do!"

"Let's get out of here then. How about I buy the chocolate biscuits and we have a coffee at my place."

I blinked. "No!"

"Aw!" He dropped his lower lip again. "How about Peanut Brownies instead, then?"

"What part of no don't you understand?"

"Your boyfriend really broke your heart, didn't he?"

"For the last time, I do not have a boyfriend!"

"I can fix broken hearts."

"Oh, spare me!" Rolling my eyes, I bit out. "Go away!"

"You're home alone right now, aren't you?"

I frowned. "Why ask if you already know?"

"We could go to your place instead."

"Daniel would shoot you!"

His mouth curved slowly. "They know, eh?"

"They?" I frowned. "Know what?"

"Your brothers know we had coffee together."

"Oh, that!" I gave my head an exasperated shake. "Yes, they know. And?"

"They haven't shot me yet."

"They will!" I curled my lip. "One day."

"Looking forward to it." He chuckled. "I'll get my kiss too, one day."

"In your dreams," I scoffed.

"I have those all the time." His look turned sly. "Dreams about a witch."

"Get lost." I turned my back on him.

Thankfully he got the message and left me to my shopping. Half expected him to be waiting outside but rather to my relief he was nowhere in sight, didn't stop me muttering annoyance at his antics all the way home.

Wendy phoned me during the week about a party on Saturday night. "Martina asked me to come. As it's at the racetrack, I wondered if you'd be interested."

I wasn't enthused. "I'm no party girl. Maybe you should ask someone else."

"There's nobody else." She sounded dejected. "I'm chronically single, you know me,"

"Whose party?" I asked feeling sorry for her. "Daniel hasn't mentioned it."

"Some racing team is hosting it and Martina's arranged taxis," she said. "I'd be glad of your company. You're welcome to come to my place first, we could go from there."

"All right, I'll come," I agreed against my better judgement. "But I'll make my own way there, I won't be staying late. What time does it start?"

"Oh, thanks so much, Kate." She sounded considerably more cheerfully. "It starts at seven."

I spoke to Daniel about it after work on Friday. "Did you know there's a party at the racetrack? Some team celebrations."

He nodded. "I would have gone, but I've got something else on."

"Well, I've been roped into it, keeping Wendy company."

"Why don't you stay over at the apartment, Dad's key is in the study somewhere."

"Hey, that's a good idea. I might just do that."

"Don't get plastered, sis." He grinned at my eye roll. "And if you need anything, just call me."

"Yes, brother darling." I pulled a wry face. "You know me, sober and boring."

I parked my car at the apartment before seven, let myself in, and dropped off my overnight bag in the spare room. Hearing music, I looked down from the balcony windows to a stage set up with a band already playing, surprised at the amount of people already milling about down at the track. Found Wendy at the track's security-monitored entrance, where we'd arranged to meet, she gave me a spontaneous hug, handed over tickets and made a beeline with me in tow for one of the marquees with Martina and her bevy of friends inside.

I could understand Matthew's fascination with Martina, she quite simply made men ogle. Loud with a throaty laugh that oozed sexy, an attractive brunette with pouting red lips and heavily made-up dark eyes. Her tight black top showed more of her eye-popping cleavage than it covered, there was no sign of knickers under the painted on white pants and her super high heels made her legs appear way longer than they were.

Her overly friendly attitude towards me was puzzling, to say the least, but also grated because of the way she'd treated my brother, but I took the red wine she handed me, sipping conservatively while pretending interest in the conversation. I found the marquee crowded and stifling, needed fresh air and wandered outside eventually to listen to the band until Wendy appeared to call me back inside for something to eat. While sampling a plate of finger food, Martina came again with more drinks, one of which I took at her insistence, thinking with a shrug that I didn't have far to walk to the apartment later.

At some point, I felt a little squeamish and headed for the toilets, wondering if the food hadn't agreed with me. With my head beginning to thump on leaving the building, I decided to locate Wendy, say my goodbyes and depart to bed. Took a shortcut behind one of the workshops and stopped dead at the sight of a couple snogging against a wall just metres away. Would recognise Martina's white pants anywhere but it was the long-haired male she was with who made me recoil—the driver of the Holden station wagon, Poke.

Whose she doing next? I thought in disgust. Matthew, you're well rid of her!

Turning away quickly, I felt a sudden wave of nausea and stumbled. Made an on-the-spot decision to forego informing Wendy and headed for the apartment block. Walked past another workshop and, at the last one, stopped to lean against the wall, waiting for my head to clear. The distant music seemed to be ebbing, peered at the ground and felt weird. Hoped I wasn't going to puke.

Felt rather than saw someone—a shadow nearby that morphed into two, maybe three. Suddenly they were right there in my space, far too close. Gasping, I put my hands up to ward them off but couldn't stop them grabbing hold. Heard the metallic sound of a workshop's utility door opening, felt myself being half dragged and half pushed inside.

"I thought she was supposed to be sedated!" A male voice protested.

Another male voice, abrupt and harsh. "Just get her in there. Hurry up!"

As they yanked something over my head, I yelped at the sudden darkness. Writhed and twisted in vain as they wrapped me in a blanket or similar, my arms tight against my sides. Someone lifted me off my feet, bundled me into what felt like the boot of a vehicle and again I tried to scream but the cloth clung to my face and muffled any sound.

Yipped as the lid slammed shut. Heard a roller door open, felt the vibration of an engine firing up. Knew I was indeed in a vehicle as it reversed, changed gear and took off at speed. Whoever was driving didn't let up, my body sliding and bouncing at every corner and bump. It seemed to go on forever. With my head now thudding madly, I thought was going to vomit, gritting my teeth against the nausea.

The vehicle finally slowed, stopped and it's engine switched off. I moaned with relief but that was short lived. Went rigid as the boot opened, tried again to scream and began writhing frantically as they pulled me out.

"Quit it!" The harsh male voice growled, "Or I'll deck you!"

That stopped me instantly. I went slack, almost falling to my knees.

Someone grabbed me by the waist and thighs, hoisting me over a shoulder in a fireman's life. Hanging upside down didn't do me much good. Whimpered as my head began to thump more painfully, tasted bile in my throat. Even in my woozy vague state I knew someone was taking me up metallic stairs, their footsteps clanging. Heard heavy breathing and low voices, then a door opening.

I was dropped unceremoniously on something that gave under my weight. Someone walked over a wooden floor and the door slammed shut, loud and final. Footsteps clanged back downstairs, voices faded away, and another door slammed in the distance. A car started up and drove off. Shaking like a leaf with reaction, I listened to silence descend before finally moving. Twisted and rolled to slowly extract myself from the blanket I was wrapped in, reaching up to remove the head covering and gulped welcome air.

It took a minute for my eyes to adjust to a space not quite dark. There was no ceiling above me, only rafters and a corrugated roof with two clear-lite panels but no windows in the walls.

A shed, I thought, remembering the stairs. A room above a workshop, maybe.

I lay for what seemed an age in the same position, trying to clear my fuzzy head and waited for the nausea to dissipate. Suddenly realised I was lying on a bed. Sat up too quickly and groaned, grabbing my protesting head. Finally swung my legs gingerly over the side, reached for the switch of a lamp on the cabinet beside the bed, instantly screwing my eyes shut at the sudden blinding light, blinking several times before squinting at the room.

It was large, with panelled wood walls, a chest of drawers, a desk and chair, and a free-standing wardrobe. The sight of the door had me on my feet, lurching across to grasp the handle. It moved, but no amount of wrenching, pushing, and desperate muttering was going to open it; the door was firmly locked. Sagged back against it, puffing out my cheeks while staring long and hard at the bed.

Thoughts tumbled through my head, made it hurt. What is this place? Why am I here?

Straightening off the door, I made my slow way around the room. Tried the handle of the wardrobe door, a hinge squeaking as it opened making me freeze. Heard no other sound as I stared at the clothes hanging inside—men's clothes. Tiptoed to the chest of drawers for a look, pulling a face at the male underwear inside, boxer shorts of all colours. Frowning, my eyes swivelled around the room. I was in a man's bedroom. Heart did a flip, breath hissing through my teeth. Swallowing down panic, I made myself sit back down on the bed to try and rack my befuddled brain.

This had to do with Poke, I was certain. Was Martina involved too? Had the quickie been staged while they waited for me? It was the Poke face I'd seen before being blindfolded and one other face had been vaguely familiar too, perhaps the Holden's rear seat passenger.

But why? What was this all about, why bring me here? Whose place was this? Something snapped in my brain, the breath leaving my lungs in a whoosh. Disbelief and shock hit me like a wave. Then anger, sharp and livid.

"Oh, no! No and no!" I yelped out loud. "I should have known!"

Douglas! I bet this is his place at the junkyard. Didn't he live in one of the sheds? He's got to be part of this, his mates doing his dirty work. A shiver of fear overlaid the anger. Was this his plan all along? Pretending to be friendly, with a suck-up to me coffee. Of course, I'd refused his second invite, hadn't I? This time he was past being nice and doubted he was just after a kiss. I don't hurt girls, he'd said. Yeah right! Oh shit! Someone, help me, please!

With that racing through my brain, I began to scout around for a weapon but couldn't find anything substantial at first—no wheel brace, that was certain. No sign of a gun either. Spotting the small three-legged metal stool beside the desk, I decided it would have to do. Turned off the light and sat cross legged on the bed with stool within easy reach. Didn't dare lie down in case I fell asleep.

It felt like hours before a vehicle arrived.

My heart began to race as the engine shut off, was on my feet with the stool dangling from my hand and padded to my planned spot beside the locked door. Heard footsteps on gravel, a downstairs door being unlocked. It shut with a bang. Scuffling sounds like boots being removed, and then nothing until the flush of a toilet, stifled a yelp at the sound of a man clearing his throat. Listening with bated breath, I heard the first step onto the metal stairs and clenched my fingers on the stool leg. No loud clanging this time, but softer treads of bare feet or socks and my arm tensed for action as the person halted directly outside.

The door handle moved twice and stopped abruptly. Heard him mutter something distinctly rude, as if he hadn't expected it to be locked. My breath hitched at the voice—definitely Douglas's. He jingled keys, inserted one in the lock, and the handle turned again.

The door swung open, and as he strode in, I didn't aim but simply took a swing up from under as if my life depended on it. The stool connected, nowhere near his kneecap this time. He didn't howl either. The sound was more like a strangled grunt as he staggered sideways against the door jamb.

Dropping the stool, I leapt for the opening but blinded by the glaring lights on the landing I hesitated, screwing my eyes shut for one second.

Douglas Willard was not only built tough, but I'd given him enough time for his lightning reflexes to kick in, and he shot out an arm, lunging for me. Recoiling desperately away from him, I lost my balance, went down on my side with a loud yelp before sliding up against the balustrade. Frantically clawed at it, hauling myself to my knees.

Too late. He was on me. Grappled my arms from behind, no amount of manic twisting on my part making any difference. He was too strong, wrestled me to the ground and held me down with his knee in my back. I screamed as loud as I could.

"Shut up!" he snarled.

I stopped screaming simply because I ran out of breath, resorting to whining and hissing instead. "Get off me! Let go, you overgrown numbskull arsehole!"

"Calm down!" he snarled again. "And I'll let you go."

That was enough to knock the fight out of me. Didn't even make a sound as he got to his feet and pulled me up too, swinging me around to face him before letting go. I stepped back hurriedly at his menacing expression but could only gasp for breath and stare.

"What the hell are you doing here?" he asked through his teeth.

"Doing here?" I managed a strangled squawk.

He took no notice of my indignation, brows drawing together in a scowl. "Why are you even in my place? How did you get in?"

"Oh, really!" I scowled back. "You're going to bluff your way out of this now?"

He blinked bafflement. "Out of what?"

"This is all your fault! Your friends brought me here!"

"What are you talking about?"

"Your friends kidnapped me!"

His scowl was disbelieving. "Kidnapped you?"

"I was at the party, they put me in a van or something," My voice wobbled, body beginning to shake again with a vengeance. "I think my drink was drugged."

"The party?" Screwing up his face as if in pain, he raised a hand to run fingers gingerly along his jawline.

"The party at the racetrack. Poke was there." I glared. "Did you plan this?"

"Plan what?" His hand moved up to rub his forehead. "I wasn't at the party."

"But you knew about it, didn't you?"

He screwed his eyes shut. "I heard about it, yes."

"And you got your mates to do this, didn't you?" I accused. "Your dirty work!"

He squinted balefully. "You've lost me."

"Why would they bring me here, to your place?" My voice was rising.

"How would I know?" he growled. "I don't know what Poke or anyone else has been up too, at the party or otherwise."

"You know nothing?" I stabbed a finger at the open door behind him, said with the utmost sarcasm. "That's your bedroom, isn't it?"

"Yeah! And you were in it." He was just as sarcastic.

"I was locked in it!"

"Well, I sure as shit didn't lock you in it!"

"Your mates did!" I hissed. "Why do they have keys to your bedroom?"

"Poke has keys, he stays here sometimes."

"There's only one bed." I curled my lip. "Do you share it with him?"

"Shit, no!" He frowned at me belligerently. "He uses the one downstairs."

"So why does he have keys to your room?"

He shrugged, still frowning. "All the rooms up here were used for storage once. He's got keys to the whole place."

"Convenient!" I bit out.

"Look, I don't need this shit!" His deep sigh was weary. "I just want to sleep."

Watched him suspiciously in silence. His hand touched the side of his face again gingerly and at that point I saw then where the stool had hit him, my eyes popping wide. A painful looking red swelling had appeared along his jaw.

The vet nurse in me kicked in. Stepped forward to take a better look, peering at his face. "You better get that seen to."

He snapped his head back and away. "Don't even think about it!"

I put out a hand involuntarily. "I'm sorry I hit you."

"Stay right there!" His venomous look stopped me in my tracks.

"You can't really blame me for reacting," I protested.

"You call that reacting?" He showed his teeth in a snarl. "You do damage every time I come near you."

I thought better of retorting and heaved a sigh. "You need that looked at; your jaw could be broken."

"What the fuck did you hit me with?"

"The stool."

He blew out his cheeks at that which immediately prompted a painful grunt.

"Douglas!" I said with sharp concern, reaching a hand again and stepping closer. "Please, I'll drive you to A&E."

"Douglas now?" Distinct sarcasm. "Not what was it? Overgrown numbskull arsehole?"

I ignored that. "We'll have to take your car."

"Forget it!" He held up a dismissive hand. "I'm okay."

"No, you're not!" I had a sudden thought, grimacing dismay. "Oh, bugger. I don't have my license, it's in my bag at the apartment."

"Apartment?"

"At the racetrack."

He almost managed a smirk. "The Playboy's den, you mean?"

"What?" I knit my brows sharply.

"That's what the locals call it."

"What next?" I muttered. Had another despairing thought, fished in my jeans pocket but blew out a relieved breath when my fingers closed over the apartment gate pass and door key. I eyed him again. "Who cares about my license. I'll drive without it."

"Don't bother." He gestured vaguely. "It's not that bad, I'll be fine by tomorrow."

"No way! You're going to a doctor, now." I was adamant.

He was about to protest but the look on my face stopped him. "Okay, but I'll drive."

"I don't think you should. You're injured."

"I don't drive with my teeth." He attempted a grin, wincing sharply and swearing under his breath instead.

"That's enough of that," I told him. "Let's get going."

His vehicle was an older model Nissan ute, which took a little getting used to, but we made it to the twenty-four-hour A&E clinic without mishap. To my relief X-rays showed no fractures, with only one loose molar needing attention and when the doctor asked how the injury had happened, Douglas merely said with a slight lift of an eyebrow in my direction that he'd had an altercation with equipment in his workshop. Didn't think the doctor believed him, judging by the narrowed eyed look he gave us both.

Two hours later, Douglas left the hospital with painkillers, instructions to rest and eat soft food. The bruising and swelling looked nasty, but he appeared remarkably unperturbed about it all, shrugged off my offer to drive, and dropped me off at the apartment in the early hours.

He got out as I did, looking up the stairs with a frown. "You'll be okay on your own?"

"It's as safe as houses," I told him. "Will you be okay driving home?"

"Ah, stop fussing. I've had worse than this."

"Yes, of course. Pub brawls."

Attempting a grin, he flinched. "Look whatever you may think, I had nothing to do with this kidnapping stuff."

I pursed my lips. "I believe you." Strangely enough I did, wholeheartedly.

"I'll talk to Poke and the others. Find out what they were up to."

"Did you know about him and Martina?" I asked. "I saw them together."

He shrugged. "No surprise there."

"Goes through the men, doesn't she?" I pulled a disgusted face. "And she was cheating on my brother."

"Sounds like Martina." He didn't sound surprised.

I looked at him more closely, saw the pain and exhaustion. "You better get home to your sleep. Thanks for dropping me off."

"Anything for you." He crooked a little smile. "Witch."

"Don't push your luck." I frowned. "I could always hit you again."

He quickly raised his hands, palm up. "Please don't."

"Scared?" I cocked an eyebrow.

"Think I should be." His chuckle broke off with a pained grimace. "Go on up, I'll wait until you're inside."

"I'll be fine. Don't wait."

He didn't reply or move, his shadowed eyes watching me.

Turning to the stairs, I said. "Take care."

After unlocking the apartment door, I turned to wave at him and got a salute in return. Waited until he drove away, the security gate shutting automatically behind his ute, before going inside but knew I was too hyped up to sleep. Made myself a hot chocolate and drank it standing at the balcony windows, seeing no sign there'd ever been a party at the track apart from a couple of marquees still standing.

My mind was full of what I'd been through. Who would have done such a thing, even planned it? An appalling thought came to me that perhaps Wendy had been involved; she'd invited me after all and Martina was her so-called friend, someone associated with Poke and Douglas's cronies. Was it all linked somehow? But why on earth would they drop me at Douglas's without him even knowing? And in his bedroom, of all places?

I didn't tell Daniel or family about the incident, thinking it best to keep it to myself, or at least for now, and hoped Douglas would find out something.

Chapter 19

I phoned Wendy next day, determined to get the truth out of her if I need be, but realised almost immediately that she had no idea about the incident and seemed genuinely concerned about my welfare, asking. "Are you okay? Martina said you'd gone to the apartment because you didn't feel well."

I decided not to elaborate. "Something I ate, I think."

"Oh, I'm sorry. I should have been there for you."

"Don't worry, I'm fine now. Glad you enjoyed the party."

"I didn't stay long either," she sighed. "It was okay, but I hardly knew anyone."

"We'll go another time," I reassured her. "When my brothers are there."

"I'd like that." She brightened. "How's Matthew, have you heard?"

"He's having a ball, even with Dad around."

"Matthew enjoys anyone's company, he's that kind of guy." She sounded wistful.

"True, but he's too sociable for his own good sometimes."

As we disconnected shortly after something made me stop and think.

Of course, why hadn't I noticed before? She likes my brother, and that's why she's hanging around me. The poor girl! First, she's had to watch Martina sink her claws into him, and now he's gone away. Ah, well, I grinned to myself. I'll have to do something about that situation when he gets home, won't I?

I waited impatiently for a sign from Douglas, but as nothing was forthcoming decided to contact him myself one day after work. Shuddering at the thought of returning to his place, I headed for the sawmill instead, in the hope he'd be there working the night shift.

I parked in front of the prefab office, spotting his ute in the staff carpark behind the building. There was no receptionist inside, but a surveillance camera on the wall behind the desk must have been operating because a burly grey-haired man appeared through a side door very soon after I entered.

"Can I help you?" he asked gruffly.

I attempted a smile. "Could I see Douglas Willard, please."

"What's he done now?" The man peered suspiciously.

I blinked. "Nothing. Um, I'd just like to talk to him."

The man frowned but didn't reply.

I felt uncomfortable. "Sorry, if it's not a good time I can come back."

"Sit down. I'll call him." He turned abruptly for the same door he'd come out of.

Sitting down gingerly on one of the thread bare armchairs, I heard the man's voice calling over an intercom. "Willard! Come to the office now."

Douglas appeared minutes later through the office entrance door, arching his eyebrows when he saw me. I stood up quickly, gawping horror at the ugly purple bruising along the side of his face.

"Oh, no!" I squawked. "That looks really bad."

"Hello, witch." He crooked a grin. "You bent my stool."

"I'm so sorry." I grimaced apologetically.

"About the stool?"

"No!" I protested. "About your face. Are you okay?"

"I'll live." He tipped his head. "Nice of you to come see me."

"I guess you're busy." Glancing at the burly man's door, I had a feeling he was behind it listening. "I'm sorry, I shouldn't have come to your work."

"But you sure as shit weren't going to my place," he smirked.

"No, I wasn't!" I frowned. "I wonder why?"

"Didn't you like the bedroom décor?"

"Funny, ha ha!" I glowered, shot another glance at the internal door before gesturing a hand outside. "Can we talk out there or some other time?"

He narrowed his eyes. "You wanna the gossip, huh?"

"Did Poke tell you anything?"

"Yep." His laugh turned to a painful grunt.

"Careful!" I frowned. "That really does look sore."

"Poke looks worse!" he growled with a glint in his eye.

"What?" I gaped. "You beat him up?"

"Bloody idiot needed a telling off."

The grey-haired man came to the door, eying Douglas narrowly before disappearing.

"I better get on." Douglas pulled a face. "What time tomorrow?"

"Tomorrow?"

"Some other time, you said."

"Oh, um, right. Tomorrow, yes, that's fine."

"How about lunch in town at the same café as last time?"

"Um, okay."

"Twelve thirty, okay?" I nodded.

He turned to the outside door, holding it open for me, and walking past him, I felt very conscious of his eyes on me. Half expected him to follow to my car, but when I looked back, he was still standing by the office building. Didn't return my hesitant little wave and turning on his heel sauntered in the direction of the main sawmill building.

The following day at work, there were no objections to my taking a longer lunch break, but after waiting for more than ten minutes outside the café, my nervousness turned to annoyance, wondering whether he'd forgotten.

Right then his ute appeared, screeched a U-turn in the middle of the street, and parallel parked. I watched incredulously as without raising a sweat, he wedged the ute into a space I wouldn't have even attempted to get my little Suzuki into, screwing up my nose when he got out with a smug grin and strode across to me.

Said snootily, "Skite!"

"It's called parking," he countered, still grinning.

I wasn't the only one who noticed his prowess, rolling my eyes at the admiring looks of three tittering girls walking by. Him turning his head to grin at them gave me a moment to scrutinise his profile—the good side without the bruising—and could see why females liked what they saw.

The stubble suits him, I thought. *Sexy! Okay, stop that! What are you thinking?*

Inside the café, we ordered coffee and lunch, an open ham sandwich for me, a meat pie and chips for him, and I refused his offer to pay. Sitting down opposite him at the same table we'd used before had me laughing inwardly.

Here we were again, having another amicable get-together, I could hardly believe it. How had we come this far? I used to detest this guy, had given him considerable grief over the years. Things were seriously out of whack, and I kind of liked it.

"And?" he asked, eying me.

"And what?"

"You're smiling," he said. "Is that dangerous?"

"Not this time."

"Sorry I was late." His lips twisted. "I'm on tank water and the pump stopped on me in the middle of a shower."

I grinned at the thought. "The pump's outside, is it?"

"Yeah. I had to run out in my soap bubbles and fix it."

"What a sight!" I smothered a giggle. "Your poor neighbours."

"The old bag next door had her binoculars glued."

"Oh, priceless!" I couldn't contain my laughter.

He laughed too but stopped abruptly, grimacing pain with a hand to his jaw.

Spluttering my own laughter to a halt, I frowned sympathetically. "Ouch."

He stared. "You should do that more often."

"What?"

"Laugh. It's cute."

I shook my head and changed the subject. "So, what's the gossip?"

"Martina," he said.

"What?"

"She planned it all."

I blinked shock. "What?"

"Told Poke that I was after you and that you were playing hard to get." He pulled a wry face. "And he believed it. She gives him some pussy and he'll do anything for her."

I grimaced my disgust. "Nice!"

"Martina gave you a drink, right?"

I nodded. "She gave Wendy and I both drinks. Two actually."

"Well, you were right, you were drugged. She put a little extra something in yours."

That shocked me even more. "What?"

"A sedative. Just to make you easier to handle."

"Why?" I gasped.

He shrugged. "I'm only guessing but I think she did it because of your brother. She's pissed off that he dumped her, nobody dumps Martina.' His lips twisted. "She also knows he hates my guts and that I er, like yours. Put two and two together and hey presto, you get mayhem, or that's what she was hoping."

"She'd do that just because Matthew broke up with her?" I shook my head in disbelief. "Drug my drink and got some guys to kidnap me?"

"You don't know Martina. She's a piece of work if she doesn't get her own way."

"I thought you liked her?" I peered at him. "You slept with her twice."

"She's an easy lay."

"Nice!" It seemed to be my favourite word.

"Martina the nympho, they call her. Rides anything, most human males that is." He grinned at my horrified look. "More than one at a time if she can and doesn't mind a crowd watching."

"Speaking from experience, are you?" I squawked, glowering disdain.

"Nah." He snorted a laugh. "Just heard stories."

Shaking my head disgustedly, I changed tack. "So, your mates took me to your place thinking they were doing you a favour?"

"Seems so." He stopped grinned, brows drawing together. "They won't do that again. I'll warn Martina off as well."

"You're not going to beat her up, I hope?"

"Nah. I'll just scare the shit out of her."

"Nice!"

"Yeah, I can be." His lips twisted slyly.

I raised my eyebrows sceptically but didn't comment.

After the waitress arrived with our lunches, we got on with the business of eating. I couldn't help but notice that we'd attracted the interest of some café customers and wondered how long before the town gossip got hold of a story about us.

Might be a good idea to let Daniel in on the latest when you get home, I told myself. As in, before he hears it, second hand and blows a fuse. Matthew will probably be on the next plane home when he finds out, and Dad will have to play referee once more.

"You're smiling again," Douglas said with his mouth full.

"Hmmm." I eyed him for a moment. "Just wondering what my brothers will do with you once they know all about this."

He slanted an amused eyebrow. "Do I look scared?"

"No." I shook my head. "Nothing much scares you, does it?"

"You do, witch. You scare me all the time."

"What?" I gaped. "Pull the other one."

He shrugged without comment, a look in his eyes I didn't understand.

After finishing my food, I sipped coffee. "Was that man at the sawmill your boss?"

"No. Patrick, one of the safety officers. Grumpy old bastard but not a bad dude."

"What do you do there?"

"I'm a jack of all trades. Cut up wood most of the time."

"Do you always work nights?"

"No, six weeks usually and then I'll change over to days,"

"How many shifts?"

"Two, eight to ten hours. Depends on how busy we are."

"And you're busy. The sawmill is doing well I've heard."

"Yep. And it's good pay."

Decided to be nosey. "Your Dad? He ran a scrap yard at the place where you live?"

"Yep. Need to tidy it up, but don't get much time for that."

"Too much work, pub brawls and women?"

He smiled slowly. "Heaps of work, not so many brawls and no women."

"I don't believe that." I scoffed. "About the women, I mean."

"Let's just say I don't have much luck," he said softly. "She's not interested."

"She?" I raised a surprised eyebrow. "There's someone special?"

"Has been for a long time."

"So, what are you doing about it?" I tilted my head. "Apart from bonking every other female in town?"

"Eh?" His eyes went wide.

"I've heard stories too." I said slyly. "And I'm not talking Martina either."

"That's a load of shit," he muttered. "Where did you hear that?"

"I have my sources." I flapped a casual hand.

"More friends from work?" He cocked an eyebrow. "Whatever you heard, I don't."

"Bonk?" Shut up now! Before you really put your foot in it!

"Not much. Not every female in town that's for sure."

"So, you haven't got anyone pregnant yet?" Are you crazy? What are you saying?

"I doubt it." His eyes narrowed. "Why are you asking me that?"

"Er, sorry," I tried an offhanded shrug. "Just being nosey."

His scrutiny had me shifting nervously in my chair.

It didn't shut me up though. "So, who is she?"

His lips twisted. "A witch who threw a spell on me, or maybe it's a curse."

"A witch?"

"A very cute witch," he said softly. "You."

Blinking, I yipped. "So, it is true?"

"Yeah, it is." His smile was rueful. "You figured it out at last."

"Well, not really." I shook my head. "My brothers keep harping on about it."

That cracked him up but instantly grabbing his jaw, the laughter turning to groans.

I eyeballed him, partly sympathetic, partly annoyed. "They said you only pick on me because you're trying to get my attention."

He blew out a breath, rubbed his face gingerly. "Smart boys, your brothers."

"So, why me?"

"Don't you look in the mirror? You're bewitching."

"You're disillusioned," I scoffed. "And for your information I'm not a witch or cute, I'm just an ordinary girl."

"Never ordinary." His mouth curved. "Very beautiful."

"Don't you start!" I scowled. "I've had enough of the beautiful, thank you!"

"Is that what he called you?"

"He?"

"Your boyfriend?"

"For the last time there is no boyfriend."

"Aw, come on. You love the guy."

"What?" My mouth opened and closed like a fish.

"Go after him, sort things out."

"Mind your own business!"

"And if it doesn't work out." He leant closer, leering. "I'm always here."

"I think you've lost the plot."

"Probably," he said cheerfully. "But that's what you do to me."

"Oh, please!" I shook my head in despair.

"It's true."

"Look, I'm glad we've cleared the air between us but that's it!" Realising I'd spoken loudly enough for anyone to hear, I added in lowered tones but just as sharply. "I'm not getting involved with anyone, okay?" Glowered for good measure. "And that includes you!"

"Understood." He nodded amicably, leaning back in his chair. "But I meant it, if you ever need anything you know where I am."

Staring at him in exasperation, I got to my feet without answering.

"And I promise I won't pick on you any more," he smirked.

"Well, that's a relief!" I wrinkled my nose.

"One other thing." Pushing back his chair he stood up too. "Don't leave unfinished business, you'll regret it if you do."

"Pardon?"

"The boyfriend."

"Douglas!"

"Kate!" He countered with a grin. "By the way, can I have your phone number?"

"No, you cannot!" I scowled. "Bad idea."

He merely shrugged and we left the café to go our separate ways.

After telling Daniel about the party incident and my meetings with Douglas, he didn't quite blow a fuse but ranted and raved for a bit.

"Okay! You can shut up now," I interrupted him. "It's all good and sorted."

"Good?" Daniel was scathing. "Willard will never be good. He doesn't know how."

"Oh, give him a break," I protested.

"Give him an inch and he'll take a mile, you mean?" Daniel curled his lip. "I've heard stories about that dude, K. You should be very careful around him!"

"Careful, how?"

"He'll have you before you can draw breath."

"Have me, how?" I eyeballed him. "What do you mean?"

"I mean, er, in his bed," Daniel muttered, avoiding my eyes.

"Funny that, I've heard stories too," I smirked. "They say girls like his bed."

"He'll do stuff you won't want to do."

"Really?" My eyebrows shot up. "Like?"

"Leave him alone, sis!" Daniel scowled. "He's more trouble than he's worth."

"You're just jealous, aren't you?"

"Piss off!" he growled. "It's your funeral, sis. Don't say I didn't warn you."

I chuckled. "Thanks, brother darling. I'll be careful."

Chapter 20

Daniel and I got over our differences in no time, jumping at Bella and Roman's invitation to a Harness race meeting down country one Saturday, the sunny weather drawing a huge crowd at the racecourse. As always, I thoroughly enjoyed being there simply to watch the horses in their element, doing what they were bred to do.

After one race Roman left us at the parade ring to check a client's horse at the stables, returning unexpectedly with someone in tow. "Look who I found," he said, laughing.

Letting out a squeal, Bella almost threw herself at the man with him while I felt the ground shift, heart leaping to my throat.

"Aren't you a lovely surprise," Bella released Kenneth to look him up and down. "Where did you spring from?"

"Been checking hooves like your man was," he told her, grinning.

"He's working for Bobby Raymond," Roman informed us.

"Bobby Raymond?" Daniel piped up. "He's one of the best trainers. isn't he?"

"One of them." Kenneth shook my brother's hand. "Good to see you, young fella. I hear you're still looking after Bella."

His drawl had my neck hairs standing to attention as per usual.

Daniel laughed. "She's looking after me, you mean."

"We all look after each other, somehow," Bella chuckled. "Don't we, Kate?"

Was certain everyone could hear my heart thudding as Kenneth turned to me still smiling but with cold eyes, neither of us making any attempt to move closer or shake hands.

"Hello, Kate," he said flatly.

Managing a semblance of a smile in return, I felt pain twist like a knife blade inside as he turned back to the others without another word.

What did you expect? I sneered to myself. Why would he want to touch or speak to you ever again? You accused him of many things, remember, even rape.

"Hey, isn't it about time you came back to see us?" Daniel asked him.

"Good on you, Daniel," Bella said. "Give him heaps."

Kenneth laughed. "I'm working on it."

"Is that a promise?" Bella gave him a narrowed eyed look.

"One day I will, I promise."

"How's the house hunting. Have you found anything yet?" Roman wanted to know.

"That's on the back burner right now," Kenneth told him. "I'm living at Bobby's stables, in one of the farm cottages there."

"Handy. What's happened to your caravan?"

"Sold it and the old ute," He grinned at Daniel. "Got myself a Ranger now, mate."

"Good choice," Daniel grinned back.

I felt removed from my surroundings, almost unaware of anything but him. My riveted eyes took their fill, wanting more and I knew right then that what I felt for him was huge, something I'd never known before and barely understood. Bella must have seen my face because she was suddenly there beside me, taking my arm and excusing us.

Somewhere in the bustle she found a free table and sat me down, barely registering her voice. "Kate? Are you okay?"

Her hand over mine brought me back to my senses. I stared at her for a long silent moment before replying. "No."

"It's Kenneth, isn't it?"

"Yes."

"Something happened between you?"

"No. I mean, yes." I croaked.

"Do you mind me asking what?"

"I was horrible," I mumbled, felt tears sting.

"Hey, now." She patted my hand. "We all do that sometimes."

"I was more than horrible."

"Okay. What sort of horrible?" she asked quietly. "Something you did, or said?"

"I thought he was taking the cabin off us." My voice trembled. "I totally lost it, called him names and accused him of…of, things."

She didn't ask what the things were, merely smiling sympathetically, "Reminds me of myself once upon a time."

"You?" I gawped. "You mean with Roman?"

"Oh yes! I wasn't very nice to him at times." She grimaced ruefully. "Sometimes I wonder why or how he put up with me."

"Oh." I had no idea what else to say.

"I know you've heard this all before." She smiled gently. "How often Mum reminds us we've got Lawson blood in our veins, how us girls take after Maria."

I frowned. "But Maria was always so nice."

"She was lovely, but she gave her men a hard time on occasion." She slanted her head. "But then some men can handle it. Bernard could. So, can Roman."

"Meaning?" I frowned.

"Meaning, I'm sure Kenneth could handle a not very nice Kate." She grinned as my eyes went wide. "All you have to do is give him a little encouragement."

"Um," I spluttered. "In case you haven't noticed, he doesn't want to talk to me."

"This isn't the place to talk, too many ears. You need to get him on his own."

I simply stared.

"Roman and I will try out best to persuade him to visit soon." She took hold of my hand. "Then it's up to you, dear girl. To work your magic."

"Magic?" I whispered.

"Your charms. He won't be able to resist."

"I don't think that will work." I shook my head doubtfully. "I'm not charming."

"Yes, you are. And he's been charmed before."

"Before?"

"He was after you at home, anyone could see that. I doubt his feelings have changed. He's just playing it cool right now, too many eyes watching."

I wasn't convinced. "Eyes watching didn't worry him before."

"Different time and place. Besides you weren't exactly all over him, were you?" Bella leant closer. "It's your turn this time. He's waiting for a sign from you."

I pulled a self-mocking face. "How do I do that?"

"Flutter your eyelashes, Kate, dear." Bella laughed. "But wait until he comes home."

We located Roman and Daniel shortly after, watching the racing together without seeing Kenneth again which in itself left me deflated and doubtful of Bella's advice.

During the next three weeks, I worked on automatic pilot and frustrated myself with dreams of Kenneth. Not a good combination to say the least, my brain and body beginning to wear themselves out and when Bella rang, I wasn't especially enthusiastic.

"Guess what?" She sounded excited.

"What?" I asked vaguely.

"We have a visitor coming to stay."

As my pulse began to race, I could only say. "Oh."

"Oh, indeed!" She snorted. "Kenneth is driving up Friday and staying all week."

"Oh." A shiver went all the way from my neck to my tailbone.

"So, my girl, you're coming over for dinner on Friday with Daniel."

"I am?"

"No excuses!"

I was a cot case by the time Friday evening came along, unable to decide what to wear. Finally donned my best black jeans and a purple top that clung which had Daniel raising his eyebrows and giving me a once over as I got into his ute.

"Wow! You look hot, K." He grinned. "Planning to knock his socks off, are you?"

"I don't know what you're talking about," I said coolly. "You don't look so bad yourself. New shirt?"

"Yeah, like it?"

"Very smart." I cocked an eyebrow. "Did some girl buy it for you?"

He looked shocked. "How did you know that?"

Leant across to tap his nose which shut him up, thankfully. With my nerves already shot, I didn't need him adding any more angst.

On our arrival, Kenneth and Roman were in the lounge having a beer while Bella made finishing touches to something that smelled delicious in the kitchen. To my relief, we all greeted each other verbally without contact, Daniel was offered a beer and I took a glass of white wine, which I promptly almost swallowed half of until I saw Bella give me an amused knowing look. Quickly put my glass down on the bench and asked if she needed a hand, to which she shook her head.

"It's all cooking nicely," she said. "Let's sit down and have a chat."

Had to force myself to concentrate as Roman began regaling an amusing incident that had happened at work that day, but couldn't stop myself glancing furtively at Kenneth. Not furtively enough, however, because his eyes suddenly locked on mine, the shock of it making my heart stop. Feeling myself go hot all over, I stared fixedly at the coffee table thereafter.

Sitting at the table for dinner with him directly opposite I kept my head down and was so intent on my plate I didn't realise he was speaking to me at first. "I understand you're working at the clinic these days."

Lifting my head with a jerk, I gulped at his intent look. "Yes, yes I do."

"Do you like it?" His eyes held a touch of amusement.

"Yes."

Bella stepped in, feeling sorry for me I surmised. "It's a busy place these days with the full-time vet clinic. A little different to when I started."

Kenneth sifted his gaze to her. "I know there's racehorses coming to the clinic from all over. One of Bobby's clients had a horse up here not long ago."

I gave myself a mental shake. Here's your chance, you idiot! At least talk to him.

Roman nodded. "It's a thriving business. Your grandfather Jason would be proud."

"No doubt, he would," Kenneth agreed.

"Not to mention he's got family working there too, Olivia and Stephanie."

"Don't forget, the Lawson girls as well," Bella grinned. "Maria's family."

"Who could forget!" Roman laughed. "The niece and granddaughter of his lady love."

Kenneth eyes returned to me. "I imagine he'd be more than rapt to know that."

Negative thoughts entered my head. And what about you, Mr Hawke? Are you rapt with me working for your grandfather's business?

"You know something Kenneth, me lad," Roman said. "You should be the one shoeing horses there. Doing my job. I reckon Jason would be stoked if you did."

Kenneth cocked an eyebrow. "You reckon?"

"Yeah, I do reckon."

"Me too," Bella smirked.

"Yeah! That would be cool," Daniel agreed. "You back here for good."

Kenneth threw up his hands in surrender. "Okay, okay! I get the picture."

"What do you think, Kate." Bella slanted a look at me.

"I'm sure his grandfather would be very happy," I said coolly, taking the bull by the horns. "But what does Jason's grandson think of us working there?"

Kenneth's eyes narrowed on me at first, then his smile flashed, which prompted not only a neck-hair reaction but did funny things to my insides too. "Jason would probably lynch me if I thought bad of any of you working there, especially the Lawson ladies."

Everyone laughed, even me. The rest of the evening passed in a blur, both enjoyable and nerve-wracking, and later in bed I was still fizzing, unable to sleep with my mind fit to bursting. I wanted desperately to apologise to him before he went away, punching in his number on my phone the next day but chickened out each time at the last digit. Let

I let out a squeak when it suddenly rang, almost dropping it at the caller's ID.

With my heart in my mouth, I breathed. "Hello."

"Hi, Kate," he greeted, his drawl making me shiver.

"You still have my number?" I asked stupidly.

"You thought I wouldn't?"

"I didn't think you'd want to talk to me again," I mumbled.

"You thought wrong, then." He paused, spoke softly. "Could we talk tonight? Meet up for dinner somewhere or if you like I'll pick you up."

I swallowed. "Um, we could meet in town."

"How about the Italian place, about six?"

"Um, okay, er, I'll see you there." Began to tremble when he rang off.

Wore the black jeans again with a different top in green, found him waiting at the restaurant entrance wearing black jeans and green shirt and after both looking each other up and down, burst out laughing. A perfect start to a night that I would never in my life forget.

I tried to apologise twice before dinner for my past behaviour, but he put a finger to his lips each time and talked about something else. When I leant forward across the table, looked him in the eyes and tried a third time he reached across and put his finger to my lips instead. That shut my mouth and had me staring like a rabbit blinded by headlights.

"Shush," he said softly. "We all say things we don't mean. Let's leave it at that."

His thumb took over from his finger to slide gently over my lower lip. As I pulled back a little in surprise at the tingling sensation, he smiled and dropped his hand.

Took a deep breath. "I wanted to speak to you at Mum's funeral, but you'd gone."

"I had to leave early." He inclined his head. "How are you coping?"

"It gets easier, but I miss her heaps," I told him. "You know Dad and Matthew are overseas? Oh, that's right. Daniel told you the other night."

"He did. Your dad would appreciate visiting his father's homeland again."

I nodded. "I'm glad Matthew's went along with him, it's a good break for them both."

"How was your trip?" He slanted an enquiring look.

"Really great." I grimaced ruefully. "It was an excuse to get away."

"I know the feeling." His smile was equally rueful. "Daniel met up with you later?"

"He did. It was such fun having him there."

"I'm sure it was, he's a fun guy."

I took a deep breath, "You didn't stay at the cabin long?"

"No. Like you I had to get away."

"Because of me?" I frowned.

"There seemed no point in staying."

"I'm sorry." It sounded inane.

"Don't apologise. We make choices, that's life."

"I suppose," I sighed.

"And sometimes we get a second chance."

I saw something in his eyes that made my breath catch. "How long are you staying?"

"I took a fortnight off work, planning to stay until after next weekend at least."

"I suppose you'll catch up with a few people while you're here?"

"Yeah, I will. It's going to a busy visit."

As our dinners arrived, we stopped talking to eat, but I couldn't stop myself looking at him and toyed with my food.

He noticed. "Don't you like the meal?"

"It's fine, really." I murmured. "I just...um, can I ask you something?"

He put his fork down to wipe his mouth. "Go ahead."

"Did you enjoy living at the cabin?"

"Loved it," he smiled. "A great place to unwind after work."

"Dad and I unwind there more often now," I told him. "Since Mum died."

"I can understand that."

I had to ask. "Do you think you'll come back to work with Roman again?"

"I'm going to give it some serious thought."

"Would you live at the cabin, um, if you did come back?"

"If I was allowed."

"Allowed?" I frowned. "Dad, wouldn't say no, I'm sure."

"I didn't mean your dad."

"Oh!" Realising who he meant, I said on a shaky breath. "I wouldn't say no either."

He didn't reply, smile enigmatic.

"Did you mean what you said er, about wanting me to live with you there?" I could hardly believe I'd asked the question and when he didn't reply to that either, I dropped my eyes to my plate and quickly began eating, feeling foolish at my forwardness.

In the ensuing silence we finished our meals, I drained the glass of wine without once looking in his direction, felt rather than saw him lean back in his chair and was very aware of being watched.

"I've made a decision," he said flatly.

I looked at him then, eyes riveted on his.

There was no expression on his face or in his voice. "I won't be coming back."

A cold sick feeling rose like bile in my throat, had the overwhelming urge to bolt.

"Unless you're absolutely sure you want me to," he added more gruffly.

I stared dumbstruck.

He tilted his head, eyes narrowed. "And there's one condition."

"What?" I mouthed.

"That you live with me, whether at the cabin or elsewhere."

Brain couldn't take it in, felt lightheaded as my heart began to pound. He was suddenly on his feet, bending over me with concern. "Kate?" His voice sounded distant. "Are you okay?"

I shook my head to clear it, beamed him a silly smile. "When?"

Laughing, he took my face in his hands and kissed me full on the mouth.

I slid my fingers up into his hair, losing all sense of time or place. It was the applause of a group of patrons at another table that brought us back to the present, Kenneth let my mouth go, turned to look and grinning gave them a thumbs up. Neither of us wanted the evening to end, we talked some more, had dessert, talked again, finished with a coffee still talking and were last to leave the restaurant.

During one of our daily phone conversations thereafter, I had no trouble being forward again. "I'm staying at the cabin Friday night. Will you come?"

"I'd like that," he said without hesitation.

Friday evening, we sat out on the deck consuming the pizza and red wine he'd brought until it got cold, moving inside for coffee, more talk and laughter. As the night closed in, I was finding it hard to conceal the tremor inside and contain my nervous excitement. He knew but was in no hurry, eventually getting up from the armchair opposite to take both my hands in his, smiling gently as he pulled me to my feet.

"I've never done this before," I whispered.

"You don't have to do anything," he murmured. "Two bedrooms, remember."

I lifted my eyes to his. "I want to be with you."

"Are you sure?" His eyes were so dark you couldn't see the blue.

Trembling or no, I managed to say with a snooty air, "Just so you know I'm not nineteen any more. I'll be twenty-one soon and you'll be thirty. You're getting old, Mr Hawke and we shouldn't waste time."

"Too much information!" He pretended affront, cocking a wry eyebrow.

I put my hand up to his face, tracing a finger down his cheek. "I love you," I said softly, adding at his rather stunned blink. "Yes. I figured that out, too."

As his arms closed around me, he touched my mouth with his, lightly. Once, then twice until the third kiss turned hot. I lost myself in it but as he broke the kiss to pick me up and carry me to Dad's bedroom door, I shook my head.

He loosened his hold as I pointed to the corner of the lounge, whispering. "This is where their bed used to be."

I walked on wobbly legs to the settee, picking up the throw rug and cushions. He said not a word as I arranged them on the floor, but his slow sexy smile told me he approved and making love with him on that primitive bed in our grandparent's cabin was indescribable.

Afterwards, he lay on his back, breathing somewhat faster than usual, and said to me, "Now that I'm old, I think I deserve a mattress."

"You're not old yet," I giggled, gulping air. "You're still twenty-nine."

"No more information, please!" he grunted. "This floor is hard, that's all I know."

He was right. I hadn't taken a great deal of notice before, but the floor wasn't exactly comfortable even with the rug and cushions. With that confirmed, we were soon snuggled under the covers in Dad's room and eventually slept until late morning.

Chapter 21

It was as if he'd never been away and the beginning of a wonderful time for me.

On completing his contract with Bobby's stable, we moved into the cabin together just after Dad and Matthew returned home, Roman and Bella were overjoyed to have him back, Anna positively gloated at her predictions being right while Leon, Karl and all the Sandford family were absolutely delighted.

I'd also lost my bet with dear brother Matthew, who couldn't wait until next winter to dunk me in the river.

My twenty-first birthday party was the best I'd ever had simply because he was there, and his thirtieth was a hoot as well. Both parties were held at the Sandford homestead at Leon's insistence, with caterers attending to food and drink and a stereo system rigged up outside belting out songs everyone sang and danced to. The musicians in our families came out to play as well; Dad and Matthew taking turns on keyboard, Daniel on guitar with Olivia playing violin, and Leon alternating flute and saxophone. Even I took a turn on piano, singing a love song for Kenneth which brought a tear to his eye and being taken in his arms for a long-sweet kiss afterwards had everyone catcalling and cheering.

After my getting together with Kenneth, I didn't see much of Douglas, there were certainly no more incidents and although he'd acknowledge me with a wave if he drove past or walked by in town, we rarely spoke. I felt curiously bereft at those moments, wondering if all the effort to become friends had been wasted but I soon shrugged it off and forgot.

Just over a year after Mum's death, on a Saturday morning at the farm, I was rummaging in my old bedroom, sorting and clearing out leftover clothing, when the front doorbell rang. Knowing that Dad was out in the sheds with Ben, I quickly went to see who the visitor was—a woman I'd never seen before. She wasn't young, perhaps a little older than Dad, but still very attractive, tall, and slim, with touches of grey in the blonde hair.

"Hello. Can I help you?" I asked, smiling.

She seemed familiar, as if I'd met her before, but I couldn't place it right then.

"Hello." She spoke softly with a slight accent. "Does Jason Von Meeren live here?"

"Yes, he does. Jason's my dad."

She blinked at that, seemed at a loss but recovered quickly. "Of course, I see that."

I pursed my lips wryly. "Apparently I look like my grandmother, Dad's mum."

She took a long breath. "Yes, I can see that too."

That surprised me. "You knew her?"

She nodded but didn't speak.

"Would you like to come in? I'll call Dad if you like, he's out the back somewhere."

"That would be very kind." She nodded. "I hope I'm not disturbing anyone?"

"Not at all." I beckoned her inside. "Come this way, the kitchen is the best place at this time of the day."

She followed, looking around. "It's certainly lovely and warm."

"It catches the morning sun, we love it." I pulled out a table chair for her, waiting until she sat before calling Dad on my mobile, saying as he answered. "Hey, have you got time to come to the house? There's a lady here to see you."

"Is she pretty?" he asked.

"Gorgeous."

He laughed. "On my way. Give me ten minutes, just helping Ben with a tractor."

"Righto." I disconnected to find her watching me intently, saying with a flap of my hand. "He won't be long. Boy's stuff, you know, playing with machinery."

"Of course." She averted her gaze, sighed. "Always the mechanic."

I was surprised to see the nervous tremor in her hand. "Would you like a drink while you're waiting?"

She shook her head but didn't look at me. "No, thank you."

"How do you know, Dad?"

She didn't answer immediately, chewed her lip. "It was a long time ago."

"You're not from around here?"

"I was born in New Zealand, lived in this district for a while, with my father."

"You don't have a Kiwi accent."

"No, I guess I don't any more." She looked at me again, smiling. "I've been living in Canada for quite a long time, almost forty years."

"They say it's a lovely place."

"It is."

We made more small talk until Dad walked in, his reaction to the visitor more than surprising. He stopped in midstride, staring as if he'd seen a ghost while she looked to my puzzled eyes, terrified and ready to bolt.

Dad finally got himself together but said just one word. "Helena?"

Woohoo! I thought. Interesting! Methinks these two have history.

She whispered. "Jason."

"Shall I make a cup of tea?" I said into the ensuing silence.

Dad glanced at me, vaguely. "Er, yes. That would be nice. Thanks, Kate."

At the kitchen bench, I put the kettle on and got out cups but kept watch. As Dad moved towards her, she got to her feet quickly but at an arm's length distance they simply stood eyeballing each other without speaking.

A thought hit me like a lightning bolt, making me narrow my eyes on the woman. She looks like Mum! Why didn't I pick it before? No wonder she seems familiar.

"Kate?" She repeated my name. "Just one daughter?"

"Yes." Dad's voice was gruff. "And two sons, Matthew and Daniel."

"That's wonderful. I'm very happy for you." She gestured a hand, frowning. "I'm sorry. I should have phoned you instead of just arriving here like this."

"It's fine." Dad slanted his head at her. "Nice of you to come."

The kettle had boiled. I set out cups while keeping one ear tuned in on them.

"Your wife. I heard she died." She spoke hesitantly.

"Zoe," Dad said. "A year ago, just gone."

"Oh. I'm so sorry for your loss."

"Thank you." Dad paused. "And your husband, he's with you?"

I made the tea, turning to see her shake her head. "No. He died three years ago. He had an accident, his truck jack-knifed in bad weather."

"I'm sorry to hear that." Dad murmured. "You're back home for a visit, then?"

"I'm back for good. Hoping to buy a house, looked at one in town yesterday."

"Oh," He sounded surprised. "Somewhere near where your father lived?"

"Two streets over."

I cleared my throat. "Sorry to interrupt." Smiled at her. "Milk with your tea?"

"Yes, just a little, please." She smiled back. "Can I help at all?"

"No, no. I've got this," I assured her, putting our drinks on the table with a plate of Patsy's homemade chocolate chip cookies.

Dad seemed to come to his senses, gesturing apologetically to me. "Kate, sorry. This is Helena, a good friend of mine from way back."

"Hi, Helena," I smiled cheerfully, shaking her hand. "Nice to meet you."

I learnt some more about her while we drank our tea, soon realising that she and Dad had history all right. Finding out the classic Ford Escort now on display in the racetrack museum used to belong to her father was a surprise, Helena herself blown away that Dad had kept it. Before her departure she exchanged phone numbers with him, the wistful look on his face as she drove away in her VW Golf making me smirk.

"Ex-girlfriend, isn't she?" I couldn't resist asking.

"Hmmm." He shot me a rueful glance. "How did you know?"

"Your body language," I chuckled. "You boys are all the same, young and old."

He pulled a resigned face at my questioning look. "She was my first girlfriend."

"Aha!" I grinned. "How long ago was that?"

"I was seventeen."

"Wow!" My eyebrows shot up. "Didn't you start young? How old was she, then?"

"She's eight years older than me, Bella's age."

"Priceless!" I squeaked. "So, you were a toy boy!"

"I was old enough," he protested.

"Old enough to do what?" I cocked an amused eyebrow.

He shook his head. "It's time I left. Ben will be waiting."

"When are you seeing her again?" I wasn't finished.

"Kate!" He shot me a narrowed look. "Leave it."

"Aw, why?" I laughed evilly. "You know what? I think she looks a lot like Mum."

"Blonde, leggy and beautiful," he sighed. "Yeah, I know."

"Your kind of woman, eh?"

"Something like that," he muttered, quickly heading out before I could say more.

As Dad and Helena's friendship slowly reignited into a romantic relationship, my brother's and I were over the moon, believing Mum would have been pleased for him and although Helena had no children, she welcomed us like her own.

Months later, while helping treat a horse's leg injury in the clinic yards, I noticed Bella's car hurtle into the carpark, the way she leapt out of her car and ran to reception drawing my attention. Approaching the building, I could see her through the glass doors gesticulating urgently to Riley, the vet on duty. As he pointed in my direction, she whirled with a look on her face that had me worried and wondering what had happened to make her so agitated. I'd never seen her like that before.

She met me outside before I reached the doors, grasping my upper arms. "Kate!" she said drawing in air. "There's been an accident."

"An accident?" I frowned. "Who?"

"It's Kenneth."

"What?" I felt my heart sink like a stone. "What's happened to him?"

"It's bad, Kate," She blinked back tears.

"Bad?" I croaked. "How bad?"

Her head shake told me instantly what she couldn't say. Staring blindly, I felt suddenly as cold as ice, a sick feeling in my throat.

"Come with me now." She took me by the shoulders. "Riley knows we need to go."

She bundled me into her car, scrubbed at her eyes before starting the engine and stamped on the accelerator. Unaware of anything but Kenneth's name resounding over and over in my head, I whispered. "He can't be dead."

Bella whispered back. "I'm so sorry, Kate."

"Why?"

"Please, let's wait until we get you home," she said. "We'll talk there."

Minutes later, we pulled up at the farm homestead where Roman, Anna and Dad stood waiting outside, their faces telling me they already knew. Dad rushed across to the car to help me out but as my legs gave way Roman lifted me into his arms, carrying me inside to the sitting room settee. While Dad sat beside me with a comforting arm around my shoulders Roman remained standing and Anna sat silent on a nearby armchair. Bella came in shortly after with a drink for me which I refused but she insisted, Dad's hand closing over my shaking one to help me sip something horribly potent that made me splutter. After two swallows I shook my head, Dad handing the glass back to Bella.

"What happened?" I asked, voice a feeble croak.

"Let's just take a moment, shall we?" Dad said.

"Now, please!" I demanded more sharply. "When?"

"It happened this morning while Kenneth was working." It was Roman who answered, a catch in his voice. "A horse kicked him at Winter's Racing Stable."

I could hardly comprehend it. "Kicked? How?"

Bella quickly went across to support Roman as he continued. "Their stable policy demands that vet's, farriers, or the like work in a restricted area, but I understand an inexperienced stable hand walked two horses through while Kenneth was there." My eyes were glued to his face as he paused again, swallowing hard before speaking again. "When one spooked and reared, she let go of them both and they took off in his direction." He closed his eyes as Bella's arm tightened around him, said on a long deep breath. "One kick, that's all." His voice cracked. "Kenneth was bent over, still shoeing... he didn't have time to get out of the way, it caught him directly on the temple."

I sat bolt upright, said shrilly. "I don't believe it!"

Dad looked me in the eye. "I'm sorry, my dear, but it's true."

"No!" I shook my head.

"Oh, Kate." Dad reached a hand to my face.

"No!" I said again. "It can't be."

Eyeballing each other, a tear slipping down his cheek was all it took. My bottled-up disbelief and horror spilled over. Dad pulled me close to rock me like a child as I began to howl wretched sobs that shook me to the core. Was vaguely aware of my brothers bursting into the room, Bella calming them down and the room filling with more people. Olivia was suddenly there by my side, clasping my hand to her cheek.

So started a nightmare few days that left me reeling. My world had been ripped apart, numbing shock and an indescribable grief swallowing me up, worse than when Mum had died. Another funeral, surreal and mind numbing. The weather seemed appropriate, grey and stormy with lashing rain, like the heavens wept. Dad, Matthew and Daniel were constantly beside me throughout, comforting and protective.

Later that day at the homestead, I went up to my old room, staring out the window for a long time at our horses, hardly able to believe that one of their kind had ended the life of the man I loved. Knew however, that in Kenneth's or even my profession there was always risk, the probability of being injured or killed by an animal of that size and strength very real and whether by accident, negligence or some mistake there was no point blaming anyone, either horse or handler. I did blame myself however, for not having spent more time with Kenneth, for those wasted months when I'd gone overseas and away from him. Deep down, I knew I should be grateful for the chance I'd had.

During the weeks that followed, he often appeared in my mind, at times so real it was if he was right there beside me and my mutterings were now directed at him, not so much myself or Trojan. I remained at the cabin, feeling closest to him there. Thankfully, work kept me busy, but the weekends weren't so easy when I had time on my own to think. There were shadows under my eyes from lack of sleep and my weight dropped.

I wanted no part of the enquiry into Kenneth's death, leaving our family lawyers and the stable concerned to deal with it. Dad and Roman were kept in the loop but I rebuffed any attempt on their part to talk to me about it. I simply shut it out, wanting only to remember Kenneth as he'd been before that fateful day.

Early one grey Saturday morning, I let Trojan out to do his business and went back to bed, curling up to hug Kenneth's pillow.

"I so wish you were here," I whispered, half dozing.

"Don't grieve too long for me, beautiful," Kenneth appeared in my mind, spoke softly in my ear. "Life's too short for grief and sadness."

Weird? Was I hearing things now as well? "Kenneth?" I murmured, putting out a hand to trace his face from forehead to mouth.

Heard his chuckle, "Yes, it's me. Did you really think I'd leave you alone?"

"You're here, talking to me." I said on a breath. "How?"

"You're not like your Oma for nothing, are you?"

"What do you mean?"

"She and my grandfather talked all the time after he died."

"What?"

"Didn't your dad tell you that?"

"He said something about dreams and things."

"Well, there you go." He chuckled again.

"I don't understand."

"Don't worry yourself now. Just remember I'm always here if you need me."

As his presence faded my eyes popped open wide, but there was nothing to see or hear except my own breathing and a tripping heart. Trojan's whine outside snapped me out of my trance, had me scrambling off the bed to let him in.

"Kenneth was here!" I told him stupidly, his answer a delighted doggy grin.

I kept the incident to myself, hoping he'd speak to me again. Felt strangely enlivened too as if I'd reached a turning point in my grief and depression, able to sleep and eat better. There were dreams of him, us running along the beach together, making love in the cabin and our laughter echoing in my head long afterwards. Trojan was ever faithful, watching me with soulful eyes and listening to my ramblings with a thumping tail.

Three months later, Dad and Helena married at the Wine Rack just as Opa and Oma had done so many years ago. The wedding day was bittersweet for me; I was immensely glad to see Dad happy, but at times during the festivities I felt removed and saddened. Wondered what might have been, when and where Kenneth and I would have married.

After Dad and Helena's road trip honeymoon, they returning to live at the farm homestead and although I had no plans to leave the cabin Dad did voice his concerns.

"Are you sure you should stay there by yourself?" He peered at me worriedly.

"I'm doing fine, Dad." I smiled reassurances. "You know me. I love the privacy and Trojan's with me, he loves it too."

"But is it good for you?"

"Yes, I think it is. I need to be alone right now."

"Well, don't forget us." He hugged me. "Come over whenever you feel like it."

"I will." I squeezed him. "That goes for you too, the cabin and beach aren't going away, you know. They're there for everyone."

"I know." He drew back. "Just take care, okay?"

"You too, Dad. Look after Helena and enjoy each other."

He heaved a sigh but didn't comment further, smiling his understanding.

Bella and Roman were ever attentive, but invitations to their home were often declined until I made an effort one weekend, Roman's sister Lara, also Bella's long-time friend, popped in with her husband Ricky at the same time.

Asking after their three grown up children, I was told that daughter Zena was now a qualified dog groomer like her mother and helping in the family's dog kennel business. Eldest son Jayden was married and running his in laws sheep and beef unit down country while Connor who'd previously also helped run the dog kennel was now pursuing a farrier career and working with Roman.

"Isn't that great?" Bella enthused. "At last, another farrier in the district."

Lara laughed. "Roman's super pleased. Aren't you, big brother?"

"You bet, I'll take any help I can get," Roman grinned. "He's a good lad, my nephew and a tidy freak. The truck's never been so clean."

Everyone except me laughed, my mind shifting immediately to Kenneth. How quickly life moves on, I thought despondently. Nothing lasts forever, even the most accomplished of farriers are soon replaced.

Gave myself a mental shake and returned to the present, nobody having noticed my preoccupation except Bella who was watching me with a concerned frown.

Said clearly for her benefit. "It's a great profession, I'm sure the horses will appreciate Connor."

Bella blinked, looking relieved. "They do already," she agreed.

"Yeah, they have a thing about his ears." Roman chuckled.

I laughed then; a genuine happy laugh that felt good.

Chapter 22

Everyone kept trying their utmost to get me out socialising, especially Bella, but I much preferred my quiet life at the cabin. My only outings apart from work were grocery shopping and visits to the farm at least twice a week, to say hi to family and ride Delta with Trojan in tow. Dad and Helena often invited me to stay for a meal, but I didn't make a habit of it.

On one such lunch occasion, it was ladies only, as the men had all gone out to a neighbouring district's agricultural show for the day. Our conversation revolved around a variety of recent happenings in town and some juicy gossip about some well-to-do husband being found with his pants down in his latest floozie's car, which had us all shaking our heads and rolling about with laughter.

The ambient mood had me staying longer than I normally would have, but as serious talk resumed, Anna's shift to the topic of Oma had me feeling immediately uncomfortable, thinking to excuse myself and leave. Why I remained glued to my seat, I wasn't exactly sure.

"She knew things, my sister," Anna said. "She had this way of looking at you."

Bella nodded. "Jason often said that, too."

"Is that where the witch thing came from?" Olivia asked.

"You can blame Bernard for that." Anna laughed. "Witchy poo was his favourite nickname for her."

"And sweet witch," Bella grinned. "I so remember that one."

"Yes, another favourite of his," Anna agreed. "He always said she could cast spells, she certainly had him under her spell that was for sure."

"He didn't seem to mind, did he?" Bella slanted a droll eyebrow.

Helena smiled. "I didn't know her as well as you all do, but I remember her eyes. Like you say, Anna she seemed to look inside you."

"The grey Lawson eyes." Anna turned to me. "Just like yours, Kate."

"Dad and Daniel have them too," I pointed out.

"Indeed, but you look most like her."

I shrugged offhandedly, hoping the conversation would change, but judging by the way Anna was peering at me I was out of luck.

"Perhaps I shouldn't talk about this now," she said, continuing, nonetheless. "But with all the goings on lately, it's as if history's repeating itself."

"What do you mean, Mum?" Bella knit her brows.

Knew I should have bolted right there and then, cringing at what was coming.

"Like his grandfather, Jason." Anna kept watching me. "Kenneth was doing his job, doing what he loved when he died."

I went rigid, reminding myself to breathe.

Bella spoke into the lengthening silence. "I don't think this is a good time, Mum."

Anna didn't heed, speaking to me as if I was the only one in the room. "Kate, my dear, you must know there will be someone else, just as there was for my sister."

I shook my head vehemently. "There will be nobody else! Ever."

Anna merely smiled gently, spreading her hands. "That's exactly what Maria said and look what happened? Bernard came along."

Bella sighed. "You could be right, Mum, but Kate needs time, a long time."

"Ah, but time waits for no one," Anna was still looking at me. "What will be will be, you can't change it."

I frowned, not understanding.

"There's a bad boy out there, just like your Opa," she told me, adding with a knowing little smile. "And I think you already know him."

My tongue stuck to the roof on my mouth.

"Mum?" Bella gave her mother a disbelieving look. "What on earth do you mean?"

"Kate?" Olivia stared at me. "Is there someone else?"

"No!" I managed a croak. "There is no one else. I don't know anyone else!"

Anna simply smiled.

At that point I decided it was high time to go, got up abruptly and said my goodbyes. Bella quickly followed me out, looking both concerned and apologetic. "Kate, please take no notice of Mum, she gets something in her head and won't let it go." Her lips twisted resignedly. "And she's getting more tactless in her old age."

"It's okay," I summoned a smile. "I know she means well."

"She thinks of Aunt Maria more often these days, I've noticed," She creased her forehead. "They say the elderly dwell on their memories and the past."

"I suppose we'll do the same when we get to her age."

"Yes, I suppose," she sighed. "Are you going to be, okay?"

"Don't you worry about me." I reassured her.

I muttered all the way home about my great aunt and her predictions. Poor Trojan watched me from the back seat with concern, likely wondering why on earth I was so grumpy.

That night I dreamt of Kenneth holding me against him, my back against his chest. As his hands and mouth roamed, I giggled, his stubble tickling my neck.

"So, there's a bad boy, eh?" he growled softly in my ear. "Care to tell me about him?"

Him talking to me a second time made me start, jerking my head to look at him. Recoiled with a yip of fright. The face wasn't his but a grinning skull, morphing suddenly and shockingly into someone I recognised. Douglas Willard.

Came awake, trashing about under the covers to sit bolt upright, heaving in air. Screwed my eyes shut as Trojan scrambled to his feet from beside the bed, whining his concern. Peeping one eye open, I quickly reached across to turn on the bedside lamp half expecting someone else to be in the room apart from my dog. There was of course no one.

"Sorry, Trojan," I whispered. "It's okay. Just a bad dream."

Swung my legs out of bed, gave his ears a ruffle and as I got up, he padded with me to the kitchen, watching me make a cup of tea. Knowing sleep wasn't happening again in a hurry, I curled up in an armchair to stare out at the night sky, Trojan flopping himself down on the floor beside me. Churning thoughts through my head, I finished the drink and resting my head back, closed my eyes.

"Don't let me stop you, beautiful." Kenneth's hand traced my face.

I gasped. "What?"

"You heard." He laughed, the familiar sexy laugh. "He's waited a long time."

"Who?" I stared into vivid blue eyes.

"The bad boy, who else? Your Opa all over again."

"Please, no! That can't be," I whispered.

"Don't mourn for me forever, beautiful," he murmured gently, his face shifting out of focus. "Take your chance. Remember time waits for no one."

Came out of the doze feeling weirdly breathless, Trojan's nose nudging my arm. Reached a hand to him, sliding it along his muzzle to his ears which he accepted as reassurance, sitting back on his haunches to give himself a scratch.

Watching him absently, Kenneth's words kept echoing in my mind. The bad boy? Opa all over again. Douglas? Felt a hysterical laugh bubbling up. What was going on here? It didn't make sense. Shook my head but couldn't rid my head of him, thoughts of the past tumbling over and over. Would I have made peace with Douglas if Kenneth hadn't gone away? The incident at the racetrack party would likely never have happened either. So what? I hadn't seen him for ages, and who knew what he was up to these days? Ha! Don't you listen to gossip? Doesn't mean I believe it! Ah, but if the stories were true? Then bedding females was still his forte, he may even have exceeded his limit of two nights with Martina. Eek! My going anywhere near him was definitely not advisable, any involvement an even worse proposition. I shuddered at the thought. He was not only bad, but trouble, with a capital T. Besides, my brothers would never speak to me again.

Sometime in the early hours of the morning, I went back to bed, Kenneth's voice coming again as I slept. "Don't be a wuss! You never listen to your brothers anyway. Don't you think you've kept the man waiting long enough for his witch?"

I couldn't believe what I was hearing, shouting out "Piss off!"

He laughed.

Waking up, I rolled over to bury my face in the pillow.

My reclusive life continued with me baulking even more against the pressures to socialise, any necessary outings such as grocery shopping or the like done with a vigilant eye open for trouble, namely in the form of a certain local bad lad. Really couldn't be bothered with the hassle.

It was Wendy who got me out there, meeting her quite by accident in town one day after work, she decided it was high time we got together for a girly outing and suggested a Friday night dinner and movie. My family not being involved was the primary reason I agreed and was rather looking forward to it.

Town was humming that night, with parking at a premium. Eventually finding a car park two blocks over from the movie theatre, I walked in to meet Wendy at a nearby bistro where we both had a light dinner, chicken and fries with salad and a glass of white wine each. The movie was a thriller, fast-paced but with a good dash of romance and humour which I thoroughly enjoyed. We chatted in the movie foyer afterwards for a short while, I thanked her for the evening out, glad I'd made the effort and felt more animated than I had for a long time as we parted ways. Threaded my way a tad cautiously once outside, the streets busier than ever with people clogging up the pavements and late-night bars full to overflowing along the way.

As if on cue, a rowdy pub entrance door burst open as I drew level. Someone hurtled out backwards, lost his footing, and fell flat on his back on the pavement right at my feet.

I didn't even flinch, merely stopping dead to look down at him. He grunted something rude before promptly rolling over onto his hands and knees, staggered up and planted his feet wide. Shaking his head like a wounded bull, he took a long, wobbling step sideways and collided with me. I let out an involuntary squeak on impact but surprisingly did hold my ground, at which point he turned his head to eyeball me, focused somehow, and although obviously very drunk, his powers of recognition were still functioning.

"Well, well," Douglas drawled, grinning like a buffoon. "It's the...witch."

"I think you need to go home," I told him coolly.

Three men simultaneously appeared at the pub entrance, the burliest and probably a bouncer shouting. "Stay outside, Willard! You're not welcome!"

Douglas curled his lip in the pub's direction, stabbing a one fingered salute as he shouted back. "Cowards! The lot of ya!"

One of the other men behind the bouncer raised his fists in retaliation and stepped forward but was pulled back.

"Come on," I said to Douglas, tapping his arm. "I'll take you home."

"Eh?" Squinting at me, he lurched backwards a step "Tis...not home time yet."

I frowned into his face. "You've had too much to drink."

He shook his head. "Never...too much!"

I grabbed his arm as he staggered and almost fell, but he managed to stay upright swaying on his feet. Said sharply. "You're drunk!"

"Nah." He laughed, a low rumble. "I'm pissed."

"Whatever." I stared into glazed blue eyes. "Did you drive here?"

"Yep." He pointed vaguely at the sky. "The ute…tis over there."

"Right. Well, you're not driving it."

"Why not?" He went cross eyed. "I can drive, I am…good driver."

"I'm sure you are most of the time," I told him amicably. "But not now."

He lurched again, spreading his feet. "Why…why not now?"

"Because," I said authoritatively. "I'm driving."

"You are?" He blinked owlishly, grinning. "That's nice."

I nodded, adding under my breath. "No, it's not nice, but I think I can handle it."

"Handle what?" His hearing obviously wasn't quite that impaired.

Whipping his head back towards the pub, he lost his balance. I took his weight with my shoulder somehow and once his feet were back under, he straightened up thankfully.

"Would you like a hand, lady?" The bouncer came towards me.

"Piss off!" Douglas glowered, raising a fist at him.

I shook my head, smiled thinly at the bouncer and tucking a determined arm through Douglas's, said, "Thank you, but we'll manage."

"Yeah!" Douglas growled. "Piss off! Th…thank you."

"Come on." Pulling him along, we began weaving our way down the street.

"Hey, witch." He turned his head, eyes glued on me. "Where…are we going?"

"I'm taking you home."

"On a broom…stick." He began to laugh, doubled over and nearly fell over.

I hung on to him. "Watch where you're walking."

"Ra…rather…watch you." He lurched into me. "Witch."

"Be careful!" I warned, pulling him away from the curb. "Not far now."

"This is nice, eh?" He chortled as we bumped into each other. "Ro…romantic like."

I thought it best not to comment, very aware of his body against mine as we continued on our erratic way and more than grateful when my car came into view.

"Let's get you in." I pulled my arm out from his, propping him against the car before opening the passenger door.

"Not the ute," he complained.

"Sorry, but this will have to do. We'll pick the ute up later."

"Later?"

"Yes, if you remember where it is?"

"Hey, I remem…re…" he mumbled, pointing vaguely. "It's over there."

"Okay, later." I grasped his arm again. "Come on, get in."

He tottered from off the car, rocking on his heels. Planting my feet, I tried holding him upright as he sidled and grabbed the open door. He lost his balance and grip as it moved, whacked his head on the pillar and sprawled across the seat, bellowing something rude.

I quickly bent forward into the car, frowning concern at his screwed shut eyes. "Are you okay?"

The said eyes popped open and went wide, ogling my front. Although my top wasn't especially low cut, me leaning in gave him an ample view.

"Wow!" He beamed a cheerfully lecherous grin. "I like…wit…witchy ones!"

His hair was longer than he usually wore it, my fingers managing to grasp a handful but yanking his head back didn't stop him grinning. Curbing the urge to slap him, I gave him my best scowl. "Get your legs in the car and buckle up."

"Wit…witchy…you're very…beautiful," he murmured, reaching a hand to my face. Knocking it away, I gave his thigh a good thump before stepping back.

"Ow!" he protested but did what he was told, pulling his legs up and in.

Slammed the door and stalked to the driver's side, getting in to watch him fumble the seatbelt. As I leant across to fasten it for him with an exasperated sigh, his hand moved again to my face, fingertips touching on my cheek.

I jerked away, glowering. "Keep your hands to yourself!"

He dropped his lower lip. "Aw, why?"

"Don't harass the driver." I yanked on my seatbelt. "And shut up."

"Grumpy!"

"Yes, I am grumpy." I snapped, starting the engine. "So be very careful."

That simply served to make him crack up laughing and was still hiccupping when I reached his driveway. Stopping the car, I gave him a baleful look before getting out to open the gate and as I slid back in, he was attempting to undo his seatbelt.

"Stay there," I told him, putting the car in gear. "I'll take you to your door."

"Should have op…opened…the gate for you," he mumbled.

"Such a gentleman." I rolled my eyes.

"I can be a gen…gentle…man."

Drove on to the shed without comment, a sensor light switching on as I parked. Before I could help him, he had his seatbelt unfastened and the door swinging open. Almost toppled out as I reached the passenger side but hoisted himself upright on the door jamb with a grunt before staggering towards the shed.

"I hope you have a key." I said following him.

Stood back to watch as he propped his shoulder against the utility door, fished in his jacket pocket and pulled out keys which he promptly dropped. He grunted again, bent down to retrieve them and teetered.

Thinking he was going to fall flat on his face, I leapt forward with a shout. "Wait!" He kept his balance however, swayed and lifting his head, stared at me cross eyed.

"Stay there! I'll get them." I told him, picked up the keys to dangle them in front of his nose. "Which one is it?"

"The…the blue one."

I found the key, the door swinging inwards with ease as it unlocked. Moving aside to let him past, he fumbled along the inside wall and turned on the downstairs lights but overbalanced as he stepped forward, hitting the wall hard with an elbow. His few choice words had me raising my eyebrows.

Blowing out my cheeks, I took his arm and helped him through into the kitchen/sitting room. He made it to the dining table, bent over it and slapping his hands flat on top propped himself there, muttering. I let him go to look around, noting another inside wall with a door standing ajar. Wrinkled a suitably unimpressed nose at the girly calendar attached to it, a brunette posing naked full frontal with over-sized boobs.

I curled my lip. Men! Dream on, pal, those are not real!

"I'm not taking you upstairs." I glanced at him. "You'll have to stay down here."

"Don't live upstairs any more." His eyes were screwed shut.

"Where do you sleep, now then?"

"There." He opened his eyes to look past me.

Turning back to the calendar's door, I walked over to peer inside and saw the double bed. "What about your mates? Doesn't Poke stay here too?"

"No one else lives here now." He straightened off the table. "Except me."

That was a relief; meeting one of his mates wasn't something I relished. "Okay. Let's get you to bed, then." I flapped a hand at the bedroom.

His eyes lit up. "Are you…gonna…come to bed too?"

"No!" I gave him an artic look. "Go in there, lie down and get over it."

"Aw." He rounded soulful eyes. "Why don't you stay…with me?"

"In your dreams." I scowled. "Hurry up."

Grinning stupidly, he lurched closer. "I dream…about you…lots."

"I really do feel sorry for you!" I rolled my eyes, making sure to keep my distance as he approached. "Come on! I haven't got all night."

"Wanna…know…about my dreams?" He stopped to stand swaying.

"Never!" I snapped, jabbing a finger into the bedroom.

Taking several lumbering steps past me, he grabbed for the door jamb but my gentle push from behind had him staggering further. He landed face first and almost dead centre on the bed. Watching his shoulders start to heave, I shook my head in annoyed exasperation as he rolled over onto his back, wheezing with laughter. Lifting his head to look at me, he gulped the laughter to a spluttering stop.

Reached a hand to me. "Hey, sorry about…"

I shook my head. "Go to sleep."

"About your boy…boyfriend," he mumbled. "Should have said so…before."

"Forget it!" I was brusque, in no mood to talk of Kenneth.

"Real sorry, sorry…you know."

I said nothing.

He stared at me, blinking a few times before finally shutting his eyes. Began to snore, little grunts. Stifling a laugh, I leant closer to prod and shake his leg, but he didn't wake. Pulled his boots off, covered him with a blanket and shut the door behind me.

Shook my head with a sigh, spying the kettle and debating whether to have a coffee. Having heard stories about drunk people getting into difficulties alone, I thought it best to at least keep an eye on him for a while. That was my excuse anyway.

While the kettle boiled, I drew the window curtains, feeling somehow safer that way. Knowing Trojan wouldn't mind a night on his own sleeping off his dinner, I reluctantly decided, for Douglas's sake of course, that staying over was a better option and with that sorted, went outside quickly to shut the gate, got my bag out of the car before locking it and once back inside checked the shed was also well and truly bolted.

Curled up on the ancient but rather comfortable sofa to drink my coffee, returning to the bedroom after finishing it to find him exactly as I'd left him.

Needing to use the loo, I located it below the shed stairs which had me glancing upwards, grimacing at distasteful memories and wondering where the steel stool was. Pushed the toilet door open tentatively, ready to hold my nose but the cleanliness surprised me, only the calendar inside the door of another naked female posing suggestively had me wrinkling my nose. Washed my hands in the also clean freshly smelling bathroom, pulling a face in the mirror before returning to the sofa, dozing fitfully with one ear tuned to the bedroom.

Woking early, I sat up with a yawn. Let out an almighty shriek, leaping to my feet at the sight of him propped in the bedroom doorway. He looked big, bad and belligerent and was eying me like he'd just spotted an undesirable alien.

"You stayed?" he growled.

"Um, well, yes." Keep it cool whatever you do. I tried a shrug. "Er, thought I should."

"Why did you think you should?" He rubbed his forehead.

"Well, they say drunk people shouldn't be left alone."

"Drunk people?"

"You were. Er, last night."

"Why?" He ran a hand along his stubbly jaw to his neck, frowning.

I gave him a stupid look. "How should I know why you got drunk."

"No!" he snarled. "I meant, why did you think you should stay?"

"I just told you why." Picking up my bag quickly, I began edging to the outer door. "I wouldn't leave anyone alone in that state."

"Wouldn't you?" He stepped forward.

"No!" I was almost at the door. "You're obviously okay now. I'll be on my way."

"What's the hurry?" He tilted his head, promptly screwing his eyes shut.

"You have a hangover." I pointed out kindly.

He squinted at me. "I don't get hangovers."

"A headache, then," I smiled sympathetically. "I have some painkillers if you like."

"Don't get headaches either." He puffed out his cheeks.

"Er, well, you're grumpy." I cocked an offended eyebrow. "Are you feeling sick?"

He gave me a deadly look. "No!"

"Do you need to use the loo?" I stepped aside to wave in that direction, adding at his questioning scowl. "Er, to vomit like."

"I don't vomit," he snarled. "I need a drink."

"Water?" I gestured to the kitchen bench. "Tea, coffee?"

"Piss off!"

"See, you are grumpy!" I said indignantly.

He didn't say anything, merely staring at me with his ice-cold killer eyes.

"Okay, okay!" I spread my hands. "I'm going. Do you need your ute picked up?"

"I can sort that out myself," he muttered.

"Fine. Have a good day," I said snootily, leaving the room.

As I reached the shed door, he spoke from behind me. "Sorry for being grumpy."

I turned to look at him framed in the living area doorway but kept silent.

"And thanks for driving me home and all that." His voice rasped. "Nice of you to bother."

I have no idea what made me do it, but I walked back to him and gave his cheek a quick light kiss, his stubble making my lips tingle.

"You're welcome. Take care." Stepping back, I turned quickly to unbolt the door.

"What was that for?" he asked, sounding bemused.

I stopped to look back, smiling slyly at his frown. "You wanted a kiss, didn't you?"

Once in the relative safety of my car, I waited and sure enough he appeared to lean his shoulder against the jamb arms folded with no familiar grin in evidence. Half expecting him to follow, I quickly exited my car at the gate to unfasten it, but he hadn't moved, making no response to my cheeky wave either as I got back in and drove away.

Uh-oh! Methinks you shouldn't have done that. The kiss, that was. A giggle escaped. At least I didn't hurt him!

Feeling strangely pleased with myself, I couldn't wipe the permanent smirk off my face, thinking how my buoyant mood after last night at the movies was nothing compared to the fizz inside me now. Got a huge welcome from Trojan, promised him a walk and after pulling on trackpants and sweater took him down to the beach, releasing some of my own pent-up energy.

Chapter 23

Still feeling more alive than I had for a long time, I went along to a car race meeting at Dad's invitation. It was also a perfect opportunity to formally introduce Wendy to my brothers; if Matthew didn't bite, there was always Daniel. Personally, I didn't think they'd be able to resist; Wendy was not only pretty with a bob of fair curls and friendly hazel eyes, but smart with a great sense of humour.

She wasn't as enthusiastic as I expected, however, but after some persuading, she accepted my offer to take her there and back. Noticing she wasn't her usual perky self on the drive over, it suddenly dawned on me that she was more than a little nervous judging by her finger tapping, and the fact that my sibling had something to do with it surprised me.

Dad welcomed her into the pits, and while introducing everyone, I saw Matthew giving her a quick up and down, but apart from a polite hello, he said no more, his concentration promptly switching back to racing mode. Daniel, in contrast, was cheerful and friendly, taking the time to speak with Wendy but although she seemed totally at ease with him, I read the signs and knew for sure that he wasn't the brother of interest.

Trickier, I thought. Matthew most likely knew Wendy was Martina's friend and would be understandably wary but if I enlisted some help anything was possible, a little word in Dad's ear between pitstops being my first option.

Matthew drove the last stint, rewarding the team with an impressive second placing and during the prize presentations caterers began getting food and drinks ready for the after-race function, the driver's and crew disappearing to clean themselves up.

I could tell Wendy wanted to leave at that point, her fingers beginning their nervous tapping again and she confirmed it shortly after, whispering in my ear. "I should go. I'm really not part of this."

"Yes, you are," I was suitably serious. "You're here with me, with our family."

She seemed at a loss. "But..."

"No, buts," I told her. "You enjoyed the day, didn't you?"

"Yes, it was great, but…"

"So, let's enjoy the wind down too."

"Oh, all right." She heaved a breath. "If, you're sure."

When Matthew returned from a shower at the apartment with his hair slick to his head, I had to admit even from a sister's point of view that he looked rather cute, certainly hunky enough to make girls ogle which Wendy was certainly doing and I wasn't the only one who noticed, grinning when Dad caught my eye. Thanks to his deft but subtle manoeuvring Matthew spent a fair amount of the evening in her company and seeing them getting on rather well, made me jump for joy, discreetly.

At the farm some weeks later while having a coffee with Dad, he told me the good news, Matthew was officially dating Wendy.

"That's so cool." I jumped for joy again. "She's such a sweet person."

"I totally agree," he nodded. "Your matchmaking skills are to be commended my girl."

I laughed. "So are yours!"

"Maybe we should try using them on your other brother as well."

"Now there's a thought. I'll keep my eyes peeled for a nice lady."

Dad pulled a wry face. "Don't somehow think he'll be so easy to please."

"I guess not." I screwed up my nose. "He likes variety, that boy."

"So, I've heard." Dad pursed his lips. "He needs to watch himself, seems us Von Meeren boys can get into trouble these days."

"Shotgun wedding, you reckon?"

Dad snorted a laugh. "Hmmm, there is that."

"Well, I suppose that's one way of sorting him out," I smirked. "We won't need to use any matchmaking skills then, will we?"

"Ha! No sympathy, eh?" Dad returned my grin. "Spoken like a true sister."

I sniggered. "As long as she's got legs all the way up, passes in the looks department and has a brain, he won't mind, I'm sure."

We both laughed until he sobered up to give me a thoughtful look. "And how are you getting on?"

"Me?" I said cheerfully. "I'm good."

"I've noticed you seem happier lately."

"I suppose I am."

"Is there someone else?"

I hid my surprise at the direct question, said too quickly. "No."

His look sharpened. "Sorry, I shouldn't have asked."

I took his hand. "You can ask me whatever you like, but there isn't anyone else."

His direct look made my nerves twitch. "It's just something Anna said."

I raised my eyebrows. "About history repeating itself, you mean?"

"Not only that. She mentioned another man, someone like my father."

"Really?" I pretended ignorance.

His eyes held mine. "A bad boy, she called him."

"There could never be another bad boy like your father, surely?" I forced a laugh.

"Well, there's definitely another girl very much like my mother," he said softly. "I know that much."

I stared at him without replying.

"Look, I just want you to know that whatever happens I'm here for you," His smile was gently reassuring. "If you ever find yourself another man, bad boy or not, that's okay."

I gave a little nod. "Thanks, Dad."

He hadn't finished. "You made your peace with that Willard lad Daniel told me."

What else did he know? I blinked. "Um, yes. We've talked." Added a lie. "But I haven't seen him for ages."

He nodded. "Well, I'm glad you sorted things out."

Leaving soon after, I felt annoyed with myself for keeping secrets from Dad. Knowing other people had witnessed me and Douglas together that night, it was only a matter of time before someone mentioned it. I had no qualms about what I'd done but the fact that my family would find out from someone other than myself or through gossip made me cringe.

And I'd do it all over again at the drop of a hat! The sudden thought shocked me. The bad boy, indeed! Was this new happiness really because of him? Had my Oma felt like this too, the same way about Bernard? History repeating? Oh great! What am I supposed to do now?

That night Kenneth came to me again in a dream; he and I were standing side by side on the cabin deck watching the sunset but not touching. The shadowy figure of a man with his face hidden appeared at the top of the beach steps and beckoned to me, but I shook my head and turning to Kenneth found him no longer there.

All I heard was his voice. "Do something about it, beautiful."

I looked again at the faceless figure, recognised the skull tattoos on one exposed arm and called out as he turned to walk away, but he didn't heed. There was no sign of anyone by the time I got to the beach steps. Came awake in bed, staring into the dark.

I stewed about Douglas all week, made plans and unmade plans. Got home after work on Friday, took a long shower after walking Trojan and braced myself to ring the sawmill.

Recognised the grumpy man's voice. "Hello, Sawmill office."

"Hello," I disguised mine, asking primly. "Is Mr Willard there, please?"

"Nope. He's gone for the day, left about half an hour ago."

"He's not working night shift then?" I probed.

"Nope. Not for two weeks."

"Thank you," I said politely and disconnected.

Felt a sudden sense of urgency, quickly pulling on a jacket and boots over my leggings and t-shirt. Left a meaty bite for Trojan, jumped in my car and tore off towards Douglas's place. At the entrance to his driveway, I stood on the brakes hard with hands clenching the steering wheel staring stupidly at the shut gate.

Leaning forward with my face almost touching the windscreen, I peered at the shed, but there was no sign of his vehicle. The place looked deserted. Blew out a despondent breath. It seemed I was too late; he was probably already out pubbing or maybe he hadn't even bothered coming home first. Crawling through town trying to find him wasn't an option, doubted he'd appreciate my help again anyway. Wished I could at least phone him, but it had been my decision not to exchange numbers. Silly me!

Thinking that the nosey neighbours would be wondering what I was parked there for, I was just about to reverse when a vehicle approached, pulling up behind mine. My heart did an almighty flip. Recognised whose it was in my rear-view mirror.

Douglas got out and approached as I wound down my window. My first thought was that his hair had grown even more since I'd last seen him, no longer shaved to his skull and surprisingly there were curls.

"Well, hello witch," he said, grin fading at my wordless stare.

"Something wrong?"

"No." I took a breath. "I like your hair longer. It suits you."

He gave me a strange look, eyebrows lifting. "You came to tell me that?"

"No."

"So, what are you doing here?"

I swallowed. "Um, er. I wanted to stop you going out."

Narrowed his eyes but didn't speak. For some weird reason I suddenly felt like laughing, clapping a hand to my mouth as a giggle escaped. His eyebrows lifted again, higher. Oh, great! He probably thinks you've gone mad.

Bending closer, he placed his hands on the door sill, asking softly. "Why?"

"You drink and fight too much."

His lips twisted. "You reckon?"

"I've heard stories!" I blurted. "And you were very drunk last time I saw you."

"So, how were you going to stop me?"

"Um." I shook my head. "I don't know."

He snorted a laugh. "Have you had dinner?"

"No."

"Do you like Thai food?"

"Yes."

"Bought some takeaways." He gestured to his ute. "There's heaps. Want to share?"

I made a feeble hand gesture. "Oh, it's okay. I didn't mean to…um…intrude."

"You're already parked on my driveway, witch," he grinned. "Come in and have dinner with me. Keep a poor lonely fella company."

At my suspicious look, his grin widened.

Pushing himself away from my car, he went to open the gate, and with an exaggerated bow and welcoming sweep of his arm, he gestured for me to drive in. I drove in. We both parked in front of the shed, but I waited in my car with the first stirrings of trepidation as he alighted from his. He sauntered to the door with his bag of takeaways, unlocked it and turned to look at me. Forced myself to move, getting with a thudding heart.

Oh blast! I bit my lip. This is not what I planned. Chasing him around the pubs in town suddenly seemed a whole lot less dangerous somehow.

Inside things were the same as I remembered except the calendar had changed months, the naked female a blonde this time with a suggestive pout and pose that made me distinctly uncomfortable. Turning my back on her, I watched him put plates and cutlery on the table.

"Sit down. Make yourself at home." He gestured to a chair. "A drink? I have wine."

"Just a small glass, thanks."

"White or red?"

"White, please." I sat down.

He poured a wine for both of us, sat down opposite and as he took the lids of two takeaway containers of Thai food my eyes went wide with a gasp.

"Wow. That's a lot of food. You'd eat all that by yourself?"

"I'm a hungry boy." He chuckled at my look. "I usually keep some for the next day."

"Oh, right."

"Eat up," he said, handing me a spoon to dish up with.

The tingle as our fingers touched was unexpected, something similar to what his stubble had given my lips the day I'd kissed him. Deciding it best to ignore it, I filled up my plate. The food was as delicious as it smelt, both of us tucking in without speaking until he put down his fork to take a swallow of wine and said with laughing eyes. "Isn't this nice?"

"The food is very nice." I deliberately misunderstood him.

"Yeah," he murmured. "And so is the company."

I eyed him with a pout. "I have my nice moments."

"Isn't the overgrown numbskull arsehole lucky then, catching you at a nice moment?"

"Did you have to remind me about that?" I protested. "I wasn't very happy at the time, you know!"

"No, shit!" he chuckled. "I wasn't very happy either, witch."

"I wish you wouldn't call me that." I gave him an icy stare.

"Witch?" he smirked. "It suits you."

"Like you suit..." I shut up to continue eating.

"Overgrown numbskull arsehole?" he queried softly.

"Just arsehole will do," I said with my mouth full.

He laughed, picked up his fork and began eating again too.

When I finished my plate and picked up my wine, he offered me more, but I shook my head. "That was delicious but I'm full. Thank you."

As I finished my glass, he picked up the bottle. "More wine?"

"No, thanks," I said. "I have to drive home."

"What's at home?" His eyes held mine.

An unfamiliar feeling made itself known; a quiver deep inside that made my pulse react. I wasn't sure that I liked it. Hearing alarm bells sounding, I didn't answer.

"What did you really come here for?" He lifted an eyebrow.

I simply stared, nerves beginning to stretch.

His lips twisted. "Did you want a comfort bonk?"

"Excuse me?" I gawped.

"Don't worry, I understand." He shrugged. "You're feeling lonely without him."

I leapt to my feet, sending the chair screeching across the floor. "How dare you?"

He remained seated, unperturbed. "I have my uses. It's okay."

I didn't remember reaching for it, but the wine bottle was suddenly in my hand. Threw it at him. Heard him grunt when it connected, wasn't sure exactly where because I was already on my way out, snatching up my bag and diving for the sitting room door. It crashed shut behind me. At the shed door I fumbled desperately with the bolt and just as he emerged, it opened. He yelled something. It didn't sound friendly.

Outside I bolted for my car, scrambling inside to lock the doors. My hand shook so much I could hardly get the key in the ignition. Let out a shriek of fright when his face appeared at the side window, shrieked again as he pounded a fist on it. As the engine fired, I slammed the car into reverse and jabbed the accelerator hard, wheels spinning as the car shot backwards. Hit the brakes, crunched first gear and saw him, no longer beside the car but in front, his face contorted and angry. As I gunned the motor, he leapt sideways, arms akimbo. Felt something thud but didn't stop, raced down the driveway and thanking my lucky stars the gate was open hurtled onto the road, tyres whining on the tarmac as I floored it.

It took me a while to resume some sort of control, realised there was no one following and eased off although my body still trembled when I got home. Trojan seemed to know something was up, sticking close and nudging me with his nose.

"It's okay, boy," I whimpered. "I've just gone and done something dumb."

I stood at the kitchen bench with my hands clenched remembering. Had I hit him? Oh no! He could be lying there injured. Serves him right! How dare he say things like that, how could he even think I'd want to bonk him. Ah, but you do, don't you?

"What?" I said out loud, utterly shocked at the thought. "No way! I don't!"

Shook my head at Trojan's worried eyes, gave his ears a reassuring ruffle and said on a breath. "Don't mind me."

Turned the kettle on to boil, got out a mug and scooped in heaps of chocolate. Tried to blank out my thoughts but my brain hadn't finished with me yet.

Oh, come on! Maybe it isn't exactly a comfort bonk you want, but you do want him! Are you mad? I will never get involved with Douglas Willard, especially not like that. Ever! Like I said before, he's bad and trouble. I don't need him in my life. So why are you hanging around him? I was trying to be nice! Ha! That's just an excuse. You said so yourself, he's improved since school days. As in improved into a sexy hunk. Don't even think about denying it! And remember what Kenneth's been telling you. Time to move on and this bad lad will surely help you with that. Big time!

"Piss off!" I snapped, hurriedly pouring the water for my hot chocolate and yipping when it splashed over my fingers. "Ouch!"

Whether my brain had lost its marbles or not wasn't relevant right now. The thought of what could happen next worried me a great deal more. I couldn't imagine Douglas would let me get away with doing damage a third time.

Oh, dear me. How exciting! Terrifying more like!

Chapter 24

Going into town to shop or do errands became exhausting, keeping a wary eye open for Douglas had me on tenterhooks. Manged to hide my agitation from family but was sure my four-footed friends noticed.

"What is wrong with her lately?" BB asked Delta.

"How would I know?" Delta shook her head.

"Doesn't she talk to you on your rides?"

"Not really. She doesn't even mutter to herself much lately, keeps it bottled up."

"Humans are not good bottled up," Kingston pointed out.

"Agreed," BB nodded. "I'd rather their fuses were out in the open."

Delta was thinking long and hard. "She's not sad any more, though. And I don't think this has anything to do with her man dying."

"You don't think?" Kingston eyed her.

"She's different. Hyped up now, not down in the dumps like before."

"Ah!" BB's eyes lit up. "Maybe she's over him and on to another."

"But I haven't seen another!" Delta frowned.

"Females are all the same," Kingston scoffed. "You think it's always about males."

"Well, that's where the trouble usually starts." BB shot him a knowing look.

"Kate's in trouble?"

"Well, she's not acting normal, is she?" BB gave him a scornful look.

"No, she's not," Delta agreed. "But if there's another man. Who is he?"

"Maybe he's a secret," BB suggested slyly.

"That's even worse than bottled up." Kingston shook his head.

"Let's keep our ears and eyes peeled," Delta grinned. "You know, this could be fun."

"Woohoo!" BB grinned back. "I like fun."

"Females!" Kingston turned his back on them both in disgust.

"Aw, Kingston," Delta spoke to his rump. "Come and join us. You're good at solving mysteries."

"Me?" Kingston rolled a bewildered eye back to her.

"Yes, you. Daniel's friend. If anyone knows what's she's up to it'll be her brother."

"She's right. He talks to you all the time." BB nodded. "I could give Bella a prod too, she knows lots of things. And Delta, how about you try talking to Kate's doggy friend?"

"He doesn't trust me or any other horse," Delta heaved a sigh, giving Kingston a pained look. "Not since a certain someone chased him around the paddock."

"I was just letting off steam," Kingston protested. "Besides he got the wrong idea, I wasn't chasing him, he just ran in the same direction."

"Whatever!"

"Maybe he'll come round," BB told Delta. "Dogs are usually friendly."

"True. I'll give it a whirl."

"We are the three musketeers and on the case!" BB bounced around excitedly.

"Oh, what fun!" Kingston was scornful.

She eyeballed him with a scowl, but ignoring her he sauntered away to a clump of juicy grass. Delta watched him for a moment before turning to BB with a shrug. "Don't worry. We'll sort it out, us females always do."

"Do you think Kate's in some other kind of trouble?" BB frowned her concern.

"I don't think so. Whatever it is she's more excited than worried."

"It's got to be a man then. What else would she get excited about."

"I can't wait to find out."

Delta was eyeballing Trojan more often lately I noticed. The poor dog wasn't sure what to make of it, keeping his distance with ears pinned back and tail down.

"It's okay, boy," I reassured him. "She won't chase you; she's just being friendly."

Trojan wasn't convinced, however, and while brushing Delta down after a good long ride, he kept his distance, staying out of the yard to watch us through the railings. Delta dropped her head to him, blowing softly through her nostrils, but as he backed away, looking worried, I had to chuckle, giving her neck a rub.

"Why so interested in Trojan lately, girl?"

Sighing she rolled an eye my way, giving me a long unblinking stare.

"What?" I slanted my head. "You're thinking about something, aren't you?"

She blew softly again, nodding her head.

"You'll have to excuse me, girl," I murmured. "I'm just a dumb human."

Certain Delta was trying to communicate something to me, I decided to have a chat to Bella or Daniel and see if they understood.

"She's probably just picking up on your vibes," Bella said when I asked her.

"My vibes?"

"Are you feeling different?"

"Um, no. Not really," I lied.

"You know horses notice the slightest difference." Bella cocked an eyebrow. "I must say you seem quite chirpy lately."

"Ha! Funny you should say that. Dad said the same."

"So, there you are. Delta's noticed as well."

"You think that's all it is?"

"Most likely."

What else was everyone noticing, I wondered. How long before the truth comes out about the other man? There is no other man! Yes, there is, the bad boy, remember.

"Are you okay?" Bella was frowning at me.

Rubbing my forehead, I told another lie. "I've had a headache since I woke up."

"There's Panadol or Aspirin inside. Do you want some?"

"No, it's okay. It's not that bad."

The following week, while doing my grocery shopping, I left the store with a half-full trolley and kept eyeing my purchases, thinking I'd forgotten something. Was almost at my car when I finally looked up. Stopped dead in my tracks with a horrified gasp.

He was leaning nonchalantly against my driver's door, with an evil smile on his face. Apart from that, he looked good, wearing a long-sleeved checked blue and white shirt, black jeans, and boots, with his hair having grown since last time, curling over his collar.

"What are you doing here?" I croaked, keeping my trolley between me and him.

"Waiting for you," he drawled. "Witch."

"What do you want?"

"Now, let me see." He slanted a sardonic eyebrow. "Revenge for starters, maybe."

"Revenge?" I gulped.

"You nearly killed me." He sounded surprisingly calm.

"I did not!"

"You ran me over."

I gulped again. "I didn't think I touched you."

"You didn't stop to check."

"You shouldn't stand in front of moving vehicles."

As he straightened off my car, I gripped the trolley handle tighter.

He grinned. "What are you going to do, run me over with the trolley now?"

"Maybe!" Unamused, I glowered.

"Well, go on." He extended his arms to me, crooking his fingers. "Try it."

I looked him up and down, "I don't believe I hit you. You don't look hurt."

"Want me to show you the damage?"

I lifted my chin defiantly but when he lifted his shirt to expose the ugly purpling bruise across his abdomen and hip my jaw dropped in shock. Turning away abruptly, I felt the ground shift. Thought I was going to be sick.

"Hey!" His voice sounded weirdly distant.

Felt his arm slide around my waist for support, closed my eyes, and willed myself back under control. The awful clammy feeling dissipated, became aware I was leaning against him and straightened up, but his arm stayed where it was. As the fingers of his other hand tilted my chin, I looked into hot blue eyes. Another shock to the system.

"Are you okay?" he asked softly, dropping his hand.

I think I nodded, tried to say something but no sound emerged.

"Where are your keys?" he asked.

Managed to pull them out a pocket with a shaking hand. He took them, walked me to the jeep still supported by his arm and unlocked the driver's door. After clambering in, I sank back into the seat as he dropped the keys in my lap.

"Stay there," he said.

Moved to the rear door, and after stowing my groceries, he took the trolley to a storage bay nearby before coming back. I hadn't moved, still felt a little queasy. He propped his butt against the car's side pillar beside me, crossed his arms, and waited. Leaning sideways, I angled my head to look up at him, but his eyes were on something distant, as if deep in thought.

"I'm sorry," I muttered.

"Don't stress about it," he said without looking at me. "I'm not that easy to kill."

"It's not funny!" I protested. "I really didn't think I'd touched you."

He looked at me then, mouth twisting. "You don't touch, witch. You do damage."

"I'm sorry. Are you okay?"

"Just another bruise. I've had worse." He grinned. "As you know."

"Did you go to a doctor."

"What for?" he shrugged.

"Internal injuries." I was appalled at his blasé attitude.

"Everything's working. I can eat, piss and shit so it's all good."

"Oh, please!" I squeaked, horrified.

He straightened off the car and turned to me, leaning in. "Are you feeling better?"

"I'm fine." I tensed at his nearness, forcing a thin-lipped smile. "I don't usually react like that, being a vet nurse and all."

He didn't seem to notice my reaction. "Are you okay to drive?"

"Yes. I think so." I broke eye contact, fiddling with my keys.

"Good. Now, how about giving me your phone number."

"What?" Jerked my head up. "Why would you want my phone number?"

"No harm being nice again, eh?" He removed his phone from a pocket, adding with a malicious grin. "Besides you owe me dinner."

I gave him a disbelieving look. "You must be crazy."

"Yep." He agreed amicably, handing me his phone with contact screen at the ready, my fingers tingling as we touched. Blowing out my cheeks, I reluctantly tapped in my details, attempting not to touch him again as I returned his phone, which didn't work. Got another dose of tingle. Yikes! What was that all about lately? Me snatching my hand back made him chuckle.

Phone back in his pocket he waited. "Where's yours?"

"What?"
"Your phone. I'll give you, my number."
"I'm not crazy."
"How about being nice?"
"Why are you so persistent?"
"Because I'm crazy," he smirked. "About a witch."

I shot him an exasperated up from under look, extracted my phone against my better judgement and gave it to him. He entered his details, deliberately touched my fingers when he handed it back and laughed when I scowled.

"I have to go," I said snootily, reaching past him for the door handle.

He moved out of the way obligingly, said before I shut the door, "Careful how you drive. Don't kill anyone on the way now, will you?"

Refusing to look at him again, I reversed out of the carpark and back home Trojan listened politely to my mutterings

My phone rang on the following Thursday evening, heart leaping to the throat as Douglas's name appeared. I didn't pick up.

A text came through soon after: **How about dinner? Friday night.**

I sat down with a thud, heart tripping over itself but again didn't answer.

Another text followed: **Don't ignore me, witch.**

My fingers trembled, making tapping an answer difficult: **I don't want to have dinner with you. Please leave me alone.**

Had a bad day?

No.

Friday night will cheer you up.

No.

Bring takeaways. I eat anything. Same time, same place.

What part of NO don't you understand?

Just dinner. Am still hurting, not bonking yet.

As I burst into hysterical giggles, Trojan grinned and wagged his tail vigorously.

I replied with tears of laughter rolling down my cheeks: **You are an idiot.**

Better than an arsehole?

Chinese or pizza.

You choose.

Friday night had my nerves screaming, wondering what on earth I was letting myself in for. Wore black leggings, knee high boots and a long green sweater that covered pretty much everything; nothing to attract his attention I hoped. Bought two dishes of Chinese food and a bottle of white wine.

The gate was open when I got there, his ute parked by the shed. He must have heard my car because he opened the door almost before I got out, watching me approach with an enigmatic little smile on his lips. Not his usual grin which worried me.

It seemed I had nothing to worry about, however, as he behaved. We ate our food with a glass of white wine each, enjoyed both and talked about everything under the sun. Except for bonking, that was. It didn't stop me thinking about it though.

Several times during the evening, he got up, which gave me ample opportunity to eyeball his delectable backside in faded blue jeans. Wide shoulders, lean hips, cute butt and a bad boy face that wasn't so bad especially now he'd grown his hair. Those riveting eyes of his that caught a girl's attention. Another point to ponder was his mouth, wondered what he could do with it apart from grinning. I watched his hands too, figured the rumours were probably true, fast and capable among other things.

The noting of his assets weren't exactly doing me much good however, the foreign little quiver puzzling. Why was that happening now? Admittedly, I reacted to him, always had and usually on a negative note, but wanting to jump him? Never! What would he do if I did? Hey! He said he was too hurt to bonk remember! Doubted it somehow, pain didn't seem to stop him much. Why was I even thinking this stuff?

I went home in a haze, unable to sleep a wink. There were no dreams of Kenneth, my head was full of a blonde brute of a man instead. Could hardly believe it.

Not having to go to work the following day, I spent all morning trying to motivate myself, glad of the peace and quiet. He didn't get in touch during the weekend, and for that, I was also grateful. When the following week rolled by and then another, I wasn't so thankful any more. The grumpy guy at the sawmill had said something about Douglas being back on night shift in two weeks; figured that was the reason for no contact.

Hoped despairingly that I was right.

Chapter 25

Two weeks later, despair had turned to morbid frustration until the phone rang.

Pulse went berserk at his number, croaked hello.

"Hey, witch." He sounded cheerful. "How's things?"

Managed a cool. "I'm fine, and you?"

"Yeah good, even better now I'm talking to you."

"Oh, really?" I pretended calm. "Is that one of your lines?"

"It's true." He chuckled. "You make me feel a whole lot better."

"I doubt that somehow," I muttered.

"Want me to show you how much?"

I ignored that. "Been working hard, have you?"

"Yep. Been at another sawmill down the line, they needed a hand."

"Oh." Ah! That explained it, not just night shifting but away.

"Sorry, I haven't been in touch. It all got a bit hectic."

"I wasn't really expecting you to call," I lied.

"Why not?"

"Why not what?" I acted dumb.

"Weren't you expecting me to call?"

"Oh, come on," I snorted. "So many girls in your life. Why call me?"

"What girls in my life?"

"I'm not stupid!" I said indignantly. "I don't believe for one second that all the stories are made up."

"What stories?"

I curbed my tongue, asked coldly. "Why are you ringing me?"

"To ask you out."

"Pardon?"

"No takeaways this time. Let's go out somewhere."

"You're asking me out, er, on a date?"

"Yep. Think you can handle it?"

"I don't think I want to."

"Aw, please," he coaxed. "No pub brawls, I promise."

I didn't know what to say, mouth opening and closing like a goldfish. "We've had lunch together before," he said. "That went okay, right?"

"Um," I puffed out my cheeks. "Yes, I suppose."

"So, let's go."

"I'm not sure it's a good idea," I mumbled.

"Please. I'll be a good boy."

"Good boy?" I let out a breathless laugh. "I don't think you know what that means."

"Let me prove you wrong."

I bit my lip, muttered. "Oh, all right."

He laughed. "Don't sound so enthusiastic!"

I sighed. "Do I need to dress up?"

"You're asking me?"

I pulled a face. "I mean, can I wear gumboots?"

"How about jandals and a bikini?"

"I've changed my mind!" I said snootily. "I'm not going out with you."

"Wear whatever you like, witch," he chuckled. "Casual is good."

Dressed in dark grey jeans, purple skivvy, long black boots, and a grey jacket, I drove to his place Friday evening with doubts and nerves going ballistic.

His soft whistle and slow scrutiny of my person didn't help. I did the same to him minus the whistle, deliberately, unsmilingly, and without comment, which made him grin. I wasn't telling him he looked good enough to eat in his black jeans, khaki shirt, black leather jacket and boots.

He drove us to a bar and grill I'd never been to before on the other side of town, a Wild West-themed place with cowboy hats, old guns and horse gear hanging on the walls. When we first walked in, I began to wonder what I'd let myself in for as one of the scantily clothed bar ladies made a beeline for him, cooed his name and reached up to kiss him.

I watched with growing scepticism, beginning to feel decidedly peeved and out of my depth when another waitress batted her eyelashes and patted his backside. There were customers who obviously knew him too, female mostly who all seemed friendly enough towards me when Douglas made the introductions. He ordered us drinks at the rowdy bar to start with, but we moved into the quieter restaurant shortly after.

At the table I eyed him. "See what I mean about the girls? Popular, aren't you?"

He laughed softly. "They're friends."

"Just friends?" I was snide.

He merely smiled and changed the subject. I began to relax thereafter, enjoying his company, conversation, good food and wine. It wasn't especially late when he drove me back to his place, as sober as a judge.

"Coming in for a coffee?" he asked when we got there.

I agreed without a second thought, deciding a hot drink would be a nice way to end the evening. Sat down at the kitchen table to watch more of his butt as he filled the kettle and got out mugs, his hair curling at his collar making me smile.

Turning to say something he caught me looking and my gut reacted to something in his eyes. It wasn't the first time that evening, even his drawl had been enough to make me quiver several times already. Broke eye contact instantly, feeling breathless.

Uh-oh! My nerves began jumping again. Time to go, like right now! Are you sure about that? It hit me right between the eyes at that precise moment. I'm falling for this guy, I thought unbelievably. And trying to halt the fall is going to be well-nigh impossible. Bugger me! What do I do now? Don't act dumb. You know exactly what to do!

As he handed me my coffee, I mumbled thanks but kept my eyes lowered. Could feel him watching as he sat down opposite, the silence almost unbearable.

"So, was I a good boy?" he asked, sounding amused.

I looked up somehow, said coolly. "This time you were."

"There will be a next time, then?" His eyes twinkled.

Tilting my head, I gave him a scornful look but didn't reply.

"There's just something I have to tell you." His voice went low.

I frowned. "What is it?"

"That kiss."

"Kiss?"

"Yeah. The one you gave me last time."

I hoped I appeared a lot calmer than I felt. "What about it?"

"It wasn't what I wanted exactly."

I eyed him suspiciously. "And?"

"Maybe you could try again?"

It really was time to scarper! "In your dreams," I scowled, standing up quickly. "You asked for one and that's all you're getting. Goodbye!"

"You haven't finished your coffee." He spread a hand.

Shaking my head, I moved away from the table towards the door. Walked straight into him. How he moved so fast I had no idea.

Stepped back in a hurry, hissing. "Get out of my way! I'm leaving now!"

He stayed exactly where he was, mouth curved.

I stepped back again, glaring daggers. It didn't make any difference. Slid my eyes away from him, scouting around the room for a weapon.

His smug laugh grated. "No stool or bottle this time, witch."

His sudden move towards me had me bolting to the other end of the table, my boots skidding on the wooden floor. We circled the table. At his next mock lunge, I leapt for the door. Stupid move. He caught hold, hands closing on my arms from behind. Yelping, I went a little crazy, lashing out and trying my utmost to get free.

He yanked me around to face him, my back flat against the door. I wasn't letting up, wrestling frantically, puffing and whimpering while he barely made a sound. Got a hand free to claw at his face viciously, felt his skin under my nails. Heard him growl as he jerked his head away, catching my wrist in a vice like grip.

"You're hurting me," I squeaked.

Letting go instantly, he took two long strides back and away with a snarled. "Shit!"

My eyes went saucer wide at the scratches on his face, from below one eye to halfway down his cheek. Saw his fingers find the wound, smearing blood.

"You're bleeding," I gasped, putting out a hand.

He shook his head, turned abruptly to grab the towel hanging off the oven handle, pressing it to his face as he leant over the sink. I watched him dab, look at the stained red towel and dab again.

"Keep pressing." I heard myself say. "It'll stop the bleeding."

"Piss off!" He snarled without looking at me. "Go on, get out!"

I heaved a shaky breath. "I'm not going anywhere. Here, let me look at that."

"A look?" He shot me a disbelieving glower. "Why not have another go?"

I ignored that. "Do you have a first aid kit?"

"You're not first aiding me!"

"Don't be stupid!" I snapped. "The first aid kit, where is it?"

"In the bathroom."

Sourced it in the basin cupboard, rushed back to the kitchen and opened it on the kitchen table, rummaging through to find what I needed before looking at him. He'd turned to lean back against the sink bench, still scowling with the towel held to his face.

"Sit down," I told him.

He didn't move.

"Sit down," I repeated. "Please."

Muttering something under his breath, he sat down. After finding a porcelain dish in a cupboard, I rinsed it with the kettle's boiled water, filling it with the same. At the table, his baleful stare watched as I spread out paper towels and utensils. That done, I reached to take the towel from him, but he bared his teeth and pulled away. Keeping my hand suspended, I turned it palm up, eyes locked on his.

"I need to clean your face," I said, trying to keep my voice calm. "Scratches can get infected, especially from claws or nails."

"No shit!" he sneered, flinging the towel on the table.

Chewed my lip a moment before peering closer to scrutinise the wound, which had all but stopped bleeding, and began cleaning the nasty-looking scratches gently while he watched me without a word or expression. Concentrating on the task, I muttered sorry several times over and pulled horrified faces at what I'd done, finally dabbing on antiseptic cream and covering the wound with a light dressing. He remained seated as I wrapped the discarded wipes in paper towels, rinsed the dish, and repacked the first aid kit.

"You should be okay," I told him quietly, picking up my bag to leave. "Any pain or swelling, please go to your doctor."

"Why do you do that?" His eyes were narrowed, mouth grim.

"Do what?" I frowned.

"Attack me every time I come near you?"

"Pardon me?" Blinking affront, I squawked. "I do not attack you!"

He frowned. "Thump me, bust my kneecap and jaw, throw things, run me over, scratch my face, what do you call it then?"

"Thump you?"

"You did that at school." His mouth twisted. "You hit harder than your brother."

"Oh!" That took me by surprise. "Well, you deserved it."

"I only hassled you a little."

"Hassled?" I shot back at him. "Bullied, is the word!"

"It wasn't that bad."

"It was so!"

"Whatever you say." His sudden rueful grin was another surprise. "Anyway, all I ever wanted was a kiss. A real kiss."

"Why would I even want to kiss you?"

The grin disappeared as quickly as it came. "Not good enough for you, huh?"

"Don't you dare start that again."

"The witch can't be seen slumming it, can she?"

He had this way of making me react that was certain. Stepped forward abruptly, took his face between both hands with no regard for the dressing and kissed him full on the mouth.

It went from angry, to sexy and then out of control. The quiver curled suddenly deep and sweet, knew right then that I wanted a whole lot more. Took all my willpower to wrench my mouth away, gulping air while staring down at him with huge eyes. Felt a purely female feeling of satisfaction at the poleaxed look on his face.

"I don't always attack," I whispered and fled.

He recovered shockingly fast, catching me before I made it to the sheds outside door. This time he did the kissing and there was no going back. We ended up in the kitchen again, me with my bum on the table and our clothes coming off in a hurry. His hands were everywhere. Found out exactly what he used his mouth for.

Douglas, I soon realised was never going to be a substitute for anything I'd ever known. He was on a totally new level and quite frankly a tad terrifying. For starters I'd never done the tabletop thing before and didn't realise every inch of a bed could be utilised quite like that either. A long time later I lay staring at his bedroom's ceiling. Breathless, boneless and blissfully worn out.

Deciding to be honest, I croaked. "Um, I've never done it that often in one night before."

"Neither have I," he murmured, watching me.

"Really?" I lifted my head a fraction, staring at him in disbelief.

His eyes narrowed. "Yes, really."

I wrinkled my nose. "That's not what I've heard."

"And what have you heard exactly?"

"All night and counting."

He propped himself up on one elbow. "So, where do you get your information?"

"Girls talk."

"Well." He leant closer, face only inches from mine. "They're talking bullshit."

"Are they?"

"What do you think I am, a machine?" We were almost nose to nose.

"Um, no! Machines don't sweat."

He snorted a laugh, sliding a hand along the inside of my thigh.

My breath hitched. "And they don't do that either."

"That?"

"What you're doing right now," I gulped.

"Want to try something else?" he leered.

"Like?"

"Like this?"

"Oh, wow!" My breath snagged as the quiver went ape.

"Let's do wow together, witch," he grinned and shut me up with his mouth.

That was Friday, Saturday we met up again at his place for a repeat session in even more motivated and innovative ways. On Sunday, needing time out to take stock or at least get my breath back, I told him I had things to do and would call him later. I didn't. Moped about the cabin all day instead, reliving our mind-boggling antics and quivering all over again while I was at it. Knew now that the rumour was true; he had fast capable hands, a demanding body that turned a woman wild and a wicked mouth. It was the other rumour that had me despairing; if he sleeps with you more than twice count yourself lucky. Couldn't imagine I'd hold his attention for that long, something painful twisting inside at the thought.

The week dragged by with no word from him.

Confirmation then, I thought despondently. Two nights happened, but they're over and all you're going to get. You're obviously not one of the lucky ones.

Late Sunday morning, I forced myself up out of bed and outside to take Trojan for a walk. On our way back he suddenly took off up the steps from the beach and hearing him bark I followed more quickly. Stopped dead at the cliff top. Heart missed a beat before beginning to race, nothing to do with taking the steps faster than usual.

Douglas was sitting on the deck steps as though he belonged there, ruffling Trojan's ears while watching me. When I didn't move, he got up to approach.

"You didn't call me," he said quietly, halting just out of touching distance.

I looked down at the ground. "I didn't think you were interested."

"Why would you think that?" He sounded puzzled.

"You have a reputation," I muttered.

"What's that supposed to mean?"

I didn't speak, didn't know what to say.

"You really do listen to bullshit do you know that?" he growled.

"Maybe." I kept my eyes on the ground. "But it's true, isn't it?"

"What's true?"

"That you don't do relationships." I felt myself shaking inside, swallowing hard before adding on a breath. "Two days max and if the girl's lucky, three."

"I admit there's been some of those. No one-night stands though."

His nonchalance was an affront. Wanting to hurl something, I jerked my head up to scowl at him but the intensely serious look in his eyes knocked the disgust out of me.

"And yeah. I suppose I don't do relationships very well." He shrugged. "But then what's the point if the girl's not the one?"

I blinked. "Not the one?"

"Like I said before I've waited a long time, witch."

"Pardon?"

"You heard."

His mouth was on mine. Sliding my fingers into his hair, I held on. We ended up inside, don't ask me how with me sandwiched between him and a bedroom door, my legs clamped on his waist and his hands on my behind.

He drew back to look me in the eye. "Which bedroom did you share?"

I rolled my eyes to the door behind me without speaking.

"And that one?" He jerked his head to the opposite door.

"My grandparents," I whispered.

"Better," he muttered, steering me in that direction.

Euphoric days turned into weeks. I had to pinch myself, our togetherness something I'd never thought possible. Douglas was indeed something else; crazy fun and frustratingly forthright but surprisingly easy to be with and talk to. When it came to sex, he turned me blind, deaf and dumb to reason. We alternated beds at weekends, kept things relatively quiet during the week or at least I tried especially with he worked night shift. It didn't however stop his seemingly boundless energy. My protests at nocturnal activities happening in daytime were often unheeded, a gnarly old fir tree behind the sawmill certainly not used for eating picnic lunches under and the front seats of his ute weren't a favourite of mine either especially the driver's side as the awkward steering wheel dug into my person. I was considerably more concerned about privacy than him, squirming with blushing cheeks on more than one occasion.

He gave my brothers grief, especially Matthew, circling each other like dogs ready to fight. He thought it hilarious. I did not and feared for my brother's safety.

He didn't let me forget my past negative reactions to him either, couldn't deny the memories of our school days and beyond to be entertaining. Anna adored him, his personality reminding her of Bernard all over again and even Dad mentioned Douglas triggering memories of his father. Perhaps they were right, although Bernard and Douglas couldn't have been more different in appearance, hair and eye colour especially, their characteristics were remarkably similar.

He was also a jack of all trades who could turn his hand to anything mechanical or otherwise, but my brothers were as usual disdainful, very uncomplimentary of his abilities and called him the Junkyard Dog! Behind his back, of course. Unbeknown to them he had an ongoing project stowed in his shed, a classic Ford Mustang once belonging to his paternal grandfather with its engine in bits and needing panel work. When he asked me to keep it secret until completed, I promised I would and couldn't wait to see the men of my family's faces when he showed them.

The one subject he did remain tight lipped about however, was his departed family and I hoped that one day he'd talk to me about them, especially his sister.

Chapter 26

Two rather overwhelming months later, Delta and I headed out to the far end of the valley without Trojan, leaving him behind with Daniel and Jonathan to herd cattle at the yards. The chance to unwind and clear my head after a super busy week at work welcome.

We loped along to where the farm bordered conservation land, halting at the boundary fence beside a dead-end access road used primarily for hunters and tramping people. After a cursory look around, I checked our gate was still securely fastened and headed back at a more leisurely pace along a track nearest the road, the river below us.

The sudden crackle of motorbike engines minutes later had me surprised, halting Delta to turn in the saddle for a look. She fidgeted in protest, swivelling her ears at the noise. Hurtling into sight behind us came two off road bikes with leather suited and helmeted riders.

I waved a hand vigorously for them to stop, intending to let them know they were in the wrong place and on private land. The green bike skidded to a halt some metres distant, the red bike doing the same. They didn't lift their visors but by body shape and set of the rider's shoulders I figured they were male but not being able to see their faces annoyed me.

"You're on private property!" I shouted, pointing back to the access road. "There's no bike trail here. You need the next road further along!"

They didn't move, but I felt their eyes watching and frowned.

"Did you hear me? You shouldn't be here, it's a private farm!" I shouted again.

A frisson of worry shivered down my spine at their lack of reaction or dialogue which for some unexplainable reason quickly turned to something else akin to fear. As if sensing my vibes, Delta jerked her head and swung her hindquarters. It made me decide not to dismount, would much rather deal with the situation on top of my horse. Had no idea what these guys were up to but getting away from them was suddenly all I cared about.

I prepared for a quick take off without drawing attention to it, tightening my hands and legs a fraction. When the green bike guy made the first move, an abrupt hand motion for me to get down, I reacted.

Delta was ready for my signal. Clamping my legs on her, I grabbed the saddle horn. For one hysterical second, I thought I'd part company with the saddle as she leapt forward in a half rear but kept my balance somehow, settling down deep to lean forward and urge her on, my voice lost in the whipping air as she bolted.

The bikers would have reacted instantly I was certain; they'd left their motors running after all and sure enough, I could hear them closing in. Fast as she was Delta would not be able to outrun them, knowing the lay of our land would be our only advantage.

To my dismay they were suddenly at our heels. Then the green bike shot up beside us, drawing level with my leg. Yipping with fright as the rider shot out an arm towards me, I laid a rein across Delta's neck. She reacted immediately, veering sharply up an incline towards a stand of trees. We were suddenly amongst them, racing through low foliage and leaping over fallen branches, but I knew our haven there wouldn't last forever.

Glancing desperately at the parallel track, I saw the green rider turn his helmeted face towards me as he hurtled along. Knew he wasn't going to give up the chase. I needed to do something drastic and very soon or this wasn't going to end well for me or Delta.

The other side of the river! I thought in panic. *It's the only place. Get down there!*

It was in plain view but seemed too far away, on top of which the green rider was between it and us. We came out of the trees heading for a narrow gully, but the only way through was back across the track. I asked Delta for more and she gave it to me. We pulled ahead, the green bike out of my line of sight, but I'd forgotten about the other.

He'd gone higher up around the trees nearer the road boundary and appeared suddenly, hurtling down the slope on our other side. I thought for one horrifying second that he was going to collide with us, but Delta's two leaping strides had us out in front. We hit the track with him right on our heels.

Delta faltered momentarily, almost stumbling. Was sure he'd touched her, likely with his front wheel. Sheer panic had me sucking in air, bracing myself for I knew not what. He tried again but this time she was prepared and having none of it, bucking and lashing out backwards in midstride. My desperate grip on the saddle saved me from coming off.

The engine note changed abruptly, a voice bellowing as the bike crashed behind us. Managed a fleeting glance back, just long enough to see clouds of dust but no bike in sight. We raced onward to the end of the gully, veering for the river. My heart stopped, began to slam in my chest. The green bike was on the lower track, still level with us and in our way.

Without really thinking it through, I didn't falter. Down the slope we went, Delta digging in her hindlegs, bouncing and sliding towards the track. My focus was on the motorbike. Before the inevitable collision, I tensed and tightened the reins.

Delta applied the brakes and so did he, slewing the bike sideways. Laying the reins across, Delta responded to pivot instantly, heading straight at him. He gunned the engine again, attempting to accelerate out of our way, but she was on him. Didn't miss a beat. Her forelegs left the ground and whether she struck him or not I had no idea. As if in slow motion I saw the bike and rider sliding under us, his visor facing upwards. My breath left me in a whoosh as she hit the ground but didn't slow.

Careering down to the river at breakneck speed, I made no attempt to slow Delta down. She barely hesitated and hit the water with a huge splash, her hooves slipping and sliding across the stony riverbed. We surged out of the water, up the opposite slope and hurtled on. I didn't dare look back for one second, the panic inside me still there, breath wheezing.

It took just one stumble, Delta lurching forward and almost to her knees. I'd let go of the saddle horn by then, wasn't quick enough to grab it again. Lost my balance, body sliding sideways and off. Hit the ground hard with my shoulder, yelped and cartwheeled. Struck my head, a sharp vicious pain and nothing more.

Woke up mumbling to find Douglas sitting beside the bed frowning worriedly, his mouth pinched. When I attempted a feeble hand gesture, he leant closer to kiss my knuckles.

"At last," he said on a long sigh. "You're awake."

"Hello." I mouthed.

Staring at each other, I tried to smile, but he didn't return it and looked away abruptly to a closed door. I looked around the room but didn't recognise it.

Blinking, I focused on him again. "Where am I?"

He put my hand down and got up. "You're in hospital. I'll get your dad."

The room was suddenly full of Dad and my brothers, hugging me and speaking all at once until two cheerful nurses appeared to check my vitals. As they left Dad sat down on the chair, my brothers perching on the bed while Douglas kept his distance standing by the door.

"How are you feeling?" Dad asked, patting my arm.

"Okay, I think. A bit woozy."

"Understandable, you knocked your head. Do you remember?"

"I remember riding Delta and falling off." I frowned. "Is she okay?"

"She's fine," Daniel told me. "It was thanks to her that we found you."

"Really?"

"Yeah, the other horses must have heard her calling, Helena saw them acting strangely at the back fence and called me," Daniel said. "Jonathan and I figured something was up with either you or Delta, rang Dad who was at Leon's and from there we all went out looking."

"Actually, it was Trojan who led us to Delta straight away," Matthew said. "She was standing right beside you, waiting for us."

"Oh, wow!" Was all I could say.

"Wow, indeed," Dad nodded. "You have yourself two wonderful heroes, your horse and dog."

"I don't remember anything after the fall." I creased my forehead. "I must have been out cold. Did you take me to hospital?"

"Yes, you were unconscious. They airlifted you to the hospital."

My eyebrows shot up. "What?"

Daniel laughed. "You missed out on all the action, sis."

"Oh no!" I clapped a hand to my mouth. "What a drama."

"Yeah, it was cool." Daniel pulled a wry face. "I mean not you, the helicopter."

"What else," I twisted my nose at him.

My brothers laughed.

"Do you remember anything at all before you fell?" Dad asked softly.

I answered without hesitation. "Yes, motorbikes."

"Motorbikes?" Matthew looked puzzled. "On the farm?"

"I told them they were in the wrong place, but they took no notice and chased us."

"Chased you?" Dad's eyebrows shot up.

"Almost all the way from the back gate." I rubbed my head. "I don't know why."

"Take it easy, Kate." Dad leant closer. "We don't have to talk about it right now."

"I'm okay," I flapped a hand, frowned. "There were two of them."

"Trail bikes?" Matthew asked.

I nodded. "Delta didn't like the noise, so we just took off."

"They followed you all that way?" Dad was aghast. "We found you on the other side of the river, almost halfway home."

"We were on the roadside to start with." Hearing the tremble in my voice, Dad took my hand. "I headed for the river; thought crossing it would get us away from them."

"Let's stop." Dad gripped my fingers. "I think this is too much for you."

I shook my head stubbornly. "I want to tell you." Looked around at each one, saw Douglas's eyes narrowed on me, his face expressionless. "One of the riders tried to run his bike into Delta from behind, I think she kicked him. The other one stayed beside us but when we turned for the river, Delta jumped straight over him." I took a breath, adding for good measure. "Think she hit him too."

"Go, Delta!" Daniel whooped. "I hope she knocked his block off."

Dad frowned at him before turning back to me. "Did you see their faces at all?"

"No, they had helmets with dark visors. I couldn't see who they were."

"What sort of bikes?" Matthew asked. "Colour, anything?"

"The guy in front was on a green bike, I'm sure it was a Kawasaki. The other one was red and white." I shrugged. "Not sure what make."

"Right, we need to talk to the cops about this." Dad touched my cheek. "But let's take a break now, you've told us enough."

They stayed until Roman, Bella and Anna came to visit, leaving soon after. Douglas had already departed before them without so much as a word to me which I found strange and, on his return, the following day he greeted me coolly with only a light peck on my cheek.

Figured he thought me fragile and let it go, but his distracted manner bothered me and when he didn't visit again, I felt curiously bereft. When deemed fit and discharged from hospital, it was Dad who collected me, not Douglas and phoning him later, I left a message as there was no reply, letting him know I would be staying with Dad and Helena for a few days

Hours later he texted: **Glad you're home. Busy at work. See you**

soon.

Two days passed before he came, peeving me off a little with another fleeting kiss.

He came two days later, peeving me off a little with another fleeting kiss. While alone with him on the homestead patio, I pointedly patted the two-seater bench seat for him to join me but instead he sat down opposite on a deck chair and stared out at the paddock.

"What's wrong?" I asked frowning.

"How could anything be wrong?" He looked at me, smiling. "You're getting better."

"I was talking about you." I eyed him, sure that his smile was forced.

"Nothing wrong with me." He shrugged. "Just tired, hectic at work and all that."

"I hope it's just work." I leaned forward. "Don't worry about me, please."

He didn't reply, again averting his eyes. There was something distinctly off, a feeling I couldn't decipher plucked at my nerves and perhaps I should have kept my mouth shut but I had to know what was bugging him.

"What is it?" I asked. "Please, Douglas. Talk to me."

As his eyes snapped back to mine, the look in them made me recoil. "Are you sure you didn't recognise those guys on the motorbikes?"

"What?" I blinked. "No!"

"Do you think they knew who you were?"

"What do you mean?" I stared wide eyed.

His eyes frightened me, I closed mine to block him out. The thought when it came had my eyes popping open again, gasping. "You could be right! The guy on the green bike, I had a feeling about him."

Douglas's jaw clenched. "Yeah, I thought so."

"You know who it was?" I stared at him aghast.

"On a Kawasaki," he nodded. "I've a fairly good idea."

"Who?"

"Poke!" He bared his teeth. "The other bike, red and white you said. Most likely a Honda and belonging to Jacko, also a mate of mine." He shook his head, snarling. "Ha! Mates of mine! Not!"

My jaw dropped. "Are you sure?" At his sharp nod, I shook my head in bewilderment. "But why? Why would they have even come to the farm?"

"They were probably waiting for you."

"Waiting for me?" I frowned. "What on earth for?"

"Poke didn't like me roughing him up last time he hassled you at the racetrack." A muscle in his jaw clenched. "He's been itching to get me back, the bastard!"

"You mean he did this to me because of you?" I was astounded.

"His chance for revenge now we're hanging out together."

"Revenge?" I squawked. "So, what exactly would he have done to me?"

"Who would know!" He stood up with a snarl, balling his fists. "But you could have been killed!"

Shocked at his words, I could only stare.

He averted his eyes, muttering to himself. "Killed by people I know."

"But I wasn't!" I said sharply, standing up to reach a placatory hand. "I doubt it would have come to that."

He turned venomous eyes on me, ignoring my hand. "This is all my fault!"

I recoiled at his look, squeaked. "No, it's not!"

"Yes, it is!" He backed away, said through his teeth. "It's always the same! Anything to do with me turns to shit!"

Couldn't believe what I was hearing. "Douglas, please!"

He didn't heed. "My sister, my mother, my father, they're all dead. My life is one big balls up, even my mates!"

"Douglas!" Whimpering his name again, I went to him with outstretched arms.

"Don't!" He put up his hands to stop me. "This is not happening any more!"

"What do you mean?" I felt my throat constrict.

"Us!" His eyes turned suddenly blank, cold as ice. "We can't go on! I'm no good for you! Never was, never will be."

I shook my head, tears welling. "That's not true."

"It is!" he snarled. "He's the one you should be with, not me!"

"What are you saying?"

"Kenneth!"

"I don't understand," I croaked. "Kenneth's gone!"

"When you woke up in hospital, I was the first person you saw." His voice rasped low. "But you said his name. Not mine!"

229

"Did I?" Tears were rolling down my face. "I don't remember."

"His name!" He repeated with a snarl.

"That doesn't mean anything." I took another step towards him. "I was sedated, probably confused, I'd only just woken up!"

He shook his head sharply, moving well out of range. "I'm not what you need, Kate. Get better for your family and move on. I'm sorry but we're over."

I sucked in air, feeling as if I'd been struck. Him saying my name instead of the usual witch word the cruellest blow of all.

With one last look, he turned abruptly to his ute, ignoring my desperate protests. Heard the door slam, the motor gun and watched him throttle away in a spray of gravel. Soon after Dad and Helena found me incoherent and sobbing wretchedly, bundling me off to bed with a sedative. Once lucid, I tried to phoning Douglas but there was no reply, left messages and texts during the following week but to no avail.

A week later back on board and able to drive, I decided to confront him after work. Arriving at Douglas's place, I sat staring disbelievingly at his gate. It was padlocked. There was no sign of life inside the property, no vehicles and the shed doors were all shut. I waited for ages, feeling more forlorn by the minute. Eventually headed home to walk and feed Trojan, took a reviving shower and resolutely contacted the sawmill.

The same grumpy man answered the phone. "Willard doesn't work here any longer," he told me. "Been gone maybe two weeks and as far as I know he's left the country."

I gasped. "You're joking?"

"No!" He retorted, belligerently indignant. "I am not joking!"

My phone slipped out of my fingers to the floor. Stared at it blankly, dry eyed and utterly disbelieving. Realised then that Douglas had meant it, we were over for good.

I told Dad days later in a chilly unemotional voice without going into details. Understandably astounded, he tried asking questions, but I wouldn't elaborate and retreated into myself. Nothing could have prepared me for the wretchedness, I'd never felt so numb and cold inside. Kenneth's death had been difficult to deal with, but the breakup with Douglas seemed even more final. Life would never be the same.

When Dad informed me Poke and Jacko had handed themselves into the police, confessing to and apologising for harassing me on their motorbikes, I barely reacted, felt no inclination to lay charges and understood they'd subsequently been let off with a warning.

Chapter 27

Delta sauntered back to the paddock alongside Kate after their ride, rolled an eye but got no response. Kate was in a world of her own, staring at the ground as she walked. Once inside the gate Delta turned to watch her as she left the paddock, Kingston and BB eying their sombre friend.

"What's wrong with Kate?" Kingston asked worriedly.

"She's not happy any more," Delta answered, sighing.

"How do you mean?" BB wanted to know.

"She's like really sad and mutters to herself all the time."

"She always does that."

"It's different now."

"Different?"

"She's not muttering to me or Trojan. She ignores us."

"She doesn't ignore you," Kingston looked baffled. "She rides you at least three times a week, that's more than Daniel rides me or Bella rides Bronc."

"I know, you're right." Delta shook her head. "But that's not what I mean. I don't know how to explain it."

"You're saying she's not really there," BB offered. "Her mind isn't, I mean."

"That's it. She's with us in body but not in mind."

"So, where's her mind?"

"With that man."

"I thought he'd gone?" Kingston frowned.

"He has gone. A long way away, I understand."

"Does she know where he's gone?"

"I'm not sure but she thinks about him heaps. It doesn't make her happy."

"I thought he made her happy."

"He did, but something's gone wrong," Delta sighed. "Ever since that horrible day."

"Those motorbikes?"

Delta nodded. "Ever since them."

"Do you think that knock on the head did something funny to her?"

"She's not gone mad if that's what you mean."

"But she was out cold."

"Yes, she was. Right until that scary noisy bird thing picked her up."

"You said she was out for ages. That's not a good sign." BB frowned.

"BB's right," Kingston nodded. "Maybe it has affected her somehow. Humans aren't that strong, you know, they don't handle hard knocks very well, like we do."

Delta was having none of it, snapped. "She's handled it and healthy enough! I don't believe it's anything to do with her falling on her head. It's all about him, okay!"

"Okay!" Kingston peered at her. "Don't get your tail in a tangle!"

BB rolled her eyes. "Here we go again. Males!"

Kingston scowled. "Hey! Enough of that. Don't blame us for all your problems."

"Females don't have problems."

Kingston snorted a laugh. "Females are one big problem."

"Watch yourself, laddie boy. Us females also bite and kick."

"I'm so scared!" Kingston wobbled his legs." My knees are knocking."

"Your knees will be doing more than knocking in a minute."

"Okay, you two! Stop behaving like children and act your ages!"

"What did you say?" BB and Kingston simultaneously turned to Delta. Delta jerked her head at their tone. "I didn't say a word!"

"You did so! You told us off." BB narrowed her eyes.

"I did not!"

Kingston also eyeballed Delta. "You said stop acting like children and act our ages."

"You're hearing things. I never said a word!"

"It must be happening again!" BB squeaked, eyes round with shock.

Kingston said nothing, his eyes flicking worriedly from side to side.

Delta looked from one to the other. "You're hearing voices again?"

"Well, if it wasn't you, it must be the voice." BB shivered.

"But it wasn't the usual one," Kingston muttered.

"The usual?" Delta was puzzled.

"Usually, it's a male voice. This sounded like a female."

"You know what?" Delta blew a breath. "I'm glad I only hear Riva, she used to scare me but your Shadow lot sound really creepy!"

"You're telling me!" BB agreed. "Be glad you don't see them, that's even creepier."

"Okay, enough!" Kingston heaved a loud sigh. "Let's change the subject."

"You started it!" BB scowled at him.

"Keep it up you two and you'll get told off again." Delta eyed them scornfully.

"Right then." Kingston sighed again. "Where were we?"

"Talking about Kate."

"What can we do to help her?"

"I don't know."

"What about her dog? He's with her way more than us, can't he do anything?"

"Trojan kind of understands what she says but he can't read her mind."

"Humans think too much, their brains are too big for their own good," Kingston pointed out. "I'm glad I'm not a human!"

"I second that." BB had to agree, said to Delta. "Anyway, maybe Kate's fella will come back one day."

"I hope so," Delta sighed. "The sooner the better."

"I don't know why they do that," Kingston frowned.

"They do what?"

"Boys, human one's that is. They always come back."

"Girls are irresistible."

Kingston choking and spluttering had the girls giving him pathetic looks.

The horses kept me motivated, the opportunity to ride Delta when I had the time helping me cope and although Dad and Helena worried about my going out on my own, I reassured them, pointing out that Poke, Jacko or anyone else for that matter would hardly come back to try the same thing again.

I noticed Delta seemed calmer than ever on our outings, almost extra vigilant in where she put her feet. To my delight there was also a rapport between her and Trojan that hadn't been there before, he'd follow or run beside us as usual but when I dismounted, he often glanced to where she stood ground tied. It made me feel safe.

Almost two months after the motorbike incident, we all congregated at the farm for one of Helena's yummy roast dinners, Matthew pulling me aside after we'd eaten.

"You probably don't want to know," he said quietly. "But his place is up for sale."

Knowing immediately what he meant, my throat constricted. "For sale?"

"The real estate signs went up last week and Daniel saw in on the net. It's definitely listed for auction."

"When is the auction?" I breathed.

"Two weeks from now. Everything's being sold, what's inside the sheds and all."

"Are you sure?" I frowned.

"That's what it said. The auction's being held at the real estate office, not on site."

"Everything?"

"Yep. Apparently, there's a classic car for sale too."

I shook my head in disbelief. "The Mustang?"

Matthew eyes widened in surprise. "I didn't know he owned one of those."

"He didn't really talk about it," I sighed, didn't somehow think it mattered if I told my brother now. "He was restoring it, his grandfather's car."

"I could find out more." Matthew eyed me. "If you like."

"Please, do," I nodded. "I'd like to know."

"Sure, sis." He cocked an eyebrow. "And if it is for sale?"

A lightbulb went off in my head. "I'll bid for it." I told him softly but surely.

"You will?" Both his eyebrows went up.

"Yes!" I was adamant until another thought hit me. "Will he be there?"

"Does it matter if he is?" The panicked look of my face had him shaking his head. "That was a stupid question. Sorry, sis."

I shook my head, flapped a hand. "It's okay. I could ask Dad to go, he knows more about auctions than I do."

"Good idea," Matthew nodded. "I'll find out about the Mustang soon, eh?"

"Thanks," I smiled thinly. "Nice of you to let me know all this."

"Anything for my little sister."

"Anything?" I eyed him a little sceptically. "Even if it's to do with him?"

"Yeah, well." He pulled a face, shrugged. "You're the one in love with him, not me."

I looked away. "Was."

"You still are, huh?" I could feel him watching me closely.

Sighing, I looked at him again. "Probably always will be."

He screwed up his nose. "Spare me the gory details, please!"

Shaking my head, I thumped his arm.

He and Daniel found out that the Mustang was indeed being sold at auction separately from the property with several other machinery parts and the like. They also told me that everything was being handled by lawyers with no owner present.

I still felt it was too risky to attend, not wanting to come face to face with any of Douglas's cronies and judged it time to enlist Dad's help.

Cornered him the following day. "Could I ask you to do something for me, Dad?"

"Sure. Anything for you, my girl."

"Careful now!" I tapped his nose.

"Now you've got me interested." He tipped his head at me, smiling widely.

"There's an auction coming up with something I'd like to buy."

"You want me to go with you?"

"I don't really want to go at all." I said sheepishly. "Would you go on my behalf?"

"Is this the Willard auction you're talking about?"

"You know?" I was surprised.

"I've heard about it," he nodded. "Everything's up for sale, I believe."

"Yes. So, Matthew told me."

Dad narrowed his eyes. "You're wanting to buy Willard's place?"

"No." I shook my head. "Just the Mustang he owns, it was his grandfather's."

"Ah, yes, The 69 Mach 1. I heard about that, too." He smiled again, brightly. "The same model Dad first raced with the 428 V8 engine."

"Really? Opa raced one of those?"

"Yes, but unfortunately it was written off, he was involved in a bad pile up."

"Oh! Was he hurt?"

"A few bruises Mum told me," Dad said. "One driver died though."

"That's sad."

"That's the risk when racing I guess," he shrugged. "Anyway, about this car. I'll be very happy to bid on it for you."

"I'd like to go but…" I petered out.

"You don't want to see him?"

"He won't be there. His friends could be though." I grimaced.

"Totally understand." He touched my cheek. "I'll be happy to go."

"The body's intact but the motor's in bits." I began telling him all I knew.

The auction was well attended, the property went for an exceptionally good price and Dad successfully acquired the car although up against four other enthusiastic bidders.

It left me relieved and quietly proud to be the owner of a classic Mustang, detached motor or otherwise. Dad organised it being shipped to one of the racetrack workshops with every part intact, all the petrolhead lads there drooled over it with Matthew positively itching to take it on as a project.

For me, it was a part of Douglas, something of his that I could hold on to. Made me feel somehow better and more able to deal with him gone.

Chapter 28

Having the privilege of a long meaningful chat to Anna some months later, kind of helped me move on a little more.

"I know you think I'm an old lady rambling." She tipped her head with a gentle smile. "All this about history repeating itself."

"You believe it though, don't you?"

"Yes, I suppose I do. As I've said before you're like my sister and I'm not just talking looks and attitude. These happenings of late are so similar."

I didn't reply, still not convinced.

"It will all be okay." She took my hand. "Eventually.

"How can you be so sure?"

"Your Oma and Opa split up when they were married, but they got back together after about a year. I believe it made their relationship so much stronger."

"Does Dad know about that?"

"His parents didn't keep secrets from him. I'm sure he knew they had their ups and downs." Anna gave me a wry look. "I'm not sure he got the detailed version however."

"I suppose everyone has their ups and down, even the best relationships."

"They certainly do."

"But me and Douglas." I sighed. "I really don't know."

"Why do you say that?"

"We didn't know each other that well, we'd only been together a few months."

"But you love him." She eyed me. "And he was absolutely smitten, that was obvious."

"It wasn't enough to keep us together though, was it?" I gave her a soulful look.

"We will see." She patted my hand.

We celebrated our New Year family festivities a little differently the following year, off the farm and at the racetrack instead. The organised night event was chocka full of people of all ages, colourful and noisy with car races and a fireworks display.

Finding the crowds and hype too much for me as the night progressed, I slunk away for a reprieve. Headed for the workshops and relative quiet, fingering the keys in my pocket and deciding to take a look at the Mustang while there.

Stopping to lean against a workshop wall, I tipped my head to look up at the stars. Although still able to hear muted music it was another sound that penetrated my brain, a scuffling somewhere close by but out of sight. Sidling further along the path to peer around the corner, I squinted in the glare of the workshop's security lights. Saw what looked like two male bodies writhing around on the ground in the shadows, thumps and grunts indicating a fight going on. Hesitated momentarily before moving cautiously closer for a better look.

A contorted face showed pale in the lights. Recognising Matthew, I let out a horrified gasp. He was flat on his back, held down by a larger male. Wasn't bothering to find out who the guy was, didn't like what he was doing to my brother and promptly scouted around for a weapon, spotted a pile of discarded broken pallets and yanked out a good-sized slat of wood.

"Stop fighting, you two!" I shouted in exasperation and swung it.

The wood made a dull thwack as it connected with the guy's head and broke. Not expecting it to have much effect the guy's instant reaction was a surprise, body jerking and slumping forward across Matthew without a sound. Morbidly satisfied, I decided to repeat my handiwork, raising the leftover piece of wood to aim again but Matthew began waving frantically before clawing out from under, his eyes on stalks.

"Kate! No!" he spluttered. "Don't!"

"What is the matter with you guys?" I glared at him; weapon still held high. "What on earth are you fighting about now?"

"It's okay, sis," he puffed and sat up, turning to give his sparring partner a prod, heaving a breath when he moved.

The guy eased up on his elbows, raised one hand gingerly to the back of his hoodie and grunted. I froze immediately at the sound, felt the ground shift.

"What the fuck?" I heard him mutter.

Promptly fainted.

Sounds came back to me first, my own breathing and the distant thud of music. Felt someone supporting my head, blinking rapidly as Matthew's face came into focus.

"Kate?" he frowned. "Are you okay?"

I stared upwards past him, certain I was dreaming. A face minus the hoodie showed clearly in the lights. Giving myself a mental shake, I glowered and whacking Matthew's helping hand away scrambled up to eyeball him.

"What is that overgrown numbskull arsehole doing here?" I asked through my teeth.

Matthew suitably shocked eyebrows shot into his hairline. Mine did the same when Douglas cracked up laughing. Reacting spontaneously and without thought, all the pent-up emotions I'd bottled up for so long simply boiled over as I rounded on him, stepping forward to aim an open-handed slap at his face. It didn't connect. Swung my other hand but that didn't hit the target either, both my wrists caught in his grip.

"Your sister's more dangerous than you!" Douglas grinned at Matthew.

Matthew slowly came to his senses, "Yeah, I already know that."

I yipped indignantly, shooting Matthew a venomous look. Douglas loosened his hold on me and let go, stepping back well out of range as I rubbed my tingling wrists.

"He came here to look at the Mustang, sis," Matthew muttered.

I eyed Douglas balefully, said with spite. "It's not yours to look at any longer."

"Exactly what your brother said," Douglas merely smirked. "And he told me never to show my ugly mug around these parts again."

"I wonder why!" I spat sarcastically.

"Thinks it might upset his little sister."

That shut me up. I turned my back abruptly on them both as to my horror sudden tears welled but fought to control myself, swallowing hard.

"See what I mean!" Matthew growled. "You're upsetting her right now."

Scrubbing at my eyes, I willed myself to face them.

"I'm okay, Matt!" I managed to croak, giving Douglas a defiant stare. "He wants to see the Mustang. Let's show him."

Douglas watched me in silence, eyes narrowed.

Turning abruptly, I stalked to the workshop, unlocked the door and flicked on the inside light. The red and black car stood to one side, beautifully restored and gleaming immaculately. Each time I saw it the same feeling hit me, a mixture of pleasure and sadness with a good dollop of admiration and pride at what Dad and Matthew had achieved.

Douglas walked towards it slowly, taking it in but his face remained impassive. Matthew stepped forward to raise the car's hood, Douglas leaning in to scrutinise the meticulous engine. My eyes shifted to his backside, the unexpected quiver shocking me.

No, please! Don't be stupid! I sneered at myself. Not now, not ever again!

Douglas took his time, moving around the car with his fingers running lightly along the paintwork. My eyes watched, relentless mind salivated and remembered what his hands could do. Was oh so very glad that nobody was taking any notice of me.

"You've done an awesome job," he said to Matthew. "Thanks for letting me have a look. It means a lot."

"Dad and I enjoyed working on it," Matthew replied. "The mechanical stuff was easy, most of it was already done. You obviously did a fair bit of work on it yourself."

"A few years of fiddling."

"Well, you did a good job."

Douglas shrugged, smiled and said to me. "Appreciate you letting me see it."

I said nothing, didn't move a muscle or smile.

He gave a small nod before leaving, turning at the door to look back at me. "Could I ask one last thing?"

I blinked. "What?"

"Why did you buy my car?"

I wasn't telling him the real reason, quoted Dad's information instead. "My Opa, that is, my grandfather Bernard raced one of these. It was written off in a crash."

"Right." He cocked an eyebrow. "Family nostalgia, then?"

"Exactly." I had a distinct feeling that he didn't believe me.

"Okay. Thanks, again." He raised his hand to us both and departed.

Matthew and I stared at the empty doorway, then at each other. He spoke first, raising a sceptical eyebrow at me. "Dad told you that after you decided to buy it."

"And?" I scowled.

"Why did you buy it, really?"

"None of your business," I snapped.

"Overgrown numbskull arsehole." He laughed. "Haven't heard that one before."

I ignored that. "Where did he spring from?"

"I don't know. He tapped me on the shoulder in the crowd."

"And then you came out here to fight?" I shook my head in disgust.

"It felt good," he grinned.

"And he was winning," I pointed out scathingly.

His grin changed to a defiant grimace. "Nah! I had him."

"Did he say what he was doing here? Apart from looking at the car, I mean?"

"He didn't say."

"How long is he here for, do you know?"

He shook his head. "No idea."

"Let's not tell anyone about this." I frowned. "Showing him the car and all."

"If that's what you want," Matthew shrugged. "No problem."

I kept an eye out for the rest of the night but didn't see Douglas again, wondered worriedly why he'd come back and by the time I got home I was so uptight sleep was impossible. Got up the following morning jaded and lethargic, glad that we had four days off work over New Year, giving me time to recover.

It didn't stop my nerves jumping however, knowing Douglas Willard was lurking.

Chapter 29

Time didn't ease my angst, expecting to meet him at every corner, in the grocery store or on the road, but he didn't show. Began to wonder if he'd gone back overseas.

At the family Sunday lunch, weeks later, Matthew had some news. "Old Marley Kilburn's place has been sold. Did any of you know?"

"You mean the junkyard up the no exit road past the racetrack?" Dad asked.

"Yeah. The rat-infested hole that no one wanted."

Dad frowned. "I thought the family sold it ages ago, after the old fella died."

"It even went to auction," Matthew told him. "But they couldn't find a buyer."

"I didn't know that." Dad raised his eyebrows.

"It's been empty for years," Daniel said. "The house is derelict, needs pulling down."

"There's an okay shed though, good size too. That's probably worth keeping."

"Do you know who bought it?" Dad wanted to know.

"Yeah, I do." Matthew turned his eyes my way.

Dad and Daniel looked from him to me quizzically.

"What?" I narrowed my eyes suspiciously. "Why are you looking at me like that?"

Matthew dropped the bombshell. "He bought it."

My jaw dropped.

Seeing my reaction, Dad put two and two together. "You mean Douglas?"

"Yep." Matthew nodded, still watching me.

"That guy must have a thing about junkyards," Daniel said helpfully.

"So, he's back home?" Dad eyed me with concern.

Matthew nodded again. "Yep. Came back over a month ago now."

"Ah. I knew he'd return," Anna said softly with a knowing little smile.

I closed my mouth, gave her a sharp look. This was no time to panic!

"Are you okay, Kate?" Dad gestured a hand.

"I'm fine, Dad." I found my voice, looked at Matthew. "What else did you find out?"

"Well, he's not at the sawmill. Works at one of the vineyards doing maintenance."

"Well, that's different." Daniel was surprised. "Fulltime?"

"Don't think so, but then he probably doesn't need to. I heard he made good money overseas at some massive sawmilling operation in the US, working 24/7."

"How long has he been away?" Anna asked. "Must be almost a year?"

I shot her another sharp look. "About that."

Remembering her words, I grimaced inwardly. Oma and Opa had been apart for about the same length of time. No way! Sorry, Anna, you're wrong! Not going to happen! No more men, no more hurt. I've had enough.

"Any idea what he's going to do with the place?" Daniel asked Matthew.

"Someone said he'll use the shed to live in, same as he did before at the old place," Matthew told him. "Like you said the house is stuffed. I guess he'll demolish it."

"What's he driving these days?"

"Another second-hand Nissan ute, later model."

Daniel lifted his eyebrows. "Why didn't he splurge and buy new?"

Matthew shrugged. "Maybe doing up the property's more important."

"I expect he'll know who bought the Mustang," Dad commented, eying me. "He may want to have a look at it one day."

"Yeah, Bro." Daniel smirked at Matthew. "Are you going to let him."

As Matthew glanced at me, I let him know with an indiscernible widening of my eyes to keep quiet. Lips twisting, he said to Daniel. "We could charge him a fee, eh?"

Daniel snorted. "Ha! Doubt that'll work. He'll bargain and want more, like another close up with sis," He instantly sobered at my ice-cold stare. "Sorry, K. Just kidding."

"If he's going to be living in the district, he's bound to meet us sometime." Dad inclined his head to me. "And I'm sure your sister can handle it."

"No worries, Dad." I smiled thinly. "It's all water under the bridge, after all."

I wasn't looking forward to that inevitable sometime, but the weeks passed by without any hide or hair of him. Matthew did have a progress report however, after noticing a demolition crew drive past the racetrack he went to check it out after work and found them at the junkyard, ripping down the house and clearing the place except the shed. The following week a building firm's truck went by with new timber on board, it seemed that Douglas was indeed planning on living there. I wondered where he was staying presently, wondered a whole bunch of things but decided it best not to ask or show too much interest in the man; it wasn't worth the trouble and my brothers would have plenty to say if I did.

Not in the mood to cook dinner after a hectic Friday at work, I drove into town for Chinese takeaways but returning to my parked car found a tyre completely flat to the ground. Muttering a few choice words, I shook my head in disgusted disbelief.

What is it with this place? I grimaced. Here I was again parked in the exact same carpark as the brace/kneecap incident so many moons ago.

That thought had me casting a quick apprehensive look around but there was nobody about, no arseholes or any other males for that matter and with a resigned scowl got down to business, extracting the spare wheel, jack and the said brace. Removing the nuts was a mission again, huffed and puffed over two before standing up to take a breather.

"Need a hand?" The voice almost sent me through my knees.

I dropped the brace with a clang, spinning around to find him standing in front of the car beside mine. My tongue froze. He moved forward, bending down to pick up the brace as I shuffled back away from him. Watching him straighten up, I could do nothing but stare into narrowed eyes that showed nothing, his familiar grin not in evidence either. Without a word he got down on his haunches, proceeding to finish the job while I watched, heart thumping like a mad thing.

Get a grip! I sneered at the tremble inside. So much for water under the bridge. One look from the guy and you're a blithering mess.

The lights at the racetrack hadn't done him justice. In daylight he appeared leaner than I remembered, the cheekbones of his face more pronounced but otherwise he looked just as good as ever, tattoos covered with long sleeves and his hair curling.

He got the wheel nuts off easily, replaced the wheel and finished in minutes. It was only after he'd stowed everything away that our eyes met a second time.

"Thanks," I croaked.

"You're welcome," he said quietly.

I felt curiously disappointed when he didn't finish the sentence with the familiar witch name. "You're back for good then?" I asked inanely.

"Yep."

"I heard you bought the Kilburn place near the racetrack, er, Matthew mentioned it."

"Yep."

"Are you going to live there?"

"I'm living there now, had a shed renovated." He seemed in a hurry to leave, inclining his head. "You better get that tyre looked at."

As he turned away, I blurted the question. "Why did you come back?"

He turned back, shrugging. "Had enough, it was time to come home."

"You're not working at the sawmill any more?"

"No. Time for a job change as well."

Words dried up in my throat. I looked at him in silence, unable to read his eyes.

He spoke again on a harsher note. "Sometimes a person needs to take time out, get things sorted."

"And you've done that?"

"Kind of," he nodded. "I thought going away was the best idea, for everyone."

"Everyone?"

"Yeah. You, me, everyone."

"You didn't even ask me what I thought!" I accused sharply.

"You were on the rebound and not thinking straight."

"Pardon me?"

"You just wanted comfort, someone to take your mind off him." He shook his head wryly at my scowl. "Be honest. I was never going to replace him or make you happy, was I?"

But you did exactly that! Staring aghast, I wanted to scream at him. You made me so incredibly happy after Kenneth, then left me to feel loss and grief all over again. Frustrated anger swamped me, wanted desperately to hurt him back and make him pay for what he'd done; for deserting me. "You're right, you weren't!" I said bitterly. "And just because I let you see the Mustang, don't get any ideas!"

His eyebrows lifted a fraction. "There's always hope."

"Hope?" I sneered. "For what? To carry on where you left off?"

"Oh, to be so lucky," he drawled mockingly.

"You won't ever get lucky!" I curled my lip. "You're not anything I need."

"I knew that before you did remember." He barked a sarcastic laugh. "But then need and want are two different things. Are you sure you know what you want?"

"I don't want you!" I spat. "That's for sure."

"Shame." He grinned without mirth. "Not even for a comfort bonk?"

I gawped at him like a stunned rabbit.

His grin widened sardonically at my look. "I'm not that good a replacement but if you ever change your mind about the comfort, let me know."

"You flatter yourself!" I found my voice, hissed. "I wouldn't touch you with a barge pole and if you come near me again, I'll call the cops. Do you understand?"

"Why bother with them?" His laugh was derisive. "Put a curse on me instead, witch. It'll be easier, don't you think?"

The familiar name was too much, made me want to hurt him more. "Oh, if only!" I curled my lip disdainfully. "Watching you disappear forever in a puff of smoke would make my day!" *This is insane! Am I really saying this crap?*

"You disappoint me, a puff of smoke?" He laughed again. "I was expecting violence, steel stools, wine bottles and stuff like that."

Memories hit me between the eyes as he stepped forward. Recoiling frantically with raised palms, I needed to do something drastic before he touched me, almost shouting. "Keep away from me! Don't you get it? I want nothing to do with you now or ever again!"

It had the desired effect. He came no closer.

"I suppose even arseholes like yourself have their uses," I added into the tense silence, sneering. "Thanks for changing my wheel."

He watched me with eyes that bored holes, drawled coldly. "Next time this arsehole won't be helping or coming anywhere near." Turning away, he threw over his shoulder. "Can't have you or your cop friends stressing now, can we?"

Watching him stride away, I felt almost physically sick. How had him helping me with a flat tyre turned into this mess? My vindictive bitchiness astounded me. Went home cursing myself, picked at my takeaway dinner with no appetite and hardly slept. Was still stewing miserably Saturday morning, even a brisk walk on the beach with Trojan not helping.

It went against my nature to be so horrible or at least I hoped so. Had to make it right, couldn't live with myself leaving things as they were. Thought of taking the coward's way out and phoning him but knew that wasn't going to work for me, needed to speak with him face to face, besides, it was highly unlikely his old phone number was still active.

Late afternoon, I got myself ready, dressed warmly in jeans and sweater against the chill, made sure Trojan was content and headed out.

Approached the racetrack with trepidation, hoping no one would chance to spot me but to my relief the workshops looked deserted, everyone having gone home already. Turned down the no exit road to Kilburn's junkyard with my nerves beginning to scream, slowing down to a crawl. As the place came into view it looked weirdly familiar, corrugated perimeter fence and steel railed gate which was shut. Got out of the car slowly to look in, feeling a jolt of surprise. The land area was probably one acre, had been cleared except for one decent sized shed to the rear left-hand side of the property. Three beautiful old oak trees lined that side of the driveway with four others on the right, their leaves rustling in the breeze.

Nothing moved otherwise and seeing no vehicle parked by the shed, I pulled at face, thinking. He's probably gone out already, boozing or some such.

Didn't know what made me do it, but I opened the gate and drove through, closing it again behind me. Thankfully now, there were no immediate nosey neighbours nearby, the nearest being at least half a kilometre away. I decided not to advertise my presence there however, driving on past the shed and parking my car behind it out of view of the road.

Getting out, I tiptoed along the shed past the two huge ceiling to floor roller doors at the front to the utility door. Waited but hearing nothing tried the handle, letting out a smothered yelp when the door opened unexpectedly. Nobody appeared or made a sound. Giving the door a little push, it swung open wider on silent hinges. Peered in cautiously expecting darkness but several clear roof panels let in a considerable amount of natural light.

Stepping inside, I immediately spotted a vehicle parked to my left behind one roller door and guessed it was his ute, the later model Nissan that Daniel had mentioned. The smell of new timber permeated the place, a large internal room almost directly opposite had been built recently with one solid door and glassed window in the nearest wall. Tiptoed across to sneak a look through the window, but the slatted blind inside made it difficult to see beyond. Further along the wall to my right was a bench and cupboards, taps and tub, washing machine and dryer with a smaller window above in the shed's external wall.

My eyes turned to the solid internal door. Swallowing down nerves I tried the handle and again to my surprise the door opened easily. Waited momentarily before stepping inside, waiting for my eyes to adjust to the semi-darkness. I was in a ceilinged open plan living space with kitchen, a glass ranch slider with curtains half drawn across on the outside wall.

No sign of life but the smell of stale alcohol filled the air. Wrinkling my nose, I closed the door quietly behind me, saw the switch beside the door jamb but decided against turning on lights.

My heart stuttered at a sound. Waited with bated breath and heard it again, a low groan coming from a door in the opposite wall. Remembered to breathe. Crossed over on tiptoes to press my ear against it and this time heard a muffled thump. Controlling the urge to bolt, I froze.

Telling myself to be brave, I opened the door tentatively to a passage beyond where a night light illuminated another closed door at the far end, one on the left wall and two on the right. Another louder groan had my breath hitching. I was certain it came from behind the first right hand door where a slit of light shone through underneath.

A weapon would be good, I thought, casting my eye around. As there was nothing but bare lino floor, fists, knees or the element of surprise would have to do.

Quickly opened and pushed the door ajar. My eyes popped wide. The grumbling noises came from a man on the floor beside the toilet wearing nothing but a pair of old jeans, propped against the wall with his legs splayed out in front of him and his chin on his chest. Very obviously paralytic drunk.

I instantly crouched down to him. "Douglas?"

Muttering something unintelligible, he lifted his face to squint at me with bleary eyes. Seconds later his head rolled on his shoulders and hung back down again.

"Come on," I said. "Let's get you out of here."

Attempting to get him to his feet was well-nigh impossible, but him shirtless didn't help, giving me nothing apart from his jeans to hold on to. Huffing and puffing, I folded his legs under him and got him up on his knees. Slung one of his arms across my shoulders and managed to lift and prop him against the wall. With slow progress we got out into the passage and from there I headed for the door opposite the living area, figuring it was the bedroom. He was almost unable to put one foot in front of the other, his knees buckling every step and it took all my strength to get him there. Finally, I fumbled for the handle, swinging the door open to reveal as I thought, a bedroom. A very spacious bedroom with a huge bed. Dragged him in that direction to simply let him drop.

He landed face first in the bed's centre. Quickly scrambling up beside him, I turned his head to one side and satisfied he was moving air in and out quite happily I pulled and pushed, repositioning him onto his side. Once I got my own breath back and my heart rate down, I propped a pillow under his head and before covering him with a blanket, couldn't resist taking a moment to admire the view and drool. I hadn't had that privilege for a long while, after all.

"You should try changing your drinking habits, mister," I scolded giving my neck a twist and rub. "This boozing is not good for you or me, I think you've put my back out."

He stirred, mumbled something but soon began snoring. Cute little snores.

The bedroom I noted was almost as large as the living area extending to the back wall of the shed with a side window and front ranch slider. I went across to pull the curtains, took one last long look at him and left the room. Turned on the light in the passage, stopping for a nosey behind each door except the toilet's, good sized bathroom with shower unit and a storage cum laundry room with hot water cylinder and linen cupboard on the other side.

Nice, I decided. Like the layout. Better than his old shed and brand new to boot.

Back in the living area I turned on lights, grimacing disgust at the tabletop laden with at least twelve or more beer bottles and two wine bottles, all empty. Sincerely hoping he hadn't finished all of them in one go, I began tidying up, discarding the bottles into a large recycling bag I found in a kitchen cupboard and once full took it out to the shed, propping it by the utility door. Slid across the inside bolt before going back to check on him.

He hadn't moved and was still snuffling. Perched on the bed, I brushed my fingers across his face, down his neck and took his pulse. Had another satisfying eyeball fix before returning to the living area with a sigh. Smiled at the comfortable looking sofa there, remembering his old ancient one and curled myself up on it after making a cup of tea and finding a biscuit to snack on. The temperature in the room was pleasant and I suspected would be warmer in the winter than his previous shed especially with the brand-new log burner he'd installed.

Coming out of a doze, I sat up blinking and realising a couple of hours had passed quickly went to the bedroom. He'd pushed the blanket away, looked positively sexy bare chested. Couldn't help myself, fetched my phone and took photos.

Something else to remember him by, I stifled a giggle. And he won't even know.

Waking late Sunday morning, I rubbed my eyes and found him on his back still sleeping. Used the toilet and bathroom for a freshen up, made myself another cup of tea and chewed on two more biscuits. Decided to explore around the shed inside and out, returning half an hour later to find he hadn't move but looked decidedly better, a tinge of colour in his face. After another photo session I figured he'd be okay to leave alone.

Unable to resist, I leant across to give him a soft kiss on the lips. Froze when his eyes flickered open. We stared at each other, noses mere millimetres apart. I couldn't have moved if I tried. He blinked once, squinted and shut his eyes with a long sigh.

"Witch," he mumbled, drifting off again.

"Don't worry," I whispered. "I won't put a curse on you. Ever."

Slithering off the bed slowly so as not to wake him again, I gave him one last lusting look before turning for the door.

Made a promise out loud. "One day I'll apologise properly. Please, take care."

Chapter 30

At work, the following Monday morning, I walked into the lunchroom before clinic opening hours to find most of the staff there talking about a weekend incident, the shocking rape and murder of a local teenage girl.

Sheena, a stable hand was especially distraught, mentioning she knew the girl in question. "June Moseley. I saw her out night clubbing on Saturday night. She left the Night Owl at about eight thirty with her friends and I think they went to the Firepit afterwards."

"Her friends noticed her missing after midnight, didn't they?" Stephanie asked.

"Yes, they thought she'd gone to the toilets but when they checked they couldn't find her." Sheena's chin wobbled. "The night club staff phoned the police straight away."

"They were really on to it," Brett, another stable hand said. "Out searching all night."

"But they were too late," Sheena whispered before bursting into tears, head vet nurse, Dianna pulling her close with a comforting murmur.

Brett spoke again. "They found her this morning I heard."

"What a terrible thing!" Stephanie looked horrified. "I've never heard of anything like that happening around here before."

"Neither have I," I agreed, shaking my head. "Who would do such a thing?"

"Some sick bastard," Brett muttered. "They're not saying much yet, but I heard rumours she'd been beaten up as well."

"Oh, that's vile!" Stephanie grimacing her disgust.

The rumours continued to roll in during the week, horrific stories of June having been raped repeatedly and subsequently strangled to death. She'd put up a fight apparently, but to no avail, left lying naked, beaten and dead. Her being found in the sawmill forest astounded me, memories of my antics with Douglas in the exact same place leaving me dumbstruck.

Police were working around the clock on a manhunt but were finding the going difficult; the perpetrator having left no evidence on her body or the area she'd been found in. Local people, especially young women had been warned to stay close to friends and watch themselves out late at night; it wasn't a good feeling. When Dad voiced his concerns about my being alone in the cabin, I reassured him it was locked up vigilantly, Trojan was always close by and that we lived a good distance from town.

Wasn't at all prepared for the tragic event's effect on me, however.

It all started the following Saturday while having lunch at the farm with family, a jovial affair to start with until Helena mentioned the tragic incident which prompted Matthew's eyes sharpening on me.

"Have you heard. Sis?" he asked.

"Heard what?"

"Willard's been taken in for questioning."

My mouth gaped. "What?"

Dad nodded. "I'm afraid so, Kate. They picked him up yesterday."

"I don't know what they've got on him," Matthew said. "But he knows that sawmill like the back of his hand which has probably got something to do with it."

"And the fact, he's not long back in town," Daniel added.

"That boy has always had a reputation," Dad frowned. "The cops know him well."

"No!" I heard myself say. "He'd never do something like that."

"How well did you ever really know him, sis?" Matthew peered closer. "And he's an arsehole, you said it yourself."

"No!" I bit out. "They've got it wrong."

"How can you be so sure?" Daniel said. '

"Saturday night she went missing, didn't she?" I returned Matthew's stare. "They found her on Sunday, when?"

"Sunday morning about ten, I believe."

"He couldn't have done it!" My heart thudded like a drum.

Everyone was watching me, looking puzzled and unsmilingly doubtful.

"Kate, my dear girl." Dad leant towards me, speaking gently. "The police must have something to go on, otherwise they wouldn't have brought him in."

"I know he didn't do it." My voice wobbled. "Because I was with him."

You could have heard a pin drop. The stunned looks on their faces were almost comical, but I didn't feel like laughing.

Matthew recovered first, his eyebrows into his hairline. "You were with him?" he spluttered. "You are joking!"

"No! I am not!" I croaked.

Dad blinked hard, creased his forehead. "With him? Where?"

"At his place." I lifted my chin defiantly. "The junkyard by the racetrack."

"You've been to his new place?" Daniel's eyes were like saucers.

"Yes."

"Why?" Matthew's eyebrows were still up way higher than usual.

Swallowing, I took a long deep breath. "I went there to speak to him."

"What for?"

"It doesn't matter." I got my cool calm voice back. "I found him totally off his face instead and ended up staying the night because I was worried about him."

"You stayed the night?" Daniel went cross eyed.

"Yes," I said, meeting Dad's eyes again. "And I have photos to prove it."

"Photos!" Matthew almost squeaked.

"Photos of him, um, in bed."

"No shit!" Daniel choked at first, snorted and began laughing uncontrollably.

As Anna also began to chortle Dad looked poleaxed, Helena glanced from him to me before winking and getting up to clear dishes while Matthew's mouth simply worked silently.

Waiting resignedly for the onslaught, I added snootily for good measure. "Would you like to see them?"

"I would!" Anna promptly nodded, looking positively gleeful.

I got up for my phone, handing it to her with the photos on view as Helena came across to take a good long look herself.

She spoke first, smiling slyly. "Oh, my! What a body."

Anna glanced up at Helena, grinned and licked her lips. "Hmmm, exactly! Now if I was younger his boots would be welcome under my bed any day."

Matthew eyes nearly popped out of their sockets, Daniel gagged on his laughter while Dad wasn't quite sure what to do, looking both shocked and suspicious. I remained silently stony faced.

Dad recovered, speaking sharply. "Okay! This is serious, we need to sort this out!"

"Yes. I agree, Dad." I nodded primly. "Let's go to the police right now."

Dad eyed me owlishly before shaking his head. "I think it would be best if I go alone, Kate." He extended a hand to Anna. "With your phone, if you don't mind."

As she passed my phone across, he glanced at the screen briefly, tightened his lips but didn't comment and pressed the off button before putting it in his pocket.

"There's a date and time on those photos." I told him, narrowing my eyes. "By the way who arrested him?"

Dad frowned. "He hasn't been arrested. He's been taken in for questioning."

"Where is he now?"

"At the police station."

"He's been there since yesterday?" I frowned.

"Yes."

"So, he's in a cell?" I couldn't keep the sarcasm out of my voice.

"Well, yes. He stayed overnight, so he'll be in the cells."

"Who arrested him?" I asked again, shifting my gaze to Matthew.

Matthew averted his eyes before mumbling. "Caleb Robinson."

I curled my lip. "Ah! Funny that. He doesn't like Douglas does he, just like you?"

"Kate!" Dad protested.

"It's true, Dad!" I snapped. "Caleb may be a cop, probably a good one but there's history between those two. He'd use any excuse to nab Douglas."

"Okay. Let's calm down." Dad put up a placatory hand. "I'll go as soon as we've finished lunch and speak to Adrian or Wayne. They'll get this all sorted."

"They'd better!"

Dad went to the police a short time later while the rest of us waited for his return. Unable to sit still, I wandered out to the front paddock, leant against the fence with my chin on my hands and watched the horses, trying to relieve my tension.

"Sis?" Matthew had followed me out.

"Did you really believe that he'd do something so horrific?" I rounded on him.

"No!" He shook his head quickly. "He's not that kind of arsehole."

I heaved a sigh, didn't speak.

"Can I ask why you went to see him?" Matthew asked after a moment. "I thought you weren't getting involved any more."

"I'm not. I just needed to talk to him about something."

He raised disbelieving eyebrows. "You did more than talk, that's obvious."

"I wasn't in the bed with him, Matt." I pulled a rueful face. "Besides he was in no fit state to do anything."

"But you took photos?"

"Well, yes." I flapped a hand. "He looked er, cute asleep."

"Right." He snorted a laugh, his look turning sly. "Does he know?"

"I doubt he even knew I was there." I shook my head. "I left before he woke up."

Matthew grinned. "He's going to wonder why the cops let him go so quickly."

"Maybe." Shrugging, I changed the subject. "I truly hope they catch the monster,"

"So, do I." Matthew grin fell off his face. "That bastard's a nasty piece of work and cunning. There's no biological evidence, they reckon he used condoms and gloves, threw them away after."

"That poor girl."

"Yeah, bloody horrible."

Dad returned to tell us that the police were completely satisfied with my evidence, Douglas immediately cleared and let go. His account of Douglas walking past Caleb inside the station, giving him lip and a one fingered salute before being hurried out of the station by Adrian and colleagues was amusing to say the least. Even I couldn't help but laugh.

Back at the cabin I paced the floor, knowing my relief at the outcome wasn't enough. There was still unfinished business between myself and Douglas, I needed to apologise, but whether I could summon up enough guts to try speaking with him again I really didn't know.

Didn't need to summon anything in the end. We did the bumping into each other thing again almost at the exact same corner in town as the first time. I stood on his foot hard, yipping as he let out his breath in a whoosh and then stepping back quickly, we eyeballed each other in silence. I felt something akin to dread at the coldness in his eyes.

Recovered enough to mutter, "I'm sorry." But the coward in me, dropped my eyes and made to walk hurriedly past him.

"Wait!" he barked, turning with me.

I halted but didn't look at him, concentrating fixedly on the pavement instead.

"Is it true?" He asked, voice low and harsh.

"Is what true?" I breathed.

"That your dad talked to the cops. Got me out?"

"Um, yes."

"And his daughter had something to do with it?"

I swallowed. "Most likely gossip."

"Most likely?"

"Does it matter?"

"Yeah. I think it does." I saw his boot take a step nearer. "What did you do?"

"Me?" I looked at him then, heart in my throat. "Um, nothing."

His eyes were no longer cold, something burning in them made me gulp.

"I'll find out one day," he said equably. "You may as well tell me."

"I just happened to know where you were that night," I squeaked.

"You just happened?" He raised an eyebrow. "So, I wasn't dreaming?"

"Dreaming?"

"I had visions of a witch lurking."

I bit my lip to stop the giggle, managing to say politely with pretend disdain. "You have a problem, I think, er, with witches, I mean. Visions of witches? That's weird."

"Very weird," he agreed, lips twisting. "What were you doing at my place?"

I hoped my innocent wide-eyed look appeared plausible, heart thudding merrily as I tapped my head. "Try not drinking so much, it's obviously affecting your mind."

He tipped his head. "Not that much. I saw you."

Time to change the subject. "Look, I'm glad things worked out okay. With the cop thing, I mean. I knew that you had nothing to do with that horrible...um, you know."

"Yeah, gruesome stuff!" he growled. "I hope they catch the bastard."

I nodded. "I hope so too. And soon."

He took another step nearer, eyeballing me. "Thank your dad for me, won't you?"

"I'll do that." I flapped a hand. "I've got to go."

"Thanks for your help, too." His mouth curved.

I pretended puzzlement. "Help?"

"You cleaned up my kitchen."

My mouth went slack.

He grinned.

Spinning away, I hurried out of sight into nearby store to puff out my cheeks and calm down, chiding myself for not taking the chance to apologise properly. Ah, don't panic! I reasoned. You'll see him again, no question. He lives in the same town remember!

Sure enough, I did see him again the next week, but didn't go near him. He was leaning back against the side of a white Mercedes behind the main street shops looking down at a woman who couldn't have got any closer if she tried. There was nothing between them but clothes. When she reached up to kiss him, I fled. Sat in my car with teeth gritted, eyes screwed shut and the old cold bitterness twisted like a knife inside of me.

What did you expect? I sneered to myself. He's moved on! Stop acting like a lovestruck teenage and do the same. And how am I supposed to do that?

The following day, Dad learnt that the police had made significant progress regarding the crime, all thanks to Douglas. At his suggestion they'd checked an old unused forestry track further out from the sawmill and there they found tyre tracks, a cigarette butt or two and boot prints. It was the break-through that within days linked DNA testing to a rapist/child molester who'd been released from prison the year before, lived in a neighbouring district and when they found remnants of June's clothing in his flat, was arrested and charged.

The residents of our district resumed their normal lives, but the loss of one of our own in such devastating circumstances would never be forgotten. A vigil was held for June in the main street which was full to bursting, people leaving flowers and messages on the town hall steps.

Douglas was there too. My heart jolted at the sight, dressed all in black and looking drop dead gorgeous. People not only stopped to shake his hand but a fair few females gave him hugs and kisses too. I'd never known myself to be capable of such jealous thoughts.

You could always go and give him the same treatment? a sly little voice suggested. *It'll make you feel better.* And then what? I doubt a hug and kiss would be enough. *Well, it'll do for starters, surely?* Go away!

Stopped breathing when he saw me and approached.

"Hey," he said softly. "Nice to see you here."

Took a breath, managing a tight smile. "Isn't this a wonderful turn out for June?"

"Yeah, bloody awesome," he agreed. "Her family are blown away."

"You know her family?"

"I knew her eldest sister quite well."

Quite well? That kicked me in the gut. How long, two days? Or more?

He narrowed his eyes as if reading my mind, added. "She was my sister's best friend."

I changed the subject quickly. "Um, I heard that you helped the cops."

"With some geography, that's all."

"Of course. The sawmill and forest, your old domain."

"I suppose you could call it that." His eyes burned.

A sudden flash of memory of us against the ancient old fir tree had the quiver purring. Mouth dry, I could only stare like a stunned rabbit.

He raised a questioning eyebrow but when I didn't respond, changed tack. "Have you seen my old place lately?"

"Yes." I gulped. "Have you?"

"Hmm, yep. Didn't recognise it with the four townhouses."

"They cleared the lot." I saw him frown. "Does it bother you?"

"Not really." He shook his head. "Things change."

"Do you like your new place?"

"Sure do, I like it a lot," he nodded, grinning. "Coming to visit me again soon?"

"Again?"

"Yeah, to help a poor lonely man with his empty bottles."

I eyed him snootily. "You're not poor or lonely. You just need to curb your drinking."

"Why do you worry so much about me drinking?"

"I worry about anyone who drinks themselves to oblivion." I was indignant. "Are you trying to kill yourself like your father?"

His eyes narrowed. "What exactly do you know about that?"

I bit my lip. "I'm sorry. I shouldn't have mentioned it."

Taking a breath, he said harshly. "It's no secret that my father got pissed every day. He used to puke heaps too and then one day he choked on it. End of story."

I was taken aback at his bluntness.

"And don't forget I told you that I don't," he added.

"Don't?"

"Puke."

"Oh, right. And you don't do hangovers or headaches either." I wrinkled my nose.

"Good memory." His lips twisted. "What else do you remember?"

"Hey, Doug." Someone spoke from behind me, saving me from answering. "Good to see you, man."

I stepped aside for three men, one of whom apologised for butting in, but I was more than grateful for the interruption. With a quick nod and stiff little smile, I made a quick getaway without looking at Douglas again.

Good memory, indeed! The conversation had shredded my nerves. Although pleased we were at least talking again I wasn't particularly looking forward to our next inevitable meeting.

Chapter 31

Immediately after Kate returned Delta to her paddock after their ride, she did a skip, a buck and raced around in circles. Kingston and BB glanced at each other and shook their heads before watching their friend again with worried eyes.

"Methinks she's lost the plot," Kingston murmured.

"Hey, Delta!" BB called out. "Haven't you already had enough exercise?"

Delta finally skidded to a stop, snorting with glee. "She's happy again!"

"She? Oh, you mean Kate?" BB looked surprised. "Really?"

"Yes, really! She's absolutely fizzing."

"Is fizzing happy?" Kingston looked doubtful.

"I'm positive. She's nervous too, but it feels good."

"Do you know why?"

"Ah!" BB eyes went wide. "So, he's back."

Delta nodded. "I think you're right. She's behaving like before."

"Silly boy!" Kingston muttered. "Why do they do that? Come back every time?"

"Not every time," BB Frowned. "Sometimes they die remember."

He pulled a gloomy face. "True."

"Don't be so pessimistic, you two," Delta chided. "This fella is alive. She wouldn't be fizzing if he wasn't."

Kingston brightened. "Well, let's hope he's fizzing just as much as Kate."

"You should ask the dog what he knows." BB said to Delta.

"I will."

Trojan told Delta he hadn't seen anyone yet, but if his nose didn't deceive him Kate had been close enough to touch a certain man, the bad boy from past times. Both of them quietly hoped things were looking up for their beloved owner.

Willing myself to take the initiative, I contacted Douglas, by text, of course, like the scaredy cat I was. It bounced back. Forced myself to call him but a recorded voice informed me that his old number was obsolete. Initially my nerves sighed with relief at the outcome but that soon changed to despondency, wishing almost desperately to at least hear his voice.

Another voice in my head made its presence felt soon after my phone attempts. Why don't you try something a little more drastic, girl? What do you mean? He's waiting for another visit, remember? I have no wish to visit a drunk man again! Aw, come on. He wasn't so drunk that he couldn't recognise you. Recognise me? Pfff! He was having visions! Ah, now, there's a thought. How about giving him visions he'll never forget? Excuse me? You could dress up or should I say dress down. You know, like sexy underwear? Are you quite mad? Get on with it, girl! Let him know you still want him. Stop wasting time!

"I don't believe I'm even thinking this," I said aloud, shaking my head violently. "It's over between us! He said it, I said it. I'll apologise to him, but that's it!"

Another event at the racetrack was scheduled for the weekend with all manner of cars racing and a chance for any classic car owners to run five laps of the track during the lunch break. I was in two minds about going, worrying myself stupid that he would be there but, in the end, decided to face whatever came and went along with family.

When Matthew asked me to join him as passenger debuting the Mustang on the five-lapper track run I agreed, meeting him before the lunchbreak in the viewing paddock. He appeared agitated but I cast it off as excitement or nerves until he stopped to grab my arm on our way to the collect the car from the workshop.

"There's been a change of plan, sis," he said, frowning.

I creased my forehead, puzzled. "What change?"

"Do you mind if someone else drives?"

"Sure, if that's what you want." I shrugged. "Who?"

He heaved a breath. "Um, the previous owner."

It didn't sink in immediately. "What?" I gasped. "You mean…? Crap!"

"Yeah. Willard." He grimaced. "Sorry, sis."

"Why?" My eyes darted around nervously. "Did he ask you to do this?"

He shook his head. "No, he didn't. Dad suggested it."

"Where is he?"

"In the workshop with Dad."

I backed away. "You don't need me then. I mean you or Dad can be passenger."

"He'll only drive if you go with him." Matt eyed me, spread his hands. "Old and new owner, he reckons it'll be fitting."

I scowled. "Does he now?"

Matt shrugged. "I can understand where he's coming from."

I chewed my lip and relented. We walked into the workshop to find Dad and Douglas with their heads in the Mustang's engine bay, both looking up as we approached. Dad gave me a slow wink and Douglas smiled. I didn't return the smile; my immediate concern was simply to appear calm.

"So, we're going out in her together, are we?" I asked coolly.

"Thought she'd like that." Douglas inclined his head to the Mustang.

I turned to Matthew. "Next time, then."

"Next time is good." He gave me a lopsided smile before turning to frown at Douglas. "You look after my sister out there."

"You bet." Douglas gave him a thumbs up.

Inside the car, I buckled up as Douglas revved the motor, grinning at my eye roll. He drove us to the track starting grid, slotted in amongst thirty or more other classic cars with the engine growling contentedly at idle. The Mustang got its fair share of admiring looks from the watching crowds, but I didn't take much notice. Stared fixedly out the side window, trying to ignore the man beside me. Impossible!

"This is nice, isn't it?" he said softly.

I didn't look at him. "Glad you think so."

"Beautiful girl, beautiful car. What more could a man want?"

"Whatever turns you on." I turned my head to eye him coolly.

"Sure am." He chuckled. "Turned on."

Turned the cool look to ice. "Please concentrate! They're almost ready to let us go."

"I am concentrating." He cocked an eyebrow. "Any plans for later today?"

"What?"

"Are you going out anywhere after this?"

"None of your business!" I snapped.

"Aw." He dropped his lower lip.

"Look!" Suddenly needed to get everything off my chest and over with.

"I apologise for being a bitch when you fixed my tyre and I'm sorry for whatever else. You're back, I'm still here and we're bound to meet up sometimes. I suppose I'm glad we're at least speaking to each other, but that's all we're ever going to do, okay?" With that I gulped in air, staring into eyes I couldn't read.

"I'm sorry too. I should never have left," he said flatly.

That stumped me.

He heaved a sigh. "It seemed like a good idea at the time."

I swallowed. "So why did you leave?"

"Wanted to get away from my past but found out I couldn't." He shook his head at my frown. "I don't mean you. The other bad stuff."

"Bad stuff?"

"My family, all dead." His lips twisted. "And me being an arsehole."

"Hey, you!" An official shouted, waving his arms at us. "Time to move!"

I jumped but Douglas barely reacted except to throttle the car away down the track. My acute awareness of the man beside me or my churning mind didn't make for an enjoyable outing, but the Mustang behaved impeccably, growling around the track at a modest pace and as we finished the run, Douglas grinned at the cheering crowd before driving on past towards the workshop access road.

"Thanks for coming with me," he said.

I smiled thinly, not looking at him. "Hope you enjoyed the drive."

"Very much." We almost at the workshop when he spoke again. "I'm having a barbeque at my place tonight; you're welcome to come over."

Heart tripping, I didn't reply and was out of the car almost before he braked inside the workshop. Dad and Matthew walked in behind us, smiling widely as Douglas got out, glancing across the car's roof at me before turning to them.

He shook both their hands. "Thanks for that, guys. I'll never forget it."

"You're welcome," Dad replied, looking at me. "So, how was it, Kate?"

"Great," I said stiffly. "She goes well."

"She sounds and looks the part, that's for sure." Matthew grinned.

As they began chatting enthusiastically about all things mechanical, I made my escape. Back home I paced all evening, muttering like a mad woman until finally talking myself back into the jeep. Set off for his place as the dark of night closed in but parked out on the road, a good distance from the open gate before peering in around the fence.

Ten or more cars were parked along the driveway with the shed well lit up inside and out. Through the open roller doors, I could see the party was in full swing, people chatting and laughing with music playing, the smell of a barbeque wafting to my nose.

He's lucky these days, I thought wryly. No neighbours close by to complain. No old ladies with binoculars spying on him.

Hesitated before entering, moving furtively to an oak tree. Passing the first vehicle, I pulled a face at a couple making out on the back seat, skirted them quickly and carried on. Arrived at the last oak tree undetected, saw a covered wooden deck had been added since my last visit, built along the living and bedroom area. There was nobody on the deck, but lights inside showed several people in the kitchen area and three females in the bedroom.

They appeared to be having a party of their own, gyrating about holding glasses aloft with one bouncing on his bed in nothing but her underwear. Wondered in mesmerised disgust what they planned to do with him when he arrived and was out of there, antics in his bedroom definitely not something I wanted to watch. Bolted back through the gate to the jeep before skidding to an abrupt stop.

He was propped against my driver's door, asked quietly. "Leaving already?"

I hiccupped to breathe, hand to my mouth.

"Are you all right?" He came off the car, stepping nearer.

I backed up, croaked. "What are you doing here?"

"I saw you come in, figured you weren't planning on staying since you parked out here." His lips twisted. "Thought I'd catch you before you left."

"Oh."

"Why did you come?"

"Being nosey, I suppose." I waved a nervous hand. "You're right, I wasn't planning on staying. I'm really not a party person, plus I don't know anyone here."

"I'll introduce you if you like."

I shook my head. "I think I'll go."

"Why don't you stay for a bit? They're an okay bunch, really." He moved closer, teeth gleaming in a smile. "Even the one's in my bedroom."

Knowing he'd been watching me the whole time grated. "So, why are they even in there?" I snapped.

He chuckled. "Being nosey, I suppose."

I screwed my nose at him, "They're all over your bed."

"As long as they stay out of my sheets."

I didn't respond to that.

He tilted his head. "Did you put me to bed that night?"

"You were on the floor of the toilet," I pouted defiantly. "You didn't look very comfortable."

"So kind," he laughed. "You should have stayed for breakfast."

"With a bleary eyed, grumpy man at the table. No, thanks!"

"Now, that sounds more like the witch I know." He inclined his head to the gateway, gesturing a hand. "Coming in?"

After one second's hesitation, I heaved a breath and went with him.

They were indeed an okay bunch, a little rough around the edges but friendly and welcoming. There was no sign of Poke or Jacko which I was grateful for but did ask him about them at one point, Poke apparently behind bars for some misdemeanour involving drugs and Jacko had gone to Australia.

"I believe you dropped charges against them both." Douglas cocked an eyebrow.

"I just couldn't be bothered." I shrugged. "I'm guessing you had something to do with them handing themselves in?"

"A little friendly persuasion shall we say." He smiled wryly.

"Right." I raised disbelieving eyebrows. "Very friendly, I'm sure."

The three females from the bedroom appeared too, fully clothed and obviously on the hunt for someone. Their surprise and malignantly jealous looks when they spotted me with Douglas were comical to say the least, the bitch in me gloating. Two enjoyable hours passed relatively quickly and with a tummy full of delicious, barbequed chops, potato and lettuce salad with a glass of juice later I excused myself. He insisted on walking me to my car whereupon my nerves livened up again at being alone with him.

"Good of you to stay," he said as we walked out. "Hope you enjoyed it."

"I did, thanks." I shot him a glance. "How are you finding it out here?"

"Yeah, good. Quieter for sure."

"I love the oak trees." I frowned. "You're not going to chop them down, are you?"

"Don't worry, they're staying," he grinned. "Good for hiding behind, eh?"

"I wasn't hiding," I protested.

"Hugging them then?" he offered as we got to the jeep, laughing at my exasperated head shake. "You're welcome to hug them anytime. Me too if you like."

I ignored that, quickly getting in. "Enjoy the rest of your night. Thanks again."

A week later, we bumped into each other in town again, somehow ending up having a coffee together which turned into a friendly catch up. He didn't even flirt. We met several times again, random meetings which had my head full of him afterwards especially at night, dreaming about the touchy feely stuff we used to do and waking up in a sweat. Poor Trojan got an earful.

Hanging around town ever hopeful of a Willard fix was becoming a habit, but even when he did show nothing changed. I couldn't deny the friendly sterile stuff between us was doing my head in. Wanted him back, but my fear of rejection kept me silent, doubting I could handle another dose of pain and loss again.

"Your phone number still the same?" he asked at one of our coffee meetups.

"Yes." I felt suddenly breathless, hoping things were looking up.

"Good." Was all he said, leaning back in his chair.

"Is yours?"

"Nope." He lifted an eyebrow. "Do you want it?"

"Hmmm," I pretended to think hard. "I suppose."

As he reached out a hand, I returned his knowing smirk with a snooty look, gave him my phone and watched him tap in his details. Handing it back our fingers touched again, the tingle making my breath catch.

"Gonna phone me?" The smirk was still there.

"Who knows," I replied coolly.

"Any plans for the weekend?"

"Not really." Shrugged oh so nonchalantly as my heart flipped.

"There's a four-wheel drive competition on." He tipped his head. "Wanna join me, petrolhead gal?"

Keep it cool! "Um, where do they do that?"

"On a farm not far from here. You haven't been before?"

"No."

"Come to my place on Saturday morning if you like. I'll take you."

"Isn't there someone else you'd rather take?"

He shook his head. "Ten o'clock. Does that suit you?"

"Um, well, yes, okay." Oh, la la! Was this a date? Felt like grinning from ear to ear, gave him an insipid little smile instead.

Saturday dawned chilly with mist slowly ebbing away, pulled on warm leggings, jumper and thick jacket with casual boots. Underneath was a different story: not my usual underwear. Black cheeky knickers and a push up bra, kinda hoped they made my boobs look bigger. Not that he'd notice but who knew, a gal could get lucky! Ha! Or get hurt again! Either way, nothing else to do but deal with it.

Arrived to find him looking hunky in jeans, thick bush shirt and work boots. Forced down my reaction to his welcoming smile, pretending calm on the way to the venue. The sun had warmed the chill air nicely by the time we got there, deciding my jacket wasn't needed I left it in his ute and as we walked in from the parking area several men called greetings to Douglas, politely acknowledging me as he made introductions.

The place was well patronised with people sprawled on a hillside overlooking a wide shallow gully where several obstacle courses had been set up, steep inclines, bogs and sharp twisting turns for specially built competition V8 buggies. We wandered around, buying a coffee each before sitting down in the crowd. I found it to be an entertaining spectator sport; loud throttling engines, buggies doing spectacular antics with mud spraying in all directions. Being with Douglas, us laughing and cheering together talk simply added to my enjoyment.

Feeling peckish around lunchtime, we made our way to the food stalls where two females in scanty t-shirts and short shorts descended on Douglas. As it wasn't exactly summertime their display of flesh was quite unnecessary, I thought but judging by Douglas's admiring scrutiny and friendly grin it appeared he wasn't of the same opinion, my annoyance further fuelled at being largely ignored but they weren't long, looking decidedly pleased with themselves after a brief chat with him.

Turning my back I joined the queue without a word, only glancing around when another female cooed his name, watching in disbelief as she fluttered her eyelashes suggestively at him and aimed a kiss at his face.

Jerked my eyes away instantly, muttering under my breath. "Well, that's three for you, aren't you a lucky lad?"

"What was that?" he asked softly in my ear once she'd gone.

Surprised he'd heard me, I yipped. "Nothing! Just talking to myself."

"Enjoying it so far?"

"Yes, thank you. It's great." I shot him a forced smile.

I was absolutely certain the next female deliberately bumped into him, rolling my eyes derisively as she stepped closer to apologise and talk.

Muttered again. "Whoop de doo! A foursome's even better for an orgy."

He heard, asking in my ear as she departed. "You think I should try?"

Gagging, I didn't dare look at him. "Try what?"

"A foursome?"

"I have no idea what you're talking about?"

"Yes, you do." he murmured. "Orgies."

Hoped desperately that no one was listening, gasped. "Do you mind?"

"Mind?" He snorted. "I don't know, I've never tried it. Have you?"

"Don't be ridiculous!" I snapped, turning on him.

His wicked grin had me spinning back again to hide my red face.

"Give me a onesome any day," he drawled softly. "One witch, that is."

Wishing the lunch queue would hurry up, I refused to rise to the bait. No more females accosted him thankfully, we ate our filled rolls in relative silence and shortly after I excused myself to the toilet, agreeing to meet him back at our spot in the crowd. Didn't immediately return however, needing space to myself mulling over negative thoughts.

Douglas's popularity with the opposite sex, my subsequent jealous reactions and his amusement had put a dampener on the day. Realised the boot was on the other foot now, he was no longer the needy besotted one or bewitched. Why would he be with so many other women to choose from? The thought sickened me. Had to get away from him and out of here, him finding out how I felt would be the last straw.

Forced myself to go back and sit with him, feigning an enthusiasm I didn't feel. He noticed of course, asking if I was okay. Shivering a little, I pointed to the sky, taking advantage of the sudden cloud coverage and change in temperature.

"Actually, I might get my jacket out of your car," I mumbled not looking at him.

"Sure." Fishing in his pocket for keys, he gave them to me.

I hurried to his ute, looking around in all directions guiltily before hopping into the driver's seat. Drove out with nerves screaming, stopping some distance along the road before pulling over to text him: **Had to go, sorry. Have taken your ute. Your friends will give you a lift home, I'm sure.**

Not waiting for a reply, I carried on until the self-service petrol station just off the racetrack road appeared, drove in to fill up and checked my phone but found no messages, vaguely aware of a Harley Davison motorbike pulling in at the roadside as I drove out. At Douglas's place, I parked beside my jeep at the shed with a relieved sigh and on exiting the ute, heard the sound of a motorbike's exhaust. My jaw dropped incredulously as the motorbike I'd seen previously appeared through the gateway and pulled up next to me. Knew immediately who the rider was before he removed the helmet.

"You stole my ute," he said.

I gawped, spluttered. "I, um...I. No! I just used it."

"Why not tell me?" He eyed me narrowly. "I would have taken you home?"

I spread my hands inanely. "I didn't want to spoil your day."

"Our day," he corrected, frowning as he got off the bike. "I was enjoying it with you."

"I'm sorry," I muttered.

"Was it something I said?" He hung the helmet on the handlebars.

I shook my head, told a lie. "I didn't feel well."

"But you drove home?" His eyebrows went up.

Sighing, I changed the subject. "Where did you get the bike?"

"From a friend," he said with deliberate sarcasm.

"Oh." I swallowed. "Sorry, I hope it didn't mess up his day, er, transport wise."

"Nah, someone's bringing him over later to pick it up." His lips twisted. "And he's happy, always glad to help mates catch their runaway ladies."

Something snapped inside of me at that. "I was not running and I'm not your lady!" I scowled, adding angrily. "Why did you even ask me out when there's very obviously plenty of other females on offer?"

"Ah." He tipped his head, smirking. "Now, I'm beginning to see."

Gritting my teeth, I spun away and stalked to the jeep.

"You're not jealous, are you?" he drawled.

"Jealous!" I turned on him. "Of course, I'm not jealous. Look, I'm sorry for taking your car and embarrassing you in front of your friends but I didn't ask you to follow me."

"You didn't embarrass me."

"Whatever! I mucked up your day anyway. Don't bother asking me out again."

He rolled his eyes. "Complicated witch."

I stared. "What?"

"Make up your mind."

"About what?"

"What you really want." He tipped his head. "And when you do, let me know."

"Excuse me?"

"Go home. Drive safe," he smiled gently. "I'll be in touch."

Mouth hanging open, I watched him disappear inside the shed without a backward glance. Drove home in a daze where Trojan, concerned at my mutterings kept his soulful eyes glued on my face until I ruffled his ears reassuringly. While undressing to take a shower I remembered the black underwear, the sight making me cackle stupidly.

"What a waste!" I said aloud, poking my tongue out at the mirror.

I hoped he wouldn't get in touch but as the week passed by, I wished he would.

"He's totally right," I told myself scornfully. "I am complicated, don't think I even understand myself." Trojan grinning and wagging his tail had me pulling an indignant face at him. "You don't have to agree!"

The following weekend I dared to text him: **I'd like us to be friends, that's all.**

I hoped almost desperately that he'd contradict me, but I wasn't so lucky.

His reply: **Suits me. See you around.**

Threw my phone down, thumped the kitchen table and with a frustrated sob buried my face in my hands. "Crap! Now what am I going to do?"

Trojan gave me a sympathetic prod with his nose.

A fortnight later, I did my usual grocery shopping, glumly dropping merchandise in the trolley without thought.

Let out an almighty shriek when he spoke in my ear. "Got time for a coffee?"

Whirling around, my elbow caught him in the gut to which he grunted, stepping back quickly with both hands palm up in surrender. Noticing every other shopper in the vicinity ogling us, I felt embarrassed and foolish.

Hissed. "Don't creep up behind me like that!"

"Wasn't creeping," he grinned, rubbing his belly. "And I'm damaged again."

"That's your own fault!" Scowling, I had to turn my back on him. The thought of the body underneath his shirt making me react inside, his grin not helping either.

"So how about that coffee?" he asked again, moving up beside me.

"I'm busy," I muttered, keeping my eyes firmly fixed on the shelves.

"Aw, come on," he cajoled. "Friend."

Silly idea, looking at him! "Okay. Okay!" I relented. "I'll meet you outside."

We had our coffees and talked, but I couldn't quite relax, finding it increasingly difficult to meet his eyes. A noisy group of people at the café entrance distracted him, giving me time to really ogle and drool before quickly averting my gaze as he turned back to me.

"Any plans for the weekend?"

"No!" I shot him a frigid glance.

It didn't deter him. "Don't waste weekends, they're for fun and friends."

"I know that."

"Good." Grinning, he got to his feet. "So, make plans."

I followed him out, both of us halting on the pavement to face each other.

"You said you wanted to be friends, right?" he asked.

What I said, not what I want! Replied. "Well, yes."

"So, let's be friends and go somewhere." He laughed at my frown. "I'm not asking you on a date. Forget who I am, just have fun,"

"Fun?" I scoffed. "And exactly what is your kind of fun?"

"What kind would you like?" he leered. "Two nights and counting?"

Heard my hand connect with his face, felt the sting on my palm. "Don't flatter yourself!" I spat, feeling ridiculously proud I'd executed a slap at last. Turned on my heel and stalked off, expecting him to retaliate but all I heard was him laughing.

Then sudden loud blips stopped me in my tracks. A cop car screeched to a halt beside me, two officers leaping out and rushing past. Whirled to watch them confront Douglas, shouting in his face and backing him up against a parked car hands in the air.

It felt incredulously like watching a scene from an action movie, I could hardly believe what was happening. Other people too had stopped to watch in astonishment.

"Miss Von Meeren!" One officer called out to me. "Are you okay?"

Couldn't believe what I was hearing either, stared poleaxed. "Yes! What's wrong?"

"He assaulted you."

The other officer kept an eye on Douglas, instructing him to keep his hands up and visible which he did with a shrug, looking amused.

"No! No!" I was horrified. "He didn't touch me!"

"Pardon, ma'am?"

"He didn't do anything!" I exclaimed. "I hit him!"

"Are you sure?"

"Yes! Of course!" I nodded sharply.

He turned to his partner with a headshake, Douglas curling his lip and lowering his hands as they reluctantly stepped away from him.

"Sorry, ma'am." The officer inclined his head, both men returning to their car.

I stood rooted to the spot staring at Douglas, unable to say a word.

"Well, well, Von Meeren witch," he drawled sardonically. "Seems I'm not the only male under your spell." And with a mocking salute he strode away.

Realising we'd attracted quite an audience; I made a quick exit for my car. Got home to pace the cabin floor, worrying myself stupid.

Needed to contact him. A quick text: **I'm very sorry.**

He replied surprisingly quickly: **For what? The slap. Everything!**

His reply: **Shit happens. I'll get over it.**

I jabbed back: **But it shouldn't have happened.**

He said nothing more while I kept right on stewing about it. Seemed I had good cause when to my horror the incident went viral with Anna unable to resist regaling my family with all the details and showing off the photos of me, Douglas and the cops. Made me realise rather shockingly that Von

Meerens were indeed news even these days. When my darling beside themselves brothers began rolling about in stitches I scowled at them disdainfully down my nose, Dad trying vainly to keep a straight face got the same treatment with only Helena appearing to show any sympathy.

Gave the photo of Douglas leaning back against the car with his hands up another secretive peek, my insides letting me know exactly what they thought of the man and his wicked smirk. Figured he'd know soon enough he was news and dreaded our next meeting, doubting he'd be wanting friendship, fun or coffee any time soon.

Chapter 32

There was no sign or contact from him whatsoever for weeks but frustrated pathetic me didn't have the guts to do anything about it.

Helena's suggestion of a girl's night out didn't initially ignite enthusiasm, but after some deliberation, I decided to take Douglas's advice and have some fun. Even if it wasn't with him.

Helena had tickets for all us girls to attend a concert/music festival at a local vineyard on Saturday evening, we dressed up, piled into two cars and made our way to the venue. The event proved popular, a huge marquee set out with tables humming and full to overflowing. Shown to our designated table near the stage we sat down to chat and enjoy ourselves while catering staff wandered through the crowds with drinks and a delicious array of finger food.

By the time, the concert began, I was beginning to feel quite merry after a second glass of red wine. The first performer, a young female violinist playing classical pieces received a standing ovation, the next act a country band of three got everyone clapping and singing along and the third act, an older male pianist playing ballads sent shivers down my spine.

While talking enthusiastically about the music during the break, Bella and Olivia eyes lit up at something behind me.

"Hello, ladies," a man drawled.

The shivers were not a patch on what I felt right then.

"Hi, Douglas," they cooed in unison, smiles beaming.

"Douglas! How nice to see you," Anna welcomed, gesturing for him to come closer.

Moving into my line of sight, he took her hand. "Nice to see you too. Enjoying it, so far?"

I salivated, thinking he looked good enough to eat in black trousers and white shirt.

"Oh, yes. It's wonderful," Anna nodded. "Such good musicians."

"We're looking forward to the rest of them," Bella told him.

"Where are you sitting?" Anna asked.

"Other side," he pointed. "I'm with work colleagues."

"You work for a vineyard, don't you? Is this it?"

"No, but my boss and the owner of this one are friends."

Anna nodded. "The fruit and vegetable growers all seem to know each other, don't they? Like farmers, one big family."

"Yeah, it seems that way."

He looked around the table, smiling slowly when he saw me. I forgot to breath, only remembering to when he broke eye contact, his attention back on Anna.

"So, it's just the girls tonight then?"

Stephanie giggled. "Yep. We've been let out."

"Would you like to join us?" Olivia laughed. "Invitation to special boys only."

"The ones that make headlines," Glenys added with a glint in her eye.

Oh, no! Please don't remind him! I despaired, dropping my eyes to my lap.

"And get into trouble," Stephanie added for good measure.

He chuckled. "It's usually girls that get us fellas into trouble."

"Oh, dear," Bella giggled. "Not any of us surely?"

My icy up from under look only served to make her widen innocent eyes at me.

"Well, actually," Douglas drawled. "She is one of your relations."

"It runs in the family, my boy," Anna chortled. "Lawson girls are a handful."

He laughed. "Add Von Meeren to the mix and it gets dangerous."

Jerking my head up at that, I returned his teasing grin with a baleful stare just as a disembodied voice informed us the show was about to continue

"I better move." He inclined his head to us all. "Thanks for the invite, ladies, maybe later."

"You're very welcome, Douglas," Anna told him.

We all watched him walk away, didn't know what the other girls were looking at, but my eyes were on his backside. He returned to a large table of perhaps ten people, my heart stopping as he sat down beside a woman. The same woman he'd been kissing in town against the white car. Tore my eyes away as she smiled, leaning in close to touch him.

The sudden pounding of drums as the African inspired group began their music was a thankful distraction, the second act a soulful jazz singer and saxophone player wasn't as effective, but the loud rock band next did the job of erasing any feeling sorry for myself thoughts and another glass of wine during the second break kind of helped with that too.

"Don't worry, Kate dear," Anna looked straight at me. "She's not his girlfriend."

Blinking dismay, I realised it wasn't just her who'd noticed my reaction to Douglas and the woman, all the other girls watching with sympathetic eyes.

Bella frowned at Anna. "And you know that how, Mum?"

"Body language," Anna replied, cheerfully matter of fact. "Conveniently partnered up for the occasion, I'd say."

I shook my head. "No, you're wrong! I've seen them together before." When nobody said a word, not even Anna, I added sharply. "And can we talk about something else!"

That had the desired effect, Olivia changing the subject quickly and chat resumed. Trying my best to concentrate I failed miserably, staring back defiantly at Bella's raised eyebrows as I grabbed another glass of wine. Subsequently needed to use the ladies in rather a hurry, pulling a face as the floor shifted weirdly on my weaving way there. In the toilet cubicle I screwed my eyes shut, breathing deeply and convincing myself I was fine. At least the floor appeared to behave better on the way back to my seat.

Another three acts followed, a harpist who played beautifully, three lads singing country and a rock and roll group that pounded out some old songs for us to sing along with. Afterwards everyone seemed to be talking at once, voices eddied around me and with a fresh glass of wine in my hand and a plateful of savouries to nibble on I felt suitably mellow. "Hey witch," Douglas's voice in my ear gave me such a fright I screeched, flinging wine up into his face. Spun around to watch him squint, wipe a hand across his eyes and shake his head, droplets flying almost as if in slow motion.

"Oh, crap!" I yelped, leaping to my feet.

Not a good move. Swayed, staggered and felt my knees buckle.

As always Douglas moved fast. Stepping forward, he locked an arm on my waist and took my weight. I heard surprised voices, saw faces and wide eyes before everything went hazy and then black. Came to being carried in his arms with Bella and Olivia scuttling alongside, their voices concerned and breathless. I peered at him, tried unsuccessfully to lift a hand to his cheek as he looked down at me.

"Hello...gorgeous," I giggled at his hair standing up on end. "Your hair's wet!"

He simply raised his eyebrows and kept walking.

"I think you're ad...adorable," I giggled again. "And...you smell nice. Like wine."

"Oh, dear." I heard Bella say. "She's had way too much to drink."

"I'm dangerous too," I hiccupped. "You...know."

Watching his mouth twist, I spluttered more giggles.

"You're so strong...and did I say you were ad...adorable?"

"Sorry about this, Doug," Bella said.

"No worries." He showed his teeth in a grin or a grimace; I wasn't sure.

"You're puffing." I frowned my concern. "Are you going to...drop me?"

"No," he said looking down at me again. Positive it was a grin, I grinned back.

"Where...where are we going?" I eyed his mouth. "Sex...sexy lips."

"You're going home," Olivia told me.

"Nice!" I fluttered eyelashes at Douglas. "Are you... coming too?"

"Are you sure you don't mind taking her home?" Bella asked him.

"Not at all." He turned his head side on to me. "You go back and enjoy yourselves."

"Sex...sexy lashes too," I observed. "Don't you...think so, girls?"

"Absolutely." Olivia snorted a laugh.

"I'll phone Jason. Let him know you're on the way," Bella said.

"Good idea." He nodded, halting beside his ute as Olivia unlocked it.

Once bundled gently into the passenger seat, he reclined it a couple of notches and leant across me to do up the seatbelt. Took my plucking at his shirt and giggling in his stride, buckled up and shut the door with me continuing to make silly faces at him through the window.

"She's going to hate herself in the morning," Bella grimaced.

"We're so sorry about this," Olivia apologised.

He snorted a laugh. "Sorry for what? It's been entertaining."

"She ruined your night and your shirt."

"Douglas shook his head, "Not my favourite shirt anyway and nobody got hurt."

"So far," Olivia laughed. "Make sure she keeps her hands to herself."

"I'll be careful," he grinned.

"Thanks, so much for your help." Bella patted his arm.

"Anytime."

As he drove, I told him over and over between giggles that he was gorgeous, adorable and sexy. Made feeble attempts to touch, stroked his arm and thigh but he very patiently removed my hand and for the most part concentrated on his driving. Things got considerably hazier, I must have dozed or blacked out and only came too again in my old bed at the homestead with Dad fussing over me. Next morning my body didn't feel as if it belonged, my eyes protested loudly at daylight, my head wanted to roll off my shoulders and although painfully befuddled my mind remembered.

Oh, please. No! Aren't you supposed to forget when you've got a hangover? No such luck! Every single detail of the night before played like a slide show.

Moaned, screwed my eyes shut and wished I could turn back the clock. As my stomach complained, I staggered from the bed and hung over the toilet bowl. With Dad and Helena keeping a sympathetic eye on me, I managed to drink copious amounts of water, nibbled at a piece of bread and by evening drove myself home.

Like the adult I was supposed to be I apologised to Douglas via text: **I'm sorry, again.**

No reply.

I tried again: **I need to apologise. Please can we talk?**

No reply.

Third time and desperate: **Please, Douglas.**

He replied: **Count us even. You took care of me when I was pissed.**

It wasn't enough. Texted back immediately: **Can we meet?**

A minute later, he replied: **No need, apology accepted.**

Face to face, please!

Another minute passed: **Okay. Coffee on Monday after work same café.**

Thank you!

I waited inside at our usual table for ages, gazing forlornly out the window thinking he'd changed his mind. Sat up straighter as the ute braked hard almost directly outside and reversed effortlessly into a park it shouldn't have been able to fit into. He strode into the café as I stood to my feet, met my eyes without smiling and gesturing for me to sit back down, he ordered our coffees.

As he sat down opposite, again with no welcoming grin, I blurted. "Thanks for coming. I really needed to apologise properly."

"You already did." His eyes were emotionless.

"Properly," I repeated. "I'm sorry for my behaviour, for slapping you the other day and I didn't mean to throw my drink in your face Saturday night."

"It just happened, right?" A hint of amusement in his eyes. "My face got in the way."

Attempting a wane smile, I felt better. "I'm truly sorry. I ruined your night."

He shrugged. "No harm done."

"Ruined your night with your girlfriend," I muttered, staring at the tabletop.

"Girlfriend?"

"You were sitting beside her at the concert."

"Natasha?" He sounded surprised. "She's the boss's daughter, not my girlfriend."

"I saw you both in town once," I hesitated. "Um, next to a white Mercedes."

He nodded amicably. "That'll be her car."

I scowled. "And you were, um, kissing her." Oh, save it! Why even bring it up?

Our coffees arrived; I stirred mine as if my life depended on it without looking at him.

He said quietly. "If I recall, she was kissing me."

I shot him a sarcastic up from under look but kept my mouth shut.

"She's friendly." His lips twisted. "And likes kissing."

"Is that all?" I was scathing.

"Yep." He took a long swallow of coffee.

I sipped mine in the silence, plucked up courage. Didn't even know what made me ask. "Did you have girlfriends in the US?"

"No."

"Ha!" I stared at him in disbelief. "None? Not even two nights?"

"None." He shook his head. "We worked all hours. It was hard slog and I lived on site. There were no women and even if there were, I wasn't in the mood."

"Oh."

"Nobody since you, sweet witch."

I blinked, said in a strangled voice, "Why did you call me that?"

"Witch?" He knit his brow. "I nearly always do."

"Not the other, you don't," I croaked. "Where did you get that from?"

"Sweet?" His eyebrows lifted. "It just popped into my head."

"That's what Opa called Oma," I whispered.

"Sorry." He leant closer. "Didn't mean to upset you."

"It's okay. I was just surprised, that's all." Averting my eyes, I drank more coffee.

"What did she call him?" he asked softly.

My eyes met his vaguely. "Who?"

"Your Oma. What did she call your Opa?"

"Oh." I came to my senses. "Big Bad Wolf."

He chuckled. "That figures."

"Do you know what they call you?" Could be a good idea to shut up now!

'No."

"The bad boy." I pursed my lips. "And I'd be inclined to put a very in front of that."

"The very bad boy, you reckon?" he grinned. "What have I done to deserve that?"

Finishing my coffee quickly, I stood up. "Gotta go. Thanks for the coffee."

He remained seated. "So, when's the next coffee?"

"I'm not sure that's a good idea," I muttered, avoiding his eyes. "Maybe it's best we stay away from each other."

"Is that what you want?"

"No."

"Glad to hear it." As my eyes shot back to his, he grinned. "I'll be in touch."

"Why?"

"Because staying away isn't what I want either."

I shook my head in protest. "But we don't do together, very well."

"We can do friends, can't we?"

Wasn't entirely convinced but nodded anyway.

In town several days later on return to my jeep, I found him propped against it. The delight at seeing him almost floored me. He raised his eyebrows at the stupid look on my face, helped me load my groceries and we stopped for another coffee.

"Good week?" he asked politely as we sat down in the café.

"Okay, so far," I gazed out the window pensively. "How about you?"

"Yeah, good," he answered softly. "What's up?"

I glanced at him. "Nothing."

"Watching for cops?"

"Look," I spread my hands. "I'm really sorry about that."

He made a slicing gesture across his throat. "Forget it."

I persisted. "You do know it went viral?"

"Yep."

"Why would the cops even do what they did?" I shook my head, appalled.

"VIPs need protection, I guess."

"What?"

"Very important people," he grinned smugly. "Like Von Meerens."

"We are not!"

He shrugged. "Opinions differ."

"Whatever!" I scowled. "Why would they even be watching? I mean both of us?"

"Cops watch bad boys, especially when they hang out with good girls."

"Oh, really?"

He didn't comment but his grin turned evil.

I wrinkled my nose at him, said indignantly. "But they shouldn't blame you for something you didn't do. That's the second time."

"Second time?"

"They tried blaming you for what happened to June too, remember."

"Don't stress about it. I'm used to the cops waiting for a slip up."

"Douglas, please." I looked at him with huge eyes. "Don't."

"Don't what?"

"Get used to it. You're not a bad person."

"Thought I was a bad boy in your eyes too," he smirked. "A very bad boy."

"Not like that."

"Like what then?"

"Let's not go there, please," I sighed. "Do you really want us to be friends?"

He snorted a laugh. "She whacks me over the head, slaps me and throws her drink in my face. Of course, I want to be friends."

"Whacks you over the head?" I gasped. "When?"

"Your brother was beating me up."

"Oh, I forgot about that," I grimaced, added indignantly. "You were beating him up!"

"She also steals my car and gets the cops onto me."

"Oh, please! That's not true."

I felt terrible, biting my lip and eying him worriedly.

"What more could a guy want?" He snorted a laugh. "Besides I'm gorgeous, adorable and sexy, aren't I?"

"What?" I gave him a scathing stare. "Who told you that?"

"You did. At the concert and all the way home, don't you remember?"

"Oh, that. Thanks for reminding me," I glared. "Not!"

Our coffees arrived with two delicious pieces of banana cake with chocolate icing which we scoffed. The conversation turned to more amicable subjects, I decided being friends was a good idea after all and positively fizzed with warm fuzzies.

At home, I de-fizzed, the annoying little voice in my head beginning with a question. You really want a sterile friendship with the man? Sanity answered. Yes, it's safer! I'd rather die that go through heartache again. You're a wuss! He's a hot-blooded male, he'll start looking elsewhere if you don't do something. So what? If it makes him happy, let him! I clapped my hands over my ears, but the malicious voice drummed on. And what makes you happy? Other females all over him. No, it makes me feel sick. So, hurry up and nab him. But I don't want to get hurt again. It's part of life, get on with it!

Chapter 33

Another week passed by with no fizz at all, poor Trojan getting an earful of more frustrated mutterings. I wasn't even in the mood to eat, picking at my dinner one evening.

My phone rang, didn't recognise the number and said a lack lustre hello.

"Hey, witch," he said cheerfully.

The phone slid out of my fingers, bouncing off the table to hit the floor with a clatter. Yelping, I hurriedly scraped my chair back and went down on my knees to reach for it.

With it back on my ear I squeaked. "Are you still there."

He snorted. "Wow, that was loud! Did you drop it in the sink or something?"

"No, on the floor," I muttered. "Sorry."

"Have that effect, do I?"

I was indignant. "You surprised me. It wasn't your number."

He laughed. "Using a spare from work. I ran over mine with the vineyard mower and haven't had time to get a new one yet."

I giggled. "Oh, well done!"

"Yeah, bummer. Hey, there's another concert on Saturday night. Want to go?"

"Oh, um." I blew out my cheeks. "Yes."

"It's outdoors at the sports ground, laid back style this time."

"Er, sounds great." Uh oh! Sounded like a date and a bad idea!

"I'll pick you up," he said, ringing off before I could protest.

The venue was definitely more casual than the vineyard had been with food stalls not caterers, no tables and limited bench seating. We bought hot chips, kebabs, a beer for him, a fruit juice for me and relaxed on the grass bank. After finishing our food, he lay down on his side propped on one elbow while I remained sitting, leaning back on my hands.

Although not as many musicians, the acts were longer with several songs a piece, but the best part was having the man beside me. The long-sleeved shirt hid his tattoos, clung to the body underneath and had me lusting.

One of the acts was a well-endowed woman with a sultry voice and seductive sway accompanied by a male piano player. Douglas didn't take his eyes off her like every other male there and when he glanced at me afterwards, I very deliberately held his gaze and fluttered my eyelashes.

"Gives you the shivers, doesn't it?" he murmured, smiling.

"If you say so." I pursed my lips.

"Didn't you feel it?"

What I felt had nothing to do with music! "Er, no."

"Like fingers on skin."

Yikes! Too close to home! "You're imagining things, I think."

"Maybe it's not just the music." Sitting up, he edged closer.

"You're talking weird."

"You make me feel weird, witch."

Swallowing hard, I hissed. "Stop it!"

"You started it," he said amicably.

"Started what?" I was indignant.

"Flirting."

"Flirting?" I blinked indignation. "I did not."

"Eyelashes," he murmured.

We were almost nose to nose. Felt the quiver, immediate, sweet and shocking. No! No and no! Not here! I jerked my head back and away from him, gulping air.

Stabbed a finger. "Look, the next act is coming on."

He leant back nonchalantly without a word.

I turned my face so he couldn't see it, closing my eyes. How did that happen? What am I doing here? I should have trusted my instincts. Friends? My foot!

A rock and roll band played several songs, got everyone clapping along which eased my nerves a little. A female threesome in cowboy hats were next, harmonising beautifully with the lead singer's voice low and sweet.

"There it is again," he said.

"What?"

"Shivers," he smirked.

"Definitely the music," I told him coldly.

My nerves were back with a vengeance, thought seriously about a glass of wine to steady them but decided a repeat of my performance at the previous concert didn't bear thinking about. My stressing and rubbing clammy hands down my trouser legs were a waste of effort, he made no moves and cheerfully wished me goodnight without even getting out of the ute.

I spent the rest of the night wide awake, suitably frustrated. Figured we weren't on the same wavelength about being friends and his talk of shivers didn't make sense. I doubted they were anything like my quiver and if they were, he had a problem which I decided wasn't mine to solve, there were it seemed plenty of other women who'd gladly do that for him. As our spasmodic get togethers continued, I wondered why I was torturing myself. He was always friendly and talkative, but barely touched me and it drove me crazy.

The day I saw him walking into the café we usually frequented with Natasha I gagged in disbelief, turning on my heel to fume all the way to my jeep. Stalked past his ute parked at the roadside and stopped in my tracks. The temptation was too great. I glanced around furtively, making sure no one was watching before crouching down to let air out of a front tyre. Vindication had me grinning all the way home but soon felt as deflated as the tyre, scolding myself for childish stupidity while Trojan cocked a soulfully understanding head.

Douglas rang that evening, "Hello, witch. How goes it?"

As my conscience went into immediate overdrive, I gulped a curt. "Hi."

"Are you okay?"

"Yes." I breathed. "Why wouldn't I be?"

"You sound stressed or something."

"Work probably."

"Time for a relaxing weekend then. Any plans?"

"No."

"Want to go somewhere with me?"

"Don't you have any other females to ask?" I couldn't help myself.

"A few." He sounded amused.

"Well, go ask them then!" I snapped, promptly disconnecting.

He phoned back immediately but I didn't answer. When no message or text appeared, I quickly locked up, turned off lights and sat in the dark stewing, sure he was on his way over. No sign of him. Silly me didn't sleep well again, forcing myself to work the next day. Got in a tizz driving home but again no bad blonde boy came to harass me.

Serves you right! I mocked myself. Ring him, you idiot! Tell him you're available before he takes another option, Natasha maybe. Bugger it!

I stabbed out a text: **Have you asked someone else yet?**

No reply. As Friday evening turned to night, I felt bereft and mortified.

Why do you do this to yourself, I sneered. Give up! Have a sterile and safe life.

He replied late Saturday morning: **Complex lady, aren't you?**

I ignored that: **Slept in, did you? Must have been a good night.**

It was.

Good morning, too? I berated myself as soon as I pressed send.

You want to know if I'm on my own?

Could see him grinning in my mind's eye, decided to be blunt: **Are you?**

No hangover, no headache and no witch here.

I couldn't help myself: **No boss's daughter either?**

Her daddy wouldn't like that.

I was sarcastic: **And you're scared of her daddy?**

No. Scared of a witch who lets down tyres.

My heart went to my mouth, stared at the phone idiotically.

He added: **You were spotted.**

I felt pathetic, had no idea how to reply.

He sent another: **Can I ask why?**

I bit my lip, stabbed at the phone: **You know a lot of women, don't you?**

Not a lot. I have a few lady friends.

Do you take all of them to the same café?

You don't approve?

Baring my teeth, I stabbed another text: **None of my business!**

My flat tyre's your business.

Sorry, stupid thing to do.

You're forgiven.

That made me feel even worse. Pathetic complicated me had to face facts. Forced myself to text again: **I think we need to move on.**

Meaning?

This isn't being friends. I stuff things up every time.

That's okay, so do I.

All we do is hurt one another.
Whose scared now?
I'm being sensible for once!
It doesn't suit you.
I'm serious! I can't do this any longer.
Is that what you want?
Yes. I think it is.
We have fun, don't we?
It's not fun!
What's a few bruises?
Stop it! Us together doesn't work.
That's it then?
Yes! Please leave me alone.

There were no more texts. I threw my phone viciously across the room, collapsed into an armchair and sobbed like a baby. Trojan was outside whimpering at the door, but I didn't get up. Eventually the tears dried leaving me wrung out and morbid, made myself move eventually and took Trojan down to the beach for a long exhausting walk.

It's over and better this way, I convinced myself. No bad blonde boys in my life, no sterile friendly stuff, no more flirting and hurting. I've had enough.

Chapter 34

Douglas listened and left me alone. The indescribable hurt of him being out of reach was worse than being near him.

I buried myself in my work, taking on overtime hours if they were available and coped with my secluded little life as best I could. My family, especially Dad and Bella tried communicating but came up against a brick wall. I kept out of town and out of sight, doing my necessary shopping elsewhere whenever possible and found solace in wine, bottles of it on Friday and Saturday nights. Trojan and I walked the beach and headlands often, but I didn't visit the farm and felt bad about it.

Delta voiced her concerns. "Kate isn't herself again. Something's wrong."

Kingston rolled an eye at her. "Okay, so she isn't riding you. That doesn't mean there's something wrong."

"Don't worry, Delta. She's probably just too busy." BB was more sympathetic.

"Her not riding me isn't the worry," Delta said. "Haven't you two noticed?"

"Noticed what?" Kingston frowned.

"She's not coming here, full stop."

BB frowned. "You're right. She doesn't visit her dad either."

"She's at the vet clinic though, I've seen her car," Kingston commented.

"So have I." Delta eyed him. "At all hours which is weird."

"Why weird?" Kingston looked puzzled. "She works there."

"Well, aren't you observant, Kingston." BB rolled her eyes at him.

"And?" He curled his lip at her.

"All hours, I said," Delta pointed out. "She's there more often lately, even at night, but she doesn't come to the farm and it's just a hop, skip and jump across the road.'"

"I agree, it is weird," BB nodded. "She always made the effort before."

"Exactly." Delta heaved a sigh. "There's something wrong, all right.

"Okay, I get it," Kingston muttered. "So, what do you think it is, this time?"

"It'll be a man problem again, I'll bet you," BB pulled a scornful face.

"Of course!" Kingston was sarcastic. "What else could it be?"

"Things were okay between them," Delta said. "Not the same as before but okay."

"Maybe they've had a tiff," BB offered.

"Human tiffs are bad news!" Kingston shook his head sadly "They lose the plot and go silly, get really loud, like much louder than normal and throw things."

"And give us the willies," BB added for good measure.

Delta pulled a resigned face. "Let's not stress about all of that. We'll just have to stay alert, try and help her somehow if she comes here. Right?"

"Sounds like a good plan," BB nodded.

"Good plan indeed. Always stay alert and be ready to help. Your human friends need you more than you'll ever know."

Delta started in surprise as BB and Kingston both suddenly leapt off all fours, jerking their noses in the air and ogling each other with wide eyes.

"What's up with you two now?" She frowned at them both.

"Did you say something?" BB spoke to Kingston, ignoring her.

"No! Did you?" His eyes bulged.

"Voices again?" Delta tilted her head.

"Um, yes!" BB blew out a breath. "Obsidian this time, I think."

"What did he say?"

"He said we should always be ready to help our human friends, they need us."

"That sounds like good advice," Delta nodded.

"She's onto it," Obsidian agreed. "Smart lady, your friend."

"Yes, we know," Kingston sighed. "Smarter than me anyway."

"Females usually are," Obsidian grunted. "Unfortunately."

"Ha! See, how many times have I told you that, Kingston?" BB chortled.

"Don't get too big for your hooves, young lady!" Obsidian chided. "Us males have our uses."

As BB face fell, she spluttered. "Sorry! Didn't mean any offence."

Kingston chuckled at BB's panic, "Ha! See, that'll teach you."

"Okay, enough!" Obsidian growled. "Remember who you are, Shadow horses. Look after your friends, human or otherwise and listen to the smartest in the paddock. You could learn something, I should know."

"Okay!" Kingston and BB said in unison.

"Good!" Obsidian faded. "Until next time then."

BB and Kingston stared at each other in silence before turning their heads to eyeball Delta. She'd been listening to the one-sided exchange with interest, eyeballed them back and waited with a question in her eyes.

"You're the smartest in the paddock." BB informed her.

"Says who?"

"Obsidian. He said we should listen to you and learn something."

"Don't count on it," Delta snorted.

"We already have," Kingston said. "Smarty pants."

Delta scowled. "Call me that again and you'll learn something all right."

"Okay, enough!" BB tried imitating Obsidian's growl.

While keeping watch for Kate, they saw her visit the homestead several times briefly but although she acknowledged them calling out with a quick wave she didn't come across to chat. Even from a distance they could tell all was not well, her body language and drawn face had them worried.

I was a fool to stay away from the horses as they'd always helped me cope in the past, hoped desperately to get myself together soon and knew Daniel and Bella would take good care of them in the meantime.

One weekend morning I made a quick dash to a country market for fruit, vegetables and the inevitable wine but wasn't expecting to see Natasha and a man I surmised to be her father advertising their vineyard at a stall, trestle tables laden with grapes, berries and avocados. Certainly, made no attempt to inspect their wares, bypassing them quickly and continued shopping until I glimpsed the back view of a blonde-haired man.

Shock had my heart galloping and without thought I bolted, hiding behind a stall to catch my breath. Telling my imagination to stop playing tricks, I quickly purchased two bottles of wine and headed for the carpark.

Stopped dead with a slack jawed gasp as Douglas straightened up from leaning against the jeep's rear door, my desperate head shake stopping his approach thankfully.

"Go away!" I croaked.

His mouth twisted sardonically. "You can run but you can't hide."

"What are you doing here?"

"Did you really think we'd never meet again?" He spread his hands, smiling evilly. "We live in the same town, witch."

"I don't want to talk to you!" I snapped.

He ignored that, looked me up and down. "You've lost weight."

"I'm going now!" Gritting my teeth, I took a step forward

"I'm not stopping you." He gestured to my jeep. "Go if you want."

He didn't move as I sidled past him, eyes averted. Felt rather than saw his body turn towards me and reacted spontaneously. The bag in my hand swung out in a wild arc, the wine bottles clanging together as they connected with his leg. With a horrible grunt, he staggered but stayed upright, instantly shifting his weight to the opposite leg. Bent forward to clutch his molested knee, breath hissing through his teeth. Dropping everything with a yelp, I reached out to help him.

He thrust his other hand in my face, snarling. "Don't come any fucking closer!"

I recoiled at his bared teeth. Saw his eyes screw shut in pain before opening wide again, a stare of pure venom directed at me. Hobbling to the car next to mine, he leant against it for support and gripping his thigh hard, blew out his cheeks.

Horrified, I realised it was the same wheel brace knee. "You better get that looked at. Shall I ring an ambulance?"

"Piss off!" he snarled.

"But you need help."

"If I want any help, it won't be from you!"

"Your knee could be broken!" I squeaked. "Again."

He shot me another lethal glare. "Fuck off before I do something you'll regret."

"Watch your language!" I told him sharply. "There are kids around here."

"Who gives a shit?"

"Please! I'll give you a lift to the doctor."

"Get lost! I'm not going anywhere with you!"

"Be sensible."

"Piss off!" Straightening up, he clenched his jaw and dragged himself away without a backward glance.

Rooted to the spot, I watched him disappear out of sight, feeling both appalled and horribly inadequate. Looked down at my bags of shopping on the ground, picked them up in a stupor and found the wine bottles unexpectedly intact. After stowing them in the jeep, I paced indecisively before finally concluding he'd most likely prefer help from his boss or girlfriend than from me. Went home to stress some more, visions of his pain eating me up.

Finally summoned up courage to text him: **How are you?**
No reply.
I had to try again: **Please let me know if you're okay.**
Nothing.
One last time: **I'm so sorry. I didn't mean to hit you.**
No answer.

Sighing deeply, I shut my eyes as tears seeped out down my cheeks. He hates me, I shook my head despairingly. Do you blame him? You're a bitch!

Couldn't leave it like that and dialled his number with shaking fingers. Waited with bated breath, but when the answer phone kicked in I disconnected without leaving a message. Curled into an armchair with Trojan keeping a watchful eye on me, I sat staring at the phone like it lifeline. Yipped when it rang less than an hour later, my heart tripping and beginning to pound at the number.

"Hello," I gulped.

"Had an X-ray," he said curtly. "Knee's bruised, that's all."

"Oh, that's such good news!" I breathed relief. "Thanks for letting me know."

"Good news?" He was sarcastic. "Thought you'd be disappointed."

"Please! I'm truly sorry."

"Those bottles, apart from attacking me with them what were they for?"

"I didn't attack you!"

"What's in them?"

"Um, wine."

"To drink on your own?"

"Yes."

"How about sharing? You owe me."

"I don't think you should be drinking right now."

"Why the fuck not?"

"Not a good idea, mixing alcohol and drugs," I said primly sharp.

"Prescription or otherwise."

"Any other advice for an overgrown numbskull arsehole, vet nurse?"

"Do you have to be so nasty?"

"Nasty?" He barked a laugh. "Me?"

"Did Natasha and her dad take you to hospital?" I had to ask.

"What have they got to do with anything? I drove myself."

"Oh, um." I hesitated. "They were at the market."

"And?"

"I thought you were there with them."

"You think too fucking much."

"Please stop using the f word. It's not nice."

"Shit! These painkillers aren't working," he muttered. "I need a f…bleeding drink."

"Please, don't do that."

"What are you going to do? Stop me?" he snarled and hung up.

I phoned him back immediately, but he didn't pick up. I stewed, debated and gabbled to Trojan. Made up my mind. Grabbed essentials and jumping in the jeep, tore over to Douglas's place. As the gate was open, I barely slowed, slamming on the brakes at the shed. Scrambling out, I ran for the utility door to hammer on it. No response. I leapt for the deck, along to the living room ranch slider but found it locked. Peered in to see him lying prone on the sofa, a large bottle on the coffee table beside him. Calling out his name, I thumped desperately on the glass and to my relief got a response. He raised his head and scowling, gave me a one fingered salute.

"Open up, Douglas!" I shouted. "Please."

"Piss off!" He dropped his head back down and didn't move.

I thumped some more to no avail, sidled along to the bedroom ranch slider which to my surprise slid open. Rushed inside to snatch up the half empty rum bottle, meeting his baleful stare defiantly.

"No more of that!" I told him, placing the bottle on the kitchen bench out of reach.

"So sensible," he sneered.

"How about going to bed?"

"Nothing wrong with the sofa."

"Can you stand up?"

Still glowering he sat up with a grunt of pain but kept his injured leg straight.

I watched him. "Do you need help?"

He snorted a derisive laugh. "Why don't you hit me over the head with that bottle, more your style, isn't it?"

I ignored that, sighed deeply. "You can lean on me if you like."

"Like shit!" he growled and got to his feet.

I followed as he hobbled to the bedroom, watched him sit down gingerly on the bed with a muscle in his jaw clenching and met his sardonic stare. "What's next, vet nurse?"

"Lie down and rest," I said more calmly than I felt.

Let out a shriek as he lunged forward, just leaping out of reach as his fingers brushed my arm and heard him laugh, whirling in the doorway with a suitable scowl at the ready

"Come here and be my painkiller," he leered, patting the bed.

"Lie down and go to sleep!" I bit out, my heart thudding madly.

"Aw, how bloody boring," he mocked. "And sensible."

"Just like me!" I shot over my shoulder, legs trembling all the way to a kitchen chair.

Coming here was a bad idea! I thought, breathing hard. Ah, come now! The little voice retorted. Here's your chance. For what? To call a truce! It's what you really want, don't deny it. I can't! We bugger it up all the time. Who cares about that? Live in the moment. What's that supposed to mean? The voice turned sly. Why not take him up on his offer? Be his painkiller, give him a comfort bonk. What? Are you mad? You'll enjoy it as much as he will. And then what? You'll get two more nights and counting, guaranteed. No way! Not again! I've made my decision. Spoilsport!

Hearing no sound from the bedroom, I sneaked a look some minutes later to find him lying on his side, eyes closed. Returned to the kitchen to make a hot drink, deciding against my better judgment to stay over as I drank it, checked him again a few times and eventually fell asleep on the sofa, waking with a start to early morning light streaming in.

He was seated at the kitchen table watching me, face expressionless and unsmiling.

I came off the sofa in an instant, swallowing nervously. "How are you?"

"Not too bad," he said quietly.

"Did you get some sleep?"

"Yeah."

"Have you taken any painkillers?"

"Yeah."

"Okay, um, well." I swallowed again. "You'll be all right on your own?"

"You're not having breakfast?"

"You want me to stay for breakfast?" I was disbelieving.

"I'm over it." He shrugged. "No hard feelings."

I shook my head. "I have to go."

"Why?" He cocked an eyebrow at my frowning silence. "Come on, friend, have breakfast with me."

"Friends don't hurt each other!"

"Exciting stuff." His mouth twisted wryly. "And if you're doing the hurting, I don't mind really."

"You need your head read!" I squawked incredulously. "I busted your knee again, um, well almost! "

"Like I said, sensible doesn't suit you."

Shaking my head, I blew out my cheeks. "I really don't think I can do this any more."

"Tell me something honestly."

"What?" I breathed, nerves jumping.

"Are you happy?" He tilted his head. "I mean, really happy right now?"

"No! I'm not!" I blurted. "But this stuff with you, isn't making me happy either."

"Stuff?"

Stomach tying itself in notes, I took the bull by the horns. "The friend thing, it's not enough! Neither is just having fun!"

"And?"

"I want serious," I gulped. "Like we were before."

He stared for a long silent moment, "Are you flirting or what?"

"Flirting?" I narrowed my eyes, not understanding. "Of course not, I'm serious."

"I'm confused." He rubbed his forehead. "You want to be friends, then you don't. One minute it's on, then it's over and now you want to be more than friends?"

"Well, you said it yourself. I'm complicated."

"Very!" he nodded. "You give me eyelashes, then I get clobbered."

"Eyelashes?" I blinked bafflement. "You've lost me."

He rolled his eyes heavenward. "You flirt, witch. Then you piss me off."

"I do not!" I snapped. "Flirt, I mean. Piss you off, that's kind of easy."

He shook his head, grimacing wryly. "Okay, let me get this straight. You want what we had before I went to the US?"

"Um, yes."

"Are you sure about that?"

I breathed deeply. "Yes,"

"Those aren't the signals I'm getting."

"Signals?"

"Every time I get close, you either give me the cold shoulder, run or attack."

"I'm no good at signals."

"Join the club." He laughed through his nose, sobering quickly to peer more closely at me. "So, you really want this, us back together?"

"Yes."

He frowned. "Think it'll work again, huh?"

"Yes."

"Didn't end very well though, did it?"

I swallowed, speaking again in a voice that wobbled. "We had our moments, but I thought it went very well considering. Why not try again?"

His narrowed contemplative look had me bracing myself for rejection, but he finally shrugged and said softly. "Okay. I'm game if you are."

"Really?"

"But." He tipped his head. "This time we take it slow, like real slow."

I sat back down on the sofa with a thump. Grinning at the stupid look on my face, he stood up stiffly favouring his knee and turned to the kitchen bench. Helped him prepare breakfast, made coffee and toast and sat down at the table to eat and talk.

"So, why the leave me alone stuff?" he asked.

"What do you think?"

"I'm male, complex lady," he chuckled. "Enlighten me?"

"Other women."

He frowned. "What other women?"

"I saw you with them a few times."

"I have friends, some of whom are female."

"I know." I screwed my nose up at him.

"So, what's the problem?"

"Your boss's daughter, I saw you take her into the café. Our café." I grimaced derisively. "It made me angry, um jealous…whatever! Anyway, I took it out on your tyre."

"Ah, I see." His smile was teasing. "Well, I was only the chauffeur. If you'd come in you would have seen a crowd, not just her daddy but her fiancée too."

I blinked. "She's getting married?"

"Yep. He was with her at the market."

"The old guy was her fiancée?" I looked stunned. "I thought he was her father."

"Very rich dude and the family like him."

I narrowed my eyes. "But you were kissing her."

"She was kissing me."

"Before or after she got engaged?"

"Not sure of the exact dates." He laughed at my appalled look. "The spoilt little madame just wanted to let her hair down before the official hitch up."

"What?"

"She listens to gossip like you do," he smirked. "Thought the bad boy could help."

"And did you?" I asked coldly. "Help?"

"Not sure, but she seemed happy enough er, kissing."

"And were you?" I glowered. "Happy kissing, too?"

He shrugged. "Nothing like a witch's kiss."

"You have this thing about witches, don't you?"

"Yeah." He grinned smugly.

Chapter 35

He took it slow, too slow. I didn't like it.

We progressed to a degree of hugging, which was an improvement but my attempts at arms around his neck and fingers in his hair were skilfully thwarted. Kissing on the mouth was out and pecks on the cheek were in.

Couldn't understand him being satisfied with what we were doing, previous experience told me otherwise and my belief he used work as an excuse to keep me at bay was frustrating to say the least, even our meet ups appearing to dwindle rather than increase. I complained but all he did was tell me to be patient.

There was also no let-up of Von Meeren gossip which had nothing to do with me, however, my brothers appearing to be in the firing line of late. Daniel sported a black eye after a night out, felt rather sorry for himself but didn't want to talk about it. With a distinct feeling Douglas knew something and not trusting the rumour mill, I confronted him during one of our coffee encounters.

"What happened to my brother?" I demanded.

"Which one?"

"Daniel this time." I watched him suspiciously. "He's got a black eye."

"Wasn't me."

"I'm not stupid."

"Ask your brother."

"He's not talking!" Frowning, I said peevishly. "Come on, friend. What happened?"

"He had women problems."

"You expect me to believe that?" I was sceptical.

"Some girls at the nightclub got fresh with him and some boys didn't like it."

"What?"

"Your brother was outnumbered. I kind of felt sorry for him and calmed the boys down," he grinned smugly.

"Kind of."

"Yeah."

"You rescued my brother?" I was incredulous.

"Well, since I am friendly with his sister, I thought I should."

"So chivalrous."

"Difficult word," he smirked. "What does it mean?"

I wrinkled my nose. "So, at this nightclub? Did any girls get fresh with you, too?"

"Nope."

"Who were you with?" I narrowed my eyes.

"A few mates." He laughed and added for good measure. "Fellas, that is."

I curled my lip. "Drinking?"

"That's what you do at nightclubs?"

"Any girls on poles?"

"Some."

"How nice for you."

"Nothing like a witch on a broomstick," he smirked.

I gave him an extremely sour look. "Whatever turns you on."

"An upright broomstick."

"Oh, shut up!" The sour glare turned ice cold.

The next incident concerned my other brother when a leaking fuel line ignited in the racetrack workshop. Douglas had dropped by to see a mate nearby on his way home from work and saw it happen. He reacted immediately, sprinting across the carpark to smother Matthew's burning clothes, pulling him out into the forecourt while others doused the flames inside. Thankfully, Matthew suffered only minor burns and the workshop no damage.

"I heard about the fire." I spoke to Douglas on the phone that same evening after hearing the news from Dad. "Thank you for helping him."

"There were heaps of other people helping." He was offhand.

"But he was on fire!" I was adamant. "You stopped it and got him out of there."

"It wasn't only me."

"Did my brother thank you?"

"No need."

"He should have," I said indignantly.

"What for?"

"For saving his life."

He heaved a deep sigh. "Leave it, sweet witch."

"How many times?" I hissed. "I am not a witch or sweet!"

"I'm biased."

"And crazy."

"That too."

One other incident didn't appear in the gossip columns, didn't concern my brothers either. Bella, Daniel and Roman were asked to demonstrate some of their skills at a nearby district's horse show which most of our family went along to. Douglas accepted my invitation to come as well but an unexpected drainage problem at his work needed immediate attention which meant we didn't arrive until after lunch, enjoying the afternoon together watching Bella's horse training demonstration in conjunction with Roman explaining the importance of hoof care and Daniel's stunt riding performance as well as several cutting and jumping competitions.

Later as Douglas took me home, we turned off the main highway on to a much quieter road with barely any traffic while I continued babbling enthusiastically about the morning activities he'd missed. Became aware that his attention was elsewhere, watched his eyes flick again to the rear vision mirror and stopped talking to glance backwards. Saw a large black SUV with a bull bar driving too close behind but not perturbed at that point I turned back to Douglas.

"Do you know that car?"

"Yeah."

"Who is it?"

"Just another dickhead."

"Excuse me?"

He didn't reply as the vehicle suddenly pulled out onto the other side of the road, speeding up to draw level. I let out a horrified gasp at the gun pointing at us through the side window, thought stupidly that it looked nothing like the rifle we had on the farm. Wasn't what terrified me most, the face behind it had my neck hairs running scared, bearded from cheek to jowl with an evilly grinning hole of a mouth.

Douglas shot a glance at me, growling. "Hold on!"

Obeyed without protest, instantly grabbing hold of my seat. Felt the seatbelt jerk tight as he slammed on the brakes, yelping involuntarily as the ute slid sideways. Lifting his foot, he wrestled with the steering wheel and straightened her up before braking, the ute stopping on a dime. The SUV shot ahead some metres before brake lights came on, smoke wafting off the rear wheels as it skidded to a halt. Douglas waited with his hand on the gear lever. As the SUV's reverse lights came on, he hit the accelerator and swung the steering wheel, sending us into a wild U-turn, tyres squealing on tarmac.

For a split second, I thought we'd roll over, but the ute righted itself, snaking as we took off back the way we'd come. Way too fast. My stomach lurched with fear, think I whimpered. Swivelled my head to stare goggle-eyed at Douglas who appeared quite calm, except for a muscle twitching in his jaw. The SUV had more speed, quickly gaining on us. Back on the wrong side of the road, it drew level. I definitely whimpered then, eyeballing the pointed gun in terror.

Douglas flicked another glance my way, snarled. "Don't let go of your seat!"

He turned his eyes to the vehicle beside us, tapped the brake, once, twice. They didn't slow quickly enough, the ute's front bumper suddenly level with their back panel as Douglas gave the steering wheel a quick vicious jerk towards them.

Cringing at the hideous screech of metal on metal, I saw the SUV slide sideways, tyres howling. Almost in slow motion it fishtailed, ploughed off the road and hurtled into a wire fence, the rear wheels lifting off the ground and slamming back down. Douglas braked hard then, the ute skidding a little before stopping dead.

Looking at me, he asked through his teeth. "Are you hurt?"

Shaking like a leaf, I could only shake my head.

"Stay here!" he growled.

Leaving the motor running, he unbuckled his belt and was out of the ute before I could protest. Watched him sprint across to the SUV, wrench open the passenger door and haul bearded guy out by his shirt front. The gun fell out at the same time. Douglas grabbed it with one hand while shoving the guy down on the ground face first, planting a foot on his back. Could hear Douglas's voice but didn't understand the words. Gasped when he suddenly snarled something and lifted the gun, pointing it into the vehicle's cab at the driver.

A skinny weasel faced guy scrambled out the other side, almost falling in his haste before stumbling around the SUV with his hands in the air. Douglas said something to bearded guy before stepping off him and grabbing weasel face's shirt. I clamped trembling hands to my mouth as Douglas shoved him back against the SUV, the muzzle of the gun in his chest. The guy looked terrified, whining loudly and shaking his head frantically. Douglas lifted the gun away, kicking him hard in the shin at the same time. Weasel face dropped to the ground screeching, rolling around in pain clutching his leg.

When Douglas spoke again, Weasel face shut up. Slithering quickly across to bearded guy, he rolled onto his stomach and lay prone. Douglas stood still for what seemed ages, looking down at them with the gun aimed while I watched in stunned shock.

My breath left me in a whoosh when he finally moved, emptying bullets out of the gun before throwing them far into the paddock beyond the fence. He walked back towards me, flung the gun into bush other side of the ute and got back in. Gave me a long expressionless stare before revving the motor, doing a sharp U-turn and driving off without so much as another glance at the men.

Breathless and shaken, I eyeballed his impassive face in silence.

"Are you okay?" he spoke at last, his voice hoarse.

"Yes!" I squeaked. "Um, no! I'm not sure."

"I'll stop soon." He glanced across frowning.

Once back on the main road he pulled over into a petrol station carpark, heaving a long breath before saying through his teeth. "Sorry about that."

"You know those guys?"

"You could say that but they're not my mates."

I cackled stupidly. "I would never have guessed!"

He gave me a long look before reaching for the door handle. "Give me a minute. I just need to check something."

Getting out, he went to the front of the ute, bending to inspect it.

"Is it okay?" I asked as he got back in.

He half grinned. "Built like a brick shit house."

"Did you have to do that. I mean, hit their car like that?"

He shrugged. "It's the only language they understand."

I frowned. "And you understand that language too?"

"I suppose." He slanted an eyebrow. "Have you changed your mind?"

"About?" I didn't understand him.

"Us being friends."

I sighed. "No."

"Pleased to hear it." He grinned, his usual show of teeth. "So, are we moving fast enough for you now?"

I glared. "That's not funny."

"Come here." He pulled me close into a tight hug. Could have gladly stayed in his arms all day, but he let me go gently to tweak my chin.

I wasn't finished. "Why did they do that to us? Who are those guys?"

"Don't worry about them," he said mildly, sounding unconcerned.

"That's all right for you to say. I'm not used to guns pointing at me!" I was indignant.

His lips twisted. "It was pointing at me."

"Why?" I persisted.

"Ancient history," he sighed. "Nothing important."

"Tell me, please!"

"I roughed up the dickhead with the beard and his younger brother a few times." His lips curved at the appalled look on my face. "They started it."

"Really?" I rolled my eyes. "And he was going to shoot you for that?"

"He's never forgiven me." Douglas pulled a derisive face. "And unfortunately, he likes guns. Been in trouble for waving them around in people's faces before."

"Nice!" I shook my head. "And the driver?"

He shot me a sidelong smirk. "The skinny runt's sister wanted a bonk. I said no and laughed in her face and he, er, kinda took exception to that."

"Delightful!" I couldn't stop the giggle escaping.

"It's true. She looks worse than him, a rat face with buck teeth," he chuckled. "Like I told you before I don't bonk every girl in town."

I gave him a snooty look. "Obviously not."

He snorted, said no more and drove off.

Almost at home I asked on a more serious note. "Shouldn't we report this?"

"And then what?" He shot me a sceptical look. "The cops will think Willard's been a naughty boy again and they'll likely arrest me for involving you."

Decided he was probably right. "But what if those guys try that again?"

"They won't."

And so it was, we never did see the bearded gun wielding guy, weasel faced guy or their SUV again or at least I didn't.

With Douglas in my life again, albeit not in quite the way I wanted things reverted to a semblance of normality. Hadn't realised how much I'd missed the farm visits, vowing that whatever happened in the future I would never neglect my family and horses like that again. Delta, BB and Kingston seemed as pleased to see me as I them.

"She's got over the tiff, if that's what it was," Kingston said to the girls.

"She's better, I agree," BB frowned. "But not quite there yet."

"You feel it, too?" Delta slanted a look at her.

"Yep. She's hiding something deep down, I reckon."

"Exactly what I thought." Delta nodded.

"Maybe that man of hers isn't giving her exactly what she wants."

"Here we go again." Kingston sighed his exasperation. "Blame the man."

"We're not blaming anyone," Delta protested. "To be honest I think it's her."

"Well, that makes a change!" Kingston said sarcastically.

"Listen here, you!" BB thrusting her face up to his. "Males are supposed to rescue damsels in distress! How about helping the situation instead of mouthing off!"

Kingston blinked affront. "How many times? I'm an equine, not a human."

BB exaggerated an eye roll. "I'd pity them if you were!"

"Okay, enough of that!" Delta scolded, peering at Kingston. "BB has a point about you helping out, you know. What about Daniel?"

He frowned. "What about him?"

"He's human and your friend. Doesn't he ever talk to you about girls and stuff?"

Kingston shook his head. "Well, he likes them but that's all I know."

"You're so helpful!" BB scoffed.

"If you want help, why don't you ask the ghosts?" Kingston sneered.

BB blinked. "Ghosts?"

Sweeping his gaze around the paddock, he shouted sarcastically. "Come on out, ghosts! How about some wonderful advice right now! Aren't you supposed to see, hear and know everything that goes on around here?"

BB looked horrified. "What are you doing?"

"Don't get smart, dude!" A voice bellowed. "Want advise, ask nicely!"

Kingston and BB leapt off all fours, Delta's eyes popping wide at their terrified faces.

BB recovered first, scowling at Kingston. "Idiot! Now look what you've done!"

"I was only joking." Kingston cowered, eyes darting in all directions.

"Wimp!" Obsidian growled. "I'll haunt you later."

"Please, don't," Kingston whine. "I'm sorry, really, I am."

"Don't mind, Obsidian, he's just teasing." A female voice spoke gently. "But do take note, we only give advice when we think you need it."

BB heaved a breath. "Thank you, we'll remember that."

"Are you two, okay?" Delta eyed them both. "What was that all about?"

"Good advice, again," BB told her, shooting Kingston a scornful sidelong look. "Don't mess with the Shadow horse ghosts, eh? Smart Dude!"

He kept his mouth shut and sulked.

Although the horses were good therapy, they weren't able to help instil calm every hour of the day and certainly not during the night. It was all Douglas's fault, his going slow was doing my head in and if the tension inside didn't find a relief valve soon, I'd probably kill him.

Friday after a mad week at work I'd had enough, texting him first: **Are you at home?**

He answered: **At staff happy hour. Home by seven. Are you coming around?**

Wondering belligerently who was at the staff happy hour, I jabbed a reply: **Do you want me to?**

Silly question, witch.

How about I bring dinner, cold chicken and salad?

Yum. See you later.

He'd just got home after I arrived, greeting me a polite cheek kiss before taking a shower. When he appeared again barefoot in old jeans with a long-sleeved shirt hanging open, I had to drop my eyes hurriedly and damp down the quiver. Busied myself at the table, pouring white wine into two glasses with a hand that shook slightly.

Meeting his eyes as we sat down to eat, I knew he'd seen my nervousness and stared back defiantly. His mouth curved but he made no comment as I lifted my glass to him before swallowing half the wine in one gulp. Although conversation was stilted at first eventually his anecdotes about a colleague getting a tractor stuck in a fence that day and the subsequent rescue efforts had me laughing and relaxing. Didn't last forever thought, nerves returning as I watched his butt at the kitchen sink after he'd cleared the dishes.

Time to put my plan into action, I thought and stood up with knees knocking, excusing myself to the bathroom with bag in hand.

Heart in mouth I squared my shoulders and strutted back into the living area. He wasn't there. Heard him out in the shed disposing of rubbish, propped myself against the closed hall door in a suggestive pose and waited. Stopping in his tracks almost immediately he walked in, I saw his eyes go wide and take me in, slowly up and down.

"Wow!" he mouthed, eyes lingering on the black underwear and high black heels before asking mildly. "What are you doing?"

"What does it look like?" My voice trembled.

He didn't move or answer.

"All we do is talk, nothing else happens!" I blurted in exasperation.

His face showed no expression except for a slight lift of his eyebrows.

Pouting, I flapped a derisive hand. "Okay, maybe that's not quite true, um, we do hug and kind of kiss."

He still didn't speak.

"Remember I said you were a bad boy...er, a very bad boy." I blew out a trembling breath. "And you asked me why?"

Just a tightening of his jaw and slight narrowing of his eyes was all he gave me.

"Doesn't this tell you?" Speaking in a wobbly whisper, I gestured to the underwear.

'Okay." He looked away. "Put some clothes on and we'll sort this out."

My jaw dropped.

As he stepped to the kitchen bench and turned his back, I fled to the bathroom and locked the door. Utterly mortified, I dragged on clothes, shoved my high heels into my bag and after making sure he wasn't waiting in the hallway, tiptoed through his bedroom and out the ranch slider door. Sneaked around the shed to my car, snipping the door shut immediately I got in. My hands were shaking so badly I could hardly get the key in the ignition and when I finally did, the engine wouldn't fire. Tried turning it over again but to no avail.

Shook my head desperately. "No! Please, no!"

Looked up through the windscreen and saw him standing in the shed doorway with his arms crossed, a very bland look on his face. Knew instantly.

Winding down my window, I screeched. "What have you done to my car?"

With a smug little smile, he propped his shoulder on the doorpost as I leapt out, slamming the door in frustration before approaching him.

"I want to go home!" I hissed, scowling angrily. "As in right now!"

"We talk first."

"What's the point? You're obviously not interested in making things happen!"

He ignored that. "Come back inside."

I stalked back inside past him, ready to attack if need be but he kept his distance, the knowing look in his eyes making me fume even more. When he pulled out a table chair, I shook my head and remained standing, tensely waiting.

With a shrug he leant back against the kitchen bench. "Making things happen would be good," he said. "But is it what you really want?"

"Isn't it obvious?" I glared.

"No, it's not that obvious." He cocked an eyebrow. "You're a complex lady."

"Oh! Really?" I was scathing. "Says the most experienced ladies' man I know!"

"Stop listening to gossip," he said equably.

"I'm not that complex!" I protested. "You know just about everything about me."

He shook his head. "Not so much."

"We've been together before."

"Not for long."

"Whose fault was that?" I frowned.

"Mine." His lips twisted. "I've told you before, I'm no good at relationships."

I couldn't think what to say.

"And what we had before happened too fast." He let out a long breath. "Let's get to know each other better this time, huh?"

"Sterile then?"

"Sterile?"

"Platonic! Whatever!" I bit out. "You know what I mean."

He crooked a grin. "What's the rush, witch?"

"So, when?" I shot him a painted look.

"We'll see."

I heaved an exaggerated sigh. "You really want no touchy feely at all?"

"Better that way for now, hmmm?"

"Anyone would think you were scared!" I curled my lip.

"There's that." He snorted a soft laugh. "Besides this very bad boy bruises easily."

"Ha! Since when has that stopped you?"

"I'm not stopping, just slowing down."

"Humph!" I gave him a beseeching look. "Can we at least hurry it up, please?"

He nodded amicably. "We'll move a little faster if you want."

"Only a little?" I protested.

"Patience, witch." He smiled slyly. "But you could give me another look at the sexy underwear from a distance like."

Deciding to give him a taste of his own medicine, I pouted snootily. "No! You missed your chance."

"Aw." He dropped his lower lip.

"Now, how about fixing my car?"

"Sure," he grinned. "On one condition."

"No way!" I scowled. "I'll work out what's wrong with the car myself!"

Laughing, he shrugged and followed me out with a spanner, opening the bonnet to reattach the battery cables. Shooting him a disgusted sidelong look, I got in with a peeved slam of the door, childing my pride mercilessly on the way home.

Should have let him ogle my underwear again! It may have changed his mind.

Chapter 36

His version of faster obviously wasn't the same as mine and when he rang one Saturday suggesting a dinner out my frustrated feelings boiled over.

"Why bother?" I snapped.

"Pardon me?"

"This is pathetic! Why are you even asking me out?"

"You don't want to go out?"

I let the breath hiss out between my teeth before answering, "What I want doesn't seem to matter does it?"

"What do you want?"

"I want us to hurry up!"

"Be patient, witch," he said quietly. "It'll work out better this way."

"Patient!" I almost yelled. "You never used to be patient if I remember."

"I've learned."

"Well, you're too patient! I want faster."

He sighed. "Let's go out for dinner and see what happens."

"Are you joking?" I was sarcastic. "I know exactly what happens and so should you!"

"How about I pick you up?" He sounded resigned.

"What would you have done if those women had stayed in your bedroom?"

"Pardon?"

"At the barbeque remember! You would have bedded them, wouldn't you?" I hissed spitefully. "Oh, I forgot you don't do orgies! Well, there's always a first time, isn't there?"

He sighed again. "Look, how about…"

I butted in, shouting down the phone, "Don't you want me that way any more? Is that what this is about? I'm only good for sterile hugs and kisses? Well, try your pal Natasha instead, I'm sure she'll oblige! I've had enough!"

"Bad day?" he asked mildly.

Imagining him rolling his eyes was the last straw.

"Go screw yourself!" I shrieked.

Let the phone drop as I slumped to the floor, beginning to sob in earnest. Reached for Trojan as he nudged me gently with his nose, burying my face in his fur until I ran out of tears. He waited patiently for me to lift my head, giving me a sympathetic look.

"Sorry boy." I said forlornly. "Think I just stuffed that right up."

Getting up, I trudged to the bathroom for a freshen up, lying down on the bed afterwards feeling sorry for myself with Trojan nearby. Less than an hour later I almost jumped out of my skin when someone rapped on the bedroom's window.

Scrambling off the bed, I glared icily at Douglas through the glass. Trojan was far more welcoming than me, wagging his tail and whining excitedly.

"Go away!" I yelled. "I'm not going anywhere with you! I'm not going out!"

He didn't move. "Let me in then."

"No!" I bit out. "You're wasting your time. Just leave!"

"Either you open the door, or I'll break it down."

Knowing he meant it, I scowled. "The front door then."

He met me there, gave my trackpants and sweater a quick up and down before holding out his hand. "Where's the gate remote? I've got takeaways in the car."

"I'm not in the mood for takeaways," I muttered defiantly. "Or visitors."

"I'm not a bleeding visitor and I'm hungry," His hand came up as I opened my mouth to retaliate. "Be nice, witch. And don't tell me to screw myself again."

"I'm not feeling nice," I snapped.

"Make an effort."

"Go…" I shut my mouth at his warning frown.

He shook his head. "Like I said, a complicated lady."

"I'm complicated?" I was flabbergasted. "Have you any idea what you're doing?"

"What am I doing?"

"Driving me around the bend!"

"Well, now you know what it feels like."

"Excuse me?"

"I've been driven around the bend by a witch for years."

"What?" I gasped. "You're doing this to annoy me?"

"Annoy you?" He laughed harshly. "You have no idea. I'm annoying the shit out of myself." He took a deep breath. "Look I'm just trying to do things properly this time."

"It doesn't seem to be working!" I snapped. "Not for me anyway."

"Okay, so, let's talk about it." He rubbed his forehead wearily. "But can we eat first."

Glaring at him balefully I relented. "Oh, all right."

He walked down to the gate, drove his ute up and brought in Italian takeaways plus a bottle of Pinot Noir. I wasn't expecting to have much of an appetite, but I ate a good plateful of delicious pasta with meatballs, enjoying two glasses of wine as well which steadied my nerves and got my mouth working on a more amicable note.

"So, what did you mean?" I asked eventually. "About doing things properly?"

He wiped his mouth before answering. "We hardly knew each other last time."

"We were getting to know each other," I protested.

"It exploded in our faces." He shook his head. "Well, it did in mine anyway. I wasn't expecting what happened between us."

"Neither was I." I chewed my lip. "But it was good and um, we both wanted it."

"I wanted you, have since I don't know when," he frowned. "But I don't believe you wanted me. I just happened to be handy."

"Handy?" I was astounded.

"Come on, you hated my guts once!" His mouth twisted sardonically. "I was a novelty, a distraction and someone different. At times that's all that matters, helps take one's mind off things."

"What do you mean?" I frowned, not understanding.

"Your boyfriend died," he said flatly. "You needed something to ease the hurt and I happened to be available." With a self-mocking laugh, he added. "I'm good like that."

"You weren't a novelty, ever!" I said indignantly, frowning when he didn't reply. "You really believe I was on the rebound?"

"Sandford was the one, it was obvious."

"I loved him dearly, but he's gone. He never wanted me to mourn him, told me to move on and I did." I finished on a whisper. "I moved on with you."

He shook his head. "Neither of us moved on, we just got in each other's way."

I frowned at his words. "Okay, I admit you did take my mind off things, but you also made me very happy."

"Happy?" He looked away, muttering. "I helped for a bit, that's all."

I ignored that. "I don't hurt any more, not since you came along. You were never second best or second hand, not then, not now." Swallowed hard. "I want you back!"

His jaw clenched but he didn't speak.

"You don't believe me, do you?"

He still didn't look at me, said gruffly. "I'm not sure this…us, will ever work."

"Are you listening to me?"

As he rubbed a hand along the back of his neck, I stood up and went to him. Took his face in my hands, looked him in the eyes and bent to kiss him. He pulled back as our lips touched, but I was having none of it. Straddled his legs, gripped his hair and took his mouth again. This time the response was more to my liking, but I wanted more. Fumbled for his shirt buttons.

He stopped my fingers. "Hey, hey! Slow down."

"Don't want to."

"Stop it, witch." His hands gripped mine.

"Please." I rounded imploring eyes.

He shook his head. "Let's cool it, huh?"

Aimed a kiss but he turned his head away. Moaning a protest as my lips grazed his jaw, I pulled my hands out of his grasp and slid fingers into his hair. Turned his face back to mine and giggled as he went cross eyed.

"You've had too much wine," he told me.

"Nothing to do with the wine," I pouted. "It's all your fault."

He pulled a wry face. "It's always my fault."

We touched noses as I aimed for his mouth again. Got my kiss but not for long.

He broke it and breathing a tad faster, growled. "Okay, enough."

"Whose being sensible now?" I muttered.

"Not sensible," he sighed. "Just trying to be good for once."

I knit my brow, looking at him in disbelief. "Why would a bad boy want to be good?"

He didn't answer, took me with him as he stood up and stopped me reaching up to clasp my hands at his neck, grimacing at my pout. "Behave, witch. There's no rush."

"You were always in a hurry before." I looked down at myself. "Is it my clothes?"

He rolled his eyes. "How about we do dinner out tomorrow, hmmm?"

I curled my lip. "What? Another slow date?"

"It's good for us."

"And what happens afterwards?" I tilted my head, eying him. "Slow sex?"

He merely shook his head, snorting a laugh without comment.

"I don't believe it!" I was sharply incredulous. "You're saying no?"

"I'll pick you up at six tomorrow, okay?" He turned for the door.

"Douglas, please!" I whined.

Hesitating, he looked back. I began to undress fast, dropping track pants first and then pulling the sweater over my head. My boring grey and white cotton underwear would have to do. Went into slow mode, lifting my hair off my shoulders to let it fall and posed.

"If you leave me again, I couldn't bear it." My voice wobbled.

"I'm not leaving you again," he muttered, eyes narrowed.

"I love you, Douglas Willard. More than anyone."

I watched him close his eyes, clench his jaw and take a long breath before turning back to approach me. Pulled me against him, mouth taking mine roughly. It wasn't slow sex; it was fast, wild and exactly what I wanted. Up against the wall. We got to the bed eventually where he slowed it down. My fingers caressed his skin afterwards, felt him shiver.

"So, it was my clothes?" I breathed.

"Nothing to do with your clothes," he murmured.

"Better without though, huh?" I nibbled his shoulder.

"Just couldn't say no."

"You said no to the black underwear!" I blinked indignantly.

"That wasn't easy."

"You could have fooled me."

"I thought you wanted…" He blew out a breath, didn't finish.

"Comfort?" I offered.

"Yeah, that." He grimaced self mockingly.

"You're not what I call comfortable," I pouted.

He heaved a deep breath before growling softly. "Look, sex with you was wicked right from the start, but I didn't want it to be just that this time round."

"It never was just that."

"Like I said you're a complex lady," he sighed. "And I'm good at stuffing things up."

"So, am I." My fingers splayed on his chest.

"And I didn't know you loved me." He narrowed his eyes.

The words shocked me upright, staring down at him incredulously. "I assumed you knew!" I exclaimed. "I never said. Oh, how could I not have?"

"Hey, it's okay." He put a finger to my lips. "I'm not exactly communicative either."

I kissed his finger. "I've loved you since that first time you were drunk."

His frown was disbelieving. "You what?"

"Or was it before then?" I pretended to think deeply, peering at him. "That's right, I remember now, dreaming about you. That was the turning point I think."

"Eh?" He looked bemused. "You dreamt about me?"

"I did and Anna talked about you too. History all over again, she said."

"What are you talking about?" He eyed me like I'd lost the plot.

"You know, there's something about this very bad boy when he's drunk." I pursed my lips. "He goes all soft and mushy and you can do anything to him."

His eyebrows shot up. "Anything?"

"Hmmm." Fluttering my eyelashes, I ran a hand down his chest.

"Like what?"

"Would you like to see the photos?" My hand went down further.

"Photos?' He halted my hand. "Are you kidding me?"

I shifted to straddle him, leaning forward to touch his mouth lightly with mine. "There's this feeling I get," I whispered. "It only happens with you."

"About these photos?"

"I don't know how to describe it, like lots of shivers that go nuts."

"Where are they?"

I tugged at his lip gently with my teeth. "In my tummy first, then down low."

"The photos, I mean."

"I gave them to Anna and Helena."

"Eh?"

Shutting him up soundly, I got physical, very energetically physical. We slept like the dead afterwards, waking late morning. Found myself lying behind him, face between his shoulder blades with an arm around his middle. He stirred and took my hand, running his tongue across my palm. Made me giggle. Slid up against him to plant a kiss at his nape, Gasped at the marks on his neck. "Oh, crap! I mean, ouch! You have bruises!"

He snorted. "I told you I bruise easily."

"I'm sorry!" Remembered using my teeth on him, not something I did very often. "Are they sore? Did they hurt? Why didn't you say something when…er…they happened?"

"I was concentrating on other things," he drawled.

"Like what?"

"Like this."

He rolled over and proceeded to show me. Lying facing each other afterwards, cooling off and still puffing a little he narrowed his eyes and closed a hand over my hip.

"Are you for real about those photos?"

"Didn't you know about them?" I blinked surprise. "I thought the cops or Dad would have told you."

"Cops, your dad?" He looked baffled. "You've lost me."

"The photos were your alibi." I traced fingers down his chest. "I took them the night June was murdered."

He didn't reply, seemed deep in thought. My fingertip found his bellybutton.

"I took them with my phone," I told him softly. "You didn't even know I was there."

"I knew a witch had been." His eyes locked on mine. "What sort of photos?"

"You were lying on your bed," I smirked, tickling his tummy. "Don't worry you were wearing clothes, bottom half anyway."

"Why did you take them?" His fingers closed over mine.

"I couldn't resist. There's something about Douglas Willard's butt in jeans."

"My butt?"

"Oh, didn't you know? I've got a thing about man butts and that swagger of yours is a real turn on." I purred. "My Oma was the same, they tell me."

"Is that all you like?"

"Um, no." My breath caught at the heat in his eyes.

"You got rid of the photos?"

"No." I gulped.

"Where are they?"

"They're still on my phone and Anna has a copy too, on her computer." His eyebrows shot up. "Why?"

"So, she can show all her lady friends."

"What?" His eyebrows came back down, knitting together.

"And guess what she said?"

"Do I want to know?"

"If she was any younger, she'd welcome you parking your boots under her bed," I giggled at his slow blink. "Helena approved too, made Dad jealous. You're a pin up boy, Douglas Willard."

He rolled his eyes, growling. "Enough of this shit!"

"No shit!" I pouted, fluttering eyelashes.

His mouth stopped any words coming out of mine for a long while after.

Chapter 37

It was the beginning of a new chapter in our lives, we got to know each other in every sense of the word and when he spoke hesitantly for the first time about his parents and sister I wept. We alternated beds like we had before mostly on the weekends, Friday night until Sunday, making the most of our time together. My brothers had plenty to say about my getting back with Douglas, taking every opportunity to give him lip but deep down I knew they were happy for me.

Weeks later with a nasty storm forecast for Tuesday night, Daniel and I put covers on our horses and shifted them to a lower more sheltered paddock that morning, making sure everything else was stowed away and battened down in the farm sheds. I hadn't been in touch with Douglas since the weekend, texted him that evening and he replied, saying he was going out but would be heading home before the weather hit.

With gale force winds and lashing rain keeping me awake, I ended up sitting in the lounge with Trojan watching the lightning at a safe distance from the windows. The car radio was full of news about the weather's aftermath on my way to work on Wednesday; roofs blown off buildings, trees down with some roads impassable, flooding and power outages. The sky was still grey, sodden with rain and the wind continued to buffet but the worst of the storm had passed.

Thankfully the clinic hadn't been affected, we got on with another busy day and during my morning break, I texted Douglas, but he didn't reply. Although he worked four ten-hour shifts with Wednesday his usual day off, I figured he'd probably been called in to help with any storm damage and decided to phone him later at home.

That evening when there was no response to my call, I left a message for him to phone me when he got in.

An hour later, I texted: **Answer your phone, Bad Boy.**

No reply. Early Thursday morning before heading to work I tried once more. Again, no answer. Felt the first real twinge of worry. Phoned the vineyard but to my dismay was told by concerned workmates that he hadn't turned up for work that day or the one before. Tried Matthew next at the racetrack apartment where he'd been living permanently since returning from overseas.

"Hey, sis," he answered promptly. "Bad storm, eh? Everything good?"

"Everything's fine. You too?"

"Just lost part of a workshop roof out here, no other damage."

"That's not so bad, then." I paused. "Could I ask you to do something for me?"

"Yeah, sure." He sounded amused. "What's the junkyard dog been up too now?"

"He's not answering his phone," I said.

He heard the worry in my voice. "You want me to check his place?"

"Would you mind?"

"No problem. I'll go there now and phone you back. Give me ten minutes.'

"Thanks, Matt."

He phoned me shortly after. "Nobody there, sis. I jumped the gate and looked in the windows. The bed's made and I couldn't see his ute anywhere."

"That's weird. He's not at work either." I blew out a breath. "I'll ring them again I think, see if they know any more."

"If you need anything call back, sis." he said. "Dad and I will be at the workshop."

Thanking him, I hung up. The vineyard hadn't seen him since Tuesday, I asked if anyone knew of his whereabouts that night and was told there'd been a sawmill birthday bash which Douglas had been invited to.

Phoning the sawmill immediately after, I spoke to the grumpy man.

"Hello. Do you remember Douglas Willard?"

"Of course, I do." He sounded indignant.

"Could you tell me if he was there for someone's birthday on Tuesday night?"

"Yep. He was here."

"Oh." I breathed relief. "When did he leave, do you know?"

"Well, everyone moved out before the rain started, about eight thirty I suppose."

"You didn't see him go?" My voice wobbled.

"Can't say I did really. Er, what's the matter?" The man's voice softened a fraction, sounded almost concerned.

"He's not answering his phone and hasn't been at work."

"That's not like him," he muttered. "I could get the boys to check along the road."

"Would you?"

"Yeah, sure. No worries."

"Oh, thank you. We'll come out for a look as well."

Phoned the clinic to tell them of the situation and very soon after Dad, Matthew, Daniel and I met up with three of the sawmill workers and began driving slowly along the route we thought Douglas would have taken home. Dad and I went first in his SUV while Daniel drove his Ranger behind with Matthew hanging out of the passenger window checking the deep ditches and using binoculars to scan the ravines. After covering more than half the road, I began to despair until Dad idled around one of the sharper corners and suddenly braked, pointing ahead through the windscreen.

"Someone's skidded." Was all he said.

Daniel's ute stopped immediately behind us, both my brothers getting out to have a good look. I watched Matthew go down on his haunches where the skid marks which disappeared over the road edge, saw Daniel pointing downwards.

Heard him shout. "There's been a collision here, someone's gone over!"

Scrambling out of the car quickly, I gasped. The ravine was several metres down, a steep slope with rocky outcrops. Dad held me back, sucking in his breath as Daniel had a better look.

"There's something there," Daniel called again. "I can see the side of a vehicle."

Matthew turned his head sharply to me. "Looks like a ute, grey with black stripes."

"Douglas?" I whispered, knees buckling.

Dad supported me back to the car, sitting me inside. "Stay here. I'll phone emergency." He promptly got out his phone while keeping one eye on me, speaking to rescue and ambulance within seconds.

Daniel was talking to Matthew. "We need a rope or something to get down."

The sawmill guys passed us to park ahead, fishing out a long rope from their vehicle which they attached to their axle while Matthew tied it under

Daniel's arms and around his chest like a harness. Dad was off the phone and not exactly enthusiastic at what they planned to do, calling out a warning to Daniel who took no notice and slithered over the edge.

Matthew and the sawmill guys stood stock still, eyes fixed on what was happening below them while I watched, body trembling. Dad stayed with me, grasping my hand as we waited. It felt like an eternity but was perhaps only minutes later that Matthew shouted out, punching his fist in the air and looking back at us with a huge grin splitting his face.

"He's alive and talking!"

Whimpering, I lurched to my feet as Dad grabbed me in a bear hug.

As if on cue we heard sirens and an ambulance, rescue crew vehicle and police car came into view along the road. The place was suddenly a hive of people, police officers put cones down to restrict access and after conversing with Matthew the rescue crew prepared to make their way down the ravine with a medic. After making a thorough inspection of the scene, the cops spoke to Dad who kept a reassuring arm around me.

"Looks like there's been a two-car collision." One of them said.

"He hasn't just run off the road then?" Dad asked.

"Nah, there's definitely been contact." The cop replied. "And I'd say the vehicle down there tried swerving out of the way."

"How can you tell?" Dad frowned.

"His tyre marks confirm it." The other cop gestured a hand, showing Dad how he thought the crash had played out. "He's braked hard as well, but the other car still hit him side on I reckon, hard enough to push him over."

"But where's the other vehicle?"

"Taken off!" The reply was brusque. "Must be damaged though, there's debris. Looks like a white car."

"Hit and run then?" Dad murmured.

"Yeah, fraid so."

I didn't speak, eyes riveted on the roadside where several people stood looking down.

"The rescue chopper's on the way, gonna winch him out," someone said.

It wasn't long before we heard the helicopter, appearing with a clatter of rotors over the hillside and hovering beside the road. I could see two helmeted men peering down from inside, signalling to someone on the ground and then one began his descent attached to a cable, disappearing out of sight into the ravine. Heard nothing except the engine and air buffeting around us. Almost forgot to breath as the man in the helicopter door signalled once more, the winch pulling the cable up and a laden stretcher appeared, it's precious cargo disappearing inside the helicopter. The cable came back down to hoist the other rescuer back up and shortly after the engine note changed, the helicopter turning as if in slow motion before flying off to disappear quickly. The silence seemed almost deafening until someone shouted. Only then did I lower my gaze to see Matthew approaching.

"He's in good hands now, Kate," Dad said into my ear. "And he's tough."

Hearing him Matthew nodded at me. "Yeah, he's a fighter, sis." His mouth twisted ruefully. "As we both know."

I managed a little nod in return, looking past him to rescue crew and medics clambering back onto the road. Daniel followed shortly, giving us a thumbs up as Matthew went to join him, both helping the sawmill boys stow away their rope.

One medic, a wiry man of perhaps thirty came across to speak with us. "I understand that's your boy?" He said to Dad, thumbing over his shoulder in the helicopter's direction.

"My daughter's partner."

"Ah, right." The man smiled at us both. "Well, he'll be at the city hospital very soon."

"How is he?" Dad asked.

"Got some broken ribs and a possible collapsed lung."

"Will he be okay?" I croaked.

"He's in pain and dehydrated but remarkably chipper and lucid." The medic was upbeat. "Once he's in hospital they'll sort him out, don't you worry."

"We'll head that way now," Dad said. "Thanks so much for all your help."

"Just doing our job and you're very welcome." He shook Dad's hand and mine.

Dad and I headed to hospital while Daniel and Matthew went back to work. At the A&E department, we were ushered through to a waiting area while doctors examined Douglas, Dad phoning Helena and I the vet clinic with an update on what was happening. Over an hour later a doctor spoke with us, explaining that Douglas had suffered three broken ribs, but his lung was functioning normally and other than severe bruising he was surprisingly unscathed. Although allowed to see him, he was heavily sedated and unaware of us.

At the sight of him lying inert in the bed, I rushed across to touch, murmuring all the while. Eventually straightened up to Dad waiting patiently at the foot of the bed, smiling gently. "He'll be fine, Kate."

I forced back tears. "I thought I was going to lose him too, Dad."

"Not this time, my dear girl." He shook his head. "This lad wouldn't let that happen."

"No, I suppose he wouldn't." I sighed tremulously.

The following day I visited him alone, surprised to find him awake and propped up in the bed.

"Hello, witch," he croaked with a valiant attempt at a smile.

"Hello, you very bad boy." Cupping his face in my hands, I kissed him. "Don't you ever do that to me again."

"Why? Too much excitement?"

"Way too much," I frowned. "Do you remember what happened?"

"Most of it." He breathed deeply, grimacing pain.

"Please, don't do that." I pressed a hand to his forehead. "Stay still."

"It's okay. Just a niggle," he muttered.

"A niggle?" I looked incredulous. "You have broken ribs, Mister. And more."

"Could be worse." As he patted the bed, I perched beside him. "The cops were here earlier too, asking questions."

"Oh, and?"

"I told them all I knew." He knit his brow. "There was another car on my side of the road. I tried to miss it. Couldn't. I remember going over, rolled a few times."

I shuddered. "You rolled down a ravine. Were you knocked out?"

"I don't think so. I must have dozed sometimes but the cold kept me awake. I tried moving but it hurt. I didn't know where my phone got to, couldn't see it anywhere."

"You were there for almost two days."

"Sort of lost track of time. Didn't hear much traffic, not many cars use that road."

"You were very cold and dehydrated. I'm glad we found you." I bit my lip.

"You were there," he murmured.

"There?" I peered at him. "It was Daniel who found you, I was up on the road."

"I saw your face, must have been dreaming, I think."

"Really? You saw me?"

"Yeah. You made me feel better."

"Oh." I blinked at him. "That's nice."

"Witchy spells, eh?" He moved closer.

I shook my head. "I don't do those."

"Ah, but you do, all the time." His face was only inches from mine.

"I think you need to rest, bad boy."

"It's those bewitching eyes of yours, they make a man do things." We were almost nose to nose.

I swallowed. "Okay, um. How about you settle down, hmmm?"

"Why don't you try some more of those spells in this here bed?" He touched his lips to mine.

"Douglas!" I squeaked, jerking my face out of reach. "We're in a hospital right now!"

"And?"

"And you have broken ribs and all that remember!" I scowled exasperation. "Besides shocking the staff is not a good idea, I'd probably get thrown out and told not to come back!"

He eased back against the pillows, muttering something rude about broken ribs and hospitals. As he closed his eyes, I heaved a sigh of relief.

Saturday afternoon he was discharged, given several weeks off work to recover and I took him to his place, staying over to keep an eye on him. He wanted me in his bed, but after persuading him to have a good night's sleep alone, I spent the night on the sofa, quite comfortably but very aware of the man in the next room. I stayed with him all of Sunday, went from there to work on Monday with Dad and Matthew more than happy to pop over occasionally from the racetrack workshop to check on him during the day.

"Please be nice to him." I instructed Matthew.

"No worries, sis," Matthew smirked. "I'll keep him restrained."

"Restrained?" I frowned.

"Well, if he doesn't behave, I'll tie him up, maybe sit on him or punch his lights out."

"Don't you dare!" I exclaimed while Dad rolled his eyes at us both.

Trojan and I settled into a routine at Douglas's, my dog surprisingly protective of him, often lying beside the bed or near his feet when he got up and when Trojan raced madly around the oak trees like an overgrown pup, or we played ball together Douglas sat on the deck watching like a benevolent parent. He often complained about our separate sleeping arrangements however, my determination to stay on the sofa a sore point.

A week after Douglas's release from hospital I'd just arrived from work when Dad called in, sitting down at the kitchen table to give us the latest news.

We already knew that the police had ruled out drink driving on Douglas's part, his ute had been winched out and was written off, irreparably damaged with confirmed evidence of a collision with a white vehicle. The search began shortly after for the said vehicle which would, they were certain have had extensive frontal damage.

"A woman came into the police station yesterday with information," Dad told Douglas. "Looks like they've found the car that hit you."

"She was driving?" I frowned.

"No, but it was her car," Dad said. "Her son borrowed it the night of the storm but never returned it."

"Is he missing?"

"No. He just kept making excuses to keep the car for longer at his mate's place which made her suspicious."

"What sort of car?" Douglas frowned.

"A white Mazda station wagon."

"The cops, have it?"

"Yes. They found it at the mate's place, hidden in the garage."

"Still damaged?"

"Sure was. A write off too, they reckon. The bonnet, side panel, front grill and bumper, all the lights smashed and damaged underneath. They found dark grey paint, matching your ute."

"Is he okay?" I asked.

Dad nodded. "Yeah, not a scratch. He had two friends in the car as well, also uninjured." He heaved a breath. "The idiot boys panicked."

"I can understand that." Douglas grimaced empathy. "Young and stupid."

I frowned. "So, what happens now?"

"He'll face charges and be disqualified from driving I'd say."

"His poor mother," I exclaimed.

"I heard she's a solo mum and there's a younger sibling," Dad said resignedly. "She's got a lot on her plate all right and she's lost her car."

"Hopefully he'll learn from his mistake," I sighed.

"Some are slow learners." Douglas pulled a wry face.

"Are you speaking from experience?" I slanted him a look.

"Better slow than never," Dad commented.

In the early hours of Saturday morning three weeks later, I heard Douglas moving about. Turned on the lamp as he appeared at the living room door, looking good enough to eat in black boxer shorts and nothing else. Standing up and very aware of his eyes taking me in from top to toe, I self-consciously pulled my night shirt further down my thighs.

Asked quickly. "Do you need painkillers?"

"I need a witch's spell," he replied softly. "Come to bed."

Ignoring that, I shook my head and padded to the kitchen bench. "You need to rest properly and take some of these."

With paracetamol tablets and a glass of water at the ready, I turned to find him right behind me. Taking the glass, he put it down and leaned in for a kiss. As the tablets dropped to the floor, I protested against his mouth, but he was having none of it. From that point rational thought ceased, ended up doing what he wanted in his bed, enjoying myself immensely in the process and making enough noise to raise the shed roof.

Gulping air afterwards, I swivelled horrified eyes his way. Spread eagled on his back, drenched in sweat with his eyes screwed shut, he was breathing hard through clenched teeth.

Panic stricken, I squawked. "You crazy idiot! Are you totally out of your mind?

"Nothing wrong with my mind," he growled, popping open an eye.

"We've probably just done you internal damage!"

"Nah!" He crooked a grin. "Best painkiller ever, witch. There's nothing like you."

I scrambled up on my knees. "I think you need a doctor!"

He pulled me back down beside him, shaking his head. "No, I don't. I feel good."

"Good!" I eyeballed him in disbelieving dismay. "You look like crap."

"So honest!"

He slept soon after, still on his back with a smug smile on his face. I watched him worriedly, finally drifting off as well and when we woke up late morning he was in good spirits, still sore but with decidedly more colour in his face.

"You are unbelievable!" I shook my head in exasperation.

He merely grinned widely, kissing the tip of my nose.

"How many guys would even think of doing that?" I asked sharply.

"You'd be surprised."

I shared his bed every night after that, tried my utmost to tone down our lovemaking which was well-nigh impossible and could only hope that we did him further injuries. Thankfully, there were none.

Less than six weeks later, he was back working and dangerously fit. Couldn't deny it was a relief to get back to the cabin and my own bed during the week.

Chapter 38

Time rolled on with my life still very much part of Douglas's. Although continuing to live apart in our own homes we met up fairly often, making up any excuse for steamy weekends which he couldn't get enough of. Mind you, neither could I.

The Mustang shifted from the racetrack to his shed, Douglas still referred to her as mine while I kept reminding him that she was ours. He enjoyed taking her out on good weather days with me as passenger, visiting old haunts and going places we hadn't been before. He purchased another Nissan ute, same model as previously, but painted blue and silver instead of grey. I no longer had my faithful jeep, it failed a warrant of fitness because of rust but Matthew soon sourced a Toyota station wagon for me through workshop contacts.

With regards my brothers and Douglas, they called a truce which I sincerely hoped would last.

Matthew and Wendy married at the Wine Rack, a wonderful casual affair that we all enjoyed immensely. At the after party, the musicians in our family got everyone singing and dancing along to piano, guitar, saxophone and violin, even managing to shock my brother's socks off with a surprise addition.

To me, Douglas's deep and oh so shiver down your spine voice singing in the shower was both a surprise and delight, but it took a considerable amount of persuasion on my part to get him to sing at the wedding, the look on Matthew's face when Douglas crooned out an Elvis number quite frankly priceless. The applause and catcalls were testament to his prowess, my heart swelling with pride when he was cajoled into singing twice more.

During the following years, I became aunty to four new Von Meeren family members, three nephews and a niece. Matthew and Wendy's two boys and a baby girl, all born just over a year apart reminded me of my brothers and I. Luke Jason the eldest, almost three, sandy haired and blue eyed like Matthew, Jake Daniel next, dark haired with Wendy's hazel eyes and Alice Kate, dark haired and blue eyed. Hearing the pitter patter of tiny feet in the farm homestead once again was a joy to Dad who continued to reside there with Helena.

Morgan Ron was Daniel's son, a Von Meeren all over again with black hair and black eyes so like Opa Bernard's. His late mother Chantelle, a petite dark eyed slip of a girl visited our racetrack one time, the only daughter of her famous race car driving father. Daniel was instantly smitten the moment he saw her, but she refused to become involved because of her health, having been diagnosed with terminal cancer and departed back to her homeland France. He followed determinedly, finally persuading her to take him on and to everyone's amazement they produced a child, but sadly only had six months together with their son before she died. Daniel was an utterly devoted father, continued to share the cottage with Jonathan and divided time between the farm, working horses with Bella and keeping in touch with his son's grandparents, having promised to visit them in France as often as he could. Dad and Helena planned to travel with Daniel and Morgan next visit, a week in Austria at the Von Meeren Estate included.

Morgan adored our horses from the outset and they him, watching him toddle amongst them without any fear magical to watch. Anna and Bella genuinely believed he had the potential to follow in the footsteps of another great horseman, his namesake, our great uncle Morgan.

"He's like his father, another Daniel," Kingston watched the family at the fence.

"A cool kid," BB agreed. "I like his name, it suits him."

Delta nodded. "Named after someone special I believe."

"If he's anything like the old Morgan he'll be special all right!"

"The old Morgan?" BB slanted a quizzical glance at Kingston. "You mean the uncle that Bella always talks about?"

Kingston eyed her back. "I didn't say that."

"Yes, you did. I heard you."

"It wasn't me!" Kingston shook his head. "I think that was Obsidian."

"You think right," Obsidian said.

"Is Obsidian talking to you again?" Delta eyed her startled friends, who both nodded.

"You knew the old Morgan well?" Kingston eyes swivelled left to right.

"Morgan was my best human friend," Obsidian told him.

"Like Bella is to us?" BB asked.

"Yep. He taught Maria and Bella everything he knew."

"And Daniel's son could be just like him." Another voice spoke up quietly. "He's got the Lawson blood. Just like us Shadow horses, it keeps carrying on."

"Who are you?" BB whispered.

"Mika, another relation of yours. Maybe one day you'll meet the Shadow clan."

"We'll be glad to." BB was in awe. "Thank you for telling us this."

"So, take good care of that boy," Obsidian instructed, his voice fading. "He's the future, for this farm, for all the horses that follow. You hear me?"

"We hear you!" Kingston nodded, his eyes like saucers.

"Wow! That was amazing," BB grinned. "I'm not so scared of them any more now."

"I wish I could have heard the whole conversation," Delta pouted.

BB and Kingston proceeded to fill her in and later in private, standing in the shade of the majestic paddock trees she told Riva all about it.

Douglas and I did converse about offspring once, but he wasn't keen because of his own family history and as I didn't think myself the maternal type, we quite happily left it at that. Although I adored my family's kids it was furry four-legged babies that made me go gaga and like Bella I understood animals better than humans most of the time.

However, a niggle in my brain surfaced on occasion regarding only Daniel and I having the trademark Lawson eyes. Selfishly and unbeknown to him I entrusted Daniel with the responsibility of carrying on the grey eyed lineage, finding himself another lady-friend and producing a second child, but he'd made no moves so far and seemed more than content with his lot.

Maybe it's up to you, said a voice in my ear. Ha! Not going to happen! If Douglas and I ever had a kid, he or she would be blonde with his ice blue eyes, of that I was certain.

A second niggle was to with the Von Meeren side of things. Since all the genetic flaws and family dying out hype, I was pleased there were boys carrying on the name but as Alice and I were the only living girls and knowing there'd been just one other before us I found it kind of provoking.

Was I the infertile one? The fact that during these last years, Douglas and I hadn't taken any precautions made me wonder. You're curious, aren't you? The little voice again. Do you have the genetic flaw? Don't you want to find out? It's only a blood test away.

In hindsight, I should have spoken about it to someone, Douglas at least or even Dad who would have known everything there was to know about such things having been through it all himself, but I kept my thoughts to myself, made discreet enquiries on-line about tests and laboratories and eventually it got the better of me.

I went to an out-of-town clinic/laboratory to have the test done secretly, reassured by the nurse that it wouldn't hurt when she assumed my nervousness was due to the procedure and needle. Little did she know it was my being found out that worried me more, sneaking out my car hurriedly afterwards half expecting someone to pop out and recognise me. The test results came through to my email a week later and were negative, I had no sign of genetic problems. That didn't in any way make me relieved or satisfied, the anti-climax leaving me feeling deflated and still anxious about keeping it to myself.

Weeks later, we were invited to a vineyard function Friday evening, I went straight to Douglas's from work, showered, got dressed and found him waiting in the lounge, looking hunky in a silver shirt, black trousers, jacket and boots. He gave my green and silver figure-hugging dress an extra-slow admiring look, wolf whistling and chuckling at my pout.

"Can't wait to take that off later," he murmured.

"You could get lucky." I screwed my nose up at him.

"Your phone went when you were in the shower, a text," he said casually, picking it up from the kitchen table to hand over. "I thought it might be your dad, so I had a look."

"He and Helena are meeting us there, he rang earlier." I told him, unperturbed until I read the text: **Please contact us at the Eastfield clinic if you'd like any other information or additional tests done.**

"Right." His voice sharpened a tad. "What are you needing tests for?"

Oh, crap! I gulped. "Er, nothing. It's just routine."

"Eastfield clinic?" He narrowed his eyes. "That's not your usual doctor, is it?"

"Um, no." I bit my lip. "A skin thing I had checked."

"You didn't tell me."

"It's all fine really." I attempted a lame smile. "Don't worry."

"Are you sure?"

"Yes." I nodded quickly. "Look we better get on."

Didn't enjoy the evening as much as I should have, my mind churning over Douglas having seen the text. Carefully went through my phone later deleting anything relating to the tests and the clinic.

He arrived at my place the following weekend with a scrummy Thai takeaway but seemed preoccupied, barely speaking during the meal and when he leant back in his chair afterwards to watch me with narrowed eyes, my nerves began to twitch a warning.

"That clinic has nothing to do with skin problems, does it?" he asked quietly.

Oh, dear! Found out! I could only stare like a petrified rabbit.

He tipped his head. "A genetic and infertility laboratory I believe."

Swallowing hard, I lowered my eyes. "Um, I just needed something clarified."

"The Von Meeren curse?"

My eyes jerked back to his. "You know about that?"

"Your brothers mentioned it." He raised an eyebrow. "Doesn't seem to be causing them any problems, does it?"

"No, it doesn't."

"But you wanted to know if you were affected?"

"I was curious, that's all."

"I thought we both decided we weren't interested in having kids?"

"We aren't."

He eyed me for a tense moment, "Why didn't you tell me you were doing this?"

I shook my head, unable to explain.

"So, where does that leave us?" He spoke flatly, his eyes cold. "Would you like me to have a test done as well, see if I have any problems?

"No! This has nothing to do with you." My voice cracked.

"Nothing? Aren't you curious about whether I can breed?"

"No!"

He shook his head. "Why don't I believe you?"

"Please, Douglas!" I hated the whine in my voice.

"I'll get myself tested, don't worry," he drawled sardonically. "Just for you."

"It's not like that!"

He stood up abruptly. "Enjoy your dessert, I'm really not in the mood."

"You're leaving?" I squeaked.

Without answering or a backward look he strode out.

There was no reply to any of my calls or texts all weekend, even my desperate attempt to talk face to face proving fruitless, finding his place locked up and deserted.

On Tuesday he texted: **Have appointment with my doctor this afternoon.**

His palpable sarcasm stabbed like a knife, I refrained from replying simply because I didn't have a clue how to.

The following text was even worse: **It's no secret. Would you like to come with me?**

Another jab, making me feel dreadful and pathetic. Didn't answer.

The next text was a change of subject, but just as painful: **By the way I won't be home this weekend, going fishing with mates.**

The weekend after he'd been out fishing, I didn't see him either, my attempts to communicate also ignored. The following Friday determined to catch up with him I rushed over to his place after work but to my frustration and despair he didn't show. Saturday afternoon after another attempt, I sat staring at the closed gate in dismay when the sudden growl of a familiar engine penetrated my brain. Felt indescribable relief at seeing the Mustang approaching along the road but that quickly changed to trepidation as he pulled up, giving me a cold unsmiling glance as he got out to open the gate. Driving through with him following behind, I parked at the shed and watched him alight again before doing so myself.

Making no move to open a door or invite me in, he said sarcastically. "You needn't have come all this way. I was going to text my results to you."

I saw red. "I don't care about your results! I just wanted to see you!" Tried toning down the anger, voice rasping. "I was worried, you haven't answered your phone."

His laugh was derisive. "Don't worry, I'm still alive and kicking."

Gritting my teeth, I changed the subject. "Are you coming over this weekend?"

"No." He was blunt. "I'm busy."

"Busy doing what?" I curled my lip. "Taking the Mustang out fishing?"

"She needed a warrant of fitness," he said mildly.

Feeling stupid, I blew out a breath. "Can we at least talk?"

"About what?" He slanted a sarcastic eyebrow. "Secrets?"

I took a deep breath, spread my hands. "I know I should have told you, but it, um, just didn't seem that important."

"Well, here's something even less important." His lips twisted. "According to my test results, I'm a healthy specimen, just like you."

"As I said before I don't care about that!" I snapped.

He ignored me, his smirk evil. "The wiggly little fellas are all present and correct and there's plenty of them."

Ordinarily I would have found his comments hilarious, but this wasn't in the least bit funny and left me gawping speechlessly.

"So, what do you wanna do next, prove if their tests are right?" he sneered at my owlish blink. "We could try fucking all night and day if that suits you."

I recoiled with an indignant gasp.

"Ah, but no! Hang on a minute!" He exaggerated a frown as if thinking hard. "What's the scientific bullshit, just do it in cycles or maybe at full moon, huh?"

His sarcasm was too much for me, I turned tail with a humiliated whimper.

Think he shouted something, maybe my name but I didn't heed. Leaping into my car, I floored the accelerator as soon as the engine turned over. Tore out of there like a mad person, dragging in air and blinking back hot tears.

On the cabin road, I rounded a corner too fast. The car slid sideways, tyres protesting. Letting out a yelp, I wrestled frantically with the steering wheel as the Toyota fishtailed, the rear wheel catching the edge of the road. Slid into the ditch, tilting alarmingly before coming to an abrupt halt. The engine stalled. I sat rigid, gasping for air and gripping the steering wheel hard.

Blinking dazedly in the surreal silence a sudden shocking thought hit me; this was the same stretch of road that Opa died on.

When an engine's growl penetrated my subconscious, I thought for one incredulous second that I'd somehow conjured up his ghost. Jerked my head sideways to stare stupidly at the car pulling up alongside. It wasn't the blue late model Mustang I remembered from my childhood but the familiar red classic of more recent times.

Locked eyes with Douglas as I fumbled for the door latch. He was already out of the Mustang and approaching fast when I exited on wobbly legs, leaning back against my car.

"Are you hurt?" He frowned his concern, reached a hand but didn't touch me.

"No, I'm fine." I shook my head. "I was going too fast. The car skidded, that's all."

"You were going fast all right," he muttered. "You left me behind."

"Oh." I blinked, said inanely. "I think the car's stuck in the ditch."

"Okay. Let's have a look," He went around to Toyota's front, bent down to peer underneath but straightened up shortly after. "No damage as far as I can see."

He got in and started the engine, rocked the car back and forth through the gears but although the rear wheels spun, they dug in and the car wouldn't budge.

Shaking his head, he got out. "It's not coming out by itself. Needs towing."

I frowned. "With what?"

"The Muzzy. She's got a tow rope in the back."

"The Mustang? Are you sure?"

"Piece of cake." He slanted me an amused look. "You okay driving yours?"

"I think so." I grimaced dubiously, flapping a hand at the Mustang. "I hope I don't do any damage to that."

His grin was teasing. "You only do damage to me, remember?"

I shot him an exasperated scowl, but kept my mouth shut.

"Just don't floor it," he instructed. "Keep the wheels straight and you'll be fine."

After attaching the tow rope to both cars, making sure I was comfortable in my driver's seat and with the Mustang's back wheels skidding on tarmac, he pulled me slowly but surely out of the ditch. With the Toyota's four wheels back on the road, he towed me some metres further and as he removed and stowed the tow rope away, I waited beside my car eyeballing his butt.

Flicking an unexpected glance over his shoulder, he caught me looking and said with a grin. "How about I follow you home? Make sure it's all good."

Face flushing, I nodded, trying to curb the excitement at his suggestion. "Okay, um, thanks."

As we exited our cars at the cabin, Trojan bounded around us, grinning and wagging his tail in greeting. Douglas gave him an enthusiastic ruffle up before looking underneath my car again, sliding across the grass on his back and disappearing to his waist. I got myself another eyeful, this time of skin and taut belly when his shirt rode up. Drooled.

"Your car looks fine." Sliding out from under, he stood up. "But if you notice noises or anything, let me know."

"Thanks again," I breathed. For pity's sake, do something to keep him here, idiot!

"No worries," he smiled.

"Would you like to wash your hands?" I gestured to the cabin door. Oh, so polite! And pathetic. He's your man, not a stranger!

"Nah, it's okay. There's a rag in the Mustang." Opening the boot, he proceeded to wipe his hands on the said rag.

Hurry up and try something else! Quickly now before you miss your chance! Blurted. "Would you like a drink, coffee, tea or a beer?"

He grinned. "Yeah, sure. A beer sounds good."

He didn't follow me inside, sitting down at the deck table instead while giving Trojan's ears another ruffle. I quickly went to the fridge, took out a beer for him and poured a glass of juice for myself. Back outside, I handed him his drink and sat down opposite.

Took a breath and asked. "Why did you follow me?"

"I wanted to apologise for upsetting you," he replied. "What I said back there was unnecessary shit. I was being an arsehole. Sorry."

"I'm the one who should be saying sorry," I mumbled. "I started this mess."

"Well at least we've found out something," he said with a wry twist of his mouth. "Both of us are as healthy and normal as we'll ever be."

Sipped my juice without replying and stared out to sea, wishing I could turn back time. As the silence lengthened, I sighed and looked at him again. "You know, I've driven this road so many times and never crashed before."

"We get blasé sometimes. Same way, same car."

"Opa died not far from that ditch."

"Yeah, I remember talk of the accident. Bernard Von Meeren in his Mustang."

He shifted his gaze to the sea, giving me an opportunity to scrutinise his profile, the chiselled cheekbones and sensual mouth. Feasting on what I'd been missing these last weeks created a gnawing ache inside and when he turned his head without warning, my heart somersaulted and began to pound.

Those intense eyes of his locked with mine. "Blue, wasn't it?"

I blinked. "What?"

"His Mustang was blue?"

"Um, yes," I swallowed, gulped. "All his Mustangs were blue."

"The good old Ford colour," he nodded. "Always looks good."

"The red does too."

His eyes slid away to our Mustang. "Yeah, that was the old fella's choice."

Glad he was no longer looking at me, I blew out my cheeks. Every time, I thought, smiling inwardly. What is it about him, that makes me react like this? Had my Oma reacted the same way to Opa? Probably, if the rumours were true.

His eyes returned to mine. "What are you thinking?"

I bit my lip. "Um, nothing really."

"You were smiling."

"Oh, just memories." I flapped a hand. "Grandparents."

"Yeah," he said softly, not looking away.

Wanted to leap out of my chair and jump him. Curbing the urge, I said as casually as I could. "Will you stay for dinner? There's leftover smoked salmon and salad."

He smiled a slow sexy smile. "I'd like that."

I poured wine with the meal, telling myself I deserved it. We ate out on the deck with a sea breeze wafting in and talked. It was divine. Didn't want the day to end.

So, what are you going to do to keep him here? The thought popped into my head. You could try seducing him again. I'm not wearing black underwear. Who cares, just strip. Take your time and dance, like real slow moves. There's no pole or broomstick. How about using the Mustang? What? Slither all over the bonnet, sorry, hood. Are you nuts? No way, he'll tell me to get off and not scratch it. You won't scratch it if you're naked, idiot! Oh, right! Now, there's a point.

"Do you ever have fantasies?" he drawled.

"Um, what?" I gagged. "No!"

"I do."

"Oh."

"I have one about the Mustang."

My jaw dropped.

His eyes were on the car. "You and the Mustang."

"Me?"

"Yeah."

As his eyes slid back to me, the smile came again, slow and suggestive. I blinked hard, glancing away with a disbelieving scowl. The ache had morphed into a quiver, mocking me. "Driver seat or passenger," I asked snootily.

"Neither."

"Oh?"

"On the hood."

"The hood?" I spluttered.

"It's American for bonnet."

I blinked indignantly. "I know that!"

Eyes holding mine, he grinned knowingly.

I don't believe it! He can read my mind! Bonnet, hood whatever, with me on it! I looked down my nose. "That wouldn't be at all comfortable,"

"Who cares about comfortable? Drink some more wine, witch," he drawled. "And you won't even notice."

"Excuse me?" I glared.

"Another time maybe?"

"No!"

"Never?" He cocked an eyebrow.

I could only blink.

"Okay, I should go." He stood up. "Give me a call if you need anything."

"I mean no! Not another time," I told him breathlessly. "Don't go."

We eyeballed each other as I got to my feet on legs that threatened to give way. There was no need for wine; I ended up on the Mustang's hood. Primal and not as uncomfortable as I feared. If there'd been a moon I would have howled. We eventually staggered inside to bed where he drove me wild again. Later stretching like a satisfied cat, my back against his chest I turned in his arms to look at him.

Murmured. "I wonder if Opa and Oma ever did it on his Mustang."

"If the rumours are true Bernard Von Meeren would have," he laughed. "Besides he had a witch like I do, they make you do things."

"Excuse me!" I tapped his nose with a finger. "I don't make you do anything."

"You'd be surprised." He nibbled my finger.

"I'm glad you stayed," I whispered. "No more secrets. Ever."

"Agreed," he said, pulling me close.

In the morning, I left him sleeping and got up quietly to take a shower. Turned on the taps and was about to step under when the bathroom door opened, my mouth dropping open in surprise as he entered.

The shower was my own private space, we'd never shared it before. I wasn't at all enthusiastic about the intrusion, but my squeaking protests weren't heeded. Wasn't expecting what happened next either; mind-blowing sensations of slippery hands on soapy slick skin and steamy antics that had me almost passing out. Afterwards out of the shower, I stood staring at him in a daze, legs trembling and clutching a towel to my front like a shield.

"What was that for?" I spluttered gulping air.

"I get the impression you liked it," he grinned while towelling his hair.

"I get the impression," I hissed. "That you know a lot about what women like."

"Wrong impression."

"Ha!" I scowled.

"But I do know there's witch I have a lot of fantasies about," he chuckled. "And I'm working through them slowly."

My jaw dropped.

Reaching a finger under my chin to shut my mouth, he leered. "How about trying another one?"

"No way!" I spat and fled.

Heard him laughing as I slammed the bathroom door behind me. Dried off fast, got dressed faster and once in the kitchen shook my head with a rueful giggle wondering if somehow, I'd ever get used to his surprises.

Chapter 39

One night lying in his arms, I murmured, "Don't you think we should start taking precautions, those, um, wiggly things could get us into trouble."

He grinned. "We've been at it this long without trouble. If kids happen, they happen."

I ran a finger across his lips. "Can I ask you something?"

"Sure." He traced a hand down my spine.

"It's about kids, actually?"

"Okay."

"If we ever do have any, what would you want."

"Human ones, I hope." His hand stroked my hip.

Shaking my head in exasperation, I giggled, "No, you idiot! Boy or girl?"

"Doesn't matter," he shrugged. "As long as they're healthy with all the right bits."

I spluttered another giggle, thumping his chest lightly.

After a moment I spoke again softly. "Your sister's and mother's names, Esther Lynette. They'd be nice for a girl, don't you think?"

He squeezed his eyes shut, letting a breath out through his teeth.

"Oh, crap!" I took his face in my hands, whispered. "Forgive me, I shouldn't have said that. I'm sorry."

He opened his eyes, turned his lips to my palm and said after a pause. "That's a nice idea, but no boy will ever be named after my father."

"You don't like Edgar?"

"Shit, no!" He crossed his eyes.

Giggling, I kissed his nose. "Aw, come on. Eddie's not so bad."

He shook his head, adding after a moment. "How about Kenneth."

I blinked huge eyes, managed a squeak. "Really? You mean that?"

"Why not?" He smiled, his hand leaving my hip to cup a bum cheek. "Good memories, right?"

"Actually, I really like your second name." I returned his smile. "Harrison. How about Harrison Kenneth Willard?"

He raised his eyebrows, looked suitably impressed and nodded. "Not bad."

I sighed happily, snuggling against him. His fingers stroked downward to the back of my knee, tightening to hitch my thigh over his hip. My breath caught.

"While we're on the subject of names," he murmured, his hand skimming slowly back to my bum. "How about we concentrate on changing yours?"

"Pardon?" My mouth was against his neck.

"Kate Maria Willard. What do you reckon?"

As I jerked my head back to eyeball him, he laughed at my dumbfounded stare and before I had a chance to comment covered my mouth with his.

We were married less than six months later, a laid back and delightfully raucous affair at the farm and afterwards went overseas for a honeymoon cum break, two months through the US and across to Europe, meeting Dad and Helena in Austria at the family estate.

We made our home together at the Junkyard, now it's official name with a wrought iron sign to prove it made especially by Roman. Most of our weekends were spent at the cabin unless someone else in the family was using it, Trojan didn't seem to mind where he lived and acquired a playmate to keep him company, a pitch black, yellow eyed cat Douglas named Diesel who appeared at the Junkyard as a skinny, flea riddled stray kitten, possibly dumped nearby. He was hardcase with a loud strident meow when demanding food, purred like a V8 when curled up on the floor against Trojan or napping on the sofa and the oak trees were one of his favourite playgrounds, scampering up and down them like a monkey.

I continued to work at the clinic and Douglas changed jobs, working for the Von Meeren Trust as vineyard and Wine Rack restaurant maintenance manager which pleased Dad no end. Occasionally Douglas stayed behind at the restaurant on Friday nights adding his sexy baritone to the music and I loved to listen, often enjoying dinner with him afterwards and staying overnight in the vineyard flat that my Opa built.

I remembered the first time very clearly. I'd made more of an effort to doll up that evening in a slinky halter neck silver top with no bra underneath, short black skirt, black knickers and black high heels. The heat in Douglas's eyes during dinner had the quiver going rampant, the subsequent night turned long, wild and positively exhausting. Something about the flat lingered with me for ages, couldn't pinpoint it at the time and kept it to myself.

"Do you feel the vibes in the flat?" Anna asked me a few days later.

"Vibes?" I looked puzzled.

"It's where Maria and Bernard got back together after their year-long split."

"Really?"

"Yes," she grinned widely. "I told her to seduce him, and er, she listened for once."

"Oh."

"She looked stunning that night. I'll never forget it," Anna closed her eyes, remembering. "Silver and black she wore with hardly anything underneath. I knew he wouldn't be able to resist. He absolutely adored her."

I said not a word, staring blankly.

"I'll never forget the next morning when they arrived at the farm together, it was so wonderful seeing them together and happy again. I was over the moon," Anna continued. "They were such a beautiful couple, just like you and Douglas."

My mind went over and over her story, Douglas noticing my preoccupation later at the cabin. "You're miles away." He tilted my chin. "All good?"

"Yes, it's good." Smiling, I told him what Anna had said.

"Wow!" He looked a little stunned. "That explains it."

"Explains what?" I gave him a baffled look.

"The good vibes in the flat."

"You are joking?" I stared at him poleaxed.

"Joking about what?"

"You felt it too? The warm fuzzies?"

"That's them," he grinned. "More hot than warm, though."

"Amazing!" I grinned back.

"Nothing compared to the shivers though."

"Um, not like the quiver, either."

"Want one of those?"

"What, now?" My eyes went wide. "It's daylight."

"And?"

"Too early."

"Never too early," he leered and proceeded to prove his point.

We were lying on the bed with me face down on top of Douglas, unable to move and gulping for air. His hand stroked, fingers brushing my spine.

"Have you heard?" His voice was hoarse.

"Heard what?" I mumbled against his neck.

"What they call you now?" His fingers moved lower.

"They?"

"The gossips." His hand settled on a bum cheek.

I sighed softly, pressing my lips to his ear. "Do I really want to know?"

"Willard's witch." I felt the chuckle rumble in his chest.

"Oh, how lovely!" I bit his earlobe.

"You are." He turned his head, eyes laughing into mine. "Very lovely, sweet witch."

"And you're a very bad boy," I giggled. "Gorgeous, adorable and sexy."

"A beautiful couple then, eh?"

"Just like Oma and Opa."

"History repeating," he murmured and kissed me.